Wanting you Always

LIZZIE MORTON

© Lizzie Morton 2022
All rights reserved.
Editor: Hayley Ramsey Editorial

Adeen Print
978-1-7391175-6-6

Kris and Babs — For helping me find my voice.

Prologue

Sam

A bum guitar note fills the room. Though it's only my ears hearing it, it still makes me flinch.

Aunt Rachel gave me her guitar for my fourteenth birthday, the same one Dad gave her when they were younger. It's the only connection I have to my dad besides Shaun, and I've spent weeks practicing one song. Practice being the key word, not perfecting, because there's nothing close to perfect about the sounds I've been creating.

I'm annoyed I can't get it right. I'm getting better, but the progress is slow, and more than once I've wanted to give up. I can't though, because this song means everything to me. It's *the* song. The one that ignited my love for music.

Eyes burning, I set the guitar down on the bed.

"Don't stop, you're getting really good." Sophie hovers in the doorway, wearing a bright, floaty dress, similar to what I see her mom and sister wearing sometimes. "Do you mind if I come in?" she asks, tucking her newly blonde hair behind her ears.

"Sure."

She looks away as I wipe beneath my eyes and the bed shifts when she sits next to me.

"Does it get easier?" I look up and hold her gaze, waiting for her to expand. Her eyes drop and her throat bobs. "I couldn't imagine losing my dad or mom. Ever."

My stomach sinks. "No," I answer. "The only thing that gets easier is creating distractions."

Sophie gives me a small smile and shifts, sitting straighter. She tosses her hair over one shoulder, and I get a waft of honey. "What's your favorite distraction?"

Listening to you sing each night.

I'd never say that out loud, so I don't answer. We sit in silence until Sophie picks up the guitar and plays the same song I've been trying to master. I watch the way her fingers move effortlessly over the strings.

"I didn't know you could play."

When she giggles, my heart skips a beat. "You know who my mom and dad are, right?"

"*The Parkers*." I overemphasize their name the way everyone does, including the media.

To say Sophie's parents are local celebrities would be the understatement of the century.

I love music and I love to sing. After already losing two of the things I loved most in the world, I refuse to lose anything else.

Somehow, Sophie's parents have managed to walk their own path and stay true to the music they wanted to produce.

They're inspiring, even if they do have to leave a lot. Sophie and her siblings never seem to mind. They filled their walls with the happiness and laughter I prayed would fill ours when we were younger, because their parents always come back. Whenever they invite us around to Friday Feast Night, it's the best part of my week. It means I get to see *her*, in the place where she's unforgivingly herself, even when she's bickering with her siblings or being embarrassed by the force to be reckoned with, otherwise known as Grams.

"Music is like breathing in our house," continues Sophie. She focuses her attention on the guitar, and when she does, her face transforms into what can only be described as euphoria.

I wish it would do the same when she looks at me.

"I get that." I watch as she carries on strumming. "Will you do something with music when you're older?" She stops playing but doesn't answer. "Red?"

Her eyes snap up and find mine, searching. Pink creeps up her neck, and suddenly, I want to kiss her. The thought comes out of nowhere; a simple one, but one that once it's there, refuses to budge. It feels like the start of something; a seed planted in my chest, growing quickly with each second that ticks by, making my heart race faster as the urge gets stronger.

She lets out a long sigh, her shoulders slumping. "I want to be seen, Sam. It's almost impossible when you have a mom and dad like mine."

I study her a moment. "I see you," I say eventually.

Later, when she's gone, with the skin on my fingers almost raw from playing for so long, I lay back on my bed, staring at the ceiling and waiting for Sophie to go about her nighttime routine. Afternoons like the one we've just had mean even more when you've walked through the unbearable pain life can sometimes throw your way. You learn to appreciate and hold on to the happy moments, no matter how small or fleeting they might be.

And the girl who spent most of the day selflessly sitting beside me has become my happiest memory.

One I refuse to let go of.

Chapter One
Sophie

"At what point are we supposed to get our shit together?"

"Never," replies Zoe. The only interest she shows at a pivotal moment in my career is to her nails. After a quick glance around the showroom, I zero in on the almost life-size bronze tiger statue guarding the door. The one with a price tag sitting around its neck that makes my eyes bulge. It's *that* kind of store. My lips form a flat line and I focus on the task in hand—staring between two desks.

A couple of weeks ago, Sooz, our bun-wearing ringleader, left for Cape Town to visit her family. With Next Level PR in the hands of the rest of us—Abby, Zoe, Amanda, and I—she left me with *this* task. The Desk Task. Capital letters included. It's my opportunity to pull a win out of the bag for the team, but I can't help feeling lost, like an underdog dressed in sample clothing. Like I shouldn't be here doing this. Like life has another plan for me. I just wish I knew what.

When I told her we needed to go shopping, Zoe's eyes had lit up. The spark was put right back out the second she had realized it was for furniture. Work-related furniture.

"Why is this so hard?" I groan, glancing between the two desks again.

When I crossed into the land of thirty, I thought making decisions would get easier. The answer should be simple. After all, there are only two obvious choices. Pink or white. Yet we've been standing for over thirty minutes in the same store, still no closer to deciding.

I smooth my hands over the black suit pants I'm wearing, and a wave of irritation passes through me when my fingers catch on a loose thread. The store assistant hovering in the background—the one wearing a snooty expression that complements her outfit from Saks—is probably wondering why we're here. We don't exactly fit the vibe, thanks to Zoe being dressed like a Japanese Anime character. Apparently, it's trending on TikTok, and because ignorance is bliss, I didn't get her to expand any further as we left the office. I don't want to spend my time worrying what she's planning to do, dressed like she is.

"Because you're overthinking it. It's a desk, Soph."

Zoe literally sparkles at me.

"Are you wearing face glitter?"

She wiggles her eyebrows. "You likey?"

"You look like a raver." My gaze settles on her feet. "Are those moon boots?"

She spins on the spot with a grin, throwing her arms out as she goes, teal hair windmilling through the air. "I'm reliving my youth. Lucky for me, nineties fashion is set to be a firm favorite for the rest of the year."

"Zo, you were in diapers for a chunk of the nineties."

"Technicalities," she sniffs, then glances at the desks. "I like the pink."

"Of course you do," I sigh, glancing at the white.

"Oh, is that orange?" She walks off, and I'm left staring at the two desks on my own.

Pink or white. White or pink. Zoe's right, the pink does have a certain allure to it.

The store assistant walks over and stands at my side. Pink is what old Sophie would pick, but standing here, right this second, I'm trying to be new Sophie in every way I can. White is good. It screams clean and crisp. Mature and all things Scandi.

"Five of the white please," I say, before I can second guess myself.

The assistant's eyes widen to the size of tennis balls. She was totally expecting us to walk out without buying anything. I don't blame her. This store is expensive. Like, life-size-bronze-tiger kind of expensive.

With my decision made, I quickly search for Zoe, finding her perched on a desk chair deeper in the store, cheeks glittering in the light as she spins way too fast, singing the lyrics to "Need To Know" by Dojacat with her phone in the air.

Why the hell is she doing a TikTok transition *here*?

I cringe, knowing what comes next.

Don't do it, Zo.

The words pussy, dick and ten out of ten fill the now silent store.

She did it, and everyone heard, including the lady creeping up to ninety right at the back perusing the fur rugs. The one wearing the mink coat, despite the fact it's sweltering.

I clear my throat, trying to draw the assistant's attention away from Zoe. "Like I said, five of the white, please."

She arches a brow. "Five? You're sure? The price tag is … erm … large."

I wave the designated company card in the air. Who would have thought a thin piece of plastic could ooze so much power?

"Five," I repeat firmly. She narrows her eyes. "Please," I finish, softening my voice.

So much for being badass.

The assistant wanders off with the card at the same time my phone starts vibrating in my pocket. Sooz. She's checking in, like she does all day long, regardless of the time difference.

I scurry to Zoe. "I've placed the order. Can you make sure it's right?" I gesture at my phone, still ringing in my hand. "I need to take this outside."

She shrugs and turns toward the checkout. The store assistant looks bemused by all the teal and glitter heading her way.

I don't have the chance to worry about it, and make my way outside, being hit by two things I hate: heat and noise.

"Hey," I answer, pressing a finger into the ear unoccupied by my phone to block out the noise of some construction work being carried out further up the block.

"Have you ordered the desks?"

No hello. No how are you, how's things? She's grumpy. I would be, too, if I were working when I should be sleeping. Sooz is the definition of workaholic.

I squint in the bright sunlight, contemplating my answer. I quickly come to the conclusion there's nothing to contemplate. "Yes. They're perfect," I reply, content with my choice.

Scandi vibes for our new office fill my eyes. Black beams. Hardwood floors. Plants in all the right places.

"I knew you could do it, Soph. I can't wait to see them." The smile in her voice makes my chest swell with pride. "I've got to go," she says, ending the call and hanging up.

We've got this. I've got this.

A quick glance through the window shows Zoe chatting animatedly with the store assistant. I'm about to pocket my phone when I decide I need to share my positive step with the world.

Me: *Ordered the desks. Go me!*
Brendan: *I'm currently in a meeting and can't respond. For anything of urgency, please contact my PA.*

I frown at the automated response that takes up about eighty percent of my message storage. Nothing can dampen my mood today, so instead, I text the one person I know will get it and who *always* responds.

Me: *I did it. I ordered the desks.*
Sam: *Didn't doubt you for a second.*

Warmth fills my chest, and for the first time in a really long time, I feel like I can take on the world.

Sam

Quickly looping back on myself, I walk along the sidewalk I've paced six times already, finally making my way to rehearsals after spending the best part of an hour procrastinating. We—S.C.A.R.A.B.—have a gig coming up. A small one. Some might say intimate compared to our latest performances, but nerves are getting the better of me already.

For the first time in my career, my steps are reluctant ones.

Ten minutes later, I head inside the Music Hall of Williamsburg. From the outside, it doesn't look like much with its Art Déco glass facade and kitsch signage. It's a blast from the past. A stark contrast to some of the new, bigger venues where we've been performing. Inside screams old school rock vibes. Just a room with raised levels and balconies running along each side. And, of course, a stage. It's the sort of venue where the floors rarely see a mop and the stickiness isn't just down to spilled drinks. A place like where our careers started. All about the music, nothing about the image. It's the kind of place I used to think was awesome. Now, I can't wait to get out of here, and I've only been inside a couple of minutes.

I used to love this, but everything changed a few weeks ago when we performed our new single at an intimate performance at The Angel Orensanz. Well, as intimate as you can get when the whole thing was being streamed live on more than a handful of major TV networks … globally. We've come a long way from the group of young guys who started by messing around with cover songs in high school.

And what was supposed to be the catalyst for our careers … was the catalyst for my nightmares.

Thanks to my procrastinating, the rest of the band is already setting up on stage and I'm hit with a wave of nausea when the smell of stale beer and sweat reaches my nose. My palms go clammy. I try to ignore it like I have been doing the past few weeks.

It might not be that bad, I tell myself.

John West, the band's manager, and I guess you could call him our mentor, walks over from the left side of the room. "Sam," he beams. "We thought you weren't coming."

"I got caught up with something, sorry," I reply, eyeing up the execs he's left behind, all in almost matching suits. Expensive-looking ones. The different shades of blue and gray are the only things making them distinguishable. They give off the vibes I hate; all serious expressions and business, meaning something is coming. They don't *just* turn up to rehearsals like this. "Special occasion?"

I didn't think it was possible, but John's smile gets even brighter. "We have some news. Can you get the rest of the band, please?"

"Sure," I mumble and walk over to the stage. "John wants to speak to us," I call to the guys.

Jake stops strumming his guitar and looks up. A flicker of annoyance crosses his eyes when they land on me. Zach gives him a look that says not to start anything, then sets his bass down on the stage. Meanwhile, Ryan gets up from behind the drums and jumps down off the stage, oblivious to any of the animosity simmering between the rest of the band. Jake and Zach follow him silently.

"Where have you been?" asks Jake under his breath, so Zach can't hear, as we trail behind him and Ryan.

"I was busy," I reply. Busy walking a hole into a long stretch of concrete, but he doesn't need to know that part.

A dark brow raises. "Right."

He doesn't believe a word, because friends tend to have a sixth sense about these things, and he knows something's been up with me recently. We've yet to discuss what and why, because of his three-year-old mini me, Clara. His chaotic home life might not work for the band, but recently, it's worked in my favor. No time equals no prying.

"So, we have great news," says John. I wasn't aware execs knew how to be giddy, but there he is, clapping his hands together excitedly. "We've been given the go ahead to record and release your new single at the end of the summer, and the label wants an album to go with it." The rest of the execs pull off an excellent impression of a group of nodding dogs. "We're thinking of coinciding the release with a world tour." He winks. "Let's give the fans what they want."

Fuck. My stomach drops lower than my balls.

Standing in a daze, I try to digest the information John dumped on us like it's nothing. This is endgame shit. World tours are for bands where every member is at their peak. Unfortunately for S.C.A.R.A.B., there's one member nowhere near the peak, summit, whatever you want to call it. The front man. The singer. Currently sitting at the nadir. Rock bottom, if we're avoiding being fancy. Basically, I'm fucked, which means the whole band is fucked.

"I thought world tours took more time to plan than this?" I croak.

"We've managed to pull a few strings and lucky for us, we have a great team to get everything set up. Orensanz is all the publicity you need. You've done the hard work, now you just need to enjoy the ride."

"Great." I grimace.

Jake stares at me like I've lost my mind. Maybe I have.

"We can discuss the details later," confirms John. "I'll let you start your rehearsal."

What follows is the worst. I consistently come in at the wrong times, miss the notes I'm supposed to, and at one point, even forget the goddamn lyrics, dragging the rest of the band down with me.

Jake corners me at the end when we've climbed off the stage. "I hope this isn't a sign of things to come." He runs his hands through his dark hair, like he has what feels like more times during this rehearsal than the entirety of our career.

"It's not," I reply tersely. Jake doesn't say another word as he walks away.

John West takes his place, standing at my side, watching the guys leave to get food.

"I think I might come watch your next gig," he says, his expression thoughtful. "It's been a while since I've seen you guys play a full set."

I nod, trying not to read too much into what he's saying, which is hard because he no longer looks excited, more like he's contemplating taking us off his label. He walks back over to the rest of the execs, and they all leave together. None of them look my way.

Standing alone, I glance at the stage.

The sweet smell of warm batter fills the kitchen, along with music from the radio. The song changes to Fields of Gold and I grin, knowing what comes next. Dad pours batter in the waffle maker, sets the timer, then turns the volume as loud as it will go.

He grabs the wooden spoon from the mixing bowl and Shaun and I both giggle when he raises it in the air to sing along and the batter pours down his arm. We both jump to our feet and join in, only stopping when the shrill ringing of the timer puts an end to our fun.

"I want you both to make me a promise ..." he says, grabbing two plates from the kitchen cabinet. He places one waffle on each and grabs the maple syrup, stopping right before he pours it on top. Shaun groans. Dad always bargains when there's syrup involved. "That you'll never give up on your dreams."

Dread seeps into every part of my body.

I'm not just letting the band down. I'm letting Dad down.

Maybe it's a good thing he isn't here to witness how I might be about to screw my life up.

The room's deafening silence is broken by the opening lyrics of "Rapper's Delight" by The Sugarhill Gang. My somber mood lifts when I pull my phone out of the pocket of my jeans.

"Hey ho."

"You know I hate it when you call me a ho," replies Sophie.

"We still on for later?"

"Is it a Friday?"

"Yes."

"Then that's a stupid question, don't you think?"

I grin into the empty room. "Is there anywhere you want to go?"

The line goes muffled and I make out faint chatter in the background. "Sorry about that," says Sophie when the line becomes clear again. "I called to say I might be late."

A pang of disappointment hits me. Fridays are Feast Night; a tradition we've continued since being young, whenever I'm not in another state or country, and when Sophie isn't helping to run functions for the rich and famous.

Fridays are sacred. Fridays are for Sam and Sophie.

"Okay," I reply, trying to keep the disappointment out of my voice.

"I'll grab us something on my way to yours?"

My brows draw together. "We can go out, Soph. I'm not Mister Pr—"

"Don't, please. I'm in a great mood and I don't want you to ruin it."

I let out a ragged breath and back down, because a Friday is the only time when she lets her hair down and acts like herself. Like the old Sophie.

"Okay, I'll see you at my place."

We hang up and despite the rehearsal being a disaster, I feel lighter knowing I'll see her later.

Chapter Two

Sophie

Still on cloud nine after completing The Desk Task earlier, I walk into the large room that has become my sanctuary.

The old wooden floors gleam, complimented perfectly by thick red velour curtains, grand chandeliers and melodies floating through the air. I drink it all in, even the musky scent I'm sure has a hint of mothballs to it. The place is ancient and kind of shabby. Perfectly imperfect, just like the group of people smiling in front of me who have become like a second family.

It feels like home and provides a sense of one to those who need it the most.

The Parkapellas.

My parents wave from the left corner of the room where they're conducting a warmup. Everyone has split off into smaller, more manageable numbers, like we do at the beginning of every rehearsal. Grams is off to my parents' right with the younger kids, and my older siblings, Aurelia and Hale, are in the middle of the room with the largest of the groups.

Only the youngest Parker, Xavier, is missing—probably on a date. Either a girl-related one, or, more likely, a drum-related one, with Ryan from S.C.A.R.A.B. Their bromance over rhythm and beats often brings into question his loyalty here. Not that he really cares. At fifteen, he goes to the beat of his own drum. Excuse the pun.

After voice warmups, everyone merges with Hale and Aurelia's group, creating one huge one. Mom, Dad and Grams stand with me at the front, ready to give the usual briefing slash pep talk. Mom clears her throat and catches my attention. I turn my head, and her eyes, the same color as scotch, widen, then drop to the sheet sitting in her hands. The one outlining the song list for the night and the key areas that need working through on each one, where the melodies don't quite slot together and the transitions aren't smooth.

My stomach flips. What the hell is she doing?

Grams and Dad stand at her other side, directing tight smiles at the group, trying to act like there's nothing out of the ordinary occurring. Hale and Aurelia might as well have a box of popcorn ready to watch the spectacle unfold for how excited they look as they glance back and forth between the two of us. Sibling humiliation at its finest.

Mom clears her throat again and tries to pass me the sheet. I shake my head no and her eyes bulge. My cheeks burn, knowing everyone is standing, watching.

"Xavier's going to be gutted he missed this," I hear Aurelia snicker quietly to Hale. You'd think she was ten, not thirty-two.

"I need to take this," I mutter, pulling my phone out of my pocket.

Mom frowns at the blank, lifeless screen in my hand, and watches me skulk away. Right before I slip out of the room, I glance back and watch as she tosses some of her long, more-strawberry-than-blonde hair over one shoulder. She plasters on a smile only a true performer knows how to. After all, she's one half of The Parkers. Dad, the other. They're music royalty. Think The Carpenters, minus the sibling thing. A husband-and-wife duo and key players in the music industry since I was little.

My shoulders slump and I leave. I might have created this group, but I was never made to lead it. I'm not my parents. I've never claimed to be like them. The talent gene skipped a generation when Sophie Parker made her way into the world.

Leaders are bold, confident, inspiring. Leaders don't have their mistakes following them around like a cheap, nasty tattoo that everyone comments on when they think the person isn't listening. Leaders are the opposite of what I am. Thirty and still without a clue what I really want to do with my life. They're driven to achieve and, in the process, help others to as well. How can I encourage others to heal and chase their dreams when I can't even do it myself?

What advice can I offer on the occasions when the group might mess up, other than, *"Hey, it's fine. It was just a bum note. At least you weren't caught on camera swinging from a roof with a male stripper in a video that then went viral."*

Or *"Don't worry about it. At least you're not 'The Flaky Parker Child'. 'The Loser One', who spent most of her early twenties getting wasted and puking. Things could be worse!"*

The door clicks shut behind me, blocking out the sound of my mom's voice. My breaths come out ragged, rattling against my chest. Black spots fill my vision. If this is how I react from just the suggestion of leading the group for the night, imagine what would happen if I had to take over completely.

There's nothing to imagine. We'd fall apart. Simple.

I press my forehead against the wall, focusing on how cool it feels against my skin, telling myself everything is fine. No one apart from my way-too-observant siblings noticed anything was up. Or at least, they didn't let it show if they did.

After a few minutes, and more than a few long, deep breaths, I stop panicking and my vision clears.

Get your shit together, Sophie. You are not this person anymore. You've moved on from all of this.

I pull away from the wall, ignoring the other little voice in my head; the toxic one, telling me if that were the case, then I wouldn't be out here.

When I finally feel ready to go back into the room, The Parkapellas are already in full swing. I don't hover in the background like I want to. I remind myself of the badass bitch I want to be, like Amanda and Sooz, who own whatever they put their minds to when it comes to Next Level. I throw my shoulders back and walk right to my mom's side.

Never one to let things slide, when the group completes an acapellariffic mash-up of Beyoncé's "Run the World (Girls)", Kate Bush's "Running Up That Hill", and "This Is Me" from *The Greatest Showman* soundtrack, and disperses for a break, she decides to pick apart my absence.

"That was a long call," she says, giving a small blonde girl, one of her biggest fans, a wave.

With stars in her eyes, the little girl walks off, bouncing off at least three people as she goes.

"Work," I lie, and with a shrug, finish with an extra peppy, "What can you do?" I throw in an over enthusiastic eyebrow wiggle for good measure.

Mom purses her lips. Something flashes through her eyes, turning the scotch in them to a bourbon. Something that unsettles my gut, telling me there is no way in hell she's going to leave this, because The Parkers aren't just talented in all things musical, they're expertly talented in being meddlesome. I wait for her to say something.

Instead, she claps her hands together loudly. "Back to it, everyone!"

Huh. That was way too easy. I don't get a chance to think any more about it, because practice becomes all-consuming, and I forget there's even an issue.

Three hours later, I curse when I see the time. It isn't usually an issue, because rehearsals aren't usually on a Friday. This week, our Wednesday slot had to be moved thanks to routine maintenance being carried out on the building.

And now … I'm late.

So late.

Sam is going to kill me.

"Guys! We're done for the night!" I call out to a sea of weary faces.

It's been a long hard practice, but thanks to my parents' perseverance, the progress made has been significant. Hope fills my chest. It's there. Everyone's goal. The dream that's been sitting in arm's reach for the past few years is getting closer, almost ready to grasp.

Mom comes over and stands by my side as I watch the group filter out slowly.

"They did good tonight," she muses, giving a final warm smile to her biggest fan, leaving with her parents.

"Yeah." I can't keep in my excitement and grin. "They did."

"They're going to be great at the showcase."

Just hearing her refer to it out loud makes my insides churn.

The American Showcase. If you want to get noticed, this is where it's at. Think the *New York Times'* bestseller list of the music world. The cream of music competitions in the US of A. They decide who really makes it big. The prize money would also be an incredible opportunity for a group outgrowing their premises but unable to afford a bigger rent … kind of like us.

"Yeah …" I pause. "I'm not sure if they're ready."

Mom turns to face me, her expression serious. "*Them* … or *you?*" She reaches up and tucks a rogue piece of hair behind my ear, then trails her hand through it. A couple of lines appear between her neat brows when her fingers linger on the ends. She rubs the blonde between them and sighs. I wait for her to make a comment about missing the red, but it never comes. Instead, when I don't answer her question, she says, "It's time."

"Time for what?" I balk, praying to God she isn't about to suggest what I think she is. She can't have forgotten what happened literally a couple of hours ago.

Mom drops her hand back down to her side. "It's time for you to lead the group. It's yours after all."

"Wait?" My eyes widen. "What? Why?"

"Your father and I have been talking. We want to record another album. We need to do this and could use the extra time."

My mouth drops open. She's lying. I know she is. It's been years since she and Dad have produced something new. With their loyal following still flooding to their tours, plus two and a half decades of success prior, they never have to release anything new again if they don't want to.

"It's a few hours a week, Mom!"

Her eyes sparkle with amusement. "I could say the same to you …"

"This is different, and you know it." I cross my arms with a huff, fully aware I'm being bratty, but the thought of doing what she's suggesting makes me feel physically sick. "I can't lead a singing group when I can't sing."

I can't lead anything when I'm barely able to keep my own shit together.

"We both know that's not true," she replies, her face relaxing, the corners of her mouth lifting.

"Could you not, like, postpone it till like after The Showcase? It's in a few months. Please. You can't leave me like this."

I will absolutely drop to my knees and beg her if I have to.

Mom gives me her 'you're not going to change my mind' smile.

"You're going to do great."

We both know that's not true. I bottled it at having to read through a list. How the hell am I supposed to lead a whole group every week?

She leans in and presses a kiss against my temple, one that does nothing to settle the impending doom that's replaced my euphoric mood from earlier.

"Don't leave me," I whisper. "I can't do this."

Dad stands at the door, waiting for her so they can leave together. As Mom walks over to him, he gives me a small smile. He's a man of few words, unless he's bickering with his life partner over the air conditioning. He prefers to speak with his music. If only the rest of the family were as reserved, life would be considerably more peaceful.

Before they disappear, Mom looks back over her shoulder and gives me a reassuring smile. "We're not leaving you, but it's time for you to spread your wings. It's time for you to believe in yourself like we believe in you. We'll be right here rooting for you."

They both leave before I can race over and cling to them—just like I did as a kid whenever something terrified me—or point out there's been no other mention of this idea for a new album which has miraculously appeared. Traitors.

I want to quit. I want to puke. I want to do anything apart from what they're suggesting.

"Motherfuc—"

I stop cursing when a small hand tugs mine. Russ.

Well, his name's actually Josh, but when we introduced him to the rest of the group, he asked that we call him Russ. It was his third practice, during a refreshment break, when he told me about his favorite movie.

The one set in Roman times filled with blood, gore and sex.

The one with Russell Crowe.

My eyes move over to the antique clock ticking on the wall. I'm no longer *just* late for Sam. I'm *unacceptably* late. I push the thought away, because it's not the most important thing right now.

All that matters is this. It's all that's really mattered since the night I bumped into him walking home from one of the

Parkapellas' sessions months back. A seven-year-old alone in Brooklyn in the dark. The streets around him were empty and my stomach twisted uncomfortably. His brown eyes looked almost black in the darkness, pleading with the unsaid words, *"Please don't tell anyone. I won't be allowed to come back."*

Russ tugs on my hand again, breaking me from my thoughts.

"Ready, buddy?" I ask, smiling down at him.

Russ opens his mouth to answer, but his stomach does the job for him with a growl. My gut kicks in, telling me deep down there's more to this than Russ simply walking home alone, something I should tell someone about. Something I should have told someone about months ago. What the hell am I doing?

An hour later, after a quick detour and a stop for takeout, Russ shovels the last of the food, including what I bought for Sam and I, in his mouth. He lets out a large belch as the four boxes settle in his stomach and my brows raise. When he grins, I laugh.

"Better?"

He nods. "Thank you, Sop—" He doesn't get a chance to finish what he's saying as a large yawn takes over.

"Come on." I stand up from the bench where we've been sitting. Russ copies, albeit sleepily. "Let's get you home." It doesn't take long to get to the edge of Bedford, and right before Russ runs up the steps of the apartment block, which is as tired as he is, I stop him. "This is for you."

I hold out a small phone in my hand. It doesn't have all the fancy extras and apps that most come with, but it will do the job.

Russ reaches out, then right before his hand connects with it, he snatches it back and glances up. I've never given him a reason not to trust me, but the uncertainty I find in his eyes gives me my first real glimpse into the past behind them.

"Why?" he asks, reinforcing the lack of trust.

I keep my answer as simple as the object in my hand. "Everyone needs a phone." I shrug, attempting to brush my gesture off like it's nothing. "Just in case."

Russ frowns and stares at it for a few seconds. When he finally snatches it from my hand, he slips it straight into his pocket and throws a quick glance over his shoulder, as if he's expecting there to be someone there when it's only the two of us.

"Thank you."

"Hey, Russ," I call after him, as quiet as I can, being that it's well after ten at night.

He turns back around. "Yeah?"

"I saved my number in there. If you need *anything*, call."

He doesn't reply, and a second later the door is closed, leaving me wondering how I'm going to explain to Sam why I'm turning up to Friday Feast Night when it's almost Saturday.

Chapter Three
Sam

Sophie's hours later than she estimated. I stare at the empty surface of the kitchen island, the one that should already be filled with takeout boxes, while swiveling my phone in circles with one finger. The sound of the plastic case moving over the gleaming marble feels like the only sound in the entire house. Jake's doing his usual, stopping with Abby and Clara, while Zach and Ryan are at Riffs.

I'm tempted to open the Findmyphone app.

The one I haven't had to use since Sophie hung up her partying shoes a few years back, but came in especially handy one night in particular. The night before S.C.A.R.A.B. left on our very first tour along the West Coast. The same night my brother, Shaun, decided to throw a leaving party at his bar Riffs. In standard Zoe and Sophie style—or Zophie as Ryan likes to call the two of them together—they got wasted and disappeared. Thanks to said app, I caught them right before they left on the last boat of the night to Staten Island … dressed as monks.

Deciding the app is a little on the extreme side, even if it will give me the answers that I need fast, I opt to call her. My chest grows tighter with each unanswered ring. My heart all but stops when it cuts to voicemail. If I was panicking before, I'm ready to lose it now. Sophie doesn't ever not answer, unless she's pissed. Because recently I've been on my best behavior, I hit call again, as my mind jumps from one worst-case scenario to another.

I'm at the front door in seconds, ready for flinging it open and searching the whole of New York, when there's a rhythmic knock that I associate with only one person. I twist the handle and pull the door open. Light floods into the night and bounces off bright blonde hair, emphasizing the all-black ensemble Sophie's sporting. She looks like a dark angel.

She glances up from her phone where my name is flashing on the screen, waves it in the air and says, "You rang?"

"You're late," I bite out, despite feeling relieved.

She frowns at my tone. "I told you I would be."

"And then you told me a time you thought you were going to be here for, which was nine. It's now two hours past …" I make a show of tapping my wrist as if doing so reinforces how late she is.

"Sam, you're not wearing a watch." She smiles and I feel some of the tension leaving my shoulders when she starts to explain. "I got tied up at the office and traffic was bad. Then Chow's got our order wrong." She lifts a white bag in the air with our usual order scrawled across it.

The familiar smell of meat and noodles reaches my nose and my stomach growls.

"Sam." Sophie grins and pokes me in the chest. "Are you hangry?"

"It's after ten and this is New York. I thought something had happened to you," I snap, still reeling with the images of Sophie in all kinds of crappy scenarios running through my mind.

Maybe I need to nip the late-night *True Crime* binging with Ryan in the bud. My overactive imagination doesn't need any more encouragement.

"Technically, this is Brooklyn," she quips, lowering the bag and shooting me a look that tells me she thinks I'm overreacting.

I'm one hundred percent not. Brooklyn has two areas ranking in the top five most dangerous areas of New York— one in the top spot. I'm not fucking around.

"We're still in New York City, Soph." When she bites her lip, my anger evaporates, and I find myself apologizing. "I'm sorry. I was worried, that's all."

"I'm sorry for losing track of time." She glances up through thick lashes, coated in the tiniest amount of mascara. The statement 'less is more' was made for her, and she gives me the look she uses when she wants something or knows I'm pissed. The one I'd say yes to every damn time, regardless of what she's asking. "Can I still come in?"

"That depends. Is the Chow's order right?" She nods and I step to the side, letting her pass.

I would have let her in, even if it wasn't.

In the kitchen, Sophie starts decanting the cartons of takeout from the bag. I pause at the door and watch as she does the thing that crucifies me every time. She sings quietly, under her breath, assuming I can't hear. But I hear her, I always do. Her voice is a siren, but instead of warning me to

34

stay away, it draws me in, just like it always has, since the first time we met.

It's day four when I see her for the first time. She's sitting on Aunt Rachel's living room couch between her sister and brother, her parents hovering in the background. She's the complete opposite of her siblings, with deep blue eyes and strawberry blonde hair hanging around her shoulders. She watches me for a second until Uncle Matt speaks.

"These are your new neighbors. Mr. and Mrs. Parker, Hale, Aurelia, and Sophie there in the middle." He pauses, giving Shaun and me a moment to take them all in. "They won't be in the same school as you, at least not yet. We struggled to find you both a place together so late in the year, but I thought it would be good for you to get to know people your own age, you know ... so you can start to set down some roots here."

I scowl at the floor. I don't need new ones. Mine are in California waiting for me to go back.

I feel her watching me again. I look up and meet her gaze. Curious? Sympathetic? Knowing? Suddenly awkward, I look away. I can't remember her name. I glance back briefly and my eyes settle on her hair. I was wrong before. It's not strawberry blonde, it's more ... red.

Ten minutes into their visit, I ask Aunt Rachel if I can leave. She doesn't hesitate in saying yes. I escape to my room, lay back on my bed and close my eyes. Exhaustion takes me away from a world where I don't feel like I belong anymore.

Later, a voice floats through the window, stirring me from sleep.

For a second, I think it's Dad. A painful stab in my chest reminds me it's not, but there's something about this voice that has me climbing out of bed and tiptoeing to the window.

It's dark out and when I glance at the clock on my nightstand, I find it's after nine.

At first, I stand and listen, trying to figure out where the voice is coming from. Then I lean out of the window, just enough that I can look around, and find a window from the house next to ours cracked open.

The Parker's house.

Movement catches my eye in a large mirror positioned just inside. Strawberry blonde hair flies through the air. The source of the singing: Red. I pull myself back through the window and settle on the floor. Leaning against the wall, I close my eyes and listen.

One song merges into two, two into three. I don't recognize any of them.

Until I do.

My chest grows tighter with each second that passes, listening to the lyrics of my dad's favorite song. "Fields of Gold". When it becomes unbearable, I jump up and go to slam the window shut. I stop myself at the last second.

The lyrics resonate deep inside me. They talk about promises, some broken. That one day a path will be walked, in fields golden and full of new ones.

I grip the window frame tightly.

Instead of closing it, I sing along, pouring every ounce of pain I feel out into the Brooklyn air. Toward the end, my voice grows stronger, dancing in the night with the girl next door, and somewhere in those few minutes, parts of me start to heal.

Ones I thought might never be fixed.

I pad across the floor, thankful I opted for no shoes because I don't want to disturb Sophie while she's lost in her own world. When I reach the central island, she's none the wiser I'm at her side, until I place my hands on the countertop. They must creep into her vision because her shoulders tense and she glances to the side and up, searching my face for signs I've heard her.

My stomach flips, then does a couple more somersaults for good measure. I force my eyes to drop to the food spread across the counter and my jaw clenches when I read the words steamed veg and plain boiled rice.

"Seriously?" I arch a brow at the steamed rainbow when she opens the carton. "What the hell is that?"

Sophie keeps her focus lasered on the carton, then snatches her hand out to the side and grabs a pair of chopsticks. "Food," she sniffs, snapping them apart.

"You do remember what we refer to Friday nights as, right?" She doesn't answer, choosing to busy herself with an attempt to retrieve a green bean with the sticks in her hand. "*Feast* night." I place extra emphasis on the word feast, because there is absolutely nothing feast-worthy about Sophie's choice of cuisine.

"We're in our thirties. We have to start taking better care of ourselves and taking life more seriously. We're not young anymore."

I'm tempted to grab her food and dump it in the trash when she gives the cartons surrounding me filled with fried goodness a disdainful look.

"You make it sound like we're one foot in the grave."

"Maybe we are. We're midway through life, Sam."

"Technically midway is forty, and if we're gonna go for semantics, then fifty is the new forty. I'm more interested to know if this is a new thing. Are Fridays always going to be this morbid? Because if they are, I'm recruiting a new partner."

Sophie sets down the chopsticks and holds my gaze. "You know what I'm getting at."

"Yeah," I agree. "I do. But why not see this as a sign to enjoy life more, rather than a sign to take the enjoyment from it?"

Our eyes lock and neither of us blinks. We're as stubborn as each other when the occasion calls for it. "It's none of your business."

I'm about to tell her that everything to do with her is my business, but I stop myself.

"Maybe we need to think about changing the name for Fridays …"

"You're overreacting," she huffs and goes back to sorting her food.

I feel it everywhere when her shoulder brushes against mine. I take a step to the side, increasing the gap between us.

"Am I really?" I soften my voice in an effort to make her really hear what I'm saying and avoid more bickering. "You're losing sight of who you are. Why don't you go after what you really want in life rather than doing *this*?"

My eyes move over the all-black outfit she's wearing, like she wears every day, the one that almost camouflages her against the counter tops and kitchen units. If it weren't for the blonde hair and white Lycra she opts for when she goes to the gym, she could audition for a part in *The Addams Family*. Even the ribbon in her hair is black. Goth Sophie, who hilariously made a brief appearance in high school, considering she doesn't even like rock or metal music, would be jealous of the quality of her black clothing.

"It takes one to know one."

Her comment makes me pause. Somehow, she's turning what was meant to be about her back round on me and I wonder where she's going with it. "What's that supposed to mean?"

"I see you, Sam."

"And what exactly do you see?" Time slows and I swallow. My heart thuds hard against my ribs. She can't know how I feel. Can she?

"I know there's something wrong, and it's related to the band." I let out a small breath of relief that what she's claiming to know isn't what I've spent most of our friendship trying to hide from her. Just like I'm in tune with her, she's in tune with me. There's no hiding from each other and I can't decide if it's what will save or break us. "I'm not an idiot. Is that what she's for? Is she a distraction?"

"What, you mean like Brendan?" I scoff.

Sophie shakes her head vigorously. "Don't."

"What? We're speaking the truth, right? I'm not gonna stand under the spotlight on my own." Sophie grabs her boxes of shitty, bland food and stalks toward the reclaimed wood dining table. I scowl. "What are you doing?"

She slides along one of the benches. "Ignoring you until you eat something and stop being grumpy."

And this is where we always end up. Too often I find myself at the blurry, muddy, slushy line that is our friendship, prepared to lay it all down. Every time I think I might have worked up the courage, Sophie walks away before I get a chance. I can't decide if I'm relieved or not. The thought of crossing it and the result not being what I want is frightening. Equally, the thought of getting the desired outcome scares the hell out of me and messes with my head even more.

What if she said yes? What if she felt the same? Those are the thoughts that make me feel ready to take the risk. It's the question that swoops in after and taints everything which stops me. What if somewhere down the line we turn into my parents?

A chill trickles down my spine, one that tells me to play it safe and remain on the right side of the line, no matter how tempting it might be to cross over.

I drag a hand through my hair while Sophie tucks into her vegetables. It's late and I'm not in the right place to have this kind of conversation. After setting our usual playlist going, I pick up the additional cartons of food and amble to the table. Each step feels like I'm walking on eggshells. Sophie makes a show of being overly interested in a lump of spinach.

Her eyes remain on her food when I slide into the chair opposite her. I open all the containers until I find what I'm searching for. My lips twitch and I fight the urge to smile, clamping my jaw together. Humming along to the song in the background, I absentmindedly slide the golden container across the table, then grab my own chopsticks and dive into my usual order. Thanks to Sophie being late, I'm ravenous, and the food tastes better than normal. Impressive considering Chow's is my all-time favorite.

Sophie doesn't take the bait at first, so a few mouthfuls in, I push the container closer. Still nothing. That's the thing about her. To most, she appears amenable. To some, she comes across as a pushover. But when you truly know her, you get to see the side not many do. The side that gets my dick harder than any woman ever has. The stubborn-as-fuck side. The side which if she put her mind to it could do whatever and take on whatever she wanted.

I love it. I love irrational Soph. I love every single side of Soph, especially the flawed parts. I love her flaws more than anything because it's flaws that make a person human. No one is perfect and owning your mistakes shows true courage and resilience. Her flaws are also why people are drawn to her, even if she doesn't see it herself, because perfect is intimidating, while being flawed connects us all.

"I know what you're doing."

Conveniently, my mouth finds itself way too full of noodles and bean sprouts. I shrug, trying to figure out how soon is too soon to shovel more in. Thirty seconds is the safe bet. When I've chewed a good amount and swallowed, creating more space, I fill my mouth again without missing a beat.

I take a keen interest in a piece of chicken when a hand creeps out and drags the box all the way across the table. I knew she wouldn't be able to resist.

"I hate you sometimes," Sophie says to herself.

"Of course you do," I chuckle and bite the inside of my cheek when I catch her taking not one, but three huge mouthfuls of the container without the steamed contents. The one with the deep-fried prawns which are heaven in a mouthful. I mentally pocket the moment as a point to me and high-five myself.

Inhaling my first box of food without another word, I'm halfway through the second when Sophie clears her throat.

"Did you not eat again?" she asks, staring at the rogue bean sprout swinging from my chin.

I suck it up with a slurp and grin. It's a grin which makes everything appear fine. Not like this is the fourth Friday in a row where I've been ravenous for our feast thanks to my singing-related lack of appetite.

Adding a carefree shrug for extra measure, I throw a bone to keep her off the scent that something might be wrong. "I'm on my world tour diet."

She stills and her eyes widen the moment my words sink in.

"You're kidding?!" she shrieks. The animosity of the past ten minutes is obliterated thanks to my news.

I keep my face serious: jaw tight, lips flat, eyes almost slits. "I don't kid," I say, deadpan, then take another mouthful of food.

The room is filled with whoops and the next thing I know Sophie barrels around the table and toward me in a way all her Insta inspirations would frown upon. She works her way into my lap, wrapping her arms around me while I'm still chewing.

Too soon, she pulls back and beams. "I'm so proud of you."

My gut twists painfully at the tidbit of information I'm keeping private. Not that there's much keeping. From the comment she made a minute ago, it's clear she's on to me like a sniffer dog and knows there's something I'm not telling her.

"How was your day?" I ask, attempting to change the subject. "You sounded like you were in a good mood in your texts?"

"It's *that* surprising?" The smirk I give her receives a playful thump to my arm. "Ass."

"I'm being serious. Tell me about your day."

"Well, as you know, I picked the desks."

That text was surprising. I figured there'd be at least another two outings for her to commit to something. There's one detail I'm intrigued about.

"And which color did you go for?" I ask, playing with the ends of her hair, which are resting against her back in a loose ponytail. For a second, my mind drifts, and I wonder what they'd look like against my skin if they were still red.

"White."

42

Two steps forward, three steps back. Old Sophie never would have picked white, she would have gone for the brightest color available. I keep my expression neutral. "You know white isn't a color, right? Was it to compliment the black? What is it they call the two together ...?" I make a show of tapping my chin, knowing exactly what it is. "Monochrome."

She narrows her eyes and shifts in my lap, something I wish she wouldn't do. "No."

"Were there other colors to choose from?" I ask, trying and failing to keep my mind focused on the conversation when she shifts in my lap again.

"Yes."

"So, why did you go for white?"

Sophie looks lost in thought. "It seemed like the right choice."

"Seemed?"

"You're making me second-guess myself." The muscle in her jaw twitches in the way it does when she's annoyed, and I decide to leave it.

Sliding the chair back effortlessly with her still perched on my knee, I smile. "There's only one way to celebrate us both having good news." Sophie gives me a quizzical look. "Dancing."

Her face drops. "I'm too tired to go out."

"I meant here," I reply, ushering her up from my lap.

She glances around the room skeptically. "Here?"

"Is there something wrong with our house?" *Our*, being mine and the band's. "Or is dancing not aesthetically pleasing now, either?"

I hold my breath, waiting to see how she will take my slight dig. True to her partying roots, her resolve cracks. "What did you have in mind?"

"Alexa, play Otis."

"Damn you."

My body shakes with laughter. "Come on." I reach around her head and give the loose bow holding her hair in place a gentle tug. "It's time to let your hair down."

Sophie stares at the scrap of black material in my outstretched hand, then takes it and tosses it to the side. When she grabs my hand, just in case I wasn't already hard-wired to every move she makes, electricity shoots up my arm from where our hands connect.

The song is only a couple of minutes, but as we join together and sway to Otis's cover of Stand by Me, time seems to stand still. With the bluesy melodies floating around the two of us, there's nowhere in the world I'd rather be. I bury my face in the soft waves of her hair, trying to ignore the need to inhale her shampoo. Honey and almond.

A lump forms in my throat when a little voice in my head says, *"Tell her. Tell her how you feel, how you've always felt."*

Something takes over. I pull away even though the song hasn't finished, and Sophie looks up, confused.

A throat clearing behind us breaks the moment. Coming back down to Earth, I turn toward the source of the noise. Standing in the doorway with salon-worthy curled red hair, legs bronzed and displayed to perfection in an outfit that screams *'look at me'*, is the last person I expected to show up.

"Grace?"

Chapter Four

Sam

Grace narrows her eyes in Sophie's direction. "Yes. Grace. Your *girlfriend*."

I flinch at her use of the G-word. It couldn't seem more out of place than it does right now with the three of us staring between each other.

"Wh—" My voice cracks. I blink and try again. "What are you doing here?"

Grace's face turns a color similar to the shade of her hair. "Is a *girlfriend* not allowed to come see her *boyfriend* whenever she wants?"

"It's after eleven."

"Exactly," she snaps. "So, what is *she* doing here?"

"*She* is going to leave you to it," says Sophie. I'm about to tell her to wait and ask Grace to leave instead, but pause when it hits me it's the wrong move, reinforced when Sophie shakes her head and mouths, '*Sorry.*'

Sophie bustles out of the kitchen-diner and even Otis, the traitor, goes silent, leaving me to face the ball of fury alone.

"It wasn't what it looked like." Middle ground seems like the best way to go.

"It was exactly what it looked like," Grace replies.

I drag a hand across my jaw. "Do you want to break up?"

Grace laughs so hard her curls shake. "Sam, come on. We both know what this is …"

A bitter taste fills my mouth. An arrangement.

An arrangement which was Ryan's idea. He came up with the gem right before Abby's big thirtieth birthday party, after I bumped into Sophie in Manhattan with the Fuckwit of Wallstreet, got wasted and told him everything.

"It's been a while …" Months. "Sophie's still clueless." So much for the logic that sometimes people need something taken away to realize what's right in front of them. "It would make sense."

I watch, confused, as Grace walks to my side. She fluffs her hair and pulls out her phone, opening up TikTok.

"We need to go live," is the only explanation I get. She opens up settings and types, *Live with Sam Riley from S.C.A.R.A.B.* She pretty much sets in stone the future of our 'relationship', when she flutters her eyelashes and says, "Do you think you could, like, take the dots out of S.C.A.R.A.B.? They're a pain to type in."

I blink. This woman is unbelievable. Not for the first time I find myself wondering where the hell Ryan found her. She hits the big, red 'Go Live' button, and instantly, ten thousand of her three hundred thousand plus followers are watching. It's creepy as fuck and staring at the two of us in the mirror image on her screen; my face gives away exactly how I'm feeling.

"Chilling with my boo, y'all," Grace says, then stands on her tiptoes and places a quick kiss on my cheek, leaving behind a bright pink lipstick mark. The viewers jump to forty thousand. She throws out a peace sign and blows a kiss to the camera. "We're gonna, y'ano, go …"

She winks and the comments flood in.

They're totally about to b0ne.

I'd do anything to be her right now.

Down for a 3sum?

I frown at one of the last ones, right before Grace stops recording.

I wonder if he f@cks as bad as he sings.

Who the hell are these people?

"We don't need to break up," says Grace, totally unphased by all the comments. "This is going great."

"For you," I reply without thinking.

She scowls and taps her phone a couple of times. My blood runs cold when a voice recording fills the room.

"Be my girlfriend and you can use me for whatever you want."

"Anything?"

"Yeah, anything."

Grace's brows pull together, faking concern. "I wonder what the media and the record label would think of this?"

They'd think I was a Grade A dick and Grace has just proved she's a bigger bitch than I thought.

"What do you want?"

She shuffles back to my side, raises her camera, and before I realize what she's doing, kisses me straight on the lips. She quickly posts the picture on her Instagram, along with the hundreds of others before it. She might as well have the words fame-chaser stamped on her forehead, and my Chow's takeout threatens to make a reappearance when I catch the last two hashtags that she types into the comments.

#mine #always

"I want this ..." She rolls her eyes when I wipe my mouth with the back of my hand, then rests one of hers on my chest. "And if you want all your fans to keep thinking you're the nice guy you pride yourself on being, then we keep this arrangement going." Thankfully, she slips her phone into her bag and backs away to the door. "Got to give the fans what they want, *Sammy*."

My skin prickles with irritation as she turns and disappears from the kitchen, leaving me behind, questioning how I ever got myself into this mess.

Sophie

I rush out of S.C.A.R.A.B.'s place like Bambi on ice.

The stumbling doesn't stop with the door or the steps. It carries on along the sidewalk.

What was that?

It wasn't Friday Feast Night, that's for sure. I'm never turning up late again if that's what the end result is. Messy, complicated moments that shouldn't be there.

We're Sam and Soph. Soph and Sam.

When I'm a safe distance from the offending location, I stop, taking in a younger couple walking on the opposite side of the road, as the girl giggles at something the guy says.

Sam walks close to my side, laughing at what I'm saying as we trudge along the snowy sidewalks. Flakes fall around us, glittering under the streetlights.

"... the best part was they had their friends over. Aurelia stormed out of the room and Hale almost puked in his bowl of Cheetos."

At the same time Sam laughs, my foot starts to slide, then my other follows it. I close my eyes, bracing myself for the impact my butt is about to make with the hard, cold ground.

It never comes.

After a second, I realize it's because a pair of arms have caught me. When I open my eyes, my breath catches in my throat.

"Careful," says Sam, his voice comes out all weird and raspy.

My heart skips a couple of beats as he helps me stand upright. His hands remain looped around my lower back. I put it down to ice-fueled anxiety. I love winter. Hate ice.

"And how do you feel about having a new brother?" I can taste the peppermint hot chocolate he's just drunk as his breath clouds in what little space there is between us.

I shrug. "Weird, I guess. Sometimes it feels like I'm living in the shadows. My parents ... Aurelia ... Hale ..." I carefully take a step back, needing some space from the way Sam's blue eyes search mine and the way they're suddenly making my pulse race. "They're ..."

"Big personalities?" Sam finishes, and I giggle at how tamely he's describing them.

"Yeah," I agree, staring at the ground intently as I start walking again, avoiding the ice. "I guess, sometimes, it would be nice to be seen."

I stop when I realize Sam isn't walking with me. I turn back and find him stuck to the spot, his hands hanging at his sides and a frown covering his face. "I see you, Soph."

I raise my hands to my cheeks. My skin is burning like I'm feverish. Maybe that's it? My mood lifts, the impending sense of doom shifting. That has to be it. I'm coming down with something. Fevers make people do all kinds of crazy things. It's the only explanation for why my head went cloudy and I found the way Sam's lips moved while he was talking fascinating.

49

There's only one thing that will make things feel right again. Pulling out my phone, I have an Uber requested to take me to Manhattan in seconds, where I hope the past twenty minutes will be forgotten and everything will make sense again.

The Uber appears in record time, and leaving Brooklyn behind, I head towards another of the secrets I've been keeping. The masculine one with a name that matches his preppy vibes to a tee.

Brendan Fitzgerald, one of Manhattan's elites. At first, I was surprised and thought his interest in me was a joke.

We met one morning when I was picking up my caffeine fix. It was a meeting as swoon-worthy as the way Brendan styles his hair, which makes him look like my main man Leo in *The Wolf of Wall Street* in the parts where he isn't getting wasted, lying and snorting coke. The weather was all moody and stormy; the rain pouring down and soaking me to the skin.

I was running late, sprinting through the coffee shop, when we collided in that way people do in the movies that makes it clear fate is on their side. Brendan grabbed a ton of napkins and his hands lingered longer than they should have in my breasticular region, where my white t-shirt was expertly see-through.

The rest, as they say, is history.

Brendan is the King of put-togetherness. We do things younger me imagined older me doing. When he's around, my goal of getting my life on track doesn't feel quite so far out of reach. Everything would be perfect if it weren't for the fact that Sam's been as vocal for his dislike of the situation, as he's been for his dislike of my new wardrobe and the dramatic increase in my fruit and veg intake.

When I get to Brendan's apartment, I knock loudly.

Luckily, tonight isn't one of the nights where he tries to hit an eight-hour sleep quota, and the door opens. Brendan fills the doorway, looking confused, in his blue pinstripe pajamas with a thread count higher than the Egyptian Cotton sheets I recently invested in.

"Sophie? What are you doing here? We don't have plans?"

That's the thing about Brendan. He's a planner. His life is scheduled to perfection by his PA and if it isn't logged in one of the many diaries sitting on his chunky wooden desk, then he doesn't want anything to do with it.

I step inside his apartment, greeted by the usual grandeur. Giant rugs perfectly positioned under furniture with a price tag that makes my eyes water. It's the view of Central Park which sold me on the idea that maybe money really can buy happiness. I'd happily sit on Brendan's red leather chaise lounge all day and stare out at the beauty of Manhattan. Even if, deep down, I'll always be a Brooklyn girl.

"I just wanted to see you." Turning back, I smile, taking all of him in.

I could do without the pajamas. I'm more of a sweatpants and t-shirt gal. Still, he's gorgeous in the way rich people are. Everything is perfect. Perfectly sculpted muscles. Perfectly moisturized skin. Perfectly tousled hair. The only thing that isn't perfect is the fact I feel nothing. Not even a flicker of what I usually do whenever we're around each other.

Damn you, Sam Riley.

I close the gap between Brendan and me, then trail a hand up his chest. My fingers linger on the top button of his sleep shirt. At first, he frowns. But when I toy with the small round piece of plastic, then slip it through the hole, a smile plays on his lips. A smile filled with promises of things to come.

Sadly, his looks are just that … looks.

Where his million-dollar deep pockets might be enough for some, I can't ignore what's always been lacking in the bedroom. Brendan is oblivious thanks to some faux-orgasm moaning. I keep trying not to think about what it means that he's content as long as he gets his happy ending.

An hour later, unsatiated and with an ache between my legs that Brendan didn't even try to help subside, I lay in his arms, toying with the coarse hairs on his chest. This is the part we do better. The being together. I remind myself daily that sex isn't everything. It's not part of the foundations that make a relationship strong. It's just (for some) a bonus.

"I picked the desks today," I remind him.

"What desks?" asks Brendan sleepily.

My hand stills. "The ones I told you about. For Next Level's new office."

"Oh yeah, those. Sorry, I'm tired. I forgot."

Like he forgot to reply.

Uncertainty washes through me. "You're still coming to the restaurant opening on Wednesday, right?"

A faint snore fills the room and I frown, trying to ignore the sinking feeling in my gut.

I came here needing a sign. Reassurance that everything is fine and what I felt earlier was misplaced—a blip. With Brendan fast asleep beside me, giving no reassurances whatsoever, it doesn't feel like one.

Before switching my brain off for the night and escaping to a place where I have no worries, I make a mental note to check the event next week is written in Brendan's diary.

Chapter Five

Sophie

Hot. It's way too hot.

I go to kick off my covers, but I'm stopped when a hand presses against my leg, pushing it into the mattress.

Lips skim against my neck. Teeth bite my nipple. I moan and lift my hips. A chuckle vibrates over my stomach, making all the tiny hairs covering my skin rise. My hands tangle through hair as my core aches. Warm breath hits my clit and it throbs.

I look down and my eyes connect with a pair of blue hooded ones. Sam's.

An alarm blares and my eyes fly open. I tumble out of bed and pain sears through my knee when it collides with the floor, hard.

"Shit," I hiss.

Rolling onto my back, I somehow manage to bend and raise my leg, then clutch my knee against my chest. It throbs and my eyes water. Following a weekend of mulling and stewing over Friday, this is the last thing I need. To be injured, exhausted, frazzled, and worst of all ... horny.

After a brief spell of liking Mondays, thanks to a stack of books about positivity and how to change your mindset sitting on my nightstand, I hate them again. Mondays can bite my ass, along with the thick black suit pants I'm going to have to wear to cover up the swelling and insta-bruise now attached to my leg, taking residence where my kneecap usually is. I'm already sweating from the heat and it's only seven in the morning. Or it could be from the dream. The one I can never think about again.

Dammit. I struggle to my feet and reluctantly make the painful journey to the shower.

Over two hours later, I hobble into the building housing Next Level PR's new offices. I grit my teeth, trying and failing to ignore the thundercloud that's hanging above my head. It follows me like a bad smell into the elevator.

After a five-floor journey upwards, the doors sweep open. I shuffle slowly into the reception area, then through the main part of the offices, heading toward the corner one where Sooz, Zoe, Abby, Amanda and I, all work together.

Standing in the doorway, I take in the desks, which have arrived promptly like the store assistant promised. At least there's one perk of paying top dollar for something which should have cost half the price.

"What are those?" I hiss, clenching my juice with a vice-like grip.

There should be five white. Instead, there's one orange, one yellow, one purple, one pink and finally, my white.

Sitting in the middle of the rainbow that has puked in our office is the teal-haired person responsible.

"Zo," I groan. "What did you do?"

"Added a little sparkle," she grins. "All that white was a total buzzkill."

"Buzzkill?" I repeat.

I can't believe she's done this.

"Come on, Soph. They're our team colors. Although I'm not feeling the white for you." She casts a perfectly lined, assessing eye over me. She purses her lips at my black pants, then her expression brightens like she's had an idea. "I think you're more of a rouge. You're deep, desired, a seductress in the be—"

"Zo!" I squeak. "Stop."

"What's wrong?" she asks, the excitement disappearing from her face.

What's wrong is that she's taken center stage when this was my chance to shine. It's always the same. Between her, Abby, my family, and a long list of fuck-ups following me around, I don't stand a chance at showing the world who I really am and what I have to offer.

My nostrils flare and I walk deeper into the room. When I reach my new desk, I drop my bag on the floor and fire up my laptop before setting my breakfast down.

"What the hell is that?" asks Zoe, peering around her monitor, wrinkling her nose at the concoction in my eco-friendly travel cup, like it's more upsetting than the stunt she's pulled with the desks.

"Green juice," I reply, as if the bright sludge isn't obvious enough.

Sitting at the orange desk across from me, Zoe stares a bit longer, then pulls a face that says she's personally offended by my drink of choice. I tap my pen against my desk, which matches my sleeveless white shirt, thanks to the majority of my work wardrobe being at the dry cleaners. The drink stands out against it. It's an Insta-worthy photo if ever there was one. Inspiration strikes and I grab my phone. Quickly standing, I arrange my neutral-colored notepad and pen next to the cup.

I ignore Zoe and hover my phone directly above the small setup, trying to capture the perfect flat-lay image. Happy there are no shadows to be found, and the result is something Abby would be proud of; I settle back in my seat. The longer Zoe stares at the juice, the more it seems to offend her. I'm tempted to rub my eyes and double check it hasn't grown a pair of arms and given her the middle-fingered salute. She shakes her head, making the teal strands of hair swish around her shoulders, then picks up her own pen and starts jotting notes on her leopard print pad of paper.

"You know," I say, trying to keep my tone light. "When Sooz tasked us with decorating the office, I think she was going for something a little more … uniform."

Zoe coughs and I'm pretty sure I hear the word "boring".

Choosing to ignore her, I busy myself with cropping and lightening the image. When I'm almost done, I add on a trending filter, just to be sure it's up to Insta standards. The caption is the tricky part. How to convey a perfect life when yours is anything but. I settle for 'The best start to the day is a green one …' and make sure to add all the relevant hashtags on a few lines down.

I upload it to my new streamlined profile and, a couple of seconds later, Zoe snorts.

My eyes snap up, narrowed. "What?"

She gives the juice a brief glance. "*That* is not the best way to start the day."

"You're keeping tabs on me?"

"Someone has to," she mutters under her breath. "You're losing your goddamn mind."

"Says the Teal Goddess."

"Goddess being the main word in that sentence," she bites back.

My skin bristles. Growing up, we were soulsies. We partied our way through our early (and better part of) our twenties. We had the kind of friendship where we finished each other's sentences. Knew what the other person was thinking before *they* did.

And now she's the daily source of my irritation.

"You're so full of sh—" I don't get a chance to finish, because Abby and Amanda step into the room.

"Is the purple mine?" asks Abby excitedly from behind me.

I close my eyes and count to ten.

"Oh my God, am I pink?" asks Amanda. "Ah! I love it!"

The girls spend the next few minutes oohing and aahing over the desks. If I could switch off my ears, I would. I'm contemplating stepping out of the office for a while, in need of some scenery that doesn't resemble a color wheel. All that's missing in here is a bit of bright blue … like Sam's eyes when he looked up at me in the hot, steamy dream that didn't feel like one.

My cheeks flush in the same way they did Friday. I definitely have mono or something. Maybe I can go home sick? A reset on the whole day might be beneficial.

Abby wanders over and stares at the juice. "What is it today?"

"Kale, spinach, lime, and coconut water." Bitter, just like my mood.

"Yum," says Amanda from her desk. She's all for jumping on the juice wagon.

A gagging noise comes from behind Zoe's screen at the same time a soft South African voice fills the room.

"Why does it look a rainbow in here?" Sooz stands, hair in a tight bun, wearing high-waisted navy suit pants and a navy and white polka dot ruffle necked shirt, taking everything in. "Is my desk ... yellow?"

My eyes almost roll into the back of my head when I look up, fully expecting the storm cloud ruining my day to be a literal one hovering above me. I've barely had time to process what Zoe's done and now Sooz is here to witness it, too? She was meant to be in Cape Town for at least another two weeks.

Zoe jumps to her feet and shoves her pad of leopard print and phone into her oversized tie-dye tote. "It represents your personality—full of sunshine." Sooz purses her lips like she can't decide if she's being sarcastic or sincere. "Glad you're back, but I've got somewhere I need to be. Ciao. I'm out of here." Blowing kisses through the air, she whirlwinds out of the office, leaving behind her floral scent and color explosion.

Sooz stands gawping. "What's up with her?"

"Who knows?" says Abby, walking to her own desk. She turns on her laptop and a variety of screens.

"She's getting worse," I comment.

"You're one to talk, Kenza," Abby chuckles, facing me.

"What's that supposed to mean?" I scowl as my knee throbs, adding to my sour mood.

58

Sooz and Amanda look back and forth between the two of us.

"I've seen you liking every one of Kenza Subosic's Insta posts," answers Abby, blowing a few brown strands of hair which have fallen from her standard messy bun out of her face.

I throw my hands up in the air and they come dangerously close to colliding with the juice. "Is stalking my social media activity the new thing to do around here? We have clients, lots of them. Why is everyone busy being concerned with what I'm doing?"

Abby's simple shrug tips my mood over the edge, and for a fleeting moment, I wonder when I became a grumpier version of her. Probably when she became the one in the group to start getting good sex regularly, having finally got her own life in order. Flipping her off, I grab my glass of juice and guzzle it down, breathing through my nose and trying to ignore the way my stomach churns as it slides down slower than glue and refuses to settle.

This is good for you, Soph. No gain without pain. That's what all the blogs say. Happiness comes from within. I need to double check later whether they literally mean within your gut.

Unfortunately, I didn't do the best job of blending the juice, and a leaf of kale gets caught in my throat. I splutter and almost cry when a bright green stain sits in the middle of my shirt.

I tilt my head back and take in the beams. This is Karma for acting like a bitch.

Abby, Sooz and Amanda all stare at the green stain in horror, knowing if I'm going to combust, it will be right

59

about now. Luckily for them, a deep voice singsongs its way from the elevator.

Sam. Shit. We haven't spoken all weekend and I don't have a clue what to say.

The universe is testing me.

He comes into my view over Sooz's shoulder, his face steadily increasing in size as he gets closer to the room. His brows shoot up in surprise when he takes everything in, then forces out a smile. "Cool office."

I jump to my feet, needing to be far away from all the bright colors. They're throwing off my yang and ying or whatever the fuck it's called. I make a mental note not to use the word fuck as much, starting tomorrow.

"Where are you going?" asks Sooz. "It's only just gone nine-thirty."

I grab my brown leather tote from the floor. "To the gym," I huff, moving away from my desk, wincing when I place too much weight on my bad leg.

Trying to hide my limp as best I can, considering it feels like my leg is going to snap in two each time I use it, I push out into the main office and retrace my steps from an exceptionally long fifteen minutes ago.

Before I manage to make a clear exit to the elevator, Sam steps in front of me, catching me off guard. My eyes haven't got the friend zone message because they trail to his arms, drinking in the intricate tattoos covering muscles that weren't there when they were younger.

I gulp, feeling him watching me.

He gestures at my chest. "You have something green on you."

"I'm aware," I reply, avoiding all eye contact, instead choosing to look at the bright unicorn bag in his other hand.

He steps out of my path and, with a frown, says, "See you later?"

I don't answer, too busy simmering over the desks and my ridiculous behavior as I hobble into the elevator.

The last thing I see are my friends watching me disappear from across the office, mouths parted, likely wondering when I lost my mind.

"Since when does she go to the gym?" Sooz asks, right before the elevator doors close.

Chapter Six

Sophie

No exercise endorphins are to be found at the gym thanks to my busted knee, and what I hope will improve my mood literally makes it worse.

Less than thirty minutes after going in, I struggle back outside. The oppressive heat hits me as hard as my frustrations.

How can something as small and irrelevant as missing a cardio session (something that deep down, I hate) make it feel like I'm losing a grip on everything? I'm also at risk of losing my friends if I keep acting crazy like I am.

I'm ready to go back to the office and apologize for being a complete bitch when I turn and collide with a solid wall of muscle.

The sensation of thick, tepid liquid, slowly traveling south, past my chest, then my navel and down to my nether regions, has me clenching my eyes shut and saying a little prayer to God that when I open them, this day will be a bad dream. I'm struck with disappointment when a car whizzes past and a horn blares, alerting me to the fact I'm very much in the present, and my prayer hasn't been answered.

I prize one eye open and look down. It's worse than I thought. I suck in a sharp breath. A giant, bright green stain covers my new, matching white Fabletics workout set.

Two lots of white ruined in the space of an hour.

I should have just stuck with black. This day can go to hell.

"What are you doing here?" I ask when I find that the wall of muscle is in fact Sam.

Blue eyes glitter down at me and Sam gives his signature lopsided smile. He holds the now half-empty cup of green juice in the air. Some of the spillage trails down his arm, over his tattoo sleeve. I divert my eyes before I can be caught ogling his arms … again.

"You forgot your drink," he says, unphased by the fact we're both covered in green crap.

"Breakfast," I clarify.

Sam stares at the sludge. "Breakfast?" I nod. "Soph, it looks like algae. This is not a meal."

"It's good for me," I sniff, staring at the traffic that has come to a standstill thanks to a stray dog deciding to do its business in the middle of the road.

"You seem to enjoy wearing it more than drinking it." The wink he throws on the end takes the edge off my mood.

There's a reason he's the lead singer and face of S.C.A.R.A.B. and it's not just because of his husky voice that vibrates in the pants of his millions of female fans. No, if that isn't enough foreplay for them, his boy-next-door good looks finish the job. He barely needs to do a thing to have women eating out of the palm of his hand. They'd probably lick away the sticky green juice sitting between his fingers without him having to ask.

"I'm leaving," I say, making sure to keep my voice light and less bitchy, remembering how Karma treated me after earlier.

I hobble away, leaving my questionable juice behind.

Sam walks beside me, matching my stride. Short legs combined with a minor injury make it impossible to get away from him. "Why are you limping?"

"I fell out of bed." My cheeks threaten to burn at the slight reminder of the ridiculous dream.

"What did you hurt?"

"My knee."

I catch his frown out of the corner of my eye. "Have you had it checked out?"

"It's fine, it's no—"

I stop walking when Sam grabs hold of my arm, much to the annoyance of the people around us on a mission to get to wherever they need to be. A guy powering behind us slams into Sam and looks like he's about to give him a piece of his mind until he clocks exactly who it is he's slammed into. Paling, he apologizes and walks off. Sidetracked, I don't realize what Sam's doing until he's on his knees, rolling the material of my leggings carefully up over my injured knee. Even with his light touch, I let out a hiss of air.

"You need to ice this, Soph. It looks swollen." The lines of his frown deepen between his brows. "Have you?"

I barely process his words, pain long forgotten. All I can focus on is the way my skin feels unusually warm where his fingertips connect with it.

"Have I what?"

Amusement flashes through his eyes. "Iced it."

I blink. "Iced what?"

"Your knee." One corner of his mouth twitches like he wants to laugh.

It's bad enough that my brain appears to be in a Sam-Riley-induced brain fog, but the universe doesn't seem to think that's enough, because it wants him to be aware of the fact, too.

"Sam, why are you really here?" I huff out, changing the subject.

I then make the error of trying to drag my leg from his grip. I wobble dangerously and Sam's other hand drops the juice and darts up, gripping my hip to steady me. Heat creeps up my neck and shoots to my core as Sam shakes his head, trying to hide his laughter. I'm ready to jump for joy when he finally takes his hands off my body and slides the material back over my knee.

Once standing, he slips his hands into the pockets of his jeans and his expression turns serious. "You're upset?"

I point at my stained leggings. "I have juice pooling in my pants."

Sam's eyes remain trained on my face as a small muscle in his jaw twitches. "How about we go back to my place? You can ice your knee and tell me how you really feel about the whole desk debacle."

I snort. "Desk debacle? Is that what we're calling it now?"

He smirks. "Can you think of a better name?"

"Lots. None of which are appropriate for saying out loud."

"Like I thought. Desk debacle it is." He steps toward the edge of the sidewalk and raises a hand in the air. A yellow cab pulls up almost instantly.

I bite my lip. Under normal circumstances, I'd follow him without a second thought, but all of this—thanks to my traitorous, over-excited brain—doesn't feel like normal circumstances. It feels like I'm about to step into the lion's den with no chance of survival. It's ridiculous, because this is me, and standing in front of me is Sam Riley, the lead singer of S.C.A.R.A.B.—Sam Riley who has a girlfriend, but even if he didn't, could have his pick of pretty much any woman in the world.

Plain old Sophie Parker would never stand a chance at being the center of his affections, but that's not what's concerning. What's concerning is when the hell she decided she wanted to.

"I'm perfectly capable of walking."

"Soph, I'm being serious. Your knee is swollen." I swallow hard when Sam's eyes darken. "You have a choice. Either you get in yourself or I pick you up and put you in."

My eyes dart left and right. There's a lot of people around and probably one or two papzz lurking in the shadows, ready to get the perfect scandalous snap. The last thing I need is more images tainting my already shitty reputation, which is why I hobble past Sam and slide into the back of the cab with a scowl on my face, wishing I could wipe the smirk off his.

Twenty minutes later, I'm stretched out on the couch in S.C.A.R.A.B.'s living area, trying to figure out how soon is too soon to leave. Afternoon is already creeping in, and without my parents helping to run The Parkapellas, I made the rash decision to add in extra practices, one of which is tonight. There's no way we'll be ready for The American Showcase otherwise.

Sam walks into the room with a tub of ice cubes in one hand and a towel in the other. I shift my uninjured leg, then try to hide my wince when I move the injured one. Sam's right. I shouldn't be walking around on it, not that I'm about to admit that out loud.

He sits on the other side of the couch and I watch as he fills the towel with half of the cubes then bunches the material around them, twisting it tight to keep them in place. He looks over and gives me a small smile. "Can I?"

I nod yes as my pulse quickens from one simple look.

Brendan. Brendan. Brendan. Brendan.

Repeating his name does nothing. It just makes me question why he's a part of my life. Suddenly, he doesn't seem as swoon-worthy or as life affirming as I've made him out to be in my head. He hasn't even messaged since I left his place Saturday morning. I should feel disappointed, but I'm too distracted right now by my best guy friend.

Brendan's the safe bet, I tell myself. Safe because, if I'm being honest, my heart decided it wasn't really in it anymore the second I stared at Sam longer than I should have.

He's safe because if my heart isn't all in, it means there's less chance of it being broken.

What isn't safe right now is Sam. Sam, who's ironically been my safety blanket for as long as I can remember. Sam, who I would trust with everything and anything—apart from myself.

I go to take hold of the makeshift cold compress and my fingers skim across his as I grab the towel. The skin on the tips turns warm, buzzing, and the last thing I want is to move them away. It's like floodgates have been opened and there's no chance of stopping the water pouring through.

"I can do it," I say, while clearing my throat.

Sam pulls his hand back, appearing totally unphased. "So …"

"So …?" My heart misses a beat. Has he noticed? Is he going to pull me up on my crazy behavior?

"The desks …"

Relieved, I sink back into the cushions, my hand keeping the compress in place. "What about them?"

"Only one was white."

"Zoe changed the order."

Sam grimaces. "Ah."

"Yeah." I sigh. "Ah."

"She probably didn't mean anything by it."

"I know, but that's the problem. She never does. She just does stuff without thinking about how it will affect other people."

Sam grabs a spare cushion and nods at my leg. "Lift."

I do as he says, and he slides the cushion underneath, then twists carefully and grabs the remote for the TV from the small table on his side of the couch. I'm trying to figure out what he's up to when he presses a few buttons and sets *Annie* playing. He knows *Annie* always puts me in a better mood. Anything musical, in fact, but this is one of my favorites, up there with my leading gal Piper in *Coyote Ugly* and my all-time favorite cast ensemble in *Hairspray*. John Travolta nailed it.

"Things have been rocky with you both for a while," he continues. *While* is the understatement of the century, but I don't correct him. "Have you tried talking to her about it?"

I purse my lips stubbornly. "No."

"Soph, she can't change if she isn't aware what she's doing is upsetting you. You can't always ..."

He tails off and I frown.

"Can't always what?"

"Avoid confrontation. I know you don't like upsetting people. But sometimes, the boat has to be rocked if you want things to change."

I make a point of staring at the screen and keeping my voice even when I reply, "I'm fine, Sam."

"Is that what this new wardrobe is? All the weird diets and refusing to come out with the group? It's you being fine?"

My head snaps back in his direction and our eyes clash. "This is who I am."

He sees right through what I'm saying, like I knew he would. "No, this is you hiding from who you are. Look, I know things were shitty after what happened in Berlin, but it doesn't mean you hav—"

"Stop, Sam. I said I'm fine. I don't need you trying to get inside my head, because there's nothing to figure out. Your time would be better spent focusing on your girlfriend."

I regret the words the second they're out of my mouth, but I can't take them back.

"Fine," he replies, an edge to his voice.

"Fine."

Luckily, the cast of *Annie* picks the exact right moment to fill the room with their voices, covering the tense silence.

The lyrics to "Maybe" are the last thing I remember before drifting off to sleep.

Sam

Sophie's phone has been blowing up on her lap for the past half hour. It's on silent, so she's deep asleep, none the wiser.

I stare at the name on the screen, and the preview of the message, confused.

Russ: *Where are you?*

Who the hell is Russ?

The floor creaks and I look up, finding Jake standing in the doorway with two bottles of beer. He glances between me and Sophie, then to my hand, which is holding the compress in place.

"She hurt her knee," I explain.

"And you came to her rescue. How noble."

He walks into the room quietly and hands over one of the bottles before dropping into an armchair.

"Don't be a dick." I lift the bottle. "What's this for?"

Jake glances at Sophie and smiles. "Dutch courage."

Busted. I look at her, trying not to stare too hard as I take in how peaceful she is, then take a swig of the beer.

"That obvious?"

"Kind of, to those who know you." He smiles again. "Plus, I'm an expert at wanting something you can't have. You've liked her forever. Why don't you tell her?"

Ignoring the extra details being thrown into the mix, I reply honestly, "Because I need her in my life."

"I don't follow."

"What if I tell her and she doesn't feel the same?"

What if I tell her, and she leaves, just like Mom and Dad did?

70

"And what if you don't and she does? You'll miss out on something good. Life's too short. You know that."

Sophie's phone lights up with the name Russ on the screen again. Jake catches it too. "She isn't always going to be single. There will be a time when you're both in relationships and this dynamic the two of you have going will have to stop. Friday's, too."

Little does he know that time's now, and it isn't even with the guy on the screen. I'm fully aware of how messed up the situation is and how much messier things could get. Jake leans forward and not very quietly places his bottle on the coffee table. The noise makes Sophie jolt upright. She looks between me and Jake with wide, yet sleepy eyes, then down at her phone.

"Shit," she hisses when she takes in the number of notifications from the Russ guy. "I've been out all afternoon?" She thumps me in the arm and Jake laughs. "Why didn't you wake me up?"

"You were tired."

"I'm always tired," she snaps.

She tries to move so she can stand, but I press my hand across her chest, holding her in place.

"You're not going anywhere, you're injured."

She pushes my hand away and clambers to her feet. The compress drops to the floor with a thud. "I have somewhere I need to be."

She grabs her bag and sneakers and hobbles toward the living room door. I'm standing in front of her, blocking the way, before she can get through. Jake watches the two of us in the background, amused.

"Where are you going, Soph?"

"Move. *Please.*"

"Not until you tell me where you're going. Who's Russ?"

Sophie's lips form a flat line. "Not everything in my life is your business, Sam. You have a *girlfriend.*"

I arch a brow. "Your point?"

"You're not *my* boyfriend, so stop trying to act like it."

Stunned by her remark, I'm taken off guard when she pushes past me and hobbles away, only stopping to put her sneakers on. I guess she's better at confrontation than I've ever given her credit for. The front door slams shut behind her and I turn back, finding Jake still sitting with a grin on his face.

"Yes?"

Jake raises his beer to his lips and takes a drink. "Just trying to figure out when you guys turned into me and Abby."

With a huff, I leave him chuckling to himself with the word prick for company.

Sophie

"I'm sorry," I call out, bustling into the room as much as one can bustle while hobbling.

Russ stomps over in a way only a seven-year-old can get away with and folds his arms across his chest. He narrows his dark, almost black, eyes to slits. "You're late."

"But I'm here." I reach over and flick him on the nose.

It's always been a surefire way to diffuse my youngest brother, Xavier's mood swings.

It does the trick and Russ smiles. "I thought you weren't coming."

My chest tightens at the little guy's face.

I ignore my knee throbbing in protest when I crouch, so I'm not looking down on him. "If I promise I'll be here, I'll be here." He nods, and, happy he's convinced, I straighten. "But even if I wasn't you'd be fine. You've got this."

Russ's eyes drop to the ground, and he stubs his toe against it, his worn, shabby sneakers making a loud squeaking sound. "I'm scared about the competition."

I reach over and give his shoulder a squeeze. "Remember what I said? You don't need to be scared of the competition." I wink. "The competition needs to be scared of you."

When Russ looks at my outfit, confused, it hits me: I'm still wearing my green-stained workout gear. He wrinkles his nose. "Why do you smell gross?"

"I went to battle with a swamp monster."

Interest already lost, Russ races over to the group, ready to warm up, standing with a renewed sense of purpose.

I'm terrified of doing this without my parents' help, but, equally, the thought of a new kind of challenge and a chance to do things my own way has my stomach fluttering with excitement.

This place fills me with the hope it was built on—it always has—and no matter how crappy and messed up life might get, it has a way of reminding me of what's really truly important in life. Happiness.

Chapter Seven
Sophie

Zoe and I don't speak to each other for the whole of Tuesday ... or Wednesday.

A part of me thought, with Sooz coming back sooner than predicted, that she would take the reins and run the show for the restaurant opening I've been working on the last few months. When I asked if that was what she wanted to happen, she simply smiled and said it was my hard work and I deserved the credit for it.

Dressed to the nines, even my rift with Zoe can't dampen my excitement for the night to come. I put everything that's happened with Sam the past few days in a box and toss away the key. I'm about to prove exactly why I'm part of the Next Level family, desk debacle be damned, and I'm doing it all with Brendan by my side. Him agreeing to come to the Meatpacking District where the restaurant is located feels monumental, especially as he hates venturing away from the Upper East Side, unless it's to the Financial District.

Outside Brendan's apartment, I check my appearance in one of the mirrors lining the walls of the corridor, skimming my hands over my new black Prada dress. It couldn't be further from old Sophie, and I have the urge to rip the material away with Sam's words ringing in my ears. Instead, I plaster on a smile and knock on the door. A minute passes, and there's no response. I knock again, louder. When there's still no answer, I'm hit with a feeling that tells me tonight isn't going to go as planned.

Pulling out my phone, I bring up Brendan's number and hit call.

It rings a couple of times before he answers. "Hey."

"Erm, hey," I say, looking at the door hopefully. "I'm outside your apartment, but you're not answering."

Brendan clears his throat. "Did you not get my message?"

"No," I say to the expertly polished chunk of wood. "What message?"

"I have to work tonight. Something came up. Sorry."

"But tonight's a really big deal," I reply glumly, unable to hide my disappointment.

There are muffled voices in the background and then Brendan says, "Sorry, babe. I have to go. Text me later and let me know how it goes."

The line goes dead, and I'm left alone wearing a dress I don't really like, chasing a dream that's never really been mine.

Sam

After what Sophie said on Monday, I figure the best thing I can do for both of us is give us both space and spend time with the person the world thinks is my girlfriend, before she can pull some kind of shitty stunt.

I pick Grace up just after six, dressed in my usual band t-shirt and jeans combo. She frowns when she takes in my appearance, gesturing at the fancy gold dress she's wearing. I hope she isn't asking for my opinion, because she looks like a Christmas decoration. Whenever she's dressed extra sparkly, it means she's out to impress. The problem is that it's not to impress me, it's to impress the world, and the agenda for our dates usually includes way-too-expensive restaurants and posing for photos, which I hate.

"I thought we were going to Le Blanc?"

"I thought we could do something more fun," I suggest, offering out an olive branch. "Like burgers and a game of pool?" Grace stares blankly and I start to explain, "It's a game with a table that's green. There are balls and sticks ..."

I'm about to go into the objectives of it, when Grace sighs. "I know what pool is, Sam."

"So, what's the problem?"

"Do I look like I'm dressed for it?" Of course, she isn't. She looks gorgeous, don't get me wrong ... if the devil in disguise is your type. She's dressed to impress, to be noticed ... by everyone apart from me.

I scratch the back of my head and decide to give her one last chance to show a little bit of decency and act like a normal, almost likeable, human. "I guess not. But you could get changed real quick."

Grace holds a hand in the air and closes her eyes. Her nostrils widen in a way I didn't know was possible. "No pool. We're going to Le Blanc. Everyone you need to see will be there."

"You mean everyone *you* need to see," I mutter under my breath as she walks past me, making it clear things between us will never, ever be different. She's in this for one reason only. It's an arrangement, after all.

During the elevator ride down to the ground floor and the taxi to one of the most pretentious restaurants I've ever been in, I try to figure out how I can get out of this.

I come up with nothing.

Le Blanc, weirdly, is far from white. The floors are rich and dark; the tables covered in deep blue silk cloths with gleaming silver and glass wear. There are red velour drapes and chandeliers hanging from the ceiling and jazz music playing in the background. All it needs is a bit of secondhand smoke and I might as well have stepped back into the Swing era. Needless to say, my t-shirt, with a bright red hand giving the middle-fingered salute and the words 'Fuck the System' sitting beneath, isn't the right attire. Proven when the waiter who comes to our table wearing a suit, which makes him resemble a penguin, looks at what I'm wearing with disdain.

Grace picks up on the funky vibes passing between us and says way too loudly, "So, when does S.C.A.R.A.B. start recording their next album?"

The waiter stiffens and gives me a sideways glance. He might not have known who I was before, but he certainly does now.

"Grace," I hiss, as a few customers on the tables close by look over. "Keep your voice down."

"Why, Sammy? You should be proud. Isn't this going to be a multi-platinum selling album?" Her voice gets louder the closer she gets to the end of her sentence and my skin bristles at her use of the name Sammy. The way it rolls off her lips sounds wrong. It's personal, and nothing about this is personal.

"It's not public knowledge," I grind out, making a mental note to make sure the guys never talk about shit like this when she's around again.

"Oops," she flutters her eyelashes at the waiter. "Silly me. Could we have a menu, please? And a bottle of Champagne."

The waiter nods and walks away.

"I hate Champagne."

Menus appear at record speed, providing Grace with a perfect opportunity to avoid eye contact with me.

"Sometimes it feels like everything is about you, Sam."

At least she's dropped the Sammy. I'm tempted to point out that it's the exact opposite, when the waiter appears again, setting down the bucket and opening the bottle.

"On the house," he says, pouring each of us a glass.

"Ooh, how kind," Grace preens, before ordering a handful of the most expensive items on the menu.

I order an equal amount of the dishes, the ones I can make sense of, not necessarily ones I will like. The portion sizes are questionable in these kinds of places and there's no doubt in my mind I'll be making a takeout stop after I've dropped Grace home. If we make it that far, because right now, she's pissing me off more than normal and I'm contemplating leaving.

Thanks to her little speech, after the waiter has left, he's replaced with one person after another requesting photos and autographs. I'm not even sure they're actual fans; they're more like the woman across from me—fame chasers. It becomes clear they're not fans when one woman asks if I've always wanted to perform pop music. Pop ... not rock. I could be famous for eating dog crap and they'd still love it. Meanwhile, Grace spends the entire time cooing in the background, photobombing at every opportunity she gets and re-gramming at the speed of light.

I can't do this. I don't give a crap what people think about my intentions for starting this or what the label thinks. I open my mouth, ready to tell Grace we need to talk so I can finally end this, when we're surrounded by three waiters. They set what feels like a never-ending stream of plates down.

When they finally leave and Grace has picked up her knife and fork, I clear my throat, ready to try again, but my phone lights up on the table with Sophie's name on the screen, distracting me. I frown at it and then at Grace, who is also staring at the vibrating object.

"Don't," she says, her voice low in warning.

I stare at the selection of dishes on the table, which she couldn't care less that I hate, and shake my head. Grabbing the phone, I answer and raise it to my ear, making out a sniffle over the noise of traffic in the background.

"Soph? What's wrong?"

Grace rolls her eyes.

"He isn't coming."

I grind my teeth. Fucking Fitzgerald. I don't know how Sophie found her way into his claws. He couldn't be less worthy of her if he tried. A night with my laptop revealed he's not just the Fuckwit of Wallstreet, he's The Dick of

Wallstreet. Literally. I wonder if Sophie knows as much or is sticking her head in the sand like with everything else.

"You're surprised?" I ask, coming across more abruptly than I intend to.

"Sam," Sophie says, with warning in her voice. "Please. Don't. Not tonight."

I want to say to her, if not now, when? I want to ask how many times she's going to let this idiot hide their relationship, stand her up and prove repeatedly he couldn't be further from what she needs in her life. I don't, because somehow Sophie and I have found ourselves in relationships with two of the least loyal people in New York. Ironic considering loyalty is one of the main foundations of our friendship.

It's that same loyalty which has me scraping my chair back against the wooden floors and heading to the exit of the restaurant with Grace staring after me in dismay.

I don't need to ask for the address of where Sophie's headed. "I have to change, but I'll try to get there as quick as I can."

The waiter manning the door watches me with intrigue as I pull out my credit card and motion for him to settle the bill for mine and Grace's table. He does so with as much speed as the menus appeared, and in the blink of an eye, my card is back and nestled safely in my wallet.

"I'm sorry for yesterday. I don't deserve you."

The wobble in Sophie's voice has steam billowing from my ears as I step out into the humid evening. Her confidence was already non-existent. I wish she'd see that Mister Preppy isn't doing anything to help build her back up. All he does is make her feel like she isn't worth showing up for. I picture myself driving a fist into his perfect jawline. Unfortunately, he isn't worth busting my hand over.

"See you soon, Soph."

I hang up before she can say anything else that might have me reconsidering finding Fitzgerald and rearranging his face.

Sophie

Standing in the center of Babini's, the Meatpacking District's most anticipated restaurant opening in the past twelve months, I wring my hands in front of me, taking in the hub of activity.

I feel unsettled and out of sorts. I'd like to say it's because of Brendan bailing, but I know it's not. What I don't know is which I'm more nervous about, seeing Sam or the restaurant opening. I hate it when we do our own loose version of fighting. Just thinking about how we left things makes my stomach churn. Yeah, I'm totally more nervous about seeing Sam.

Trying to block out everything apart from what needs to happen for the opening, I slowly spin on the spot, taking in each small detail, checking everything the clients wanted is in the right place. I'm ready to go over the guest list when a wave of calm washes over me. I turn and find Sam leaning against the wall by the entrance. He looks completely different from the boy I first met, yet somehow the same. His hair is tousled on top, falling across his forehead, almost hitting his eyes, but not quite.

With his hands tucked into the pockets of his suit pants, his sleeves rolled up showing off heavily inked forearms, and the couple of buttons undone at the top of his charcoal shirt, revealing even more inked skin, he looks like a rock God.

When he pushes off the wall with one foot and strolls toward me, every set of female eyes in the room watches him. The walls are about to be filled with some of the biggest celebrities around, but if Sam wanted to, he could outshine them all with a smile and a joke. Throw in a song with his voice, which makes some of the best artists sound like amateurs, and every single person would be putty in his hands.

"Finished checking me out?" A smile plays on his lips and his eyes twinkle beneath the expensive restaurant lights.

"Cocky much?" I retort, trying to sound as offended as humanly possible to hide that it's exactly what I was doing.

He throws a thumb over his shoulder. "I can leave …"

My eyes widen and the word, "Don't," is out before I can stop it.

Sam chuckles, and the space left between us disappears. The next thing I know, his arms are wrapped around me, my face is nestled in his shirt, nose pressed against the middle of his rib cage. I forget everything, overwhelmed by the smell of soap and, because he hates wearing cologne, what can only be described as Sam.

Storming along the sidewalk away from school and our first big dance, all I know is I need to get away. From here. Everything. I just need space to think.

"Soph! Wait!" shouts Sam from somewhere behind me. A quick glance over my shoulder shows him running to catch me up. I don't look back a second time. "Hey. Stop."

He grabs my arm and then I'm spinning, turning, facing him, and everything I just witnessed flashes through my mind.

My lip wobbles. "I needed you. You promised you'd come in with me. You promised the first dance." When no one else would. The last part is too humiliating to say out loud, but his grimace tells me he hasn't forgotten the fact.

"I got caught up ..."

"I saw you ..." And her. The two of them together. A lot more than that, too ... something I still can't get my head around.

Sam's face twists almost in pain and he steps toward me. I want to move back, keep the space between us, but I can't. My feet remain glued to the spot. He takes another step, and then another. The next thing I know, I'm wrapped in his arms, pretending the smell of another girl's perfume isn't clinging to his clothing.

We never fight. I hate it.

He whispers his apologies and everything feels better again.

Then, for a second, with his face nestled in my hair and his hands clinging to the back of my dress, my guard slips.

For a second, I step over the invisible line that's always there between us.

For a second, I let myself imagine I'm his.

Then, when the second is over, I plaster on a smile and pull back, reminding myself I never will be, because he's my friend, and that's all I want him to be.

"I'm sorry, too. I hate it when we fight," Sam whispers in my ear.

And just like that, everything feels right again.

"You're ruining my make-up," I grumble, glad my face is still pressed against him so he can't see how hard I'm smiling. How much I need him.

"Stop pretending like you hate it." He laughs again and his chest rumbles. I feel it everywhere, even in my toes. "You good?"

I tilt my head back. "Better now you're here," I admit, even though I probably shouldn't. Suddenly, the words feel like they have meaning behind them. They never have before. "Thank you. I don't think I could have done this without you."

So much for trying to swim at the deep end on my own. I'm clutching to Sam like I always have done, praying he'll help keep me afloat.

"You can do anything you put your mind to," he says, his voice more serious than I've ever heard it. "Don't forget that."

With a half-hearted smile, I decide to move on from his comment, because I don't really know how to reply. He always has had more faith in me than I have myself. "I don't know what I'd do without you, friend."

Why does the word sound alien now? Is this the way things are going to be? Is this the kind of thing there's no coming back from? These kinds of thoughts? What would it mean for us and everything we've been through together?

"Yeah, well, that's what they're for …" Sam clears his throat, "friends."

The room feels chilly when he steps back and the sparkle in his eyes is missing. I want to ask what's wrong, but I don't get a chance, because Amanda floats into the restaurant. She looks her effortlessly glamorous self, with her platinum hair hanging poker straight around her shoulders, reflecting the light. Even from a distance, I can tell her make-up is flawless. She looks ready to pose on the cover of Cosmopolitan or something.

As she heads over to us, she lets out a string of wows. Grinning, she shoves Sam out of the way. "You did so good, Soph. Everything looks amazing." She spins around with her phone raised, snapping photos.

84

"I'll grab us all a drink," says Sam, walking off in the direction of the bar, the surface of which is filled with Champagne flutes, ready to be filled. I try not to focus on how many there are.

When he's out of earshot, Amanda zeros in on me. "What's Sam doing here? He wasn't on the guest list? Was he?"

"No. I needed a boost." I pray she accepts my loose version of the truth without too many questions.

She arches a brow. "A Sam-related boost?"

"You know how it is."

I could tell her everything. About the weird moment we had and everything that's followed. How it feels like my eyes are being opened to something that's always been there; something I'm not sure I'm quite ready to acknowledge because it would mean *everything* would change. It would open the possibility of her telling me to go for it, and me then having to inform her why I can't, because of Brendan. Brendan, who I haven't told anyone about for nine whole months.

What I'm struggling to get my head around is that I'm less concerned about anything Brendan related and more concerned about Sam and what happens if these thoughts and feelings that keep creeping in refuse to go away. What then? Is loving someone worth the risk of losing them?

Amanda's eyes skim over my outfit. "You look nice."

"Thanks," I reply, voice lacking conviction as I try to figure out whether her comment is genuine. "It's new."

"Just make sure you don't spill anything down it. It would be a shame to see such a beautiful dress ruined."

She walks off to do whatever Amanda does, and I'm left feeling out of my depth until Sam comes to my side.

"Don't even think about chewing on your lip," says Sam, with three bottles of beer in his hands. He ignores my pout and glances around. "Where's Amanda?"

I take a bottle from him. "Doing Amanda things."

"More for us then."

"More for you." I take a small sip. "I'm working."

Sam rolls his eyes at the same time Amanda pokes her head back into the restaurant and calls me over to help her work the door. He drops his head as I walk past and says quietly, "Party pooper."

A shiver rolls through me. I need to station myself on the door all night if this is how I'm going to react just from the sound of his voice.

"I'm sure you'll take the reins and party for the both of us," I laugh over my shoulder.

That's the last opportunity I get to speak to him for three hours and the event goes by in one big, successful blur. When I've finished working the door with Amanda, we go back inside, making sure all the right people are in the right places, talking to whoever they need to. Sam spends the night chatting to pretty much everyone, and each time my nerves threaten to kick in, the sound of his laughter filling the room sends them back in their box where they belong.

"Not my usual jam, but it was fun," Sam comments, standing at my side and watching the last guests leave.

My body sags with both exhaustion and relief. "Never, ever, am I running an event again."

"But you did so good," says Amanda, smiling as she walks over. "I need to blow off some steam. Want to come dancing?"

"No way," I reply. "I need my bed. Stat."

"It's not exactly a secret," he mutters, and I feel disappointed he didn't think he could confide in me about this sooner.

"What exactly is going on?" I gesture at the building housing mine and Zoe's apartment. "I know that was kind of awkward then, but you can come in and we can, you know … talk?"

Sam shakes his head. "It's fine. I'm fine. Just promise me you'll be there tomorrow?"

Even if I wanted to, I couldn't say no, so I smile. "Of course, I'll be there."

Sam's expression brightens, and his eyes trail over my outfit. "Maybe wear something a bit more casual." I can't come up with a witty reply, because he's right. What's become my daily wardrobe isn't gig appropriate. "I'll text you the details of the venue tomorrow. Night, Soph."

"Night, friend," I reply, turning and heading into the building with a smile that only appears after spending time with him.

Chapter Eight
Sam

Nerves get the better of me the day after Sophie's big event, and rather than feeling excited for our first performance since Orensanz, all I feel is dread. Dread which is heightened each time I remember John West is going to be watching, judging, with a strong chance his verdict isn't going to be good.

Sophie agreeing to come last night appeases me for all of six hours, until around five AM when anxiety has my eyes wide open, ready to take on the day. The colossal mess that was me asking her is partly to blame. It took well over an hour to get the cringe fest out of my brain, including Sophie's reaction. The reaction that was the same as to my bit of harmless flirting. Both times couldn't have screamed friend zone more if she'd tried.

After two hours of tossing and turning, I decide I can't stay in my room any longer, and in the kitchen, I still can't figure out what to do with myself. Brewing a pot of coffee takes all of ten minutes, and then, with caffeine flowing through my system, my jitters go up a notch.

"What the fuck is he doing?" asks Ryan, leaning against the door frame, watching me with a bemused expression.

Zach scratches his temple. "I think he's cleaning?"

"Organizing," I call from where I'm crouched by the kitchen cabinets.

"But why?" asks Ryan, confused.

If I wasn't feeling so out of sorts, I'd find the pair of them amusing, standing, each in plaid pajama pants and a S.C.A.R.A.B. muscle vest—Ryan's memorabilia request, because apparently the ladies love it when he shows off his guns while drumming. I'm ready to give them a crappy, made-up explanation when Jake's head appears above both of theirs, hair sticking out in all directions. He frowns at the range of Tupperware I've begun organizing by purpose and size.

"Because he's nervous about tonight," he explains to the others, giving the answer I've been trying to avoid.

"Nervous ..." repeats Zach, his dark brows furrowing as he processes Jake's response.

Ryan laughs and walks into the kitchen. He steps over the Tupperware party I'm conducting, then grabs a cup and fills it with coffee from the second pot I've brewed. "Funny. Not. What's really going on?"

I grimace and avoid everyone's eyes. "What Jake said. It's true. Kind of. I guess."

"But you never get nervous," Ryan replies.

"It's a new thing," I mutter, each question making me resent myself more.

Ryan connects the dots. "Is this why you kept screwing up at rehearsals the other day?"

"Yes," I admit.

Zach groans, then catches himself and his face twists. "Sorry, it's just … what are we going to do tonight? Are you gonna be okay to perform, man?"

"I'll be fine," I snap, hating the sympathy in his voice. Sympathy means there's something wrong and I've spent the best part of the last month trying to convince myself everything is fine, while deep down nothing is, not even close.

Having none of it, Zach continues, "You're sure? We can cancel the set. It's better to cancel than mes—"

"I said I'll be fine," I say firmly, getting to my feet. I shake my head at Jake in frustration. "Did you really need to tell them?"

He narrows his eyes. "Yes. I needed to tell them. We're not just a band, we're a family. You know that. Whatever you go through, we go through too. We help each other."

"I don't need help," I reply stubbornly, striding toward the door he's still filling.

"Yeah, right," Jake bites back, squaring his shoulders. "Normally, you sing like a fucking canary. Want to know how many times I've heard you in the past couple of weeks? Zero." I shove past him. "We're not finished. Where are you going?!"

"Out," I reply, slipping on my DCs at the door. "I'll see you tonight."

I leave, not giving a damn how bad I look. All I know is I feel like I'm about to let everyone down and I can't breathe.

Walking toward an old, converted warehouse in Williamsburg, filled with eateries and bars, I focus on the one person, besides a certain blonde, who I think might be able to help stop me screwing up tonight. My older brother.

"If you're here, you're helping," grins Shaun. He grabs one of the many crates piled high on the delivery truck sitting outside Riffs and hands it over.

Twenty minutes later, between the two of us and the delivery driver, we've managed to stack them all in the middle of the bar and I'm sweating like a pig.

"Come on, bro. That was nothing." Shaun smirks, not even a slight gleam on his skin.

"I'm out of practice," I grunt, wiping my brow with my shirt, glancing around.

Bartending is an art. That's what Shaun always says. He might joke, but what he's crafted here really is incredible. Riffs took off the moment the doors opened. Thanks to a ton of hard work and constant effort, he's managed to create the business that isn't just a trend, but one that will last a lifetime.

"You know what the answer to that is …"

"Go on," I sigh, "Give it to me."

"You come round more."

"I've been busy." I walk behind the bar and open one of the fridges. Grabbing a bottle, I pop the cap off, like I have so many times since Shaun bought the place.

He arches a brow. "It's not even eleven."

I drain half in one go. "Your point?"

Moving opposite me, he perches on one of the stools and drags a hand through his hair. He's a couple of years older, but growing up, we might as well have been twins. It wasn't until we each crossed into our twenties, developed our own styles and collected a variety of tattoos between us, that our similarities became fewer. Shaun has more of a grunge, motorcycle rebel vibe going on. It isn't just males who flock to Riffs, and the performance at least a third of the Brooklyn females are after isn't music related.

What hasn't changed between the two of us is our values. Family and loyalty come above everything, which probably isn't surprising after what we went through as kids. Aunt Rachel and Uncle Matt did a stellar job in raising us after we moved to Brooklyn, but we each have our own demons haunting us. Shaun's determined to prove the saying, 'like father like son', isn't true, and me, well, I just don't want to lose everything I love again.

Maybe that's why I've spent over two decades keeping a certain friend as just that, a friend.

I'm terrified of losing her.

Lost in my own thoughts, I'm taken by surprise when Shaun reaches out and takes the bottle from my hand like he's plucking a petal from a daisy.

"My point," he continues, "is that the last time I had a member of S.C.A.R.A.B. here drinking before eleven, they almost ruined their career, and they were dealing with a broken heart. So …"

"So, what?"

"Which is it? Has Sophie finally put an end to the mess you call a friendship, or are you destroying your career? I know you can't handle both at the same time."

"You come across as a dick when you act like you know it all."

He chuckles. "Ah, but little bro, I'm not acting." When he winks, I flip him off and then a silence surrounds us that I'm not sure I want to break.

Tapping a finger against the top of the bar, I gaze to the side, telling myself I can do this. I can confide in him. He's my brother, and he's screwed up as many times as I have. The difference is he does it with confidence, claiming one of the things he's learned since he first got the keys to Riffs is that failures are important. He told me once that when you fail, you have a chance to move forward, to carry it with you as a reminder of the mistakes which led you to that point. Luckily for him, he doesn't have the world watching his every move, or in the case of my voice, lack of.

The only person who really understands how I'm feeling is who I should have been confiding in all along, since the moment this all started. The one person I know will never judge me, because she's spent a good chunk of her life being judged and trying to make people see who she is besides her mistakes.

I swallow hard, then say, "I can't sing."

"Right." Shaun snorts, because it really is that unbelievable. "Funny."

"I'm being serious." I give him a look that says as much, pleading with my eyes for him not to make this worse than it already is. "Ever since Orensanz … it's been bum notes and shitty practices. I'm fucking terrified I'm not going to be able to step out on stage tonight."

A moment passes, and Shaun blinks. "You're being serious?"

"Never been more serious about anything in my life."

"Fuck." He stands from the stool and walks around the bar, grabbing a bottle of Scotch and two glasses, filling each halfway.

He offers one over and I hesitate. "And you were frowning at me because it wasn't eleven ..."

"Yeah, well ..." We look at each other, not needing to say anything for a while. "What do you think is wrong?" I take a swig of my drink, wincing at the burn, but enjoying the punishment. "Come on. We've been through everything together and you've stood by me with all my shit. You know you can tell me anything."

I stare at the bar and, for the first-time, voice what's been going on in my head for a while. "I feel like I'm not good enough."

Shaun gives me a warm smile, and his eyes crinkle at the sides. "That's only natural, but you're here doing it. If you weren't good enough, this wouldn't be happening. I promise."

"I guess ..." I still can't look up.

"There's more to this. Come on, out with it."

"Orensanz. It was amazing, don't get me wrong. But ..."

"But ..."

"It was the best response we've ever had for a performance."

"And ..."

"And it feels like it was because it was Jake who was singing, not just me."

It sounds even worse out loud. The band has always been a team, always. So, why do I feel like this now? Why am I doubting myself? I spend a good chunk of time telling Sophie not to care about what people think, and here I am doing the same.

Shaun lets out an "Ah …" which sits between us like a giant pile of crap. "So, you think he's better than you?"

"No." I groan. "I don't know. I just feel like I'm not good enough and all I've ever wanted to do is make Mom and Dad proud."

Shaun's demeanor changes. The warmth in his expression disappears, replaced with an Arctic coldness. "Why would you care what they think? They left." He backs away and slams his glass against the bar so hard what's left of the Scotch sloshes over the sides. "The only person you need to make proud is yourself, Sam."

"Da—"

"Don't. I don't want to hear it. Are we done here? I've got shit I need to do."

Setting my own glass down, I walk around from behind the bar and stand in front of Shaun on the other side.

It isn't how we're leaving things which unsettles me. It's how lonely he looks, standing in front of a perfect display of liquor bottles. He has a future, everything he's worked for, sitting in his hands, but I know better than anyone that all means nothing if there isn't an army behind you, helping you to battle through whatever life throws your way.

He's one of the best people there is, but if he constantly creates flimsy, meaningless connections with people like he does, making them think he's letting them in while secretly blocking them out, there will come a time when he will be alone, and it will be too late to change anything.

He won't look me in the eye, but it doesn't stop me saying, "You have to stop hating them one day."

"I don't have to do anything I don't want to." He sounds as stubborn as he was when we were younger, and when he gets like this, there's no getting him to hear sense.

"Right. Thanks for the sound advice. Your company has been stellar as always, bro."

Tapping the bar as a signal goodbye, I leave Riffs feeling no better than when I arrived, dreading the night ahead more than ever.

"Grace? What are you doing here?"

Standing in the doorway to my dressing room, Grace gives me an unimpressed look. "You'd know the answer if you took the time to actually read my messages. A response would be nice, too."

Frowning, I try to decide whether to go with a 'sorry'. I'm almost there, about to apologize, when I remember the recording she not so kindly played the other night.

"I don't know where my phone is," I reply bluntly, despite the fact it's sitting beside me on the dresser.

Her eyes move to the side and stare directly at it. "Do you think I'm an idiot?"

I lean back in the dresser chair and my head falls back. Staring at where a patch of paint is coming away from the ceiling, I sigh. "Grace, I've got a ton of crap going on right now and I'm going on stage soon. I'm not in the mood for this."

Not getting the message, she steps into the room and closes the door quietly behind her. "That was a shitty thing you did leaving me in the restaurant …" At first, she doesn't carry on speaking. I think she's waiting for me to make a comment, but there's no way I'm talking to her about anything, because there's a strong chance she'll use anything I say against me in some way. "I think we should all go out together."

My head snaps back down. "Who?"

"Me, you, Sophie, and her boyfriend. It will be a great opportunity."

"How do y—" I don't finish my question, asking how she knows about Brendan. There's no point. She has a way of knowing everything, being everywhere. I don't want to know what the opportunity is she's going on about, either. I need to figure out how to get her out of my life before she can do some serious damage. "I need to get ready." Grace walks toward me. The next thing I know, she's standing between my legs and dropping to her knees. "What are y—"

My question is answered before I get a chance to finish it. I'm so shocked when she reaches up, starts unbuttoning my pants and pulls hard at my zipper. I barely process what's happening.

She looks up through her lashes and licks her lips. "Let me make you feel good."

Most 'single' guys would jump at the chance. But I'm not most. I don't want this, especially not with Grace. There's only one thing I want. One person. It's the way it's always been, no matter how hard I try to convince myself otherwise. I open my mouth to tell her 'no' at the same moment the dressing room door swings open, revealing the last person in the world I want to find me like this.

With no time to take in the flash of her mortified face, all I'm left with is the 'Oh my God, oh my God, oh my God's' coming from the corridor.

"Soph, wait!" I shout, quickly zipping up my pants and stumbling toward the door, forgetting about Grace scrambling to her feet behind me, her *tut* following me out of the room.

I might as well have let Sophie go and stayed in the dressing room. I wish I had, because in the minutes that follow after catching her up in the corridor, and the conversation that follows, I'm reminded of the big fat friend zone I'm sitting in, giving my already funky mood a sour edge.

"Seriously?" scoffs Grace.

"What?" I ask absentmindedly. Glancing back over my shoulder, all I find is an empty corridor with an occasional stage crew member rushing through doing last-minute prep. I turn and blink, realizing for the first time since walking back that Grace is, in fact, standing in front of me. "You got your double date. Tomorrow night. I'll text you the details."

"*My* double date?"

When I don't respond, Grace jabs me in the chest with her finger so hard it will bruise. "You're a real ass when you want to be, Sam Riley," she snaps, then spins on her heel, leaving the smell of her overly strong perfume behind.

Ryan wanders to my side, keeping me company while I watch the second female of the night storm away.

"That looked exciting," he comments, his lips twitching.

I rub at my jaw. "Yeah. It wasn't."

"You ready?"

No, I say to myself, my insides churning. I've spent all day trying not to think about our gig, but now we're here, and there's no escaping the fact I have to step out on stage in less than ten minutes.

"Yeah," I answer.

Ryan arches a brow. "Could you sound any less excited?"

"I'm just tired," I lie.

His other brow joins its partner, and they creep higher, the gap between them and his hairline virtually non-existent.

"Well, drink a Red Bull and get un-tired. We're on in …" he checks his watch. "Five."

My air supply becomes restricted when a boulder almost closes my airway. Lost in my own thoughts, I don't notice Ryan walk off.

"Sam!" shouts Zach.

I head backstage with lead feet, finding the guys standing off to one side, speaking with their heads low and in hushed voices. When Jake looks up and sees me, he stalks over with his guitar hanging around his neck.

He reads me like a book. "Whatever it is, forget it. Deal with it after the set. *Please.*"

"Sure," I reply quietly, wishing it were that simple.

The crowds cheer, getting louder with each second that passes. I only just hear them over the pounding of my heart. What the hell is wrong with me? Ever since Orensanz, the odd bout of nerves has turned into a wildfire, threatening to burn my career to the ground.

"Sam!" snaps Jake, getting my attention from the stage.

When did he get there?

Jumping to attention, I step out to the screams of our fans and blink beneath the bright overhead lights. Sweat trickles down my back. When I grab hold of the mic, my hand slips. I wipe it against my jeans and try again. With the mic this time firmly in my grip, I open my mouth to go through the introduction I always use, but nothing comes out. Not even a breath.

Starting to panic, I look to the side. Jake frowns and my eyes widen. He shakes his head and starts to strum his guitar. Zach and Ryan follow suit.

I can't do this plays on repeat in my mind while the seconds tick down.

Hundreds of expectant eyes sparkle in the darkness, waiting for me to perform.

I close mine, taking myself back to where this all began, trying to grasp onto anything that feels familiar and might break me out of whatever the fuck this is. But when I open them, they settle on Sophie standing near the front with fucking Fitzgerald by her side. He throws an arm around her shoulders and yawns. Any hope of getting out of this unscathed drops through the stage with my stomach.

And then, it's time to sing the opening lyrics to the song. I open my mouth. The room spins. My chest constricts. The mic picks up the choking sound that crawls up my throat. It pours through the speakers for every set of ears in the room to hear.

Pulse racing, I back away, shaking my head.

"What are you doing?" hisses Zach when I collide into him.

I don't register what he's saying. I don't register anything apart from the ringing in my ears.

With no other choice, I race off the stage, leaving my band and fans behind for the first, and potentially last, time in my musical career.

Chapter Nine
Sophie

Tapping my foot to the beat, I hold my breath and wait for the group to hit the crescendo of the song at the first of our extra Parkapellas sessions. It's the song we've been running through for the past three hours, and they miss the right notes by a fraction each time. The result is the end of the song falling flat—not that I'd ever say it out loud.

They miss the notes again, and internally I groan, not for myself, but for them. Disappointment fills each of their eyes, but they continue through to the end.

"That was great!" I exclaim, clapping my hands together.

Not one person looks convinced by my show of enthusiasm. My shoulders sink. If Mom were here, she'd have them hitting every note exactly how they should. I'm tempted to run out and call her, maybe even drag her here and show her exactly why this whole 'helping me find myself' plan she's got going on is a really bad idea.

Russ walks away from the group, who are now talking between themselves, with his little face the most serious I've ever seen it. "It was shit."

I purse my lips and glance in Grams' direction. "I told you this would happen if you kept cursing around him."

The thing about Grams ... she's a tyrant; she doesn't give a damn what people think and has her own unique ways. I guess she's where I get my quirks from; the rest of the Parker gang, too. She's the most loving person in my life, impressive considering how much love I've got going on, even if she cusses like a sailor.

She waves me off. "People these days are too damn sensitive about everything." After ruffling Russ's dark hair, she winks at him. "Don't listen to her. It adds character."

"Grams!" I shake my head as she walks off, trying to stifle a laugh. She's a bad enough influence as it is. The last thing I need is Russ and the other kids believing we secretly think her ways are funny and encouraging them more.

When Russ reaches up to straighten his hair, something catches my eye that makes my blood run cold. I move my eyes to the side so he doesn't sense me staring. Grumbling, he messes with his hair some more. The movement causes the sleeve of his shirt to move, revealing deep purple bruising on the inside of his arm.

Mom warned me when we started this that there was a chance I might come across these things. This isn't the first time I've found myself in this situation, but it doesn't make it any easier or less wrong. Russ has become the heart of what we are and why we do this. Unfortunately, what he's just revealed could change everything.

Swallowing hard, I plaster on a smile. "Russ, can you help me with something before I go?"

Totally unaware of what I've seen, he grins back. "Sure."

We head into the kitchen, and I task him with helping me set up the end of session refreshments for everyone. Russ doesn't so much help as stand consuming one cookie after another when he thinks I'm not looking. I take in the way his clothing hangs a little too loose on his tiny frame and curse under my breath, for a second, hating myself and questioning how I didn't put the pieces of the puzzle together sooner.

"Hungry?" I ask, keeping my tone light. Russ nods and grabs another cookie, this time not bothering to hide what he's doing. "That's a nasty bruise you have ..."

A few crumbs fall from his mouth, now stuffed full.

"I fell."

I wait a beat, chewing the inside of my cheek. "I didn't know you could get bruises under your arm from falling over."

Russ's eyes widen, but thanks to a few people entering the kitchen, he's saved from having to answer straight away.

After a couple of minutes, they leave, and I seize the moment before anyone else can come in. "You can tell me anything ..."

"It was an accident. Please, don't say anything to anyone," he replies in a rush, *because if you do, they'll send me away,* are the words left unsaid.

"Russ ..." My chest grows tight and I'm hit with a wave of nausea. As much as the thought of not seeing his face and hearing his random little outtakes on life each week hurts, I know I can't keep this to myself.

"*Please,* Sophie." Small dark orbs glisten up at me and I've never felt so torn in my life.

I'm about to tell him I have no choice when Grams walks in. Against my better judgement, I remain quiet. Grams glances between the two of us and her jaw tenses. It's so subtle you'd only notice it if you understood the context of the situation, but it gives me the answer I need. She already knows.

"Russ, are you eating all the refreshments *again*?" she says, smiling.

With a sheepish look, he grabs a handful more cookies and runs out of the room.

"You've seen?"

"Yes," I reply quietly, in case there's anyone lingering outside the door.

She lets out a long exhale and suddenly looks as old as her eighty-six years. "We can't do anything tonight. We can talk about it tomorrow, like we can talk about how you'd help more here if you demonstrated your own talents."

"There's no talent to demonstrate."

"You're a Parker. You don't have a choice in the matter, and you're wasted in what you're doing right now. Admit it, you're miserable. That's what all this ridiculousness is." She gestures up and down at what I'm wearing, kindly reminding me I need to change into the clothing I brought with me for the gig.

"I thought we were meant to be talking tomorrow?"

Grams sighs. "Yes, I suppose. Go before you're late."

I eye the doorway to the room where Russ is, carrying too many secrets for someone his age. "You're sure?"

"Positive." She gives me a tight smile, the opposite of what she's saying.

"Thanks, Grams."

After a quick change of clothes in the restroom and then a goodbye to everyone, I step out onto the street. My phone starts vibrating almost instantly with a call from Brendan. I'm tempted to ignore it, but decide if I'm aiming to be the bigger person, I should do the opposite.

"Hey." My voice gives away exactly how unhappy I am with him.

"Let me make Monday night up to you. I'm out now. We can meet."

"I'm busy," I reply bluntly.

"What are you doing?" He sounds surprised, as if I can't have plans unless they involve him.

"I'm on my way to a S.C.A.R.A.B. gig."

"Oh, right." He clears his throat awkwardly. "I could come with you?"

I stop in my tracks, not caring that I'm interrupting the stream of bodies moving along the sidewalk. "Seriously?"

"Yeah, sure. It might be fun to try something new." He sounds like it's the least fun he might ever have in his life, but I'm not about to pick him up on it. My gut stirs, telling me to say no, telling me that I've known deep down for a while something about our relationship isn't right.

Instead of saying no, I find myself saying, "Okay," because this is what I've been anchoring for since the beginning, a chance to prove to everyone that I, Sophie Parker, can obtain the unobtainable and be successful in all areas of my life.

After giving him the venue details, Brendan agrees to meet me as soon as he can. All the way, I walk in a daze, thinking how funny life can be and how things can change so quickly. Just like with Russ. My mood, which had lifted, darkens thinking about him again, but I push it to the back of my mind. Grams is right, we can't do anything about it tonight.

When I get to the venue, I get my third surprise. Brendan is already waiting for me; dare I say, eagerly. My fourth surprise of the night is when he pulls me into his arms and places a swift kiss against my lips. This is the moment I've been waiting for. I expected when it finally happened, there would be a foot pop, fireworks and all the other things that make it like a fairytale. There's absolutely nothing, apart from awkwardness when I pull away, shielding my face from a couple of papzz heading in our direction with their cameras raised.

"Let's go inside!"

"Sure," Brendan replies, as I grab his hand and drag him through the doors before we're featured on the front of all the gossip columns.

We maneuver through the crowds toward the security guards covering the area which leads backstage. When I give my name, one nods to let me though, but stops Brendan, who stands frowning, not used to having his presence questioned.

"He's with me," I explain.

The guard shakes his head. "If he's not on the list, he doesn't go through."

"You probably know me," says Brendan with so much swagger my cheeks burn. He straightens his tie, then offers out his hand. The guard stands with his arms folded and looks as if he's being offered a pile of dog turd. "Brendan Fitzgerald."

"You're not on the list." The guard looks away, clearly bored by the interaction.

I'm already over the threshold and give Brendan an apologetic look. "I just want to see Sam quickly before he goes on."

Brendan looks at me like I've slapped him across the face. "You're not seriously going to leave me here alone? I came here for *you*."

I shrug, thinking to myself that it's funny how he's changed his tune now the shoe is on the other foot. I go to say sorry, but stop myself, because I refuse to apologize for wanting to support my friend. "I won't be long. Promise."

Before he can guilt trip me into staying, I scurry along the corridor, not slowing until I catch Sam's name on one of the dressing room doors. Stage crew members hurry by wearing headsets, some with clipboards in their hands, others with the occasional piece of music equipment. Somewhere in the background, I hear Ryan's laughter.

Eyeing the door to Sam's room, I wonder if I should tell someone I'm here to see him or at least knock. Taking a deep breath, I remind myself he's one of my oldest friends and we gave up knocking a long time ago. I grab the handle and push down, swinging the door open.

I totally should have knocked.

Frozen in the doorway, I probably look as mortified as I feel. Walking in on Sam getting a pre-show blow job is the last thing I expected. Jealousy sparks inside me, then I remind myself this is normal. He can do whatever he wants. Grace, peering around his side while on her knees, is his girlfriend. There is nothing wrong with this situation, apart from the way I'm standing, gawping.

I glue my eyes shut, then reach out with my hands, trying to find my way back into the corridor, while my mouth has a life of its own. "Oh my God, oh my God, oh my God."

"Soph, wait!" calls Sam. I barely hear him, too busy bouncing between the walls. "Hey!"

I must be halfway along the corridor, thanks to the speed my feet are moving, when a hand grabs my arm and Sam turns me around.

I squeeze my eyes shut tighter. "Is your dick away?"

Totally the wrong thing to say after how things have been going recently. Now, I have to remind myself it's wrong to picture what your friend's dick looks like. God, could this get any worse?

"Unfortunately for you, yes." I make a gagging noise, because that would be the reaction I'd have if things were normal, and I wasn't acting like I've had a brain transplant. "Like music to my ears, Soph."

"You're so full of it."

"You wish you were." Sam chuckles.

My eyes fly open. "You did not just say that."

The expression on his face turns serious and his voice drops a level, so only the two of us can hear. "Would it be that bad?"

I gawp some more, then, when his words register, shudder. Sam probably thinks it's because I'm repulsed by the thought (which I should be). Deep down, I know it's because I'm secretly turned on by the thought (which I definitely shouldn't be).

Sam laughs. It's a forced kind. One that makes my heart go haywire, racing and missing beats all over the show, as I consider that maybe, just maybe, he meant it. I tell myself to get my shit together, because these few days of crazy could destroy everything we have if I let it.

"I'm done," he says, his eyes hardening, and I wonder how much he can read from my face. "I promise." It's the next comment that stings and reminds me that whatever crazy thoughts I've been having, they're just that … crazy. "You're so easy to mess with."

"I'm really sorry for walking in on …" I tail off, hoping maybe Sam will correct me by jumping in and saying it wasn't what it looked like.

"It's fine." He drags a hand through his hair and, in true rock and roll asshole style, says, "We were finished, anyway."

I close my eyes briefly, inhaling, doing what I can to block out the image threatening to creep back in; the one which makes my chest ache. Like another time …

"Hey! Is Sam in?" I ask, peering around his brother, Shaun.

Each of his arms brace the door, creating a block. "He's busy."

"Ooookay, Mister Grouch. I just need to see him for a second." I duck beneath his right arm and am halfway up the stairs before he has a chance to realize what's happened.

"Soph! Wait!" he hisses from behind.

He's too late, because I'm already at the top of the stairs seeing exactly what he didn't want me to, thanks to Rachel's open-door policy. Something I can't unsee.

"Oh …" It must come out loud, because Sam turns his head from where he's got his arms wrapped around Abby as they watch a movie together. My heart thuds hard, creating a weird sort of ache in my chest that has no right being there.

His eyes widen when it registers it's me standing watching the two of them together, but as he tries to untangle himself, I'm already running back down the stairs and out of their front door.

"Soph!" he calls, grabbing my arm before I can dart to the right and up my front steps. "Hey, wait. I can explain."

I stare at his feet. He hasn't got any shoes on. Luckily, it isn't raining. "It's fine, Sam. You can do whatever you want with whatever girls you want."

"It's not like that."

My eyes move up, narrowed. "Really? Because it looked like it."

He reaches up and scratches the back of his head. "It's just … We're just …"

"Just be careful," I say, letting out a huff of air. "She's only just broken up with Jake."

"You've never cared about who I hook up with before …" He rubs his thumb over my skin and my breath catches in my throat when I realize he's still holding my arm. "Why do you now?"

My mouth goes dry. I can't figure out if I want him to let go of me or not. Then, the image of him and Abby flashes through my mind. I throw back my shoulders and tilt my chin up. "I don't care. Do whatever you want, Sam. We're just friends."

Something flashes through his eyes and his mouth parts as if he wants to say something. Instead, he lets go of my arm while shaking his head and walks back into his house, to Abby, without a word.

"You can stop talking now," I say.

"I—" I hold my hand up to stop him talking and his face scrunches.

"You're not an asshole, so stop acting like one."

"Sorry." He rubs at his jaw, the situation becoming increasingly awkward. Then he asks the last question in the world I'm expecting. "Want to go on a double date tomorrow?"

My mouth parts, and I suck in a breath. "A double … d-date?"

"Yeah. You and Fitzpatrick. Me and Grace."

I blink when it sinks in that he means we will be on opposite sides of the table. Then it registers exactly what he's said. He knows what Brendan's name is and the way the corners of his mouth tilt up confirms it.

"We could," I reply, tilting my head to the side, trying to figure out what he's up to.

"Babini's." He grins. "Seven PM."

I'm about to ask what he's playing at when we're interrupted.

"Sam! We're on in ten!" shouts Ryan. "Hey, Soph!" A second passes and then I hear him say, "And Grace. Oh, shit." His cackles float along the corridor.

I peer around Sam and find Grace adjusting her dress. My attention is diverted when I catch the way one of Sam's hands trembles out of the corner of my eye.

"Is everything okay?" I ask, my eyes roaming his face. "You look kind of pale."

Pale is putting it nicely; a corpse would have more color.

Sam clenches his jaw. His humor from a few seconds ago is nowhere to be found. "I'm fine. See you later, Sophie. Thanks for coming."

After quickly contemplating whether to ask what's caused his sudden change in mood, I decide against it. I also decide against saying goodbye, hurt by the emotional whiplash he's just put me through. I spin around and stalk back along the corridor and into the main foyer.

"Is everything o—" I power past Brendan before he can finish his question.

I'm contemplating leaving altogether and am almost at the doors to the venue when I hear the crowd chanting S.C.A.R.A.B.'s name. Excitement hums through me. It's been way too long since I've listened to live music, so I decide if we're here, we might as well make the most of it and enjoy ourselves. I head toward the main room, the noise of the crowd the only directions I need, with Brendan following behind.

Weaving my way through the bodies, I collide with more than one person and feel beer slosh against my outfit—I'm grateful I took Sam's advice and opted for wearing something more casual and less expensive. Brendan doesn't seem to be enjoying himself, cursing multiple times when his expensive Italian leather shoes, which would be better suited at a New York Fashion Week event, get trodden on.

We find the perfect spot at the same time Jake, Zach and Ryan step out onto the stage and the room explodes with energy. It's infectious and I can't stop myself from jumping up and down, cheering with everyone around me. Well, everyone apart from Brendan. I only stop when it hits me that Sam is nowhere to be seen. It's then I notice how tense the guys look. I catch Jake eyeing the crowd uncertainly, then see him hiss toward the side of the stage.

A couple of seconds later, Sam finally steps out. The pallor he was wearing during our conversation in the corridor has been swapped for more of a green tinge, and the only way to describe his expression is terrified. Never, in all the time we've known each other, have I ever seen him look like this. Normally, he's the most confident of all the guys and has a stage presence that has even the males in the audience swooning.

Not tonight, though.

Things get worse when the crowd quietens, waiting for what is the standard intro to the gig. Everyone stands expecting Sam to crack one of his usual jokes, to get the crowd fired up, or at the very least say hi. He reaches up to grab the mic and his hand slips. Dread fills me when his eyes dart to the side and he gives Jake a look of sheer panic.

It's very obvious Sam is in a tailspin and things feel like they're about to take a turn for the worst. Jake shakes his head then begins strumming his guitar, and the crowd, which had become tense, instantly relaxes when Zach and Ryan follow suit. Sam closes his eyes as the guys go through the intro. It seems to work, and I think everything might be okay. But then, he opens them again and they laser in on me.

Of course, Brendan picks the same moment to display his second bit of affection to me publicly, wrapping an arm around my shoulders. Sam's eyes flash with disappointment, then he opens his mouth to sing, and I hold my breath.

Nothing comes out, not even a squeak.

Shit. I shift my feet as the crowd titters—and not in a good way. This isn't a little fuck up, it's a big one, and what makes it even worse is when I glance to the side and catch Abby's dad's head above the crowd, his face wearing a deep-set frown.

My eyes dart back to Sam, catching the way he sways slightly as a sheen of sweat covers his brow. I want to jump on the stage, take him away somewhere and tell him it doesn't matter, that everything will be okay, because he looks like his world is ending. He opens his mouth again and this time, a choking sound is picked up by the mic. I wince. Fuck, this is so bad. Like, really fucking bad. I can't believe I was pissed with him before. He mentioned there were issues, but if I'd known he was going through something this big, I would have tried to convince him to fake a sick bug and scrap the performance until he had his shit together.

I don't want to watch, but my eyes are glued to each movement he makes. I feel every ounce of his humiliation churning in my stomach as he backs away and collides with Zach. Jake hisses something, but the glaze in Sam's eyes tells me he's too far gone to hear anything.

He swallows hard and races off the stage.

The room goes silent, and I wrack my brain, trying to figure out a way to spin this so he hasn't just destroyed his career.

Chapter Ten

Sam

Beer feels like the only way to make things better.

Ryan offered me a spliff, which I was tempted to take, but then I decided I didn't need something else affecting my vocal cords. Maybe I'm coming down with something? That's the only explanation I've been able to come up with in the half hour I've been hiding out in my dressing room.

We've been doing this for years and I've never once struggled with stage fright. Why now?

Because it isn't stage fright, you idiot, a little voice says—one I wish I could ignore.

My stomach somersaults when there's a knock at the door.

"Come in," I say. The words come out clear as day. *Now* my voice works. Seriously?

John West steps in like I predicted he might. Closing the door behind him, he doesn't say a word. He walks and grabs one of the extra bottles of beer sitting on the dressing table, then takes a long drink and lets out a sigh that feels as heavy the emotions pressing in on me.

"How are you doing, Sam?"

"Okay," I lie.

He tilts his head and gives me an amused look. "Really?"

"No," I admit, downing the rest of my beer and setting the empty bottle on the table. The semi-transparent brown glass is apparently fascinating, because I can't take my eyes away from it, even when John asks me another question.

"What happened out there?"

"I think that's kind of obvious …" I reply, bitterness creeping into my voice.

"Yeah, but I want to hear from *you* what you think really happened."

"I panicked. That's it."

"But you've never panicked before. Unless that's what was happening during rehearsals?" I nod in reply, and he takes another drink. "What's making you panic?"

I pause, considering how to answer him. "You really care?"

His brow knits together. "Of course I care."

"Right," I say, taking in his exec suit, "because of the label." Even at gigs, he isn't off duty.

"No." He shakes his head. "Because I've known you since before S.C.A.R.A.B. was even a blip on my radar, Sam. You're one of my daughter's closest friends, and your wellbeing means more to me than the label. So, tell me what's really going on."

I watch him warily, trying to assess if this is a trap and he's attempting to get information, so the label can turf my ass out on the sidewalk.

My expression must give away what I'm thinking, because he gives me a reassuring smile. "You can trust me."

Can I? Really though? I'm not sure. I can't see past the expertly tailored suit and black shirt he's wearing. They make him look like he's a part of the mob. It's the eyes swimming with sincerity, ones that mirror Abby's, that make me believe what he's saying.

Scratching the back of my head, I let out an awkward laugh. "Could you do me a favor?"

"Sure," he replies. I scan his suit jacket up and down, letting my eyes ask the question I'm too embarrassed to say out loud. His brows shoot up. "You want me to remove it?"

"Please. It's putting me off."

"I'll do one better." I think he's going to strip when he begins unbuttoning his shirt, until I take in the black S.C.A.R.A.B. shirt he's using as a vest. "I like to think of myself as one of your biggest fans." He winks. "Don't tell anyone. I'm not allowed to show favoritism."

I start to relax and open another beer. John picks his up and we clink our bottles together.

"It started after Orensanz," I say, neglecting to add in a few of the more specific details, like the months before that, when Sophie getting with Mister Preppy started to mess with my head. Orensanz was the tipping point, the thing playing on my mind most, and that's all he needs to know. "The media were hyping everything up, saying how we were going to be one of the greatest bands the world had seen in decades. I started watching old videos of all the bands they were comparing us to, and then I started watching all our old performances. All I could see were the mistakes I made. I don't get it. I don't see what other people do. I mean, I do in the band, but not in me."

John's face softens into an expression I'd expect Dad to be wearing if he was still here. It stirs up too many emotions, making the huge pile I'm already struggling to keep upright wobble dangerously. I look away as the back of my eyes burn, feeling closer to crying than I have in years. What the fuck is wrong with me?

"That's quite a burden you're carrying on your shoulders," says John.

"Yeah. It's been a crappy couple of months." Just admitting it out loud makes everything feel less oppressive, even if I don't know what to do in order to move forward. Putting on a brave face each day and acting like everything is okay, when deep inside it isn't, is exhausting.

Silence settles in the room. I focus on my bottle, picking at the label where it's coming away with the condensation. Every now and again, someone rushes past the door. The chatter that filters in is happy and excited. It's worlds away from how I'm feeling.

Only when he's finished his beer does John say anything again. He places his empty bottle down next to my first, then leans back in his chair and clears his throat. "Imposter syndrome. Heard of it?"

I look up. "Isn't that a movie?"

"No." He laughs. "It's what I think you might be dealing with. It's common, and to be expected, especially considering how quickly things with the band is taking off."

"What is it exactly?"

"Which explanation would you like?"

"The simple one."

"Imposter syndrome is thinking you're not as good as everyone believes you to be."

"Sounds about right," I say, finishing my second beer. I eye up a third, deciding against it while John's still in the room. "Who gets it?"

"Anyone, in any situation."

"Have you ever had it?"

"Every day," he chuckles.

"Really?" That wasn't the answer I was expecting. He always seems so put together.

"Of course."

"How do you deal with it?"

He thinks about my question before answering. "I ask myself what life would be like if I wasn't doing the thing I loved, and whether my insecurities are worth destroying my happiness for."

"You make it sound easy."

"It's not. It takes time and work. But you feeling this way shows you care, and when you come out of the other side, you will be better for it. What's your happiest memory with the band?"

I pause and frown to myself.

The sound of the tent zipper being opened makes me freeze, breaking me out of my pity party.

"Soph?" I whisper hiss into the darkness.

We've always gotten away with late nights together during our annual summer camping trips with the whole group. Late nights that sometimes creep into entire nights. Sleepovers.

This year, things are different. Aunt Rachel laid down the rules firmly before we left, declaring sixteen was too old to let it pass as nothing. If I didn't feel the way I did, I would have argued with her. Instead, I kept my mouth shut, knowing she was hinting at exactly what I've wanted to happen for a long time already.

"Soph?" I hiss again when I don't get an answer.

"Hey." I can barely make out her face in the darkness, but I can hear her smile.

"What are you doing?"

"What do you think I'm doing?" She clambers through the tent, and I feel her legs at each side of my lap. She giggles when she realizes the position that she's put us in. "Sorry."

I shuffle, and she falls to my side, giggling again. "You're going to get us in trouble."

"Embrace the danger." After a few seconds, I hear her swallow. "Sam."

"Yeah?"

"Why didn't you tell me that today was the day your dad passed away?" When I don't reply, I hear her take a deep breath. "Is that why Rachel and Matt started the camping trips?"

"They're a distraction," is all I'm able to reply, thankful for the dark as my eyes start to burn.

"Move your arm."

Doing as Sophie says, I lift it, feeling her warmth everywhere as she tucks into my side, wrapping herself around me. When she stills, I lower my arm back down and rest my hand on her shoulder. I toy with the strap of her camisole absentmindedly, needing to do something with all the energy charging through my body.

Luckily, I can pass my croak off with not wanting to be caught by Aunt Rachel, or worse, Grams, when I say, "What are you doing, Soph?"

She nestles her head against my chest, and mine starts to swim when all I can smell is honey and almond.

"Replacing the bad memories with better ones."

I clear my throat, bringing myself back to the present, deciding to share a memory that doesn't involve Sophie.

"The summer we toured the West Coast. Right before Abby came back, and we signed with the label. It's when there was no pressure and we performed for the love of it."

It was a really, really great tour, back before we knew how big we'd eventually become.

John smiles. "So, do it."

"What?"

"Go. Perform. For the love of it. We can push back recording the album and releasing the next record. Nothing is set in stone. Enjoy yourself, find your voice again and figure out why you're really doing this."

I wait for him to start laughing and tell me he's joking, but it never comes. "Just like that?"

"Just like that." He grins and I frown. "What about the label? Aren't there rules against this kind of thing?"

This time, John throws his head back and laughs. "We have a mainstream band with a singer who can't sing. Believe me, what you get up to right now is the least of our worries. All that matters is that you're able to sing at the end of whatever you spend your time doing." He stands and I watch as he puts his shirt back on, tucking it into his pants before grabbing his jacket. "Whatever you need, just ask. But promise me you'll take this time to figure things out."

He's almost at the door when I say, "You're assuming I'll go off and then be able to just sing. What if it's pointless? What if it doesn't work?"

"What have you got to lose?" *Nothing* is the answer neither of us says out loud. John's hand rests on the door handle when he stills and turns back. "Can I make another suggestion?"

"Go for it." I breathe, not liking what I think he's about to suggest. They say time heals, but some things take a really, really long time and I'm still not there yet.

"It's easy to lose yourself in success, Sam. Sometimes, to understand why something is worth continuing, you need to go back and remember why you started."

"Yeah. Maybe …"

His final words haunt me hours after he's left, my mind focusing on one major flaw.

After tonight, it's clear one of the reasons I started singing could also be one of the reasons I stop.

Sophie

I didn't know until now that it's possible to feel numb while also feeling like panic might consume you.

Leaving the venue—where everything has gone to absolute shit—Brendan trails behind me. I try to ignore the muttering and not-so-nice comments from all the fans decked out in S.C.A.R.A.B. gear, because they serve no purpose apart from clouding my judgement on what needs to happen next. The gossip columns will already be getting ready to run the story and it's only been a few minutes.

I ignore my phone when it vibrates. Although she couldn't make it to the gig tonight because she couldn't get a sitter, Abby will already know, which means it's likely to be Sooz, Amanda or Zoe, wanting an update on what's just happened. That's how quick news travels. Too fast.

I decide I'll reply in a few minutes when I can hear myself think.

124

After a quick glance at the crowds hovering outside the front of the building and spilling down the steps, I hurry along the sidewalk, trying to put as much distance between myself and them as I can. It's the only way I stand a chance at getting a cab, because each one that appears is snatched up instantly.

A throat clears from behind me, and I startle, turning back with my guard up. Brendan almost crashes into me thanks to my abrupt change in direction.

He steadies himself and asks, "Where are you going?"

Mind lost in the huge list of damage control that needs working through, I'd forgotten he was with me.

"I have to get to the office," I reply abruptly, annoyed he's distracting me.

Brows drawn together, in true Brendan style, he ignores the signs there's something wrong and pulls the situation back round to being about him. "Oh, right. Can you not cancel? I thought we could go back to my place?"

I take a step toward the edge of the sidewalk and hold my hand in the air. No cabs appear. Not that I expected anything else. After all, I don't have Sam the magnet with me. I growl to myself as a streak of yellow with an empty back seat flies past.

"Sorry. I have work things I need to do."

"It's late, Sophie. Come on, let's go back to mine and I can show you a good time."

He has to be joking. If he's planning on showing me a *real* good time, then he must have a new bag of magic tricks with him, because he's yet to have achieved said goal. I spin around and take Brendan in; I mean, really take him in. He looks the part. Effortlessly gorgeous, dressed in the best clothes money can buy, with an incredible job and a steady future secured firmly in place.

But is it enough?

He knows what Sam means to me; therefore, he should know why I need to go.

Maybe he needs things spelling out?

"You saw what happened back there, right?"

"Yes." He looks as annoyed as I feel. He still doesn't get it.

"Next Level work with S.C.A.R.A.B. all the time," I explain, moving steadily into his language of love. Work. "This is my job, Brendan. What would *you* do if everything in yours was about to go wrong?" The blank look I receive triggers an epiphany. How could I have been so blind? How could I not have realized that unless it's related to him, then Brendan doesn't give a shit? Deciding there is one thing he's good for, I grab hold of his arm, tug him toward me, then raise it in the air. A cab slows to a stop beside us. "Thanks!"

"Seriously? You're really leaving?" he snaps as I slide across the back leather seat and close the door quickly so he can't follow.

I don't apologize. I'm tired of always saying sorry for things I don't need to. I'm not sorry I'm leaving.

"Wait!" I screech, right before the driver puts the cab into drive. I lean my head out the window. "You need to be at Babini's tomorrow at seven PM."

Pissed, Brendan throws his arms out as the cab starts to pull away. "I don't know where that is."

"If you'd actually planned on turning up to my event last night, then you would," I call back to his retreating form.

Settling in my seat, I replay his shocked expression and mentally high five myself. The tide is turning in our relationship. Unfortunately for Brendan, it doesn't look like it will be in his favor.

After giving Next Level's address to the driver, I pull out my phone. I frown when I see the notification that I received a few minutes ago wasn't from one of the girls, but from Russ. When I open it, it's a blank message? Weird. Maybe he's done something to his phone in his sleep because there hasn't been anything else since.

I close the thread and then call Zoe. It rings continually, then goes to voicemail. I call again, because everyone knows she never answers on the first try. It usually takes at least three.

"I'm engaged," she answers breathlessly on the second attempt.

"You need to get to the office. It's an emergency." I don't need to know the details of what, or whom, she's engaged with. The line goes quiet, followed by muffled voices. Zoe giggles. "Zo!"

"I'm here," she huffs. "Can this not wait till the morning?"

"It's a S.C.A.R.A.B. emergency."

"Give me half an hour," she grumbles, my explanation spurring her ass into gear.

Chapter Eleven

Sophie

I've been in the office five minutes when the girls begin filtering in. If shit hadn't literally hit the fan, I'd be congratulating them on their timely manner. Well, not Sooz, because she's always on time for everything. And not Abby, because she's late.

"What happened with Sam?" asks Sooz, grabbing her favorite pen and pad of paper—the ones she uses when she needs to focus.

"Did you two?" Zoe's eyes widen. "You know …" She starts making inappropriate motions with her arms and body.

"Wait, I thought this was a S.C.A.R.A.B. emergency?" says Sooz, looking between us. "And since when did the two of you start hooking up?"

"Sorryyyy!" Abby practically screeches as she rushes in. "Jake took forever to get back from the gig and I couldn't leave Clara. So, you're hooking up with Sam?" The last part comes out so offhand you wouldn't believe there was an issue with it, like we haven't been friends forever and it's weird.

"Please," I scoff, trying not to focus on the thought of me and Sam hooking up. If I think about it, my body will react and give me away. "This is Sam we're talking about."

"Right," snickers Amanda, walking back into the room with steaming cups of coffee for each of us.

I do a double-take of her before replying. Abby looks like she hasn't seen her bed in weeks, Sooz looks like she's rolled out of bed, and Zoe looks like she's literally been rolling around in bed. But Amanda looks ready to take part in a photoshoot. I need some tips on how she always manages to look so pristine.

"He has a girlfriend," I remind them, cursing to myself when my cheeks feel like they're about to burst into flames.

In return, I get *the look* from Amanda, who then gives Abby another of her *looks*. I let out a small sigh of relief when she sits at her desk instead of commenting.

"So, what happened?" asks Sooz again.

"He choked." Four pairs of eyes stare at me in horror. "On stage," I clarify.

"How do *you* know?" asks Zoe suspiciously.

"I was there. Sam invited me," I reply. Abby's lips part, ready to say something, but she pauses, and I jump in before she can. "It was bad."

Zoe arches a brow. "How bad?"

"Maybe worse than the Berlin Incident."

Definitely worse than the Berlin Incident, which might have been humiliating for me, but for Sam, the stakes are much higher with what's just happened.

"No. F'in. Way."

129

"I'm not joking," I reply. "We need to do damage control, like yesterday."

"Has anything been reported yet?" interrupts Sooz.

"I haven't had a chance to check," I answer.

"Yes," states Amanda, holding her phone in the air with a grim expression. "It has."

"Shit," mutters Abby when she catches what Amanda's looking at. "I think the better question would be what hasn't been reported." Amanda taps the screen and Abby winces. "Oh no. There are videos too."

The familiar tune of S.C.A.R.A.B.'s opening song from earlier fills the room … sans the singing.

Abby looks at me with a strange expression on her face. "You were watching, yeah?" I nod. "In the crowd?" I nod again and she purses her lips.

"Poor Sam," says Amanda, turning the video off at the point where the crowds begin voicing their disapproval.

"Where do we start?" questions Sooz. "It's already out there." She looks flustered, which doesn't fill me with hope, because I've never seen her out of her depth. I guess there's a first time for everything.

"This could destroy the band," Zoe says, voicing what none of us want to admit. "They need to get back on stage as soon as possible so they can prove everything is fine and it was just a hiccup. Maybe we can spin a stomach flu story?"

"They can't," I say. "They can't go back on stage. The same thing might happen and then they'd be really screwed." The room remains silent and I take a breath before explaining what little I know. "Sam mentioned he's been having issues. I don't think it's something that can just be switched off."

"Dammit," says Sooz.

"Dammit indeed," agrees Zoe.

Amanda appears more positive than the rest of us. "There's always a way of flipping these things. We just need to come up with a way to spin it in their favor."

"Their fans are loyal to the bone," I say. "Hopefully, they will understand. After all, S.C.A.R.A.B. are the underdogs. They've come from nothing and that's what people love about them. How normal they are."

Abby watches me with a sparkle in her eye. "You could be onto something."

I tilt my head. "Onto what?"

"The whole normal thing," she replies.

A lightbulb flickers on above my head and I sit a little straighter, starting to digest what she's getting at. "That's it! We focus on how normal the guys are. Show that even the biggest stars fail sometimes."

"Yes!" grins Sooz. "We make people empathize and then show them that they can be inspired by them."

"I know just the magazine," Amanda says excitedly, swiveling her chair and firing up her laptop.

Abby claps her hands. "We can go raw with the photos. Make it a really emotional shoot."

"And we can do Q&As on all the main radio stations. We could get Sam to inspire people to overcome their fears and past failures. This is great." I avoid the fact Sam has yet to actually overcome his own fears. We can deal with that when it comes to it.

The office goes into a frenzy, despite it almost being eleven.

Zoe moves to my side and grins. "You did good, Soph. Really good."

The office's new brightly colored desks surrounding us make our temporary truce feel all the more significant, and I give her a warm smile back. "Thanks."

The moment is broken when my phone rings. Zoe and I both glance down to where it's sitting on my desk. I frown when I read Russ's name on the screen.

"Answer it," Zoe urges when it stops ringing and immediately starts again.

Not needing to be told twice after what I saw earlier, I pick it up and accept the call before it can cut off.

"Russ?" I whisper, being careful not to draw attention from the others.

My stomach plummets when a small voice whispers back, "Sophie, I'm sorry. I know it's late, but you said I could call if I needed you."

I plug a finger into my other ear, blocking out the noise in the room. "Russ, what's wrong?"

"Who's that? Who are you talking to?" comes a much deeper voice from somewhere in the background.

"I'm sca—" He's cut off when the line goes dead.

Quickly pulling the phone away, I try to call him back, but it goes straight to voicemail.

"Dammit," I say to myself.

"What's going on?" asks Zoe.

I jump to my feet, phone still in my hand, and grab my bag with my other. "I have to go."

"Is everything okay?" calls Abby, as I power to the elevator.

My voice comes out way too high and sounds totally unconvincing when I reply, "Fine!"

It would appear the few secrets I've been keeping are catching up to me and the last thing I need is a million questions delaying me from getting to Russ and finding out if he's okay. The elevator opens and I step inside, bringing up Grams' number with shaky hands.

Right before the doors close, Zoe slides in and holds out her hand.

"Give me your phone. Who are you trying to call?"

"Grams," I croak.

She takes the phone from me, and I hit the button for the ground floor, almost tumbling when the elevator starts to move, shaken, as my mind jumps to the worst-case scenario.

What if there's something seriously wrong? This is all my fault. I never should have let what I saw earlier slide. I should have reported it. An elevator isn't the place to have a panic attack, so I try to get my breathing under control.

"Soph!" Zoe snaps.

I blink, realizing the doors have opened, and she's stepped out. "Sorry," I say, exiting, but she isn't really listening to me.

"Yes, she's here," she says into my phone, then holds it to my ear.

"Sophie, what's wrong?" asks Grams.

I nod at Zoe as a signal I'm okay and take the phone from her so we can head outside. "It's Russ ..." I can't keep the panic out of my voice as my chest constricts.

"Sophie, sweetie, I need you to take a deep breath."

I do as she says and my chest eases. "Okay." I breathe again. "I'm okay now."

"Now," says Grams gently, "tell me what happened."

"I got a blank message from him earlier."

There's a pause. "He has your number?"

I chew my bottom lip as it hits me. Maybe I've screwed up? "It was in case of emergencies." I start to explain. "He's so little, and I hated him coming to the sessions alone. I just wanted to know he was safe."

"Okay. We can deal with that later. It's not important right now." Grams' words should be reassuring but there's something in her voice that fills me with doubt. "Then what happened?"

"I've been in the office with the girls as something came up. He called once, but I missed it, then he called again. He didn't say much, just that he needed me. Grams, he sounded scared. I need to go and check he's okay."

She hums down the line. "We could get in trouble for this. His details are confidential."

"I already know where he lives. I walked him home."

The whole time I'm speaking, Zoe watches me, taking everything in.

"Sophie …" Grams sighs.

Telltale signs of anger crawl up my neck and I clench my hands, running the risk of breaking my phone while trying to keep my voice even. "There could be something seriously wrong."

"Could. We don't know there is."

"Grams, really? After what I saw earlier, we don't not know either."

I stare across the dark street, the irrational side of my brain trying to figure out why she's talking me down. The rational side gets it—gets that if we go in all guns blazing, we could trigger something there's no coming back from for no reason. Then I remember the bruises I saw on Russ's arm, and how he looked walking home alone with Brooklyn towering over him. The way he inhaled mine *and* Sam's takeout.

My rational side can do one. I'd happily be proven wrong over finding out days later I was right and didn't do a thing.

"I'm going to call the cops," states Grams, taking me by surprise. "They can check things out."

I throw my free hand in the air. "They won't see it as an emergency. Grams, I heard someone in the background. They sounded …" A shiver runs through me thinking about it. "They sounded angry. You, Mom, Dad, everyone has been telling me for God knows how many years to listen to my gut. To trust my instincts and screw the world. This is me doing that. Something doesn't feel right. I'm going to find him."

"Sophie. Wa—"

I hang up and throw my arm out into the road. The universe is finally on my side because a cab idles toward us and stops straight away.

"What are you doing?" I ask as Zoe climbs in behind me.

"What am I doing?" she looks at me like I've lost my mind. "You don't think I'm going to leave you to handle this alone, do you?" She rolls her eyes at my non-response. "Come on, Soph. Things might have been crap between us lately, but you're still my best friend." I sniffle, overwhelmed by everything that's happened tonight, and how, despite our differences, I still need her by my side. I'm ready for bursting into floods of tears when she says the words we used to say to each other all the time growing up. "In it together, no matter what."

"Thank you," I say, putting as much emotion as I can behind my words, needing her to believe after how rocky things have been, that I mean them. I then lean forward and give the driver Russ's address. When I turn my attention back to Zoe, she's sitting in silence, her funny expression appearing even weirder with the streetlights flickering across her face as we pass them by. "What?"

"I'm trying to guess which thing you're going to tell me about first. The a cappella group you've been disappearing to for years—which I'm assuming is where this Russ person is from—Fitzgerald the Fuckwit, or the fact you want to bone Sam."

I stare at her in shock.

"Does Abby know?"

She snorts as if she can't believe I'm asking such a ridiculous question. "Of course Abby knows."

"All of it?"

"Soph … we know everything about each other, including the things we don't want to. Sometimes we even know things we're not aware of. We're a unit. A team. You never have to keep things from us, no matter how lost in our own shit we get."

Hating seeing the sadness that fills her eyes, I turn my head away and stare through the window as the cab flies through the night, wishing we could go faster.

Zoe squeezes my knee. "It's going to be okay."

Thankfully, the cab stops a couple of minutes later. I stare out at the building I've walked Russ home to too many times. A siren calls out in the distance. My eyes settle on the pieces of discarded trash decorating the steps, then the old brown paint on the rendering, which is faded and flaking around the window frames. Windows that likely haven't been cleaned in Russ's lifetime. The neighborhood is one of the few that haven't had a facelift in recent years.

I should have known. I should have done something.

I can do something now.

Before I can allow any doubts to get the better of me, I climb out of the cab.

"So, I guess we should ju—" I start walking up the front steps and am already at the door when Zoe realizes what I'm doing. "Wait!" My hand is raised, ready to knock, when she darts up beside me and grabs my arm. "Do you not think we should wait for the cops?"

"They could be hours," I reply, shrugging my arm from her grip and pressing the buzzer for Russ's apartment. Some lights to the right on the ground floor come on.

"Fuck," Zoe huffs, then fluffs her teal hair, which somehow manages to appear even brighter in the dark. "We're definitely getting arrested."

I roll my eyes. "Stop being a drama queen. We're not going to get arrested. We're just going to introduce ourselves and check everything's o—"

The door swings open and we both plaster on smiles. The woman standing in front of us looks like her daily fluid intake comes from vodka rather than water, and the way she clutches the door frame to keep herself upright confirms it.

"Hi." I give a little wave. "Is Russ here?"

The woman looks at me blankly. "Who?"

Dammit. It's then I remember that Russ isn't actually called Russ.

"Josh," I correct myself. "Sorry. Is Josh here?"

"And you are?" she asks with narrowed eyes.

"A friend." My skin grows clammy from being put on the spot. "He, um, he left something behind tonight."

"Where?"

Zoe shifts beside me, and I swallow. "Um …" I should have waited, or at least had a plan. Going off-piste isn't working in my favor.

When the woman turns away, I don't miss her bored expression, or the way she sways. "Josh!" she barks toward an open door I assume is her apartment, just along the hall. I hold my breath and peer over her shoulder. When a small head of dark hair doesn't appear, my stomach churns. "Josh!" she shouts again.

When there's still nothing, she turns back toward Zoe and I and shrugs. "He must be asleep?"

I scowl at the question in her voice. If this woman is who I think she is, he's under her care and she should know exactly what he's up to. Just like she should know where he's been tonight, which I have a strong suspicion she doesn't.

"That sounds like a question and it should be an answer," comes a familiar voice.

Zoe and I both turn, finding the source slowly working their way up the front steps.

"Grams?"

"Who are you?" scoffs the woman.

"Someone who cares," Grams replies.

The woman's brows raise and her cheeks turn pink. "And what exactly is that supposed to mean?"

"That perhaps you don't …"

My head ping pongs between the two of them and I make a snap decision, one without rational thought, the kind old Sophie would make. Damn the consequences.

"Hey, what ar—"

I push my way into the building and dart through the open door to the apartment, running into answers I wish I'd never found.

Hours later, it feels like I've taken a million steps back and my efforts to change have been in vain. Zoe stares me down across the holding cell, with Grams' head resting on her shoulder as she snoozes lightly.

"I told you we were going to get arrested."

Chapter Twelve
Sam

After fastening the second button from the top on my black shirt, I step back and take in my appearance in the mirror.

"Where are you going all dressed up? Do we have an event?" asks Ryan, spooning cereal into his mouth from the huge bowl he's carrying as he enters my room in only a pair of joggers.

The guy would perform on stage half naked if we let him. He has a thing about clothing. Apparently, it interrupts his natural movement patterns or some crap like that. He's lucky that he's shredded in a way the best athletes spend hours a day striving to achieve with little effort involved.

"No event," I confirm. "I'm going on a double date."

Ryan jolts in surprise, causing almond milk to slosh over the side of the bowl. Thanks to the rainbow he's consuming, my cream carpet now has a shocking pink and blue stain in the middle. "Double date? Who with?"

"Grace."

He fills his mouth with another huge spoon, and around the large amount of cereal says, "I meant who's the other couple?"

I shrug and try to act unphased. "Sophie and some guy."

He groans. "Seriously?"

"What?" I snap. After last night, I'm not in the mood for a pep talk.

"It's a disaster waiting to happen. Why are you putting yourself through this?"

"We're just friends."

"Yeah," he snorts, "right."

He makes to leave, stopping when I ask, "Have you seen Jake?"

"Nah. Think he's been busy with Abby and Clara."

"Right." Weird, I think to myself, as Ryan walks out. Jake always checks in at least three times a day, even if he's busy with them. He likes to know what we're all up to when he isn't around, A.K.A. he likes to check we're not getting into trouble.

I drop Sophie a reminder text of the time and location for meeting. She hasn't replied to any of my other messages all day, likely because she's upset with me still, like everyone else. With a few minutes to spare, I collapse onto my bed for the first time all day and think back on what John West said about taking a break to get my shit together.

My body sinks into the mattress and it hits me how tired I am, making his suggestion all the more appealing. I've spent the day filling every minute I can with useless tasks, anything to distract my mind, which wants to keep reliving last night. I feel sick to my stomach each time an image of the crowd creeps in. I'm actually almost sick when I remember Sophie's face, witnessing it all firsthand.

Damn, I don't know what to do. What John said makes sense, but it feels like by stopping, I'm giving up. There's only one person I want to talk through it all with, despite how humiliated I feel. The problem: I don't think she wants to talk back.

I rub my hands over my face and groan, trying to figure out how it's already Friday again. It's been the longest—and equally the shortest—week I've had in a long time. Then it hits me. It's Friday. Ironic. I have a feeling Friday Feast Night is about to become memorable for a whole new set of reasons.

After a few minutes of wallowing, I get up and head out, the entirely wrong female driving my feet forward along the sidewalks of Brooklyn to catch a subway into Manhattan.

Half an hour later, with still no response from Sophie, I enter Babini's. I smile to myself as I take in how busy and vibey it is after only being open for two days—largely thanks to Sophie. She didn't just do well with their opening. She smashed it. Everyone knows in New York that if you stand a chance of success, you need to have the right people behind you. Babini's hit the jackpot when Next Level tasked Sophie with the job and she's proved yet again that she can do anything she sets her mind to.

I just wish she'd believe in herself, too. She's spent the past few years searching, trying to prove she's more than her younger self, but she's already gone above and beyond by just being her. She's grown as a person in ways she isn't even aware of. Now, she just needs to own it and leave the past where it belongs, using it as a reminder of how far she's come.

"Two of the guests are already here," the hostess informs me, after getting flustered when I gave her my name for the reservation.

Passing through the restaurant, I focus on the word two, when it should be three, then say a quick prayer that Mister Preppy is a no show again. Maybe then Sophie will finally realize he's a dick and that she's settling for second best.

She should be number one in his life. She should be the first thing he thinks about when he wakes up, the last before he goes to bed, and even then, sleeping, she should fill his dreams. Every part of him should be consumed by her and what it would take to make her happy each day and what he would have to tear down in his way if she weren't.

Brendan has proved, in the time they've been together, that in the case of the Fitzgerald family name, the apple doesn't fall far from the tree. The only person who will ever take the number one spot in his life is himself.

Approaching the table, I find Grace shamelessly flirting with Brendan. I know the moment she clocks me walking toward them, because she moves away from him and straightens the red silk dress that she's wearing so it covers her cleavage, which is currently at risk of popping out. It's wasted effort because I'm more concerned about where Sophie is.

I drop into one of the two remaining chairs and Grace preens, "This is Brendan Fitzgerald."

Brendan gives a shit-eating grin, totally unphased by his girlfriend's absence.

"I know who he is," I say to Grace, then focus on Brendan. "Where's Sophie?"

He shrugs and picks up his glass of wine, tilting the glass so the dark liquid skims around it. After making a show of raising it to his nose and inhaling deeply, he finally answers. "I've not heard from her all day."

"Yet you're here …" I narrow my eyes as he lowers his glass back down to the table. "Not concerned …"

"A bit like you …" he fires back.

"You're her boyfriend."

"You're her best friend."

The laugh I let out catches in my throat. It's more of a hacked off, can't-believe-I'm-sitting-here-communicating-with-this-asshole kind of laugh.

"I'm surprised you've taken enough notice of what Sophie says to know who I am or what part I play in her life. Do you actually know *anything* about her?"

"Sam," says Grace through gritted teeth.

Luckily, a waiter comes to the table, helping to break the tension when he asks for my drinks order. After too many beers last night, I opt for water. The waiter disappears again and Grace stares at her place setting. Brendan pulls out his phone and ignores us both while I glance around the restaurant, becoming more concerned about Sophie with each minute that passes.

"Are you going to find out where she is?" I ask Brendan.

He looks up. "Who?"

"Sophie."

He shakes his head and returns his attention to his phone. "I'm busy."

My nostrils flare. This guy is unbelievable.

143

"Too busy to care your girlfriend is missing?" Brendan ignores my challenging tone while Grace shoots daggers my way. "What? She should be here."

"If you're so bothered, then you find out where she is." She huffs and tosses some of her blonde wavy hair over her shoulder, pushing her chest out far enough to distract Brendan from his phone when he thinks I'm not looking.

I curse that I didn't just try myself to begin with, getting too caught up in proving what an ass Fitzgerald is.

"Fine." I pull out my phone and call Sophie, but it goes straight to voicemail. "Dammit."

There's no point in texting her because I have multiple times already today and had no response. Instead, I call Zoe. She doesn't answer the first or second time. I get lucky on the third.

"Hey," she answers with a shrill voice.

She knows something.

"Where's Sophie?" I ask.

"She's busy." My brows pull together at her answer.

"We had plans," I state.

"Oh."

"Where is she, Zo?"

"Erm …"

I can hear her brain working to come up with an acceptable answer, then another person on the other end of the line joins our conversation.

"Ma'am, you can't use that in here."

"Oh yes, I know. Sorry, sir." Zoe sounds overly posh in the way she does whenever she's trying to get strangers to take her seriously. "Just one moment."

"Zo, where the hell are you?"

There's a pause and a load of noise in the background.

"Well, you see, the thing is …"

Whoever's with her isn't happy with being dismissed. "Ma'am, I will confiscate it from you."

There's rustling, and I assume she's moved the phone away from her face. I still make out when she hisses, "Christ! It's a phone, not a gun!" There's another pause and muffled voices. "Why can't I say gun? It's just a word. Look at me. Do I look like I'm a threat with firearms?"

"Zoe?"

"Sam …" Her voice becomes clearer and I hear her swallow. This has the Berlin Incident written all over it. "We're in the 71st Precinct."

I choke on air, then when I've recovered, say, "Wait? What? You're in jail?" My voice is loud enough the tables surrounding ours look over.

"Don't worry, we're fine. We're with Grams." My jaw drops. Not only have they managed to get themselves arrested, but Sophie's eighty-odd-year-old Grandma, too? What the hell have they been doing? I'm all for the old Sophie making a reappearance, but this is too far. "Actually, things aren't fine," Zoe continues. "They're pretty shi—"

"Ma'am," interrupts who I now know to be an officer of the NYPD.

"I'm coming to help."

"No, don't!"

"Zoe, I'm coming." I don't give her a chance to say anything else, hanging up before she can convince me not to go.

Brendan doesn't look up when I stand to leave, making it clear he hasn't been listening, because Sophie being in jail is definitely in his interest. After all, he has a rep to worry about.

"Where are you going?" asks Grace.

I barely hear her question, busy calculating how long it will take to get there.

"Are you coming?" I say to Brendan.

"Where?" he asks, finally giving his attention to something that isn't his phone.

"I think Sophie might be in trouble."

"Of course," Grace says to herself, without an ounce of concern.

"I haven't eaten," Brendan replies, frowning at the table.

"You heard me, right? She's in trouble."

He looks up and shrugs. "She'll message if she needs me."

Clearly, he couldn't care less about Sophie, which means I couldn't care less about how I come across to him. I decide a few home truths are in order.

"You're a prick and she deserves better," I tell him, before leaving.

My feet move at lightning speed as I weave through the tables.

"Sam!" Grace shouts after me, but I'm already out the door.

The rep rockstars get for their lifestyles, for the most part, isn't true. At least, not where S.C.A.R.A.B. are concerned. In the years since the band has taken off, there has been minimal drug use, not a lot of sex, much to Grace's disappointment, and, with my voice deciding to go AWOL, now hardly any rock and roll.

I feel more like a rockstar than I ever have before as I walk into the 71st precinct and I'm not the one on the wrong side of the law.

What I expected to be a major challenge, getting to wherever Sophie, Zoe and Grams are being held, proves relatively easy when the receptionist tells me she's a fan. Some shameless flirting and an autograph see me following her to the third floor.

I hear them before I see them.

Zoe and Grams' cackles are music to my ears, filling me with the hope that maybe things aren't as bad as what I've been imagining all the way here.

I don't hold back when I get close.

"What the hell have you been doing?" My angry question is targeted at Sophie, and I get three hard stares in return. The officer behind them clears his throat. "Sorry." I focus back on a disheveled looking Sophie. "Seriously, what's going on?"

"Trespassing." The officer answers for them.

"Trespassing?" I repeat.

"These ladies refused to leave someone's property when our officers arrived after concerns were reported."

"Concerns *I* raised," adds in Grams.

I look between them all, confused about what's actually going on.

"Isn't that like a minor offence? Doesn't it usually go with a warning or something?" My attention catches on what Sophie is wearing. Exactly the same thing as the gig last night, albeit more crumpled. "When did you come in?"

147

"They were in a holding cell last night," says the officer grimly. "It was confirmed there were no charges being made this morning."

I stare at the three of them in shock. "Last night?!"

Sophie finally speaks up. "That's why my phone's dead."

"Why are you still here?" I ask glancing around the office.

"They're refusing to leave," confirms the officer.

I look at him and smile. "Sir, I was asking them. Do you mind if we have a minute?"

He steps back. One, single, step. I'm too tired to argue and hope he won't interrupt any more.

"What's going on?" I ask Sophie directly, my focus lasered her way to make it clear the question is for her and her alone.

"It's not what you think," she replies.

Her eyes move to the side of the room and settle on a door. She frowns and bites her lip anxiously while Zoe sits, wringing her hands together. I want to ask again what's going on and get some clear answers, but something deep within stops me. An inkling telling me this isn't some drunken misdemeanor—that it's something bigger than us all.

Contemplating what to do, I quickly realize there's nothing to contemplate.

"Can I grab a chair?" I ask the officer, who's still hovering in the background.

His eyes flash with something. Respect? I'm not really sure. But he looks like he's got his own internal battles going on, perhaps debating between the right answer for his job and the right answer on a personal level. A couple of seconds pass, and then he dips his chin. I nod back with a tight, thankful smile, then go about sourcing a seat.

When I return, Sophie watches me intently with watery eyes and I question to myself, for what feels like the millionth time, what the hell is going on?

"Fancy swapping?" I ask Zoe.

Despite whatever the unknown circumstances of us all being here are, the edges of her mouth curl up slightly and she stands without a word, leaving the chair next to Sophie free. I step forward to replace her, but stop when our paths cross and she grabs my arm.

Standing on her tippy toes, she lifts her chin and whispers so only I can hear, "Just so you know, I'm Team Sam. Fitzgerald the Fuckwit needs to go."

"I know," I reply quietly. I make to move, assuming it's the end of the conversation, but Zoe's hand tightens round my arm.

She drops her voice impossibly low. "He *really* needs to go. He's cheating on her. I've seen him."

"I know," I repeat, my stomach twisting in a tight knot.

And I do know, I've known all along. The evidence has been there all over the media. Reports of who his newest conquests might be, sometimes weekly. Thankfully, Sophie has avoided the media world like the plague following Berlin, unless it's related to Next Level. Hearing Zoe say she's literally seen it, though, is something else entirely. She lets go of my arm and I settle in the chair, talking myself through every reason why I can't introduce him to my fist like I wish I'd done earlier.

When I've finally calmed down, I look up and find Sophie literally hasn't moved and is still focused on the door across the room. The dark circles beneath her bloodshot eyes look alien on the Sophie I'm used to seeing, and I'm tempted to scoop her up, source the nearest bed and demand she sleeps. After a while, I look away and find Grams watching. I smile and she smiles back. A smile that tells me she knows everything about everyone, including me, and how I feel about her granddaughter.

I'm not sure how long we sit, waiting for I don't even know what. It could be hours; it could be minutes. Eventually, with the warmth of the office, the slight scent of Sophie's perfume still lingering on her clothing from yesterday, and the steady hum of the computers, I drift off to sleep.

Chapter Thirteen
Sophie

Somewhere between the hours of nine and ten, Sam's head falls to the side, landing on my shoulder.

I'm so distracted waiting for Russ to come back through the door he disappeared through a couple of hours ago, it takes me by surprise, and I almost jump out of my chair in shock. When he's settled, a wave of calm passes over me as his breathing slows into a steady rhythm.

"How are you doing?" asks Abby. "I haven't forgotten what you said at the beginning of the tour."

I glance around the VIP tent at the same time my phone vibrates in my bag and dread settles in my stomach. "I'm good. Promise."

My phone vibrates again and my muscles coil tight. When is this going to end? It's been weeks since Berlin, but thanks to a video of Zoe and I that went viral, my phone has been blowing up non-stop with notifications from all my social media accounts, and not the good kind. Because she isn't a Parker, it hasn't affected Zoe the same. When I tried to tell her what was going on, about all the trolling, she simply shrugged and claimed any publicity is good publicity.

"You still don't seem like yourself. You've been quiet," continues Abby.

"I'm just ready for change. I feel like I'm at a time in my life where I need to make some decisions and to start thinking for myself. There's only so long you can live off mummy and daddy's money."

What I really want to tell her is that I want to crawl into a hole and never come back out. I want to be seen, but not like this. Not for my mistakes. Not because I'm a Parker. And not because I'm friends with S.C.A.R.A.B.

I want to be seen for being me. Just Sophie. I want to offer something to the world and make a difference. Unfortunately, the world has other ideas and keeps kindly informing me it would be a better place without me.

"Are you sure it's just that? I haven't seen you try to hook up with any guys, either?"

I sigh. Right now, guys are the least of my worries. "I'm just over the whole dating game. I know we're not old, but it's getting old, if you get me. I'm tired of chasing guys, only to be pushed aside for a better piece of ass, as if I'm second best." Because she looks totally unconvinced by what I'm saying, I decide to give her a glimmer of the truth. "I want someone to finally see me for me."

Sam pivots around from where he's been standing. "I see you, Soph."

The concern covering his face makes me laugh awkwardly, because recently, whenever he's close by, I feel like I'm under a microscope, and he knows everything that's going on inside my head. A part of me wants him to help. I want to lean on him like I always have done. But I also want to learn to stand on my own two feet. To prove to myself that I can come back from my mistakes, which is why I purposefully say what I know will push him away.

"Whatever, Sam. I know you see me, but I mean really see me. Not just like a friend."

Hurt and disappointment crosses the face of the one person who's always tried to support and help build me up, making me feel like an even bigger failure, and it makes me question what I've just done.

"Soph." I let out a small moan. "Soph." The voice is firmer this time.

"Grblugh," I answer, twisting in my chair, attempting to bury myself deeper into the chair and escape from reality.

"Soph!"

I blink rapidly, trying to bring myself back into the present, finding a swirly version of Sam, crouching in front of me. Even distorted, he looks gorgeous, and my stomach flutters.

He gives me a lopsided smile. "Hey, Sleepy-red."

My returned "hey" comes out muffled. "Sorry. I drifted off." I rub at my eyes and then my own words sink in. I dart forward, almost knocking Sam to the floor in the process. "Shit! I fell asleep. Russ!"

Heart hammering, my eyes move around the room frantically.

Sam steadies himself and takes a step toward me. He bends his knees, leaning forward slightly and dipping low so we're at eye level, causing some of his own sleep mussed hair to fall across his head. My eyes find it fascinating and follow the movement, then his hands are covering my shoulders and his thumbs rub back and forth in a soothing pattern.

"Hey, it's okay. We were only out twenty. They're coming through in a minute."

His explanation helps my body to relax enough I'm able to get my heart rate under control.

"Okay," I say with a long exhale.

I don't get a chance to ask how he knows exactly *who* it is we're waiting for, because the door I've stared at for an unhealthy amount of time swings open. Zoe and Grams stand, and the officer who's been with us for an equally unhealthy amount of time straightens his back, towering over us all.

Another officer walks through the door, back into the main room. Following is a woman in her late thirties, five six with her clunky heels on, wearing a blank pant suit that would work wonders for her figure if it spent some time with a seamstress. She's as serious as they come, her jaw set in a hard line; her gaze as heavy as the huge pile of files sitting in her arms.

The shriek of my name bounces off the walls and Russ races toward me. I'm winded when he continues full pelt into me, wrapping his arms tightly around my middle. Arms frozen in mid-air; my body remains rigid. I don't know what to do. The woman in the pant suit stands back from the group, watching. Assessing.

After Grams' wariness over how close I've already become with Russ, I'm reluctant to do anything that could make things worse. My intentions have only ever come from a good place. I know it. The people closest to me know it. However, the woman, who is very clearly from Child

Protection, knows nothing about me apart from the fact I gave a child, who wasn't under my care, a phone, and walked him home regularly.

A lump forms in my throat and I struggle to swallow over the awareness of how bad this all looks.

Russ pulls away with a small smile, none the wiser of my internal battle. The lump grows bigger and my throat closes completely, blocking oxygen from entering my body when I take in the bruise covering his cheek. The one that maybe wouldn't be there if I'd said something straight away.

Then, I remember the woman hovering in the doorway, acting like she couldn't care less about Russ or his wellbeing. The uncertainty flooding my system is replaced with a flare of anger at the neglect he's been through. I'd charge back into that apartment a hundred times over to make sure he's safe, which is why I reach over and give his shoulder a squeeze. It's a big solid line I shouldn't cross, but he needs the reassurance more than I need to follow the rules, and when he looks up with fear, I try to tell him with a look what I can't say out loud.

I'm going to help you. I'm not going anywhere unless I know you're safe.

The woman in the suit steps forward and clears her throat. "Josh, I'd like you to go with Officer James. I'll be with you in a few minutes."

I narrow my eyes at her use of his real name. She doesn't know a thing about him, not really. He's just another case on her books. Focusing on my breathing to keep myself calm, I wait until Russ is out of earshot before I speak.

"Where is he going?"

"To a new foster home," she answers.

155

"A new home?" The words falter as they fall from my lips. "Like the one he's just been in?"

"Ms. Parker," says the woman with a level voice. "Josh explained what you did for him. Normally, it would be frowned upon, but given the …" she clears her throat, "shall we say, circumstances? No further action will be taken against any of you and the charges have been dropped."

"I don't give a shit about the charges."

"Sophie," warns Grams.

I shake my head her way. "No. Don't, *Sophie*, me. You've seen him. What he's been through."

Heart rattling against my ribcage, anger-fueled adrenaline floods my system and all I see is red.

I'm angry. So damn angry. And hurting. For Russ.

"This is the way the system works, Ms. Parker," intervenes the suit. "Where would *you* have him? On the streets?"

I turn my attention back to the woman with venom in my eyes. "What's your name?"

She blinks, clearly taken aback by my question. "Elayne," she answers after a beat.

"*Elayne*. Will this home Ru—Josh is going to be similar to the one he left?"

Elayne lifts her chin. "We have good homes in the system. Don't let what happened tonight taint what we do and how hard we try to protect the innocent."

"But it still happened," I say through gritted teeth.

"Sometimes things get missed, Ms. Parker."

"Missed? Missed?! You make it sound like we're baking or some crap. This is a *child*. Things shouldn't be missed!"

"Do you think I don't know that?" she replies, a slight snappiness in her tone, giving away her true feelings and frustrations. "No person, no system is perfect. But it's better than a reality without them."

She has a point. A good one. I know she does, but it doesn't change what's happened here, and I refuse to back down.

"He can't go to another home like that."

"And where would you suggest he go?" she asks blankly.

I can't give her an answer, because I don't have one. We stare at each other, refusing to back down, each believing we're right, because on some level, we both are. I start to panic after a couple of seconds, where I still have no answers as to how to help. Just like every other area of my life, I'm falling at the last hurdle. Failing Russ.

I'm about to bite down on my bottom lip when I feel movement behind me. Warmth envelopes my back, not quite touching. Sam.

"I see you, Soph."

And there it is, I feel it. The push I need.

"I'll take him. I'll take Josh and care for him temporarily until you can find a more suitable place."

If Elayne is shocked by my words, she doesn't show it. I'm tempted to look to the side and gauge the others' reactions.

But then I feel other things I never have before. Resolve. Fire. Drive. Certainty.

I don't look to the side or behind me because I don't need to. I refuse to question my choice and allow it to be influenced by what anyone else believes. It's the right one. I know it.

"Ms. Parker. It's not that simple. You can't just walk out of here with a child who isn't yours. There are rules. Hoops that need to be jumped through."

"Then jump. Do whatever you need to."

"He will still need to go to a home with people who meet the right criteria and have been vetted until we make sure you're a suitable candidate to take him."

"And when it's all complete, he can come to me."

"Ms. Parker ... Are you sure about this?"

I nod. "Never been surer." Elayne's expression softens, and she finally looks at me like a human. Needing her to listen, I reach out in the only way I know how. "*Please*. Fix this, for Russ." I don't bother correcting myself. "I bet there is so much you want to say but can't, right? Because there are *rules*?" Her eyes dart away, giving me the yes that I need to continue. "I can't imagine what it must be like seeing the things you do," her eyes move back to me, "and sometimes not being able to help in the ways you might want to. I don't *know*, but I get it.

"This is so much bigger than you and I. And right now, what I'm asking you to do isn't just about this situation. It's about every awful situation in the world where there's that murky fucking gray area, the one where we have to abide by rules and regulations or live in fear by the lack of them. It's scary, and I guess you, like me, and a world full of people at times, might feel helpless. Like your actions don't matter and won't change things. But they will.

"Most people can't get to the top of the mountain by sprinting. It's the small, consistent steps which get them to where they need to be. You can help this one little person who has their whole life ahead of them, who can carry your values and examples forward. Be the extra pressure that makes the droplet fall, because when it does, it will ripple through a society scared to disturb the water sitting beneath all the grays. You. Can. Help. Here. You can let me help. *Please.* Apologize with your actions when you can't with your words."

My chest heaves after my monologue. Meanwhile, Elayne remains completely still. In fact, the whole room is still. I look around, wondering what volume my voice reached and how far it carried.

"Give your details to Detective Wells. I'll be in touch," says Elayne abruptly before walking away.

I look around, confused as hell, until the officer who's been shadowing our every move for over twenty-four hours starts to clap.

"That was quite a performance you put on there." It feels like he's baiting me, and my skin bristles with annoyance.

"It wasn't a performance," I reply flatly.

"I know."

Sam places his hand on the small of my back, leans in, and close to my ear, says, "You should go home and get some rest."

Moving my attention slowly away from Detective Wells, I turn back to him so I can speak properly. "I can't go."

Detective Wells clears his throat from behind. "You need to go home, Ms. Parker. You can't fight the battle you've started if you're exhausted. Nothing more can be done tonight."

I want to stomp my foot and demand answers about what happens next, but I realize he and Sam are both right. I've slept twenty minutes in forty-eight hours and I'm dead on my feet. Admitting it to myself only makes the exhaustion worse and my body sags. When I wobble, Sam wraps his arm around my waist and draws me in to his body.

"Let's go catch a cab," he says to Grams and Zoe.

Body shutting down as the adrenaline from the past ten minutes subsides, my vision starts to go hazy. The only thing I recall before consciousness slips away is the squeak of my sneakers against the polished linoleum floors and the sweat that coats my skin as we step out into the humid Brooklyn night.

Chapter Fourteen

Sophie

My eyelids hurt as I try to open them and take in my room.

If I could sleep forever, I would. I don't think I've ever been as exhausted as I feel now, even with the momentous hangovers of my past. This is a different kind of exhaustion, the kind you get when you've really been put through the wringer.

I expect to find Sam beside me when I roll over, after a vague recollection of him tucking me in somewhere close to midnight, but the other side of my bed is cold and empty. There isn't an imprint either.

He just … left?

Trying not to focus on the why, I turn my attention to what comes next. There are so many people I need to speak with because I have an unbelievable number of questions. Then there's the list of things to do. The one that would easily be longer than my body if I put pen to paper. Yet, I find myself buried deep beneath my covers, suddenly overwhelmed by everything.

I haven't got a clue what I'm doing. I'm tempted to call my mom. I can't decide if it's to offload or beg her to come help me. Something stops me, though. A need to prove—not to everyone around me, but to myself—that I can get through this. I can figure this out.

About an hour later, I hear Zoe enter our apartment. Surprising, considering she's a champion sleeper. I'm trying to figure out what she might have been up to that would spur her to leave the apartment before me, when I hear her feet clomping in the direction of my room. I bury myself deeper in my warm cave. Never one for subtlety, she hammers her fist against my door.

"Go away!" I grunt from under my blankets.

I need more time to process everything that's happened and after Zoe made it clear on our way to find Russ that she knew *all* of my secrets; I know I'm in for the third degree. My brain can't cope with all of her questions when I have so many of my own.

"I'm coming in and you have no choice," she shouts, way too loud.

True to her word, the door flies open and a few seconds later, I bounce against the mattress thanks to the force she sits down with. She pulls back the blankets and cool air bites my skin.

"Zo, I'm not in the mood." I go to grab the blankets back, but we find ourselves in a tug of war. Zoe wins when she heaves them into her arms and dives off the bed, flattening them beneath her on the floor. She looks back over her shoulder and I can just about make out her grin through all the teal covering her face. "Whatever," I mutter.

The grin disappears, and she straightens her shirt before climbing back on the bed. She brings the blankets with her, tucking us both in. A small peace offering I don't deserve after the way I've been treating her recently.

"We have so much we need to talk about, but first, I need to know what's really wrong between us. Why do you hate me?" she asks. I focus on the paisley print of my sheets, trying to block out the wobble in her voice. It makes my heart hurt knowing it's there because of me. When I don't reply, she continues. "Is it because I changed the desk order?"

"Maybe," I admit, because partly it is, and this conversation has been a long time coming. I'm tired of being angry and hurt. If there's a chance for us to move on, then I'm ready to move.

After a pause that seems to go on for an eternity, Zoe lets out a long exhale.

"I'm sorry. I shouldn't have done it. Or I at least should have run it by you first."

Who the hell has climbed into bed with me? Zoe never admits when she's in the wrong. Like, never, ever.

I twist so I'm facing her. "Never mind me. What's wrong with you?"

She frowns. "Why would there be anything wrong?"

"Why? Erm, because you just apologized."

"We're thirty now." She winks. "Sorry, my mistake. You already know because you remind me at least four times a day."

My mood lifts, and I give her a playful shove. "I'm sorry, too. For being dramatic and uptight."

"Is that the new way of describing being a bitch?" she laughs.

163

"Pushing it, Zo."

Her eyes fill with emotion. "I've missed you."

Guilt seeps in. Guilt for every jibe, every grump, every negative thought I've had about my best friend. The world is quick to dislike her. She's bold and brash, but she is who she is. What you see is what you get, and she's one of the most honest people I've met. She might not be to everyone's taste, but she's true to herself, accepting that in order to be happy, she can't please everyone. Maybe some of the resentment I've been harboring toward her these past few years is more jealousy. Wanting to be and live my life like her, without the expectations of others weighing down on my chest.

"I've been right here," I reply.

"You haven't really been here in years."

"What do you mean?" I know exactly what she means. I've changed. I'd like to think it's for the better, but I'm losing control, torn between what I think I should be doing with my life and what I actually want to do. Although we've grown apart, she still knows me better than most.

"I wanted white desks," I say. Although now, after some reflection and my anger wavering, I'm glad we have the rainbow. It's the principle surrounding what happened that I need to get across. "Sooz gave me one job. To pick the color. It's the only major decision I've had with regards to Next Level, and you took it from me."

Zoe pales, telling me that, now she understands why I'm hurt, she regrets what she did. "I didn't know it meant that much to you."

"You never asked. You never do, because you're so busy being you. You're always disappearing …"

"Firstly," she holds a single finger in the air, "it's not what you think. And second, we can send them back …"

She watches me; her face making it clear how stricken she is by this confrontation, which has been coming for way too long. I consider what I should say next. We could keep going, but we'd be going in circles and likely end up bickering. What would be the point?

I take a deep breath, feeling like I've run a marathon or ten after the past couple of days. I could hold on to this, but everything that's happened with Russ has made me realize that, now I've voiced how I feel, that's it. It's done. There's no point harboring anger over something like a desk debacle. Not when my life is about to turn upside down if things go the way I hope they will with Child Protection.

"There's no point. It won't change that it's done." I pause and the corners of Zoe's mouth turn down. "But I appreciate the offer."

"What can I do to make this better? Please, Soph. I meant what I said. I miss you. I miss us."

"I know," I nod. I want my best friend back. I want my old life back. I miss it. I miss it all. "There's more to it than just the desks." Zoe waits for me to continue. "After what happened in Berlin, things were shit. I mean, like, really shit."

"You mean the trolling?" I nod. "Why didn't you say?"

"I did! And you told me any publicity was good publicity, but things are different for me because of my parents, you know that. The second anything goes wrong, people are there waiting."

Zoe looks distraught. "I should have listened properly." She drops her gaze to the sheets. "I'm sorry."

"It's okay," I whisper, because I think it finally is. I think this might be the start of me putting it all to bed. "You were so excited about everything you were doing … I could have told you what was really going on. I should have … I just …

I didn't want to put a dampener on everything when you were finally doing well."

My phone lights up on the bed, distracting us both. The name Fitzgerald flashes on the screen and my eyes dart up to Zoe, expecting her to look surprised. Then, I remember she knows it all.

"Why are you with him, Soph?"

"I don't know," I reply. Because I don't.

She gives me a sad look. "He's … well, he's not you, and don't give me that opposites attract shit. This isn't opposites. This is worlds apart, and not in the good sense where you can help bring the best out of each other. Think Jake and the Ross family. Stuck in their ways. Elitist." My lips twitch and my mouth parts. I don't get a chance to say anything because Zoe continues on. "Let me guess. It was his idea to keep your relationship a secret. Fly under the radar to stay out of the media, so you could have a 'normal' relationship. It's bull. You know it."

Everything she's saying is right. He's shown on more than one occasion that he's a less than stellar boyfriend. I've been so focused on my quest to prove I've got it all together, I've neglected to see what's right in front of me.

I clear my throat awkwardly and glance down at the bed, tracing the blue pattern on the sheets with the tip of my finger. "I need to end it. Especially with what's going on with Russ." I'm talking to Zoe, but I feel like I'm talking to myself. Making it clear to my brain exactly what it is that has to happen next before it can come up with any crazier ideas. "I need to get everything straight in case they say that I can take Russ." I kind of groan, kind of whimper. "Oh my God, what if they do say yes?"

I'd be over the moon, euphoric. Equally, the thought of caring for said child, an actual human, only emphasizes how far I am from the ideal parental situation.

A feeling of dread crawls through me, settling in my stomach. At first, I can't figure out why, and Zoe eyes me as I frown to myself.

"Is so—"

"Oh my God! Crap, crap, crap, crap, crap."

"What's wrong?" asks Zoe, alarmed.

"I forgot to give Detective Wells my details." I let my head fall back and it collides with the back of the bed frame, hard. I barely feel the shooting sensations across my skull. "There's no way I can look after a child!" I exclaim, my voice getting louder, and the pitch higher with each word. "I can't even remember to do something simple like pass on my details."

I'm ready for jumping on the train and rocking down to a really great pity party, when Zoe holds her hand up and says firmly, "Soph!" I look at her. "Detective Wells has all your details. You need to chill."

"How?"

"Sam went back to the station and dealt with things once you were settled. He gave them everything they needed so you wouldn't have to."

"Oh …"

"He told you, but you were so exhausted you probably didn't take any of it in."

"Right."

My heart thumps hard. He didn't just leave like I thought. He went to help. I'm such an idiot for questioning him, even for a second. He's never given me a reason to, ever.

"You will be fine," says Zoe, breaking me out of my Sam musings without an ounce of doubt in her voice.

I give her a sideways glance. "You really believe I can do this? Look after a child?"

"Soph," she says, exhaling. "Do you know what you need to do?"

"What?" I ask, unsure whether I want to hear her answer; the cold hard truth of how, in trying to correct my fuck-ups, I've continued to fuck up.

"Believe in yourself."

She makes it sound so easy because it is easy for her. She's never cared what anyone thinks, and I guess with that comes a sense of freedom; an opportunity to go after whatever you want, regardless of the outcome.

I want to answer, to say something, but I don't know what. Zoe keeps quiet and shuffles down the bed, then settles beneath the blankets, making it clear she isn't going anywhere. Needing something to do, I lean over to my nightstand, grab the remote and turn on the TV. After a few minutes of scrolling through Netflix, I settle on a reality dating series, hoping whatever drama goes on makes me feel better about my own. All it does is take me back to my twenties, to the Sophie I really don't want to remember. Without an adequate distraction, my mind detours to Russ. The phone call. How I found him. Where he might be now and whether he's safe. It makes me feel sick to my stomach that he's having to go through any of this.

I sniffle, and Zoe looks up from where she's nestled. "He's going to be okay."

"You don't know that."

"No." She pauses. "I don't. But I have faith."

I snort. "Since when did you become religious?" Zoe has always been the least likely to believe there's something out there—something bigger than all of us—that plays a hand in our lives.

A loud knock at the door stops her from responding. We stare at each other for a second, and then there's another knock.

"Are you expecting someone?" Zoe shakes her head no and we each sit, contemplating whether whoever is outside is worth climbing out of our cloud of warmth for.

"Soph!"

It's Sam.

"I thought he had a key," says Zoe.

"No key," I reply, making a mental note to rectify the issue as soon as possible.

"Come on!" Sam shouts.

I have no choice other than to let him in, because if I don't, with how much commotion he's causing, the neighbors will complain.

"I'm not moving," states Zoe. "I think they're about to bone each other."

A glance at the TV screen confirms she's talking about the dating show. Grumbling as I clamber out from under the covers, I shuffle to the apartment door.

I undo the multiple latches Sam insisted we get, then make quick work of the main lock.

"Could you take any longer?" he mutters, walking into the pokey living area.

"I was contemplating if I could get away without answering," I reply, knowing the exact reaction I'm going to get.

He spins around, shock on his face. I can't hold it in. I giggle. Sam's face breaks into a grin, then he reaches over and pulls me in. My arms move around his back, and I bury my face in his chest. I'm tempted to inhale because the slight scent that's already filled my nostrils is addictive. The thought of how embarrassing it would be if he caught me literally sniffing him is what stops me.

"You good?" he asks against my hair.

I nod into his chest, managing to get the teeniest of sniffs in. Totally worth the risk. It makes me feel all fuzzy inside and my anxiety disappears temporarily. Minutes pass, maybe an hour, but I don't care how long I stand, refusing to move. I'd happily do it forever, lost in my best friend, who right now, I don't want to be my best friend. I have enough of those in my life.

I pull away, blinking rapidly when it hits me exactly what I've just thought and who I've thought it about.

Sam.

Sammy Sam.

Oh, no. It's one thing staring at him too long, sniffing him, and whatever other actions my body has been doing without my permission. But acknowledging feelings is stepping into the red zone. There's no coming back from acknowledging the fleeting thoughts. Ones that wouldn't be so fleeting if it weren't for the major security team that I have running drills in my brain.

If Sam weren't standing in front of me, I'd be banging my head against the wall. I am absolutely on the path of self-sabotage with the best thing I have going in my life. I need to put an end to it right this second.

Sam's brows pull together, and I wonder how much of my internal battle he can read on my face. "What's wrong?" he asks, confirming he's reading it all.

It's then I realize he's still wearing the clothing he came in last night.

"Why haven't you changed? It's ..." I glance at my watch. "Three in the afternoon." My eyes widen. "Holy cow, when did it get so late?"

Urgency takes over and I try to figure out what I need to do so I can get ready and hop foot it back to the precinct. They will totally block my calls, so there's no point in trying that route of communication.

Sam snaps his fingers in front of my face. "Soph. You don't need to do anything. Detective Wells gave me an update."

"And?"

His lips form a flat line. "There is no update."

My stomach sinks. "How can there not be an update?" I snap, unfairly directing my anger his way.

He shrugs. "These things take time. You heard what that woman Elayne said. There are hoops to jump through. I'm guessing lots of them in order to achieve the outcome you want."

"Okay." My shoulders droop, my mood returning to its oppressive self from earlier.

"Actually," says Sam, scratching the back of his head. "I need to go. Sooz has been on my case all day that I have a ton of things I need to do after what happened at the gig."

I clap a hand over my mouth, realizing that with the turn of events, I've totally forgotten what happened with Sam and everything he's going through beside the extra drama I've drawn him into.

171

"Oh God, I'm sorry." I cringe. "I should have asked."

Taking me by surprise, he steps back in, cups my jaw and places a brief kiss against my head, one that sends off a swarm of butterflies in my stomach. "No need to apologize. She told me what you did. That this plan was your idea."

"It was a team effort," I mumble, cheeks growing warm.

"It's genius. Don't worry about my stuff. Just make me a promise …"

"What?" I ask, the one simple word catching in the back of my throat.

"Keep an open mind about whatever happens."

"I—" I actually can't breathe. The next thing happens in a nanosecond. Because I'm hyperaware of everything he's doing, like the way his thumbs move back and forth, burning a path against my cheeks. I don't miss when his eyes drop to my lips, then, at the speed of light, snap up again. "I don't know what you're saying."

"It doesn't matter how you get to your destination, all that matters is that you get there in the end."

His eyes move back to my lips and this time it's torturously slow, making my body heat and respond in ways it never has to Brendan, with one single look. It makes me question if his words are referring to more than just the situation with Russ.

"Red …"

My heart, already racing, kicks its pace up a thousand notches, chugging in my chest. Starting to feel faint, I sway on my feet. Sam's hands drop to my arms, keeping me in place. When I'm steady, he steps back, expression blank, totally unaffected. Meanwhile, I'm struggling to remember what my name is and questioning if it's normal to require a panty change from just one word.

I'm distracted from all my analyzing when Sam reaches into the pocket of his pants and pulls out a box, wrapped delicately, with a small bow finishing it off.

"This is for you to open later." He hands it over.

"Okay?"

"Later," he says cryptically, mouth turned up. "You'll know when you need to."

"How will I know?" I ask, watching him back away to the door.

He taps the side of his nose and winks. "Call me later."

I'd hate him for those three words if they didn't do funny things to my insides.

An hour later, I've almost recovered from Sam's visit when my ringtone fills mine and Zoe's apartment—better described as a bedsit—with a call from an unknown number.

I contemplate letting it ring through. I hate answering unsolicited calls for a variety of reasons. One being that after spending a night taking part in one of Sam and Ryan's *True Crime* marathons, I convinced myself my phone would get hacked, like in one of the cases we watched.

Remembering I'm expecting an update on Russ at any time, I snatch my phone up, fumbling it slightly as I accept the call.

"Hello?" I answer, sounding less confident than I'd like.

"Is this Ms. Parker?" comes a familiar voice.

"Speaking."

"It's Elayne Cartwright from Child Protection. We met yesterday."

"Hi!" I wince at the shrill noise that comes from my mouth.

Way to sound mature and like you can care for a child, Soph … not.

Elayne clears her throat, making it obvious she appreciates the noise as much as I do. Dammit.

"Yes. Hi. I'm ringing with an update for Josh Young."

Young. I never took note of what his family name is, like his real name has never found a set place in my mind. I've always thought of him as Russ. Is that a bad thing? Does it make me the wrong person to do this? I'd like to believe all that matters is that I care for his wellbeing, but I'm not sure it's that simple.

"Okay." I barely hear my own reply.

My voice lacks confidence, conviction, the kinds of things that would make me sound like I'd nail being a parent. Then, I remember the woman who answered the door at the home where Russ was supposed to be safe. The woman who looked the part, putting a show on for the world.

"We pushed for your checks to be carried out as a matter of urgency. You passed them all, which means you can take Josh under your care temporarily …" I let out a sigh of relief. It comes out too early because a massive 'but' follows. "*But* there was one issue which arose, and a couple of other things we need to discuss."

"Issue?"

"Your living situation," she clarifies. "In order for you to be able to take Josh in your care, he needs to have a room."

I don't need the time she gives me to make the calculation in my head. I already know this place is way too small to house an extra human, no matter how small they might be.

"Ah," I reply.

"Thankfully, you have alternative living arrangements, so if you'd still like to take Josh into your care, we can arrange for Wednesday. There will be more checks we need to carry out over the next few days."

Only one detail stands out in everything she's said. "What do you mean, alternative living arrangements?"

Elayne lets out a stiff laugh. "The apartment you and Mr. Riley have invested in together. He mentioned how exhausted you were today, and as the property is also under his name, we were able to carry out the assessments required with him. He didn't want us to bother you when he was able to be there instead and assured us the property will be kitted out with everything needed for Josh to be comfortable by Wednesday."

I feel like I'm about to throw up. Sam lied. The whitest of them, but I can't believe he's done this.

My eyes catch on the box he gave me earlier and I say to Elayne, "Can I have a second?"

"Of course," she replies.

I walk over to the kitchen counter where I left it and, with my phone balanced carefully between my shoulder and ear, take hold of the box and open it. When I've removed the packaging from the outside, I lift away the lid, sucking in a sharp breath when I see the contents.

Two sets of keys, nestled among red, shredded paper, each with a 'home sweet home' keyring attached.

I'm about to confess to Elayne that this has nothing to do with me, when I notice a small piece of white folded paper, hidden almost completely thanks to the gift packaging. I pull it out quickly, aware of how long it's been since I've spoken, and unfold it.

Sam's scrawl stares up at me, along with the words, 'It doesn't matter how you get to the destination. All that matters is that you get there in the end. Don't overthink this.'

I'm totally overthinking it, trying to figure out what it all means. Elayne coughs, signaling she's still on the line.

"S-sorry," I stammer, taken aback by what's just happened.

"Is everything okay?" she asks.

I decide Sam's right. It doesn't matter how any of us get to where we need to be. "Everything's fine."

"Great. So, as I was saying … we will also need to keep a close eye and carry out regular follow-ups, especially as you haven't done this before. I should also mention that Josh is being considered by a couple for adoption." My stomach sinks and I don't really know why. This is a good thing, an amazing thing for him. "The process has started, but it's a long one. At some point, it will be required they meet. Josh doesn't know yet. There are certain … hoops. We try not to let the older children know until the adoption process gets to a certain point, as sometimes these things fall through. This won't come without challenges, but it can still happen … if you want it to."

I barely hear her last words, because they're irrelevant. It's all the parts before that make my throat grow dry. For a fleeting second, doubt creeps in and I question what I'm getting myself into, what things will be like when we get to the end, because if what Elayne is saying is true, there will be one, and already I don't know how I feel about it.

Swallowing away what doubts I can, I say, "Sure! Wednesday sounds great." It comes out all croaky and unconvincing.

There's a pause over the line, and this time, when Elayne speaks, her voice is gentle, understanding. "You don't have to do this, Sophie."

"What do you mean? Why wouldn't I want to?"

"I …" she pauses again as if she's choosing her words carefully. "Obviously I understand the situation in its entirety after spending a considerable amount of time with Josh, or Russ as he likes to be called. What you said at the precinct last night, it was admirable, but what this child has been through … it won't come without its challenges.

"Parenting is one of the biggest challenges anyone can face. It requires you to be selfless, to put someone else first, to love them wholeheartedly, even through the hard times. Throw into the mix loss and grief, then on top of it all trauma, abuse and neglect … are you ready for what you might be faced with when the door closes and the two of you are left alone, without any *distractions*?

"He might lash out. He might withdraw. But whatever happens, he needs you to keep showing up each day, giving him hope that one day things will get better, that he will have a future worth fighting for. It's a lot … if you've changed your mind, no one would think any less of you."

Her words sit heavily between us. I take a deep breath and this time I try to sound as confident as I can, not wanting to leave any doubts in her mind, because I have none, apart from what will happen at the end—about how I will feel when it's time for him to leave.

"I haven't changed my mind. I want to do this."

Sure, the 'alternative living arrangements' have thrown me and the thought of having to care for a human in less than forty-eight hours is daunting, but this is what I want to do. I'm more certain about this than I have been about anything in my life in a very long time.

"In that case, we will be in touch again on Monday to discuss bringing Josh to you."

"Great." I give myself a big pat on the back, because my 'great' sounds effortlessly great, like I've got everything in order.

Little does Elayne know she's about to release Russ into the custody of someone who has struggled to look after themselves for the majority of their life. For a fleeting moment, I consider admitting it all while the call is still connected, but at the last second, change my mind, keeping my lips pressed shut and my secret still mine.

After the call has disconnected, I get ready to call Sam and ask him what the hell is going on, but he beats me to it. I open the message he's sent, cursing and laughing at the same time as I read the address of mine and Russ's new, temporary home, with instructions to meet him there on Monday.

Chapter Fifteen

Sam

My nerves at the gig might have been the crazy, next-level, life-changing, career-destroying kind, but they're nothing compared to what I'm experiencing at this very second, waiting for Sophie to arrive at the apartment.

It's kitted out with everything Google said she might need over the next few weeks—maybe months. Still, I find myself checking over all the details. So much so, I've gone through the list I compiled six times and it's only ten AM. Basically I'm a mess. Hilarious, considering I'm not the one who's about to have a child's future in their hands. And just in case the anticipation of Sophie's reaction isn't scary enough, child protection is en route as well.

I'm on my third watch check in under a minute when I hear two pairs of footsteps approaching from the other side of the main door. They're slow, hesitant steps, giving me enough time to glance around one final time.

It looks homely … I think.

My heart thumps hard with the sound of the key sliding into the lock a few seconds later. God, I hope I've got this right. I'm terrified I've missed something important that could hinder Sophie's attempts at helping whoever this small Russ person is. As the door starts to open slowly, I realize I've frozen to the spot. I jump to life as it opens fully, finding Elayne and Sophie standing together, looking the epitome of awkward.

"Hi," smiles Sophie.

Elayne from Child Protection gives me a curt nod, one that compliments her black suit and starched shirt. "Mr. Riley."

"Hey," I reply to both, eyes moving between them. I repeat the action when both of their expressions become amused, trying to figure out what could be triggering it.

Sophie bites down on her bottom lip briefly, then lets out a small cough. "Sam …" she mumbles.

"What?"

Her attention moves to the side, settling on Elayne, who she gives an apologetic smile, before focusing back on me. "We need to come in?"

I realize I'm blocking the way. Damn. I look like an idiot.

I do my own version of Sophie's awkward cough/throat clearing thing. "Right." I cough again and flatten my back against the wall. "Sorry."

Elayne sweeps past with a briefcase as serious as her posture, adding to her superior aura. Sophie does the opposite, rolling her lips, trying and failing to hold in a snigger. Before she passes me, my arm darts out and I flatten my hand over her left hip.

"Stop laughing," I hiss into her ear.

180

I snap my hand away when I see Elayne start to turn back. I'm already standing tall and to attention when she faces us.

The next hour is one big contradiction, moving at the speed of light yet painfully slow. Elayne has questions, hundreds of them. No exaggeration. All I want is for her to wrap it up and leave so I can get the full story from Sophie. Currently, I'm doing whatever I can to help while completely in the dark.

Finally, after an additional thirty minutes of expectations being laid out, Elayne stands from the large dining table and goes about putting away all the paperwork we've worked through into her briefcase. "So, Josh will be arriving around two PM. If you can have everything ready to assure his transition is …" she takes a breath, as if contemplating her next few words. A look passes between her and Sophie, and she shakes her head a little. "Let's just get him settled and then we can take each day as it comes."

I'm tempted to ask if she's speaking on a professional or personal level, but in the end choose not to, reluctant to give her a reason to stay when she's so close to leaving.

"If you need anything, you have my card," Elayne says to a pale Sophie.

"Yep." Sophie grins, but she might as well be grimacing for what it does to her face. There's no sparkle in her eyes; no lift to the corners of her mouth. She looks like she wants to hide somewhere and pretend all of this isn't happening.

When the door's shut and the sound of Elayne's footsteps are virtually non-existent, I let loose on Sophie before she can run.

"You don't have to do this." I don't know why I say it, because Sophie always has been stubborn. When she puts her mind to something, there's no backing down.

She doesn't meet my eye—the only sign of uncertainty. Her voice, which comes out determinedly, says, "Yes. I do."

I'm thrown by how bold her response is and take a moment to think over what I want to say next. "I need answers."

Already disappearing down the hall and into the kitchen, leaving me with only the faint smell of her perfume, she calls over her shoulder, "Can we talk over coffee? I want to christen the new machine."

She's referring to the Jura GIGA 6. Besides all the kid stuff, this purchase came top of the list. It was obscenely expensive and worth every dime for how her eyes lit up when she saw it. Sophie needs coffee in her life as much as she needs oxygen. I'd buy her ten of the same machines if it meant I got to witness the same reaction.

A happy Sophie is a happy Sam.

I hover at the entrance of the kitchen, choosing not to make my presence known when I catch her folded in half, peering at the aluminum coffee robot. It doesn't take long for me to give away I'm watching, snorting at her tapping the side. It sits, doing nothing.

"Your machine isn't working," she states, her attention set on all the buttons.

"*Your* machine," I correct her, "isn't turned on."

My answer does the trick, and she stands upright, turning to me with her mouth open wide. "Mine? How can this be mine?" She shakes her head, confusion clouding her face. "What's really going on here?"

"This place is yours," I clarify, "and everything in it." Seeing her start to panic, I add on, "It's one of my investments, but yours for as long as you need it."

"O-okay."

"I had to add your name on the paperwork. There was no other option," I reply, when it's clear she isn't appeased by my answer. She shifts her weight between her feet, wringing her hands together. "A hoop ..." I expand.

"Ah." She smiles. "Well, thanks ... I guess."

"You guess?" I chuckle, one brow raised.

"I can't confirm how happy I am until I know what the standard of the coffee is," she sasses back.

I walk across the kitchen and make a show of flicking the power button, clearly displayed at the side of the machine, on. Under two minutes later, Sophie has a perfect latte sitting in her hands. The one and a half thousand extra dollars on the price tag paid for efficiency. Sophie raises the cup to her lips, inhales deeply and takes a small sip, letting out a content moan I feel everywhere. The other one and a half thousand paid for quality.

"It's a pass," she says, the corners of her lips lifting above the rim of her cup.

After making myself a black coffee, we sit in the living area. Sophie looks uneasy and I know it's because, with the remote for the television hidden behind the cushion supporting my back, there are no distractions.

"So ..." I say when we're both settled on the ash gray couch.

"So ..." replies Sophie, twisting her body sideways after setting her cup down on the side table so she's facing me.

"How are we here?"

Her eyes drop to her lap, then she glances to the side at the blank TV screen. "Russ was in a foster home. He called me after your gig, scared. Then I heard something in the background and the call cut off. I couldn't just leave it, so Zoe went with me to find him, to check everything was okay.

Grams too. When we got there, the woman whose care he was in was wasted and couldn't have cared less about where he was or his wellbeing.

"Elayne told me yesterday that one of the older boys in the house had been bullying him badly after they found out Russ was being considered for adoption. Russ doesn't even know …" There's a long pause and I wonder what's left to come that could be worse than what she's already told me.

"Where do you know him from?"

I expect her to answer straight away, but instead she frowns and looks away. After a few seconds, she schools her expression, smiles, and focuses back on me. "Those details are for another day. But I promise I'll tell you when it's time."

I'm the one frowning now, wondering what Sophie's been hiding. We never keep secrets from each other. Well, apart from the real nature of mine and Grace's relationship.

"Sam …" Sophie looks down into her lap and I know whatever she's about to tell me next has been tearing her apart. "I bought him a phone. I told him if he needed anything to call. The bruises you saw …" Her hands twist together in her lap and she blows out a puff of air. "Russ told Elayne that the older boy who hurt him saw the phone, and that's why …" She chews on her lip as she tails off.

I can see in the way she starts to shrink inwards; the way her shoulders slump and she suddenly appears half the size.

"Soph, this isn't your fault."

Blame pours off her. "*I* got him the phone, Sam. *Me*. You saw his face …"

Her eyes water and some instantly spill over, tracking a steady path down her cheek. After quickly setting my cup down on the coffee table, I shuffle in, and without thinking, reach up and hold her face, wiping the wet away with my thumb.

"Hey," I murmur, being careful not to lean in any closer or my lips will press against hers. She doesn't say a word, so I decide to probe her for a hard truth. "Did you see anything that suggested this was happening already?"

She gives me a little nod and her throat bobs as she swallows. "There were some bruises on his arm. He was always hungry …"

I pull back. "Where did you meet him?"

Sophie finally meets my eye again. "Another time. Like I said. It's better if I show you. I think it might make more sense." I don't push again, trusting that she needs to do this her way. "Thank you," she casts a quick glance around the perfectly kitted out living room, with walls just the right shade of light gray. The color gives it a cool vibe without making it feel like a home where a child couldn't live. "For all of this."

"Wait." My mood lifts when I realize there's still something I still have to show her. I stand and hold out a hand, which Sophie takes.

"Where are we going?" she asks as we walk through the hallway.

"You missed this when you were taking a call," I explain, as we get to the right door. "Close your eyes."

She arches a brow. "Seriously?"

"Come on," I laugh, "humor me."

She does, giggling. The light sound makes my stomach flip and I feel nervous again, predicting what her reaction might be.

The door squeaks as I open it, and I make a mental note to figure out how to fix it. I've never used Google as much as I have in the past couple of days. I wouldn't have gotten us to this point without it, and so far, judging by Sophie's reactions to everything, it seems to be a trusty ally.

I step into the room and turn back, ready to guide Sophie in, but stop myself from moving as my gaze roams over her, standing, eyes closed, looking more beautiful than I've ever seen her, despite the fact she's back to wearing her non-Sophified wardrobe. All black and designer. My stomach flips harder and on repeat, each one following the last in quick succession. This time it has nothing to do with nerves, but everything to do with her. It's the little things, like the couple of light freckles, just visible under the thin layer of make-up covering her cheekbones and the way her lashes rest above them.

I could stand and watch her all day, but Sophie quickly rectifies the situation when she clears her throat and says, "Erm, Sam? What's going on?"

"Sorry. I was just checking something," I lie. Stepping forward, I hold her arms, then shuffle back with her in my grasp, urging her to follow me into the room. When we're in the middle, I stop and drop my hands. "Open your eyes."

She does as I say, and I know the moment she realizes what it is, because she sucks in a sharp breath. "Sam …"

"Think he'll like it?" I ask, following her gaze as she takes each detail in, from the checkered bedding to the TV unit set up with a games console, then the couple of storage boxes filled with toys Google said were age appropriate.

Trying to see it through her eyes, I suddenly feel uncertain, like it isn't enough—too bare, not enough personal touches. I remind myself I don't know this small person, that's why. We can add all the extra stuff later if there's enough time.

"He's going to love it," she says quietly, circling on the spot, taking it all in.

The blue in her irises turns a shade brighter, something they only do when she's either excited, filled with hope, or both. It's the second I realize they've been the other, duller shade, for way too long, that I'm hit with a sense of longing and a need to wake up each day and make sure they stay the brightest they can be, no matter what it takes. For too long, I've been scared of what would happen if I lost my voice, fearing it's the one thing getting me through my days after everything that happened with my parents. It gave me an escape from a life I didn't want to be a part of.

But without my voice leading my future along a certain path, I can see things for how they really are. If I never sang again, it wouldn't matter. I got here through sheer grit, determination and resilience to the shit life can throw your way, without a care of how old or young you might be and who it might leave you without.

Doing this, helping Sophie with all of this so she can in turn help someone who really needs her, it's helped open my eyes to everything else I have to offer in life. I'm not my voice. My voice is simply a part of me. It's a giant bonus in what is already an almost perfect life.

Almost … because there's still one thing missing. Or maybe I should say one person.

She's almost done a full turn, her face transformed with the beam her mouth is set in, when I decide that I don't want to continue living in fear of losing things. Sometimes we have to take chances to get what we want the most, regardless of the risks. The guys were right … trying with the potential of succeeding is better than living with a forever of wondering what if. Of asking yourself what could have been.

Sophie faces me, and our eyes connect. For a second, my heart stops beating, and I can't look away. When it starts again, it bangs against my ribs in a new rhythm that will only ever belong to one person.

I want you, I almost say. I want to say it more than I want to breathe, because I do want her, and every incredible thing that comes into my life when she's around.

What we are isn't enough for me. Not anymore.

I don't want to be the friend standing in front of her who she would do anything for.

I want to be the guy standing at her side who she can't live without.

But we both still have things, situations, people who we need to deal with before any of this can even be considered a possibility. That's if she even feels the same way.

I swallow hard, trying to keep the emotions bubbling up from the past few minutes at bay. "I meant what I said. This place is the both of yours for as long as you need it."

She doesn't show any sign of resistance or temptation to argue. Instead, she tilts her head to the side and smiles. "I know you've done a lot. More than you should have. But do you think you could help me with something else?"

Ignoring the long list of crap I have sitting waiting for me at home, I reply, "Sure," because I could never say no to anything Sophie asks me.

"Are you sure you want me to come with you?" I ask, eyeing the fancy building in front of us, equipped with an eloquently dressed doorman, the works.

The only time I've ever been close or really looked at the Upper East Side has been from Central Park, usually when the gang has been doing something drinking or music related. Not a lot has me feeling out of my depth, but this here does. There's something about the wealth and success walking around in front of us that has me questioning whether I'm enough. Do I have enough to offer Soph? I'm not so sure. Looking around, seeing all the tailored suits, potted plants, and shiny cars, I feel like maybe this could be what she really needs. Sure, happiness is important, but happiness only goes so far, and although money might not literally buy it, there's something to be said for financial security. It … well, it makes people feel secure, obviously. It's a drip effect, spilling into all areas of life.

What if friendship isn't all it's made out to be?

Could Brendan be the person Sophie's meant to be with? After all, he's from old money—banks full of it. I'm by no means strapped for cash, but what I do have, from my success with S.C.A.R.A.B. up to this point, will only stretch so far over the years. Especially if my voice decides against making a reappearance.

A bitter taste fills my mouth at the thought of watching *my person* ride off into the sunset with someone else.

"I'm sure," replies Sophie, heading toward the entrance of the building.

Even the doors scream money. Gleaming glass, framed with gold, not a smudge in sight.

"What are we doing here?"

It's one of those silence filler questions you ask when really you know the answer, like I know the answer right now relates to someone whose name begins with a B. One I would use for another name not close to his actual one. A name which isn't fit for public use.

"Something I should have done a long time ago," Sophie answers, walking through the doors into the grand lobby, blonde hair illuminated by the chandelier hanging in the center.

Striding in the direction of the elevators, everything about her, including the jut of her chin in the air, screams purpose. As she goes, she gives one of the concierges behind the desk a quick wave. She receives a wide-eyed look in return, and he waves frantically while keeping the phone he's talking into carefully balanced between his shoulder and cheek.

I try to ignore how much it pisses me off that she's been here enough times to warrant such a greeting.

"Lucky us," Sophie muses when she presses the elevator call button, and one of the two sets of doors opens instantly. We step inside straight away and turn, facing back out into the lobby. "Apparently, I have better luck with elevators than cabs."

I don't respond, distracted by the concierge that waved powering in our direction.

"Ms. Pa—"

His words are cut off when the doors sweep shut and the elevator moves fluidly up the building. Standing in silence, I watch with my head tilted at the display, as the number of floors we pass by increases, almost to the top. An immature part of me loves the fact Mister Preppy hasn't made it into the penthouse suite. He isn't the top dog he thinks he is.

When the doors open, Sophie steps out and I follow her along a corridor decorated with lots of mahogany, lots of rugs and porcelain vases filled with fresh flowers that likely cost more than the average American's salary. At the end, she pauses, taking a deep breath before knocking against a door, which, compared to everything around us, appears too plain, lacking, like its owner's personality.

A minute passes without a sound from the other side. It feels like an hour thanks to how nervous Sophie is. Not like she's here to say a quick hello to her boyfriend of almost a year, which makes me start to wonder why we're really here. I try not to get my hopes up, because I don't want to feel the sting of disappointment again.

"Of course," she mutters to herself, raising her knuckles and knocking louder.

With still no response, she tries the handle, and the door opens.

"Maybe we should wait," I say, hoping she listens, because something in my gut stirs, setting off a warning light.

"I need to speak to him."

I don't point out that she hasn't even clarified *who* we're actually here to speak with as she steps into the huge apartment overlooking Central Park.

"Soph, if he isn't answering …" I don't get to finish my sentence.

My warning would be pointless anyway, because Sophie's attention has already caught on something across the room, a giant red flag in the shape of a bottle of wine and two glasses. She walks, more like stalks across the vast room, stopping before one of the counters in the open-plan kitchen, where they're sitting on top of the black-and-white marble countertop. She grabs one and raises it in the air.

After a quick inspection, she lets her head fall back and, on a laugh, says, "Of-fucking-course."

Her 'of course' is probably referring to the fact she's here trying to do the decent thing so she can give Russ her all. Meanwhile, Brendan is here doing something totally indecent. I'm about to tell Sophie that nothing good can come from all of this, but she's already stalked across the room with the bottle of wine in one hand, while the other is flinging open a door.

"Oh," is all she says, startled by whatever she's found.

I hurry in her direction and, as I do, a male groan followed by a hissed 'shit' reaches me.

It's my turn to say, "Oh," when I take in Grace, completely naked on all fours over Brendan, spread across the super-king-sized bed.

Sophie takes a second to regain her composure, then hardens her gaze.

Brendan looks stunned when she says to the room, "Apparently, I have a thing for walking in on the men in my life getting head from you."

Grace's cheeks turn a shade of red; a red darker than the wine in her discarded glass.

"I can explain," says Brendan, like the idiot he is, because there's no explanation required.

"No need," replies Sophie. She holds the bottle of wine in the air. Brendan pales, clearly thinking she's going to do with it what I also think she is. Sophie catches his change in coloring and laughs. "I could. I want to. But you're not worth such a beautiful wine being wasted, not after I've wasted enough of my time on you already. We're done." She turns to Grace and proves she's better than the both of them with her final words. "Thank you for making this really easy for me."

She spins around and stalks out of the apartment.

"Sarah! Wait!" shouts Brendan, trying to cover his modesty as he darts off the bed to race after her. The door to the apartment slams shut before he makes it out of the room and his steps slow when he realizes there's no point in following.

"I knew you were a prick," I say to him before turning back to Grace. "I'll wait in the corridor. We need to talk."

She nods and I make my way out. I want to follow Sophie more than I want to have this conversation, but she's already disappeared, and, right now, she probably needs space and time to process exactly what's just happened, regardless of what her intentions were for coming here.

Grace follows me out a minute later with a sheet wrapped around her. I don't have it in me to be pissed. I don't have it in me to be anything but relieved. She's given me an out.

Because karma's a bitch, one of Brendan's neighbors picks the exact moment to come home. Grace blushes furiously, pulling the sheet tighter around her body, as if it will make the situation better.

When her neighbor's door closes, Grace scowls. "What's so important after you've been ignoring me for days?"

"It's been one, two at most," I confirm.

"Whatever," says Grace, with a roll of her eyes. "Have you been ignoring me because of *her*?"

"Who?" I ask, feigning ignorance. We both know who she's talking about.

"I'm not an idiot, Sam. Don't treat me like one. You went chasing after your friend the other night, when the polite thing for you to do would have been to stay with *me*. Your *girlfriend*."

"Firstly, you mean polite like screwing said friend's boyfriend behind my back?" The blush that's been sitting on Grace's cheeks since Sophie and I walked in on her and Brendan drains away. My eyes scan over the sheet again. I'm hit with a wave of anger. More at myself; that I've allowed her into my life. "Secondly, you've never been my girlfriend. We're done."

Grace blinks. "We have an arrangement."

"You fucked up the arrangement when you fucked someone else." I glance at the door to Brendan's apartment. "I'm sure he'll look great on your grids."

Never one to go down without a fight, Grace raises her chin and squares her shoulders, determined to have the last word. "The arrangement didn't work. You know that, right? If she felt the same, you wouldn't still be *just* friends."

She reaches out to rub my arm, but I take a step back, not needing to hear any more.

I take a deep breath before I can say something I'll regret. "Have fun with Brendan."

"She doesn't want you, Sam," Grace calls after me as I walk toward the elevators.

She says something else, but I'm already stepping inside one, trying to block out whatever toxicity she's sending my way.

Chapter Sixteen

Sophie

Forget Mister Dreamy, Brendan Fitzgerald is a Grade A prick.

I don't know how I didn't see him for what he really is. Oh wait, I do. I was too busy on a mission to reinvent myself, attempting to become the type of person who would be accepted in his world. The irony is that really, if I'm being true to myself, I don't want any part in what he's about, especially not after today.

Two hours after my second blow-job related incident in a week, I'm dancing around my room with a vodka and diet coke in hand. I've not drank like this in years, but the occasion feels fitting. There's no point trying to appear put together when everything feels like it's falling apart.

During an animated spin, my drink sloshes over the side of my glass and flies through the air, splattering over half of my designer black wardrobe that's hanging on the pop-up rack.

I laugh to myself, then set my drink down and eye the pieces of clothing warily, like they might slide off the hangers and attack me for such an offence. Truthfully, I'd willingly go into battle. I hate designer clothing. Always have.

I'm done with all this. So done. I'm done trying to be someone I think the world wants me to be, when the people closest to me love me the way I am. I'm done apologizing for my mistakes; mistakes which affect no one but me. I want to live my life the way I want to. Starting with helping Russ and making sure he's safe and cared for. I can only give him my best if I give him myself, otherwise I won't have a clue what I'm really doing.

With newfound clarity, something takes over, and in the blink of an eye, every piece ends up discarded on the floor. The planners and organizers are my next target, then all the self-help books. If it weren't for the risk of setting the apartment on fire, I'd burn them. And the clothes. The couple of foot stomps on top of all the mess lifts my mood. It's when I'm contemplating printing off an image of Brendan and graffitiing his face that I decide I need to get out of the apartment and dump my anger into Brooklyn.

I'm considering what I should wear now my entire wardrobe is out of action, when the front door to the apartment flies open, slamming against the wall behind it, followed by a round of hooting. I leave my room to see what's going on, finding my four closest friends with bottles bundled in their arms, dressed and ready to go dancing when I need them the most.

"What's this?" I ask no one in particular.

"A friendtervention," grins Amanda.

"Sam called," explains Zoe, flinching before she continues under her breath. "I filled everyone in."

I know she's expecting me to be pissed, especially after how things have been between us recently, but I'm not pissed. The opposite, actually—I'm relieved that she's saved me from the humiliation of admitting I've made another mistake. I hate that I've spent months, the better part of a year, leaning on someone I shouldn't have.

After an awkward pause, the apartment becomes busy and the girls spring into action. Sooz focuses on the music, setting one of my favorite bluesy playlists going in the background. Amanda disappears for a few minutes, then reappears with all my 'current' clothing bundled in her arms. I shoot her a questioning look and she winks, disappearing outside. Then Abby appears with a round of drinks. They're a murky color, suggesting they have a bit of everything in them and probably taste like ass.

"I thought that went in the trash?" I say, when Zoe reappears, showcasing an outfit I haven't worn in well over a year.

She shrugs. "I kept this one just in case."

"In case?"

Abby hands me one of the glasses, watching us subtly, while Sooz not-so-subtly moves her gaze back and forth.

"In case you realized you were being an idiot?" Zoe's comment comes out more like a question.

"Do you think that?" I ask her.

Sooz and Abby look between us in unison this time, being anything but discreet.

"Think what?" asks Zoe at the same time Amanda re-enters the apartment.

"That I've been an idiot."

Zoe purses her lips before answering. "I think …" she swallows, "that you might not have been doing the right thing, but you were doing what you thought was right at the time. That's all that matters. You know there's no judging here … ever."

I smile playfully, ready to take on whatever the universe has planned for the few hours ahead. "Nights without judgement are my favorite kind."

"You're happy with the outfit, then?" Zoe asks.

"It's practically glowing. It will brighten my mood." I receive a giant grin when I take the yellow Rolling Stones shirt and red tartan mini skirt out of her hands and disappear into my room to get changed. "Special occasion?" I ask, heading back into the living room, dressed in Zoe's outfit choice with the addition of fishnet tights and black shoe boots.

If Aurelia were here, she'd be rolling her eyes. She declared it sacrilege when we were younger that I dressed like a punk rocker, when I pretty much hate any kind of rock music.

"We're celebrating the real Sophie Parker being back in business." Zoe hands me a glass of Champagne she's poured, then raises hers in the air. After blowing a few crimped teal strands of hair out of her face, she toasts, "To no more white clothing. Please tell me you've given up the green juice as well?"

"For the record, Clara and I love green juice," Abby adds.

"Only when there's soda mixed in," laughs Sooz.

Abby sends daggers her way. "It's still full of vitamins …"

"But kind of defeats the point …"

"Whatever," Abby grumbles, facing me, already looking like she's drunk too much. "Remember, everyone has an opinion about something, including the choices other people make. Just because your lifestyle doesn't line up with someone else's, doesn't mean there's anything wrong with it." She takes a deep breath and continues her speech. "Being different adds flair. It stops the world from being boring."

"Are you finished?" I chuckle.

She shakes her head. "No. I could go on for hours, but the Champagne will go flat. I do have one last thing to say though ..."

"Go on ..." I signal I'm listening and open to whatever she has to say with a smile.

"Be true to yourself. Don't doubt your choices."

Russ. She's referring to Russ. My biggest choice yet. The world, if it catches wind of what's happening, likely, thanks to my family and friendship circle, is going to have a lot of opinions.

"You just want me to go out and get wasted with you," I joke, wanting to change the subject before we move onto one that I really don't want to discuss ... Brendan.

It does the trick, and Abby, Amanda, Sooz, and Zoe all laugh in unison. They make it seem so easy and I hint as much, focusing my attention on the queen of not giving a shit. "How do you do it? Not care what people say when you mess up?"

Zoe holds my gaze with a hint of sadness in her smile. "I'm human, of course I care. Want to know the real secret?" I nod. "Ignore all forms of media when you do ... mess up, that is."

I giggle. "That simple?"

"Not always," she admits. "In the early days, when my socials were small, I used to worry over every comment on whatever I posted."

"I always thought you didn't care what people thought of you," I say, surprised. Zoe always is and always has been the queen of cool, seeming totally unaffected by other people's words.

"When you know you've done wrong, there's no point in putting yourself through more pain, so I learned to just ignore it. I've learned not to be afraid to be myself, Soph, and you shouldn't be afraid either. Be one hundred percent unforgivingly you, because Abby's right, someone will still have something to say, even when you think you've nailed it." She winks. "If people want a show, make sure you give them something to really talk about."

A wave of calm washes over me. God, I've missed my best friends. I look around the room, not knowing where to even start with my apologies, so I decide to keep it simple. "I needed this. Thank you." The next thing I know, four pairs of arms fly around my body, smothering me. "I've missed you all," I say when we pull apart, then finally find the courage to say, "I'm sorry."

"This is soooo much fun," slurs Abby, completely out of context, sloshing some of her drink on the floor.

Zoe disappears into her room, so I look at Sooz and Amanda. "She's wasted?"

"Mom problems," explains Amanda.

Abby giggles as she slides onto the couch and rests her head against the back of it. "I'm just going to close my eyes." A few seconds later, her breathing turns heavy.

"Soph, you've got a message from Sam," calls Zoe. She walks back into the living area, tosses my phone at me, then, with a level of focus I've never seen on her face before, disappears into my room.

I open the message.

Sam: *He's a prick.*

I smile to myself as I reply, feeling the girls' gazes on me but choosing not to acknowledge them until I'm finished.

Me: *She's a bitch.*
Sam: *We have shit taste. Want to wallow together over food?*
Me: *Did it skip to Friday without me knowing?*
Sam: *Are we only allowed to eat on Fridays?*
Me: *No. It's just our thing. We could meet later. I'm with the troops.*
Sam: *Sorry. I told Zoe. Maybe shouldn't have?*
Me: *I'm glad you did. Saved me the hassle.*
Sam: *As long as you're okay. Message if you need me.*

I pause and consider my reply. Under normal circumstances, I wouldn't say what I'm tempted to next. It's inappropriate, hovering at the edge of the friendzone. The combination of alcohol running through my veins and the events of the past few hours has me not giving a damn and my fingers do whatever the hell they want.

Me: *I always need you.*
Sam: *I'm always here.*

I could say more, push things further, but I choose not to and go for rounding off the conversation safely.

Me: *Text you later.*

I lock my phone and look up, finding Sooz and Amanda watching me with knowing looks while Abby snores lightly.

Sooz raises her drink in the air and winks. "To guy best friends."

"I don't know what you're talking about," I reply, taking a sip of the Champagne rather than the concoction Abby created. It fizzes in my mouth and all the way down my throat, adding to the riot of butterflies in my stomach.

Does it make me a bad person having this reaction to a bunch of texts when I've only just broken up with someone a few hours ago? I quickly decide it says more about the relationship I was in over how I'm dealing with it afterwards.

"I've said it before and I'll say it again," continues Sooz, ignoring my attempt at shutting down the conversation. "Sam's a total hottie. How none of you have gone there is beyond me."

"I've known him since I was ten," I state, hating what comes out of my mouth next. "He's more like a brother."

A brother who I've found myself daydreaming about inappropriately in the last week. It's the most ridiculous answer I could have come up with and Amanda and Sooz laugh so loud Abby stirs.

"Have you seen Sam?" asks Amanda when she manages to catch her breath. "There is nothing brotherly about him. If I were you, I'd be getting out of that friendzone fas—"

"All done!" exclaims Zoe, clapping her hands together as she walks out of my room, oblivious to what she's interrupted.

"Done with what?" I set both glasses down and go to my room to check what she's been up to. I gasp when I get my answer. "You kept everything?"

I don't see her shrug, but I feel it from behind me. "Like I said, just in case."

Overwhelmed, I sniffle.

Zoe clears her throat awkwardly when I throw my arms around her.

"Not mad then?" she mumbles into my armpit.

"Totally not mad."

I pull away and she beams. "At least I've done something right." Her smile drops in the next second and she watches me, concerned. "He was never worth your time. Are you okay?"

Glancing at the clothing rack now filled with my old, familiar wardrobe, I ask myself how I'm really feeling before I answer. "I think so. Humiliated more than anything."

"You have nothing to be humiliated about. He's the one who should be embarrassed about how he behaved and what he did."

She's taking this way too in her stride. Normally, under circumstances like this, Zoe would be a total hot head and already be on the way to The Upper East Side, threatening to castrate him.

"Why do I feel like what happened today isn't new to you?"

Zoe grimaces. "I may have been keeping tabs on him."

"Zo! What the hell? How? And more to the point, when?"

"Whenever I had the chance. That's where I was always disappearing to. I was trying to catch him out. I had suspicions, but I needed hard evidence before I could say anything to you. I didn't want to upset you without it …"

I can't be mad at her, not with how genuine her intentions have been.

"You could have told me," I say. "No matter how shit things get, or what comes between us, we can always talk. We're still best friends."

"How about," Zoe replies, "we forget all this crap and do what we do best?" She wiggles her eyebrows and I laugh.

"We've been on our best behavior for way too long. Let's give people something to talk about."

I hook my arm through hers, and my chest expands, filling with warmth. "Sounds like a plan."

Back in the living area, I walk to the couch and tap Abby gently until her eyes flutter open.

"How long was I out?" she grumbles.

"Ten minutes max," I reply. "Time to paint the town red."

"Paintbrush ready," she says around a huge yawn, then grabs her 'cocktail' and downs the contents in one.

Chapter Seventeen

Sophie

"I can't remember the last time I saw you with a pitcher of beer," comments an older, taller, version of Sam, from across the bar where I'm now sitting alone.

Dancing with the girls lasted all of two hours.

Abby's alcohol tolerance has diminished as much as my own thanks to her cute little person who isn't such a cute sleeper. Sooz declared she was taking her home when she fell asleep a second time, and Amanda left with them. After three reassurances I'd be fine, Zoe went to meet her latest booty call. With adrenaline still flooding my system after the events of the day, I fired a text to Sam and made my way to Riffs.

"Shaun, are you trying to tell me I've become boring?" I quip with an alcohol fueled-wink on the end.

"You said it," he replies, holding his hands in the air.

"You sound like your assh—" I stop myself from calling Sam an asshole out loud. Sure, he might challenge me constantly over all the lifestyle changes I've made, but he's only done it with good intentions at heart. "Like your brother."

Resting his arms on the bar, Shaun leans forward and wiggles his eyebrows in a way that has an older woman beside me groaning. I glance at her and fight back a laugh. She looks like she's ready to dive over the bar and do very naughty things to him.

"What's he done this time?" asks Shaun.

"Been right … again," says a voice from behind that has me jerking to attention.

I spin on my stool, almost toppling off in the process. Tonight, like too many times earlier in the week, my eyes decide they like the way Sam looks all disheveled, tortured and broody, like a modern-day Kurt Cobain. With his usual white t-shirt drawing attention to the tattoo sleeves that have slowly covered his arms over the years, and his standard skinny jeans and slip-on combo, he looks effortlessly cool. There's something about the dog tags hanging around his neck. They do funny things to my insides.

Yeah, Sooz and Amanda were right. There's absolutely nothing brotherly about him, or the feelings that have decided to appear at the most inconvenient of times.

When he perches on the stool next to me, there's no climbing needed with his super long legs which his pants pull tight around, so tight the seams look at risk of ripping apart. I glance at the pitcher in front of me skeptically.

"Why are you looking at the beer like it's been poisoned?" asks Shaun.

I smile sweetly and avoid the question. "Please, can I have a cocktail?"

"A fancy one?"

"A strong one." I slide the pitcher in Sam's direction. "You can have this. I think there's something wrong with it."

"Sold." He grabs my glass and finishes the dregs before refilling it straight away. I watch as he guzzles over half the glass in one go.

"Want to talk about it?"

There are a few 'its' I could be referring to. A Grace-shaped 'it'. A Brendan-shaped 'it'. A Russ-shaped 'it'. And then there's the big stinking where's-his-voice 'it'. Those are the current ones, without all the crap from his past. It's not surprising that the light-hearted, carefree Sam I rely heavily on isn't in Riffs tonight.

As if he knows I've thought about him briefly, my phone vibrates in the pocket of my jacket for the sixth time in half an hour. If only Brendan paid me this much attention when we were in an actual relationship. I consider blocking his number, but there's too much enjoyment in letting him listen to my voicemail, like I have his on many an occasion.

"Not tonight," replies Sam.

He finishes the beer, then holds up a hand and catches the attention of one of the other bartenders, ordering another pitcher. We sit, neither of us saying anything, while we wait for our new drinks to arrive. I use the time to take in the atmosphere, listening to the combination of laughter and rock music in the background; the liquor bottles sparkle in front of me whenever the light from the industrial-style black pendants hanging overhead catch them. It feels like home, and I feel more alive than I have in a very long time.

"I miss coming here," I say to myself.

"Then come …" I catch Sam's grimace in my peripheral vision. "Here, I mean. More often."

"That's two in a week." I giggle, only able to focus on one part of what he said.

"Two what?"

"Comments. Of the C.U.M kind."

My foggy brain remembers that technically he said, 'you came', and I feel like a total loser because there's nothing funny about my joke. Heat travels up the back of my neck and I consider leaving. Shaun saves the day, appearing with two delicious looking concoctions, bright purple, in skull shaped glasses, with mint leaves poking out of the top and smoke rolling off them the works.

My eyes light up and I can't help an "Ooo," falling from my lips. "What are they called?"

"Zombie Apocalypse," answers Shaun. "They're British. Dan told me about them."

"She'll be wasted," Sam says under his breath.

"Perfectooo!" I grin, ignoring Sam's comment. I drag the two glasses my way and when I take a sip from one, a small moan slips out. "They're sooo good." Sam stares at me. "What?" I ask, taking another sip through the straw.

"You're adding extra o's to everything."

"And?" I hiccup.

"You only do it when you're wasted. You'll end up puking."

"Zoe's the puker. And besides … I'm thirty now." I sit a little straighter and puff out my chest.

Sam looks bemused. "Is there something about thirty I don't know? Something that stops you puking when you're wasted?" I narrow my eyes and take a long, defiant drink through my straw—one I will most likely regret in the morning. My eyes widen when the liquid fills my mouth, burning my throat as it travels down. It's seriously strong. Sam must see the glimmer of uncertainty cross my face mid-drink, because I receive a smug look. "Like I thought. Anyway, why didn't you go for something … green?"

The mischievous sparkle in his eyes has me brushing off the remark.

"Hardy har," I reply.

"I can make you something green if you'd like?" says Shaun.

"No, thanks," I reply. "The Zombie Apocalypse is fine."

"You'll feel like you've been through the apocalypse in the morning if you drink both," comments Sam.

"I was having an enjoyable night," I say, facing him. "Was being the main word in that sentence. You were supposed to come and keep me company, not question my choices, so if you're going to, please move seats." I lean across the bar and spot a stool further along. "There's one over there with your name on it. So, what will it be?"

His eyes harden. "I like my seat."

"Then leave my drinks alone."

We turn away from each other and focus on our glasses. Shaun chuckles as he walks off to deal with a group of customers at the same time Sam's pitcher of beer arrives. In the background, I hear a 'holy shit that's Sam from S.C.A.R.A.B.' from someone close by. The way Sam cracks his neck and gulps his beer tells me he heard it, too. I have a feeling, if he could be invisible for a night, he would be.

"So …" I clear my throat. "We haven't had a chance to talk about what happened thanks to everything else that's been going on." My stomach twists and not because of the five different drinks sitting in it. In three more sleeps I will have a child in my custody—temporarily—but still, a child nonetheless, and here I am getting wasted when I have a million other things to do. I couldn't have picked a better time to revert to my old ways.

Shaking away the uncertainty creeping in that makes it tempting to run from Brooklyn as fast as I can and leave all my responsibilities behind, I add on, "At the gig," in case it isn't obvious what I'm referring to. Sam refills his glass and takes another long drink. When he doesn't answer my question, I decide to leave it and talk to myself, because there's nothing better to do. "The last time I drank like this was in Europe when we worked on the to—"

"I choked. It keeps happening," he says quietly, staring straight ahead.

"Oh," I reply.

"No extra o's?" He smiles into his beer.

"What's wrong with you?" I flinch into my drink, but Sam doesn't seem phased by poor choice of wording.

"I've been asking myself the same thing."

"Are you broken?" I really need to stop drinking if we're going to continue down the line of serious conversations, because alcohol does nothing for my filter.

"Maybe."

Huh. Never in the time I've known Sam would I ever have said he was broken. Sure, he might have been pretty close, but even in his darkest times, he proved to be a wall of strength. However, in those moments, he always had singing to pull him through. My stomach twists again, thinking back on the gig. Without his voice, he has no armor to fight whatever pain the world throws his way.

"Want some of my Zombie drink?"

"Yeah, why not."

I slide the full cocktail across the bar, then hold up two fingers to Shaun, signaling for more. If we're going to do this, we might as well do it properly and make the imminent hangover worth it.

"What are you going to do?" I ask.

"Travel for the summer, maybe."

My brows shoot up in surprise. The selfish part of me ignores that he might need this so he can help himself, wanting him to stay right by my side and help me through whatever happens in the coming weeks with Russ. I guess that's the thing about having a friendship like ours. You learn to lean on each other when you need to the most. Essentially, you get all the perks of a relationship without actually being in one. The company, the memories, the moral support. But we're not in a relationship, not even close. We're friends, and friends support friends with whatever they need to do, even if they might not want them to do it.

"Where?" I ask, keeping my voice light, like there isn't an issue.

"I don't know. I haven't figured that part out yet ..."

It doesn't matter that it's Riff's peak hour. We might as well be sitting in an empty room.

Shaun walks over with fresh cocktails, which are smoking more than the first ones. "You really are both going to be wasted."

"I already am," I giggle, swaying on my stool.

"The couches have your names on them." Shaun points at a couple in the left corner of the bar. "This is a no broken bones zone."

I roll my eyes, jump down, and grab my two glasses. Walking over to the designated 'no falling corner', Sam follows me closely behind, and when I sink into one of the couches, the soft worn leather envelopes me. I'll admit, but never to Shaun, they're a safer distance from the ground.

Somewhere on the journey from the bar to the couches, Sam loses himself in thought and I leave him to it, recognizing he needs time to deal with whatever is going on inside his head; something I wish he'd let me help him with. I spend my time, while Sam mulls to himself, watching a small group of women across the room cheer as they do a round of shots. One staggers to the bar and spends a couple of minutes trying to catch Shaun's attention with the giggling. Shaun catches me watching and winks, before finally appeasing the women by walking over to their friend and leaning in to talk to her. A round of cheers fills Riffs and I chuckle to myself. They remind me of me, Abby, and Zoe when everything was simple.

Sam clears his throat, his gaze focused in the same direction. "If I ask you something, will you give me an honest answer?"

"Sure," I reply, praying it's nothing too bad.

"What actually happened?"

I shift on the couch so I'm facing him. "What do you mean?"

His eyes trail from my face to the shirt Zoe picked out for me. I feel every millimeter they pass over, wishing I didn't. I forget how to breathe when the hand that doesn't contain the apocalypse in it reaches over, grasping the hem. He runs the soft material between his thumb and forefinger thoughtfully. He might as well be rubbing them against my clit for what it does to me. Everywhere starts to ache in an unbearable way that can only be satisfied through one action.

"You never have told me what actually happened. Why all the changes?"

Okay. Maybe there is another way of solving my issue, because his words might as well be a bucket of cold water poured over me.

"You never asked," I reply.

I don't know if I'm ready to have this conversation; to relive the painful crap that's brought me to this point.

"Because I knew you didn't want to talk about it."

I look away. "Then why now?"

Sam's hand finds my chin, and he tugs it back so I can't look away. "We have to talk about earlier."

"Do we?"

"You can't just shut off from shit, Soph."

"Why not? Because you say so?"

A line appears between his brows. "Because if you do, then there will be another color to replace all the black."

"Which would you like next? White? Gray?"

"Soph ..." Sam warns.

"You say it like you're the king of dealing, Mister Broody."

"Mister Broody?"

One corner of his mouth lifts, causing a flicker of annoyance to light inside me.

"You've barely said a word since you got here. So, what, you're allowed to sit and sulk and I'm not?" His hand drops

213

from my chin, leaving the skin behind burning. He looks thoughtful as he picks up his drink. I see the moment he has an idea, because his whole expression brightens. "What are y—"

He leans over and grabs the fuller one of my two cocktails and passes it to me. I still don't get an answer to what he's up to, because he catches Shaun's attention and gestures with his free hand for two more drinks. My head throbs at the thought of tomorrow's hangover. I block it out when Sam looks back at me.

"Let's play a game."

"What kind of game?"

"A drinking one." He grins.

"I have work tomorrow," I remind him.

"Call in sick."

"Nice and responsible for someone who's about to take on a child in less than three days."

"All the more reason to let your hair down. This could be your last chance in a while, and after everything that's happened in the past week, I think you're more than deserving of a break."

Two more Zombie Apocalypse's appear at our table.

"Why are you doing this?" I ask when the bartender walks away.

Sam shrugs and takes a long sip through his straw, drawing my attention to the way the muscles in his neck move when he swallows. "If you won't give me answers, then I'm going to have to prize them from you."

"Fine," I huff, defeated. "What game?"

Pearly whites flash at me. "A game of truths. One person asks a question, and the other person has to give an honest

214

answer. The catch … the person asking the question has a chance to beat the truth with a worse one. Loser drinks."

"Seriously?" I groan. "This sounds like something we would have played in high school."

"Are you trying to say you're too good to play?"

I frown. Sam Riley is screwing me over and he knows it.

"I go first," I say, admitting defeat.

He rolls his lips. "Of course, you're a lady, after all."

It takes me a minute longer than normal to come up with a handful of questions that will work in my favor, thanks to how many drinks I've already consumed.

"Okay," I say, when I think I've got one. "What was your worst kiss?"

Sam shakes his head. I already know this story and it gets me every time.

"If this is how you're going to play, be prepared, Red." He raises his drink ready, knowing there's no way he's going to win this round. "Henrietta Burbank. Senior year. She was so nervous she took a chunk out of my lip, and I spent two hours in the emergency room getting stitches. But you know that already."

I crease over with laughter, spilling some of my cocktail on the already sticky floor. "You might as well drink," I wheeze.

"No, no," states Sam. "The rules are you have to give your truth back. Have at it."

"Fine." I catch my breath. "Liam … I can't remember his second name. It was at one of your gigs, again, senior year. It was like making out with a helicopter."

We go through a few more humorous truths before the alcohol takes over and I decide to take a risk with something that's been bugging me for years.

"Have you ever hooked up with anyone in our friendship group?"

Sam gives me an amused look before answering. "No." I give him a look back that says I don't believe him. "Do you know something I don't?"

I clear my throat awkwardly. "Erm ... Abby."

"What do you want to know?"

"Did you ... you know ..."

"Sleep with her? No."

I swallow. "Did you kiss her?" He shakes his head no. "Did you like her?"

"Yeah." My stomach sinks. "But it was different."

"H-how so?"

The breath is stolen from my lungs and the rest of the room disappears when he leans in, leaving barely a centimeter between us. "Abby and I were there for each other whenever we couldn't have what we really wanted. Anyway, that's more than one question. Your turn."

"No, I haven't hooked up with anyone in the group." At a stalemate, neither of us says a word and I force myself not to look at his lips.

I receive a tense nod before Sam drinks two fingers' worth of his cocktail. "Worst trolling comment you've ever received?"

"Sam ... this is a game."

"So, play."

"Fine," I sigh, knowing this is the whole reason he wanted to start. "I think it would be the one that said, 'You're

216

an immature waste of everyone's time.'" I make a show of thinking some more. "Oh no, wait, maybe it would be the one that said, 'The world would be a better place without talentless people like you in it. No one wants you here.'" I shake my head. "No, actually, the one that said, 'I hate your parents for making you'. That one burned. I've forgotten the rest. There were too many."

Sam doesn't say a word at first, just watches me. "Someone commented on one of the videos taken at Orensanz saying they thought S.C.A.R.A.B. would go further if Jake was the lead singer instead of me."

We both take a long drink, each needing it.

"Can we not play this game?" I ask, slurring a little.

Sam shuffles across the couch, wraps his arm around my shoulder, and tugs me to his side. When he rests his chin on top of my head, he replies, "Sure, we don't need to play anymore."

I go back to watching the group of women from earlier, enjoying the silence after bringing up crap I wish I didn't have to, knowing I needed to. It feels like we sit for hours wrapped around each other, but it's only a few minutes. I'd do it forever. Then I remember I can't and try to block out what Sam said earlier about going away for the summer. I want to tell him to stay, that I need him in ways I'm not clear on myself, but I don't have the courage to face two rejections in one day. I don't doubt that Sam's would hurt more than Brendan's.

Eventually, Sam untangles himself and moves back far enough he can look down at me. Four blue eyes bore into mine, unblinking.

"Don't ever change who you are because of what others think."

My lip wobbles. Sam catches the movement and leans in. My mind races with each millimeter eliminated. He's going to kiss me. Is he? I don't know. I want him to. I think? But maybe not now when there's a chance that I won't remember it.

Sam's thumb moves across my bottom lip in a soothing pattern. He doesn't kiss me and I'm not disappointed because it doesn't feel like our time, not yet.

What he does instead is give me what I need to keep moving forward.

"The hurtful words people feel the need to direct at us say more about them than they do about us," I recall him saying, before the rest of the night becomes a blur.

Chapter Eighteen

Sam

A new beat fills the room, and Sophie slides along the bar, letting out a whoop.

"She's really going for it," says Shaun, standing beside me with his arms folded.

We both watch her jump up, ready to go into a third run of "The Woodchuck Song", barefoot, apart from the fishnets.

"Coyote Ugly is one of her favorite movies," I explain when she swings her head in vigorous circles, creating a golden windmill with her hair. "She's always wanted to dance on top of a bar."

Shaun smirks. "Does she even know the bar's closed?"

"I don't think so."

I scratch my head, trying to decide what to do. I could take her back to her apartment, but the chances are Zoe is out, and with the amount of alcohol she's packed away, she needs someone close by for the rest of the night to check she's okay. She says Zoe is the puker, but the number of sneakers I've gone through says otherwise.

"Run the World" fills the room and Sophie stamps her feet to the beat. Shaun's jaw clenches tight.

"Why is Beyonce playing in my bar?"

Everyone knows rock is the only music allowed within Riff's walls, which means Sophie's committing the biggest offence there is. It's clear she couldn't give a crap when she crawls across the surface in front of us and starts using one of the beer taps as a mic.

"She plugged her phone in."

"And you let her?" Shaun scoffs. A list of expletives, with the odd Fitzgerald thrown in, reaches us from above. "Who's Fitzgerald?"

"Someone not worth discussing," I reply, checking the time on my phone and finding it's almost three AM.

It's been a long night, and Sophie's spent so long dancing, I've sobered, and a hangover is threatening to kick in. Deciding I've had enough, I move closer to the bar.

"It's time to go." She completely ignores me. "Sophie …" Still nothing. I place two fingers in my mouth, let out a loud whistle, and shout, "Yo! Soph!" It does the trick. Startled, her legs tangle mid-spin. "Shit," I hiss, darting to the side and catching her just in time before Riff's can no longer be classed as a no-broken-bones zone.

"My hero," she giggles into the crook of my neck. The sensation of her breath against my skin makes me almost drop her.

"You can take her upstairs," says Shaun.

My brows shoot up in surprise. He hates it when people, including me, his own flesh and blood, invade his personal space. "You're sure?"

"There's no way you're getting her home when she's like this."

"Thanks."

He waves me off as he walks across the room. "Just make sure she doesn't fuck with my things. I'm gonna finish closing up. She can take my bed. It's closer to the bathroom."

"You're lucky," I chuckle, making my way behind the bar and into the back, toward the stairs, with her in my arms. "Not even Shaun's hook-ups are treated to his bed."

There's a deep rumble against my chest. Then another. I look down and find she's passed out, snoring so hard the blonde strands of hair covering her face keep blowing into the air. I shake my head and manage to get us both safely up the two flights of stairs.

When we're in Shaun's room, I conclude the big man above is testing me. I set Sophie down on the bed and go to grab a shirt from his chest of drawers. While I'm trying to find one big enough to cover her whole frame, preferably from the top of her head to her feet, I hear her grumbling behind me. When I turn back with an adequately sized shirt in hand, she's stripped off and spread across the top of the sheets. Fighting back a groan, I close my eyes and walk over to the bed carefully, trying not to fall as I go.

Only when the ends of my shoes hit the edge of Shaun's bed, do I dare open my eyes a fraction. This time, the groan is harder to keep in. Another deep snore fills the room. For someone so small, she makes a hell of a lot of noise when she's passed out.

"Sophie," I say, loud enough to rouse her.

"No Sarah?" she grunts.

I frown. Fucking Fitzgerald. I block him out of my head, because currently, I have bigger things to worry about than why I didn't punch him.

There's no way I can leave Sophie passed out on Shaun's bed like she is. She'll die of humiliation. Trying to suck it up and act like a man, I train my thoughts on neutral subjects, like what I'm going to have for breakfast when I wake up. With a lot of effort on my part, I manage to pull the shirt over her head. Under normal circumstances, it might be a relatively straight-forward task, but she's consumed four Zombie Apocalypses, making it a new level of challenging.

Eventually, with the shirt in place, I decide, because one can never be sure what Sophie will get up to when she's drunk, to grab a pair of Shaun's gym shorts. I slide them up her legs and tie them around the waist, making sure there's no chance of her accidentally removing them.

When she's finally tucked in bed, I head into the living room and switch on the radio. The end of a soul track floats through the speakers, and I smile. One of the perks of being up at this time is the late-night stations playing old music. A familiar song starts, and I hum as I turn to get a glass of water from the kitchen.

I almost jump out of my skin when I find Sophie swaying in the middle of the room.

"Christ!" I pinch my nose and inhale deeply, trying to settle my heart as it hammers against my ribs. "You almost gave me a heart attack." The swaying stops, swapped for some foot tapping and neck bobbing to the beat. "What are you doing? You were fast asleep …"

I'm silenced when she starts to sing.

Time and experience give anything creative more depth, and Sophie's voice is a shining example of that. Her voice is different from the first time I heard it when we were young. It's full of emotion, with a level of control some of the biggest artists struggle to achieve. She hits each note perfectly, and the fact she does so while wasted is pretty damn impressive.

Sophie grabs one of the remotes from Shaun's coffee table and belts out the crescendo of the song. "I love Otis," she smiles drunkenly to herself when "Try a Little Tenderness" finishes.

A lump forms in my throat. "I know you do." Another song begins, and she drops the remote on the couch. "Come on, dancing queen." I grip her shoulders so I can steer her back to bed. "You need to sleep."

When she's tucked in for a second time, I tiptoe to the corner of the room and switch off the lamp, hoping the darkness keeps her down.

"Psych!" she shouts, jumping in front of me when I'm almost at the door.

She's like a goddamn ninja.

"Sophie," I moan. "It's late. Like really, really late."

"Sleepin's cheatin', Sammy," she chimes, shimmying back through to the living area.

By the time I get there, she's dive bombing the couch.

Shaun walks in, takes one look at her and shakes his head. "What happened to getting her to bed?"

"Easier said than done," I mutter. After a few minutes, her movements slow and I seize the opportunity to pull her into my side.

"Looks like the hands-on approach might be required." Shaun winks and laughs at his own comment, knowing exactly how much it will piss me off.

"Prick."

"You love it."

"You could help."

His expression turns serious. "Bro, this is me helping. Do you not think this has been a long time coming?"

I look down and find Sophie has closed her eyes. "No," I reply. "I don't. We're friends."

"Bullshit, you've never been just friends. Seriously, this is getting sad to watch."

"Don't, Shaun. I'm not in the mood."

He shrugs and opens his mouth to say something else, stopped by Sophie.

"Can we go to bed, Sammy?" she murmurs into my chest.

My nostrils flare, and Shaun shakes his head again.

"Yeah, we can," I reply quietly.

Shaun calls after me, "I know you're scared of losing her if things don't work out. But if you don't try, there's a chance you'll lose her, anyway."

I drag Sophie into his room and close the door before he can say anything else. Sophie stumbles over to the bed and before she can collapse on top of the sheets, I slide them back. My grip on them tightens, and I grind my teeth when her lashes flutter against her cheeks.

"Come on, get in," she says, her voice finally sleepy. "It's cold."

Now she's cold. I grumble to myself, climbing onto the bed, then lying back next to her. Sophie buries herself into my side and I wrap an arm around her shoulders, pinning her to me so she can't escape, then tuck the other behind my head.

"Sam?" Sophie whispers.

I swallow hard. "Yeah?"

"Will you sing me to sleep?"

I stare at the ceiling, trying to figure out how to answer.

"Sam?" Sophie asks again, after a couple of minutes.

"I'm sorry. I can't," I reply hoarsely, hating that I can't give her what she needs.

I can't because of what it will mean if I do, and how it will feel in the morning when she doesn't remember a thing. Sophie doesn't say anything after that, and eventually, her breathing slows into a steady rhythm.

Around the fortieth, 'What the hell am I going to do?' my mind gives in, and I fall into a restless sleep beside her.

Sophie

A ten-ton weight bearing down on my chest wakes me from the soundest sleep I've had in a long time. Moving is impossible. I'd be concerned if it weren't for the familiar scent and warmth cocooning me. Combined with the cloud I'm lying on; I'd happily never move again. Especially if it meant I didn't have to face up to whatever happened last night.

There's a reason I've stayed on the straight and narrow for so long. This. Alcohol anxiety. Waking up to the dread. The questions. Praying the answers aren't as bad as what my gut is telling me they are.

The last thing I remember clearly is ordering a pitcher of beer.

Okay, no, that's a lie. I also remember a funky-looking cocktail with smoke pouring off it. Wait. No. There were four. Oh, God. That's where things get fuzzy.

If only I could reme—

Sam.

One eye flies open, taking in the dead weight holding me in place. A long, thick arm, corded with muscles and way-too-familiar tattoos.

Oh no. Oh no no no no no.

I groan. What have I done? As far as fuck ups go, this is colossal.

Opening the other eye, I take in my surroundings. The very rugged manly surroundings that most certainly aren't my room, not that I thought they were to begin with. I could never afford a mattress this heavenly.

"We didn't hook up, if that's why you're groaning." My muscles, which had been coiled tighter than an anaconda capturing its next meal, relax. I sag into the bed, sighing with relief. "Not the reaction I usually get when I wake up with someone. I'm gonna try to not be insulted."

Irrational me receives an internal scolding, when jealousy bubbles in my stomach hearing Sam talk about waking up with other women.

The alcohol from last night threatens to make a reappearance and I cover my eyes with my hands, praying that when I remove them, I'll find myself safe in my own room. The weight lifts from my chest and then a set of calloused fingers scratches the back of one of my hands before lifting it cautiously.

"Open your eyes."

Is this the way Sam always sounds first thing in the morning?

"No." I squeeze them tighter when the tiny muscles in my lids flicker, threatening to betray me.

"Soph. Open your eyes. *Please.*"

God, he sounds even better than when he sings. Ignoring my attempts to keep them shut, my eyes respond to the gruff demand with a 'please' thrown on the end. The only saving grace is the other hand I manage to keep in place, providing some armor against what I find when they open fully. I drink in Sam, spread across the top of the sheets on his stomach, thankfully still clothed. His hair is mussed in a way the best stylists would struggle to achieve and his bodyweight rests on one elbow while his other hand still holds mine.

The whole sleep God image he has going on isn't the biggest issue. It's his eyes. Sleepy yet piercing, making my heart pitter patter in my chest when I realize how close they are, because them being close means he's close. All of him. Especially his face. If I could pull back or move away, I would, but I'm frozen against the bed.

"Nothing happened." His words coat my skin and every part of my body hums, wishing something had.

"Okay," I pant. All we need is some drool to finish off whatever look I dread to think I've got going on.

What the hell is wrong with me?

"What's going on in that head of yours?"

I drop my other hand, contemplating whether I should give him the truth, when I glance down, taking in the sheets around my waist and what I'm wearing. I frown. "Please tell me I didn't get naked."

"I grabbed you some things, and you put them on," Sam replies.

"Okay." Phew. The last thing we need is the awkwardness that comes with one person seeing the other naked; things are bad enough. Warmth spreads through me when I realize he's still holding my hand and his thumb is tracing a path back and forth. "You can let go now," I say quietly, wanting him to do the complete opposite and never let go.

My next breath catches in my throat when Sam says, "I don't want to."

I don't get a chance to over-analyze his words, because the door to the room flies open. Sam snatches his hand away, rolls onto his back, then sits up abruptly. Shaun stands, filling the frame with a tray sitting in his hands with three giant steaming cups of coffee. My stomach growls when it catches a whiff of the plate piled high with toast.

"The late-night raver is finally awake." He winks, and I scowl at the word raver. I don't want to know what I got up to. I'm happy remaining in the dark.

"Come on." He grins. "It was good to see you back on form."

"It was a one-time performance. One I won't be repeating," I reply.

Sam tenses beside me, then climbs out of bed. "I need to use the bathroom." My gaze follows his crumpled appearance to the door, taking in the moment when he brushes past his brother, shaking his head.

When the bathroom door clicks shut, Shaun smiles and lifts the tray in offering. "Figured you'd need fuel to drag yourself home."

My lips twitch at the sides. "Thanks."

He walks over and sets the tray down on the bed, handing over a cup with questionable looking liquid filling it. "I put that soy crap in you like."

I try not to laugh at the curdled mess. "Is it standard filter coffee?"

Shaun gives me a questioning look. "Yeah?"

"Rookie mistake. You either use the barista blend or the drink needs to be milk-based. Otherwise, it looks like this."

"Thank you, oh wise one," Shaun chuckles. "I'll try to remember that the next time someone requests this shit."

I wrinkle my nose. "It looks gross."

"There's a simple solution …"

"Go on …"

"You could go back to being the old Soph and cut the crap. It's not you. Never has been."

Shaun looks like he's expecting me to lash back and create a massive drama.

It could be the hangover, or it could be acceptance, that has me doing the opposite and saying, "I think you might be right." I cringe, remembering a vague snippet of the truth game Sam and I played last night. "Shaun, can I ask you something?"

"Sure."

"Did Sam ever really like Abby? Like … *like* like."

There's a pause and I catch the way his muscle twitches in his jaw, as if he's trying to decide how to answer. "For years I thought he did." He rubs a hand over his jaw. "Then I realized I was missing what was right in front of me." Shaun's face turns as serious as the night Zoe publicly humiliated him many summers ago. "My brother's unhappy. Has been for years. You make him happy in ways no one else can." I stare at him, confused. "Come on, you're not stupid. Why do you really think he can't sing?"

My mouth parts and I choke out, "He has imposter syndrome."

That's the conclusion we've all, including Sam, come to. The snippets Sam told me support the theory. So what the hell is Shaun going on about?

Shaun shakes his head. "Right, keep telling yourself that."

I go to ask him what he means, when the sound of the bathroom door opening puts an end to our conversation. Sam walks back in and settles in his spot on the bed. He looks down his nose, giving the cup in my hand the same look his brother did.

"You can have mine," he says.

"It's o—"

"You need it more than me. It's fine."

I set the swamp liquid down and pick up one of the more inviting cups, inhaling deeply. The first sip is the best, helping me to forget whatever meaning is behind Shaun's words.

"Thanks," I reply, smiling as I relax back against the pillows. I could almost feel content if it weren't for Sam's eyes lingering on me.

Shaun clears his throat. "I'll leave you guys. Remember, don't fuck with my things," he adds on the end, attempting to lighten the mood.

I laugh and watch him leave, taking his light heartedness with him. When the bedroom door shuts, the air around us thickens and my skin burns under Sam's gaze. Deciding I need to get home, I set my half-filled cup back on the tray.

I'm standing and am about to ask if he thinks Shaun will mind me borrowing his things to go home in when Sam beats me to breaking the silence.

"I tried to get you to go to bed. Multiple times. You were like a boomerang. That's why I stayed in here. I wanted to make sure you were safe."

230

"Okay."

"You know me, Soph. You know I'd never take advantage of you. Right?"

I nod, then move to grab one of Shaun's discarded sweaters too quick, making the room spin.

"My head," I moan. "It feels like I've been th—"

"Through an apocalypse," Sam finishes. We smile at each other.

"Last night was a really bad idea."

"Maybe, but the world hasn't ended because you got drunk. We had fun. That's it."

I shrug on the sweater and source my clothing from last night, finding it sitting in a neatly folded pile on top of one of the dressers.

"I guess I should go home and pack." The enormity of the few days ahead starts to press in, and my chest tightens.

Sam stands. "If you need anything, call Shaun. I have a busy week …" He must see the confusion in my eyes because he goes on to explain, "Someone did such a good job in planning how to correct my fuck up, Sooz now has me on a tight schedule until Friday. It means I won't be around when Russ arrives. I'm sorry."

"Okay," I say quietly to the ground, feeling completely out of my depth. Then, I remember a snippet of our drunken conversations and look up. "Did you mean what you said last night?"

Concern flashes across Sam's face as if he's second guessing the events as much as I am. "Which bit?" he asks carefully.

"The bit where you said you'd go away for the summer."

He lets out a long exhale and drags a hand down his face. "I don't know. After this week, I don't know what I'll do, but I need to do something. I can't not sing, Soph. The guys need me. Hanging around here like this isn't helping."

His comment stings. "R-right," I stammer and start walking toward the bedroom door to leave.

Sam steps in front of me and dips down. "That wasn't what I meant and you know it. I'd spend all day in bed with you if I could." My cheeks flush at all the potential meanings behind his words. Meanings that feel like they're creeping into what we do and say to each other, more so with every minute that passes. Sam doesn't correct himself or take back what he's said. "We can't hide from what we need to do or who we need to be. As much as we might want to when shit gets hard. This week is going to be a long one for both of us."

"We need to do our own thing," I confirm, wanting to glue myself to his side so it's an impossibility.

Straightening, he leans down and presses a brief kiss into my hair. "It's just a week."

"Or a summer ..." I refuse to leave it. I want to be there for him like he has me with Russ. I don't want him to disappear and try to fix things alone when he doesn't need to.

"Soph ..."

"Let me help you, Sam."

"You have enough on your plate with Russ."

"And we will settle into our groove in a few days. Plus, I won't be alone in all of this. I have my friends and family to help, and you do, too. Please, just give me until next week and then I promise I will help."

"How?"

232

"I'm not sure yet," I reply, gripping the clothing in my hands hard, refusing to let Sam's break in resolve pass me by. "But I will think of something. I promise."

"Fine. I guess I'll see you Friday?"

I blink. "Friday?"

"Feast night. You didn't think I'd let Russ be the reason for you missing another?"

Excitement stirs inside me, imagining us all together in the new apartment. How it could be every Friday. There's no way I'm letting Sam disappear from my life. I'll do whatever it takes. Help in whatever way I can.

"I'll put a Chow's order in for three."

Sam laughs. "Maybe don't order the steamed veggies. Apparently, kids aren't a fan."

"Says who?"

"Google."

Chapter Nineteen

Sophie

What the hell was I thinking?

I can't care for a child.

I can barely care for myself.

My big toe, spouting blood over the new flooring in Sam's—or should I say our—apartment is evidence of that.

It's already Wednesday. After a frantic two hungover days of packing, then unpacking, there's less than ten minutes until Russ is due to arrive with Elayne. I'm one hundred percent certain I'm going to puke from nerves and the sticky red liquid following me around isn't helping matters.

Grabbing my phone, I raise it to my ear when I find who I need. There are a couple of seconds worth of ringing before the call connects.

"Hale! Get here!"

I hold the phone away from my face, out of fear of an eardrum being burst.

"Grams it's me," I call into it, knowing that no matter how loud I shout, she won't be able to hear me any better, because she always manages to turn the volume on hers right down, despite the fact she can barely turn it on.

"Hale! It's been bleeping again."

I hear my older brother grumbling in the background and then his voice becomes clear.

"That's because Sophie's called you."

"It stopped though."

"Because you answered." I picture him shaking his head and the humor of the moment helps me forget what's about to happen and why I need Grams to get her urgency on and actually speak to me, not Hale. "Ow! That hurt."

"Then don't roll your eyes at me. How do I hear her?"

"You don't turn it down for one," he answers. "Ow! Stop poking me."

"Guys!" I call.

"Was that her?"

"Yes, Grams," Hale sighs. He must be holding the phone to his ear, because his voice gets louder. "Hey. Putting Grams on now. Please, don't call again if she hangs up. I'm busy."

So much for sibling support.

"Sophie?" says Grams a couple of seconds later.

Her voice sounds more distant than Hale's and I know it will be because she's holding the phone a safe distance from her face. She has a habit of hanging up mid-call with her cheek.

"Grams, I don't know if I can do this," I say, getting straight to the point as we don't have much time.

"Don't be ridiculous," she scoffs. "Of course, you can do this."

"Grams, I'm bleeding."

"Are you dying?" she asks, with no concern whatsoever in her voice.

I glance at my minor injury and quickly assess. "No. I ran over my toe with the vacuum."

"Then you will be fine." There's clattering in the background that sounds like stainless steel against porcelain.

"What are you doing? Are you even listening to me?"

"I'm making a snack," she states, as if it's obvious, forgetting I can't see her through the phone. Technically, I could if I wanted, but we tried video calling once and I spent the whole time staring at the wall after she flipped the camera and couldn't get it back to its original setting.

"Grams! Russ is going to be here in,"—I pull my phone away and check the time, wishing I hadn't—"Less than five minutes. Can you not hold off?" I gulp.

"You know I go woozy if my sugars drop. And this conversation is pointless."

"Gee, thanks," I say over more rustling.

"You need to stop doubting yourself." When I catch the sound of her chopping, I can't help but acknowledge how impressive it is that she's managing to handle technology and prepare food at the same time.

"Because it's that easy. Grams, I've spent the better part of a decade being told how immature I am. Imagine what people will say when they find out I'm attempting to care for another human."

"Sophie, dear. Stop. The other human you're referring to has no expectations. You've witnessed firsthand what he's

236

been through, and you can offer him more than what he's had so far. Love and care. Nothing else matters."

"I'm scared," I admit, giving in to the tightening in my chest that's making the simple task of breathing difficult.

"Of letting Russ down, or the world?"

I swallow. "Both."

"The only person you're letting down right now is yourself. Be that vivacious, powerful woman in the precinct the other night who fought for what was right. That's who you really are. You just need to believe it."

"Why do you sound so sure?"

Everything on her end goes silent and I assume whatever she's about to say next is serious enough she's halted preparing her food.

"Because I know you and everything you have the potential to be. Something unique. Why do you care so much about what the world thinks when you have two people standing right in front of you who see you as their world?"

Her words are beautiful and empowering, but all I can focus on is one minor detail. "Two?" I want to hear her answer, but I don't get a chance, because in the next breath I can hear the sound of footsteps approaching along the corridor. "Shit. They're here, Grams."

"You've got this. You're a Parker and we're made for great things."

"Wait," I hiss, right before she's about to hang up.

"What about The Parkapellas? Crap, I completely forgot." I slam the base of my hand against my forehead, frustrated I could have forgotten something so important.

"Leave that to me for the next couple of weeks. You focus on Russ."

The line goes silent as she hangs up abruptly. I'm left staring at the door, almost passing out when there's a knock. My feet stay glued to the floor as my phone buzzes in my hand.

I quickly open the message.

Mom: *I'm incredibly proud of you right now. Your father and I are here if you need us, but I know you can do this. Love you.*

When there's another knock at the door, I accept I have to answer.

Taking a step forward, I inhale, then press down on the handle, opening the door slowly while plastering on a terrified smile.

"Hi!" I squeak, taking in Elayne wearing another of her black pant suits, which seem even more out of place with the New York heat increasing daily.

"Ms. Parker," she says with a nod.

Her arm jolts, and she looks down with a smile I've not seen her wear before. I follow the movement and my gaze lands on Russ. I expect a smile and for this to be a grand reunion like you see in the movies, for Russ to come running into my arms. He remains at Elayne's side and his dark eyes twinkle up at me amid the bruising, which looks to finally be starting to fade. I feel nauseous, having to remind myself that he's here, and he's safe.

It hits me out of nowhere how much I want this. I don't know what life had planned for me and I've never had any plans for it myself, but I suddenly feel certain I'm where I'm meant to be. Maybe I wouldn't be here doing the right thing without having been through all my fuck-ups. No matter how hard I have to fight, I'll do whatever I can to make sure Russ gets the life he's always deserved.

"Ms. Parker," says Elayne, clearing her throat. "Are you aware you're bleeding?"

"Perfectly aware," I reply in a daze, smiling at Russ. His serious expression breaks and he giggles. Bleeding. Taking in what Elayne's just said, I blink, then look down at the mess. "There was an issue with the vacuum."

I think the world might be ending, or some serious crap is heading our way, because Elayne, completely out of character, laughs out loud. It's the belly kind, where you gasp for breath and your eyes stream, which is what hers are doing now. I'd be embarrassed that she's kind of laughing at me if it weren't a welcome reprieve from her scrutinizing.

"Come in and I'll get cleaned up. Sorry, I was running behind after a pep talk from Grams," I explain. It's something I shouldn't admit, but honesty has got me this far and I'm rolling with it.

Ten minutes later, with my foot bandaged up, I find Elayne in the living area, without Russ.

"Erm, where's Ru—I mean, Josh?" I ask, searching the couch with my gaze, as if a seven-year-old could hide behind a cushion.

Elayne smiles and I contemplate pinching myself to check I'm not in a trippy dream. One of those where it feels so real it could be, but there are weird things that make it clear it's not. Like people smiling who shouldn't be.

"It's fine for you to call him Russ," she says. I'm definitely stuck in a weird dream. "Ms. Parker, please stop looking at me like that."

"Like what?"

"Like you don't believe a word I'm saying."

I try to shake my disbelief away and think straight. "It's just … you're being very … friendly." Yeah, that was way too honest. "Sorry." I shrug. "It's just a bit weird."

Holding my breath, I wait for her to scold me. To tell me I'm unfit to have Russ in my care and drag him out of the apartment before I get a chance to say hi properly.

What she does is laugh again.

"I'm intrigued you think you could give such a good character assessment after a couple of meetings." The wit behind her reply is as surprising as her laughing. I never would have guessed that Elayne, of all people, had some sass in her.

"Only you can be the expert?" I sass back.

"Ah," she smiles. "No. You did my job for me with that fantastic speech you gave at the precinct."

"It wasn't a speech."

Her face turns serious. "I know."

There's a clatter from deeper in the apartment. Roughly in the direction of what is now Russ's room, if he's allowed to stay that is. I should go check on him, but when I hear his faint chatter with a lack of screaming or crying, I decide he will be fine on his own for a few more minutes.

"Is that why you approved me?" I ask, needing answers to fire up my confidence, ready for when she leaves and I'm left to handle all of this alone.

"No."

"Then why did you?"

"Not many people would refuse to leave a property like you did. Not unless they cared. Like a parent would care. You're a natural."

240

"So," I say, tilting my head while trying to get it around exactly what she's saying, "getting arrested worked in my favor?"

"Don't make it a regular thing. There's only so much I can let slide." I almost hit the ground when she winks. "In fact, I'm not supposed to let anything slide. But ..." My heart skips a beat. "You know we had to carry out a lot of checks on the internet. Some of them on social media ..."

The glimmer of hope that everything is going smoothly vanishes, replaced with the cold, hard truth. All my past indiscretions are about to screw me over. There's no way if she's seen everything that happened, all the videos, all the trolling, that she's going to let Russ stay.

"Right," I say quietly, staring at the ground.

Elayne must see something in my eyes, because hers warm, reaching out to me, dare I say it, like a friend. "Ms. Parker. The world can be a cruel place. The people in it can be even crueler. Our pasts don't define who we are in the now, not if we don't let them. The woman I met in the precinct the other night is not who I found in our searches."

My gaze snaps up and I search her face for any sign she might be lying. "How can you be sure?"

She smiles. "The fact you're even asking that question and the fact that you're aware proves you're different now. For a flower to grow, it needs water, food, time. Humans are no different. We all have to learn somehow. Nobody is perfect, and those flowers that weather the harshest conditions are the strongest and often most beautiful."

"And Russ's old foster Mom?"

Elayne's face darkens. "Some flowers are never meant to grow."

I nod.

"But for the record,"—she winks again—"best behavior from now on."

I beam, considering a salute, but backing out at the last second. I settle for a plain old, "Understood." Then ask, "What happens now?"

Elayne picks her super serious briefcase up from the floor, sets it on the small coffee table, and opens it. She pulls out a huge wad of papers. "Unfortunately, more paperwork."

"Great," I reply, my mouth twisting into a grimace.

"Get used to it," she retorts. "This won't be the last of it."

Half an hour passes before we get close to the bottom of the pile. I find the last few forms confusing. "Why do you need my bank details?"

"For payment," Elayne replies, her attention still focused on checking what I've just signed.

"Payment for what?"

"Caring for Jo—Russ."

I stare at the sheet of paper, my pen hovering over the line I need to fill out. "Why would I get paid?"

"Because Ms. Parker," she explains, "children cost money. The state will help somewhat."

I don't give anything away with my face, trying to figure out if this is a test. "I didn't do this for the money."

"I know." She nods at the sheet, urging me to fill out the details. "But it will help. Take what support you can. It isn't much, but it will help make things easier."

I still hesitate. A quick mental calculation of how much salary I will have left each month with reduced working hours, while supporting two, confirms I need to take whatever is on offer. The scratching of the pen against the last sheets of paper grates on me, until I finally accept that without the help, my time with Russ could be even more limited.

When all the paperwork is completed, I walk with Elayne toward Russ's room, finding the door ajar and Russ sleeping soundly on the bed.

"Well, look at that," muses Elayne to herself.

I shift my weight between my feet and peer round her. "Is this a good sign?"

"Considering he hasn't slept in days, yes. I'd say it is."

Russ lets out a small puff of air that I find weirdly fascinating. "Should I wake him up before you leave?"

"Normally, I'd say yes. But nothing about this situation is normal. You have my number. If you need anything, please don't hesitate to contact me."

"Okay." I'm incapable of saying anything else, terrified about being left alone with Russ and having to figure out all of this on my own.

At the door, I must look worse than I feel, because Elayne reaches over and gives my arm a squeeze. "Don't doubt yourself." She sounds like she's been speaking with Grams. "This will be hard. There will be some great times, but there will be more tough ones. Parenting isn't meant to be easy, but you're already off to the best start."

"How so?" I ask, my voice shaky.

"You have Russ's best interests at heart. Use that to guide you when you're unsure of what to do. Always trust your gut."

I decide I like Elayne. There's something about her, beneath the bluntness and her serious exterior. Behind the tight bun and unfitted clothing, there's a woman with a story. Maybe that's why she sees something in me she knows she can trust, because we each have our own to tell.

When we've said goodbye, I close the door behind her and turn the lock. A quick check on Russ confirms he's still sleeping. I decide to leave him a bit longer so I can check my phone, which takes longer than expected thanks to misplacing it earlier in my frenzy.

When I do find my phone, it's full of message alerts from the girls, all telling me I can do this and that they're thinking of me. Mom texted three times asking for an update and Grams sent a blank message I don't think she meant to. Sam was the last to text, a couple of minutes ago, as if he sensed my emotional wobble while I was in the full throes of Elayne's pre-departure pep talk.

His message is different from the rest. There's no ego boost, no flowers or fluff. He goes straight in for my insecurities, drawing a reaction only he knows how to.

Try to keep him alive till Friday.

I snort, then read it again.

My laughter fills the new apartment for the first time, and I feel sure that although things won't be easy and we have a rocky road ahead of us, eventually everything will be okay.

The four days that follow my drunken session with Sophie in Riffs are the longest of my life.

The band's month-long tours where we've been apart in the past haven't touched on how much I miss her now. The walls surrounding our friendship are coming down and I'm beginning to catch sight of the something more we could be. I want her near me, want some form of contact with her at all times of the day, more than I ever have before.

I no longer just want her. I need her.

It's messing with my already-fucked head, which Sooz has kindly pointed out, cracking the whip behind me all week, making sure I attend interviews and photoshoots in what could be every magazine and radio station located in New York—spinning my failure to S.C.A.R.A.B.'s advantage. Rehashing the memory of that night over and over—dissecting every little detail—is exhausting. By four PM Friday, I'm ready for crawling into bed and hiding from everyone. Friday Feast Night is the only thing keeping me going.

"Has the drill sergeant finally finished with you?" snickers Ryan when I walk into the living area, searching for my wallet.

"Hope so," I grunt, lifting a couch cushion and coming up with nothing.

I look around the room again. Where the hell is it? It's been over half an hour of searching and if I don't find it soon, I'm going to be late for Sophie. Under normal circumstances, it wouldn't be an issue, but the last thing I want to do when it's our first feast night with Russ is make it appear like I'm not taking him being there, and this huge change to her life, seriously.

"So," Ryan says, trying to appear vague. It's wasted effort on his part. He's the nosiest of us all.

"Have you seen my wallet?"

"That depends …"

I catch the faint smile he's trying to hide when he covers his mouth with his hand. "On what?"

"Whether I'm going to get an update on what's happening with you and Sophie."

I really don't have time for this.

"Come on, man." I hold my hand out, ready to receive what I know he has. "I'm gonna be late."

"For Sophie?"

"Yes, for Sophie."

"And the kid?"

"His name's Russ," I remind him, counting to ten in my head. It's pointless losing my temper. All it will do is spur him on to keep going. He thrives off prying, especially when we're not on tour and he's bored. Basically, like now.

He makes it clear he's in no hurry to end the conversation when he asks, "What's the plan?"

"There is no plan." I pull out my phone, clenching my jaw when I see the time. "Come on. I really am going to be late."

I'm stressing so hard I'm starting to sweat. Ryan must see it, because he starts laughing—one hundred percent at my expense.

"When are you going to tell her how you feel? It's a fucking sideshow watching you trying to navigate this shit." He wipes beneath his eyes, finding my situation *that* funny.

"I'm not navigating anything," I reply, getting closer to losing my cool.

246

"And I'm the President. Please, you've had a boner for Sophie since you knew what to do wi—"

"If you finish that sentence, this isn't going to end well," I snap. "You're doing this on purpose."

"Someone has to," he snaps back. Ryan never snaps. He's always totally chilled out, mainly thanks to his weed habit.

The crowds on the screen in the background cheer when Michael Becket scores a touchdown on the Jacksonville Jaguars re-run, covering up the tense silence.

"What's going on here?" I ask calmly, trying to rein in my temper. Butting heads isn't going to get us anywhere and definitely isn't going to get me to Chow's in the next five minutes to pick up the food order.

"What's going on is that whatever *isn't* going on with you and Sophie is affecting us all."

"It's stage fright," I remind him.

He lifts his hips, pulls out my wallet and tosses it my way. "No. It's not. It's Sophie fright." I'm tempted to walk out and leave the conversation where it is. My feet have other ideas, remaining rooted to the spot. "Have you even told her she's the reason you started singing in the first place?"

My ears burn. I keep forgetting about the night I joined in his weed party and admitted everything. "It's never come up."

"When you see her every chance you get? Right. She's your muse, man. You know how it goes …"

I know exactly how it goes and what he's anchoring at. My patience snaps and my anger comes tumbling out.

"What are you suggesting? Sleep with her so everyone is happy? Then we can go back to climbing the fame ladder, right?" I try to get a grip on my breathing. "She's worth more than that, Ry. I love her."

I pause. Blink.

Ryan settles back against the couch. A spliff appears out of nowhere and he lights it, taking a long drag and grinning. "Button officially pushed. Thank me later."

"Asshole," I call over my shoulder, hurrying from the room and straight out the front door.

All the way to Chow's, I replay the three words in my head.

I've always wanted Sophie. There's never been any questioning it.

But loving her … that's something there's no coming back from. Acknowledging the fact makes it impossible not to do anything about it. Ryan purposely backed me into a corner, knowing there's only one way I can get out.

Chapter Twenty
Sam

The kid I caught sight of in the precinct is worlds away from the one I officially meet when Sophie opens the front door to their apartment.

"Shit. It's Sam Riley from S.C.A.R.A.B.!"

My mouth drops open, and Sophie covers her face with her hands.

"Russ, we've talked about this. That word's banned."

"I thought that was fuck?" he replies. It could be interpreted as innocent if it weren't for the mischievous glint in his eye.

"Russ …" Sophie warns.

He ignores her and focuses all his attention on me. "Are you going to sing?"

I scratch the side of my head, trying to come up with an answer. Of all the things he could ask me, it had to be that.

"Erm, no. But I brought food?" I raise the bag of takeout in the air with no idea why I've said it like a question.

Russ wrinkles his nose. "Vegetables?"

"Google said not to." Sophie coughs and glares at me. "There are noodles and fortune cookies."

"Yessss!" Russ catches me off guard, snatching the bag and scurrying back into the apartment.

"He's fun," I say, as more of an observation.

Sophie sags against the door and closes her eyes. I take the few seconds she's giving me to drink her in. She couldn't look more unkept if she tried, in a pair of lounge pants, covered in bleach stains and a yellow checkered shirt, which, thanks to the top three buttons being undone, falls low on one side, exposing the skin of her shoulder and the green strap of her lace bra.

"What are you doing?" Sophie giggles drunkenly as I drag her along the hall toward the stairs.

"Taking you somewhere quiet so I can tell you what a bad idea this was." I hurry her up towards the bedroom where our friendship, for me, began. When we're inside the room, which Aunt Rachel still hasn't turned into a guest room, even though she's threatened to numerous times, I shut the door and turn the lock.

Sophie's already flopped back on the bed and is bouncing on the mattress.

"A surprise party? Seriously?"

"It's the big two one, Sammy. Nine years from thirty, the big three zero. Twenty-one."

"Is this a new drunken thing? Number dumping?"

She snorts as I flop on the bed beside her. "You said dump."

"And you couldn't sound further from twenty-one if you tried."

When she rolls onto her side and rests her weight on one arm, her blonde hair falls forward, catching the last orange rays pouring through the window. It almost looks red, like it should. My eyes move down to her shoulder, and I swallow hard when I find her dress has fallen, revealing the perfect shade of green lace cupping her breast and complimenting her milky skin tone.

"Ten years from now," Sophie says, oblivious to my wandering eyes, "where do you see yourself?"

"Music, I guess."

"You guess?" I shrug and she rolls her eyes. "Tell me something you know."

That I'll always want you, my brain wants me to reply.

"That I'm lucky to have you as a friend," is what I say.

Sophie grins. "Come on, let's go back down and dance."

She drags me out of the room, and I spend the rest of the night and weeks after trying to get the image of green lace out of my head.

I focus on Sophie's face and then her hair, which takes the concept of 'messy bun' to a new level with the bleached strands sticking out in all directions—doing what I can to avoid the peep of green lace beneath her shirt, which my dick refuses not to respond to.

"You look exhausted."

Sophie opens her eyes, and with her lashes lifted, I can see the dark circles they've been hiding. "It's been a hectic couple of days."

I step forward and pull her into my arms, enjoying the way hers wrap around me instinctively in the dance we've been doing for two-thirds of our lifetime. "You're not kidding."

"Sooz been keeping you busy?" she mumbles against my chest.

"That's one way of putting it." I nuzzle my face into her hair, feeling the stress of the week disappear as the smell of her shampoo turns me woozy. "I need you back." The last part slips out before I can stop it, completely unrelated to work.

"Why? Are there many interviews left?" Sophie asks, missing the meaning behind my words.

"Nah, we finished them all today." I squeeze her tighter and my pulse starts to race when I decide to take a small step into unknown territory now neither of us have any complications holding us back. Saying out loud what is normally a given in our relationship changes the dynamic of who we are together; it changes everything. "I just missed you."

Sophie moves her head and looks up. Her brows drawn together makes me consider taking what I said back, laughing it off in a 'duh, just kidding' moment. But then her lips part, and her breath warms the skin on my lips when she tilts toward me, enough to make what she wants to happen next clear.

With less than a centimeter between us, my lips tingle in anticipation and I can't stop myself from pushing the moment further. "Red …"

"Sophie?" calls Russ, his voice less confident than when he was standing beside her at the door.

She darts away from me like she's been burned and holds the back of her hand against her mouth. She clears her throat, then calls back with a flustered edge to her voice, "Coming."

The pink covering her cheeks tells me she felt it too, all of it. She wanted me to kiss her. She'd never say that, though, at least not yet. I ignore the slight disappointment when she hurries away, reminding myself I've had years to come to terms with the non-friendly side of my feelings. Even with the extra time, it's been a struggle; a constant battle between what's right for our friendship and what I want deep down.

Sophie, if she's feeling what I think she might be doing, is going to need time.

I take an extra minute closing the door, preparing myself for the night ahead, before walking into the kitchen. My throat goes dry and I struggle to swallow when I find Sophie standing behind Russ, her arms alongside his, helping him to hold his carton and spoon the contents into a bowl. The little guy's concentration breaks when I shift my feet, the movement catching his attention.

He looks up, his brows furrowing. "It's too hot," he declares.

"Which is why we're putting it in a bowl," explains Sophie, carefully.

Russ huffs and watches me as I move to the opposite side of the kitchen island and pull out the other two food cartons.

"Are you putting yours in a bowl?" he asks abruptly.

Sophie moves away from him and busies herself opening drawers, searching for a fork. I catch the way the muscle in her jaw ticks and the reason her appearance is so disheveled becomes obvious. During their first few days together, Russ has put her through the wringer.

I consider my answer, knowing there's a chance, with the scowl Russ is giving me, that whatever I say will be wrong. "I prefer mine in a carton."

"Well, that's shit. I want mine in a carton," he demands.

I chew on the inside of my cheek, unsure whether to find his language offensive, alarming, or hilarious.

With her back to us both, Sophie's shoulders rise and then, after a second, droop low. She turns back round with not one, but three forks in her hand, and a tight smile on her face. "How about …" she suggests, pausing to gauge Russ's initial reaction, "we wait for it to cool," when he just watches her, waiting, she continues, "and *then*, we put it back in the carton?"

I don't know what's going through Sophie's head, but I try to figure out, as one emotion after another flickers across Russ's face, exactly how this is going to go. It's a relief when he grins. "Can I watch TV, please?"

"Sure," Sophie answers, leaning against the countertop, gripping it tight for support as Russ disappears without another word. When he's settled on the couch, just in sight, her smile slips, letting me see exactly how she's feeling. "What are you doing?" she asks when I walk around the island.

"Getting something," I reply cryptically, with one cabinet in mind. It's one of the high-level ones that even Sophie would struggle to reach.

What's inside is a welcome sight.

With the pricier bottle I'm searching for further to the back, I stretch to my max, feeling my shirt pull tight and lift. After a few more stretches, my fingers grasp it enough I'm able to drag it closer. Bottle finally in my hand, I twist around, catching Sophie staring hard at where, moments ago, the skin around my middle was on full display.

"Wine?"

The tension from the hallway returns and I have to remind myself there's someone else in the apartment with us. When Sophie's tongue darts out and sweeps across her bottom lip, I almost forget why it would be inappropriate to ignore the takeout, lift her on the counter and tear her shirt away, so I can appreciate the green lace bra in its entirety.

"Just in case," I answer, making a mental note to ask her if it's the same one.

"Sophie?" calls Russ, interrupting another moment.

Sophie startles again, and it hits me that this is the way things will be now. Her life isn't entirely her own and everything she will do, every decision she will make, will be with Russ at the forefront of her mind for as long as he's in her care.

"It's ready," Sophie calls back, busying herself by pouring the contents of the bowl back into the takeout carton to appease the whirlwind seven-year-old.

I set the wine down on the counter when Russ rushes back in, unsure whether to open it. Maybe having something in my system, clouding my judgement, isn't a good idea. I make quick work of putting the bottle back in its place in the cabinet when Sophie casts it a wary glance, making it clear she's thinking the same.

"This is so cool," grins Russ, clambering onto one of the stools and tucking into his food.

I've barely opened my own carton when I look over and find he's halfway through his, showing no signs of slowing. I've just settled next to him and picked up a fork when he finishes, polishing the scraps he dropped on the countertop in his haste and all.

My mouth waters at the smell of my favorite Chow's meal. It's magic what they do with it, creating the perfect combination of red and yellow peppers, onion, beef and rice noodles, not egg—they're too big. The sweet, salty and spicy flavors are a party in my mouth, and I let out a little moan at the first mouthful. It would be heaven if the food didn't catch in my throat with the feeling of someone watching me.

Sophie is staring at her own food intently, which means it can only be one person.

I glance to the side, finding Russ watching, eyes still hungry. I smile through my stomach growling and slide the carton his way. He snatches it before I can change my mind and I make a mental note to order two next time. While Russ is busy filling his mouth, Sophie scrapes half of her order into the bowl he decided he didn't want. She pushes it my way and gives me a weak smile that doesn't reach her exhausted eyes. I want to talk to her about it all, but not while the one who will be the main topic of our conversation is sitting, listening.

Thankfully, Russ crashes five minutes after he finishes eating.

Sophie disappears to help him get settled and I decide I'm pro-wine after all, uncertain whether it's the big or little person who's just left the room making me feel on edge. I've filled two large glasses when Sophie returns, not showing any signs of hesitation over my drink choice this time, taking one of the glasses and a long drink without a word. I follow her lead, raising my glass to my lips, enjoying the rich flavor that coats my tongue. I'm more of a beer fan, but tonight I'd drink anything set in front of me if it promised to take away my nerves.

"Sorry," says Sophie eventually, swirling red liquid around her glass.

"For what?" I ask, literally no clue what she's apologizing for.

"It wasn't exactly a feast night."

With comedy timing, my stomach growls.

"Who knew kids could eat so much?" I shrug, trying to pass it off as meaning less than it does.

I haven't missed the way Russ's clothes hang off him, but I don't doubt for a second that with Sophie's help and care, it's a problem that will disappear in time. It's what's left behind that we can't see which is worrying, and why Sophie can't do any of this alone. She needs support and someone to hold her up just like Russ does, because I have a strong suspicion that the bruising left on his face is only a small glimpse into the life he's led up to this point.

After taking another long drink, I try to lighten the mood. "We could order pizza?" Sophie snorts into her glass, mid-drink. She lowers it as the snort turns into laughter, which then becomes hysterical. "Pizza's funny?"

"He'd eat all that, too." She bends over, laughing harder. It's only when her shoulders shake, turning into a tremble, that I realize she's sobbing silently.

I rush to her side and pull her into my arms, wanting to make whatever she's going through better, but not knowing how or where to start.

"It's going to be okay," I say quietly, in case Russ wakes and can hear us. Not knowing what else to do, I stand, holding her with one arm, running my other hand through her hair in a steady rhythm until eventually she settles.

When she pulls back, her face is all blotchy, her eyes puffy and red.

"Sorry," she sniffles.

"Stop apologizing."

She drops her gaze to the ground and her lip wobbles again. "You probably think I'm acting ridiculous."

I lift her chin so she can't look anywhere but right at me. "I think you're acting normal. How about we order the pizza with an extra one? You know, as a precaution. Then drink some more wine and talk."

"Sounds like a plan." She gives me another smile that goes nowhere near her eyes.

"I'll order. You chill. I'll be with you in a minute."

She nods and grabs the wine glasses. With our favorite pizza place on speed dial, I watch her move into the living room and let out a long exhale. I had a feeling coming here tonight that things were going to be different, and the process wasn't going to be easy for Russ or Sophie, but I never imagined I'd be walking into this.

After grabbing the opened bottle of red, I follow Sophie into the living area, finding her stretched out on the couch with her eyes closed. I pause and stand, taking her in.

"I can feel you watching me."

"Just returning the favor." Her eyes fly open and narrow. When I grin, she flips me off. I pass over her glass, then settle at the other end of the couch with her feet set on a cushion in my lap. "Pizza will be here in thirty."

"Okay."

I have a sip of my drink, then with my free hand, take hold of one of her feet.

"Mmmm, that feels good," she hums, her eyes flickering shut when I press against her arch with my thumb. Thank fuck I put the cushion where I did, or she'd know exactly how I feel about her moaning over my massage. After a couple of minutes, she reopens her eyes, albeit lazily, appearing more relaxed than she has all night. "Movie?"

"Sure."

The walls of the room flash different colors in the disappearing light as Sophie scrolls through different options, searching for something to watch. Eventually, the room fills with the sound of guns firing and more explosions than is acceptable in the opening five minutes of a decent action movie. I hold back a laugh at the bored expression on her face as she pretends to be interested in the chaos on the screen. I know exactly what she's doing. Avoiding everything, including the couple of moments we've shared.

A particularly large explosion fills the room with bright white light, and I take in the blotchiness still covering her skin. "How have things been?" I ask, refusing to let her avoid opening up about what's really been going on.

She doesn't take her eyes off the screen when she replies, "Fine."

"Just fine?" She doesn't answer. "Soph."

Her head snaps in my direction. "I'm watching the movie."

"You hate action movies."

"Well," she huffs, "I like this one."

"You're doing it again," I say, raising my glass to my lips, waiting for her reaction.

"Doing what?" she asks, her eyes narrowed at mine as Arnie's oversized face fills the screen in the background.

"Avoiding." Before she can realize what *I'm* doing, I grab the remote sitting in her hand and press pause. "You have to talk about all this."

"Talk about what?" she snaps again, pinning her anger and frustration on me. I take it all willingly, accepting that whatever comes my way will help both her and Russ. "The fact I can't do this? That I make a terrible foster mom? I haven't got a clue what I should be doing. Russ isn't happy and I don't know how to change that for him. He has nightmares and yesterday I caught him crying for his birth parents. And then, last night, just when I thought things couldn't get any worse, I was helping him get ready for bed and he took his t-shirt off so he could have a bath.

"There weren't just bruises, Sam. There were scars. Big and small ones, everywhere. The things he must have been through ... and we don't even know for how long." She rubs away the tears that have resumed falling down her cheeks. "Gah! I don't know. I don't know how to take it all in. I used to go out and get wasted every night! I don't know how to do all this deep, serious stuff."

"Keep going ..." I urge her, relieved to see she's finally talking openly about *something*, but hating every word that comes out of her mouth, especially the ones about the sleeping child two doors away from us.

"Why? So, you can laugh at me after?" Her chest heaves with frustration as she starts to roll with the momentum. "Poor old, Sophie, thinking she can take on whatever she wants and failing ... again. Thinking she can be whoever she wants. Hell, thinking she can be with whoever she wants when she can't even get the biggest player in Manhattan to give her an orgasm."

My eyes widen at that part, which I one hundred percent wasn't expecting.

"Done?"

"Nowhere near. I don't know how to do it all. Support the both of us. I mean, technically, the numbers must work, otherwise Russ wouldn't be here ..." The longer she talks, the louder and higher her voice gets. "But Elayne needs to send me the numbers because I can't figure this shit out. How do people do it? The school drops offs and then working full time. I don't know how to make it work and we haven't even started." She pauses, thinking over what she says next. "I want to give up, Sam."

"No, you don't," I reply instantly.

"Oh right. Great." She laughs bitterly. "And you know that how? Because you know *everything* about me?"

"Yeah, I do." I set down my glass and push the cushion and her feet away so I can face her properly.

"Tell me something you know …"

Sophie's adrenaline from her truth dumping starts to pass, but I've already decided to do some of my own.

"I know it all. That you *hate* anything monotone and boring, which makes the wardrobe you've been sporting for the past three years crazy. That even though your family constantly rubs you the wrong way and you feel like you live in their shadows, you love them more than anything. I know that you love winter more than summer, but you never tell anyone after Mandy Cartwright called you weird for it back in high school. Like I know Grams is most likely the one behind Russ's cursing, which you hate, but I know you laugh about it inside.

"I know that whenever your mom cooks, you contemplate turning vegetarian, because she always cooks the burgers rare, and you're terrified of dying of food poisoning. I also know you hate rock music, but you'd never say, because you're scared of hurting mine and the band's feelings, but you'd still come to every gig or practice we asked you to. Just like I know you literally peed your pants when you swapped out Ry's weed for dried grass and he claimed to be the highest he'd ever been.

"I'll admit I didn't know the bit about Fitzgerald the fuckwit and how bad his performance was lacking, which is why we're probably having this conversation, because what you might really need is to come hard. Maybe a few times to really scratch that itch."

A cushion collides with my head for the last one and I laugh right along with Sophie, who then starts crying as well.

It could be considered a talent that she's managing to do both at the same time.

When she stops laughing and crying, and her expression turns serious, a lump threatens to close my throat, because I know what question is coming next.

"H-How do you know all that?"

"Because I see you, Soph. Just like you saw me that first day in my aunt and uncle's."

Then, I remember what everyone keeps telling me about moments passing by. What Shaun, Jake and Ryan have all said about missing out on something because of fear, knowing it roots back to all the shit with my parents.

I want it all. I want this life, with Sophie, challenges and all. That's if she wants me back, something I won't ever know unless I tell her how I feel.

I don't want to be afraid anymore, which is why I take a deep breath and swallow before saying, "I want you. I always have."

Chapter Twenty-One
Sophie

It's almost forty-eight hours after Sam's declaration and I'm still walking round in a daze with no clue how to process everything he told me.

"Earth to, Soph," says Abby, clapping her hands as she walks in my direction from the tire swing.

"Sorry," I mutter, watching my younger brother, Xavier, in his element, jumping between pushing Abby's daughter Clara, and Russ as high as he can after some guidance from Abby on safety limits.

"He's great with kids," states Zoe, fanning herself. Even beneath the thick trees of Central Park, there's no hiding from the heat.

Abby and I decided by mid-morning there was no better time for strength in numbers. Clara was struggling with overheating, and Russ, well, he just needed a break from reality and time to act like the kid he hadn't been able to.

"That's because he's only just stopped being one himself," I reply.

"True."

Abby reaches us and flanks my other side on the bench where we're sitting, then we all take a minute, relishing in the almost silence, bar the squeals in the distance.

"What's on your mind?" asks Abby, eventually.

"A lot," I reply, and she smiles—a knowing one. It tells me Jake is fully aware of some of the 'lots' and has made Abby aware of them, too.

"Which do you want to start with?" she chuckles. "The fun or the serious stuff?"

"Honestly," I sigh. "I feel like all I do is talk. I'm literally bored of my own voice."

Zoe starts laughing, then stops abruptly when a child—which isn't ours—almost rolls over her toes with a scooter. "Watch it!"

The young girl, maybe a year older than Clara, wearing tiny overalls with her hair in braids, looks back and sticks her tongue out before speeding off.

"She's cute," says Abby, oblivious to the anarchy she's sending Zoe's way.

"Yeah. The cuter they make them, the worse they are," says Zoe under her breath.

"True that," Abby agrees, staring ahead at the two humans now relying on each of us. "Serious stuff it is." She waits a moment, then asks, "How is he?"

I watch Russ laughing with Clara. "Not great," I reply honestly. "Behind closed doors, he isn't the same kid I met." I take a breath before explaining further, aware of how bad my first statement sounds. "What I mean is ... he's hurting. When I met him, he was smiling, then I learned that he was hiding all this." I gesture around me, not even close to touching on what *this* is. *This* isn't a book or some stupid drama show. *This* is as real as it gets, and I don't have a clue what I'm doing. "I keep asking myself why I've done this and whether he'd be better off without me trying to help. Does that make me a bad person?"

"The fact you're even trying to help him, knowing just a small part of what he's been through, proves you're one of the best there is," says Zoe, without taking a breath.

"I agree," says Abby. "In the best scenario, fostering must be hard. But in the worst …"

"Yeah." I say, catching the moment his laughter falters and he looks over to me for reassurance. I give him a small wave, which seems to do the job, and he goes back to laughing with Clara and Xavier. "It's really fucking hard."

"The best things in life don't come without a fight," says Abby, staring at years' worth of Jabby history flying through the air.

"And when you don't fight, it's shit," says Zoe.

"Basically, you can't win." On my last word, Russ's laughter filters over to us and I smile. "Today's been a better one. Thanks for coming with me."

"There will be good and bad," agrees Abby. "Hold on to the good ones with a vice grip, because they can be limited, but when they come, they make up for all the crap."

I turn to her, needing some advice, which, out of our friendship group, only she can give, as she's the only one of us with the experience. "Can I ask you something?"

"Sure," she replies, tucking a piece of dark hair behind her ear and waving at Clara with a grin.

"Am I doing something wrong if Russ is being …"

"Difficult?" she laughs.

265

"That's the nice way of putting it." My mouth twists, remembering the 'hiccup' we had this morning, which ended in a minor tantrum on both our parts—all over what is the correct amount of milk to pour over a bowl of cereal.

"I remember asking my mom the same thing after Clara turned one."

"What did she say?"

"That if they're acting out, it's a good thing?"

I frown. "How is it a good thing?"

"Because it means they feel safe to do so. No one's perfect, Soph. The three of us know that better than most." Zoe laughs at her side. "What's important is creating an environment where they can make mistakes, act out, throw tantrums when they need to and learn from it, while knowing, through it all, you will be there behind them no matter what."

"That sounds fun," I muse, wondering how many difficult times Russ and I have got to come.

"Yeah, it's not. But it's part of being a parent. You're going to do amazingly at it."

"Thanks," I reply quietly, not quite believing her yet.

My phone bleeps, providing a break in the conversation. My heart flutters like a bird flapping its wings against my ribcage when I pull it out of my bag and find a text from Sam.

"Now onto the fun stuff," says Zoe, casting me a sideways glance.

"One minute," I reply, opening the message.

Sam: *I have a solution.*
Me: *To?*
Sam: *The school drop-off situation.*

My fingers hover over the screen before I reply, as I try to figure out how he knows it's even an issue. Then I remember Friday night with my huge info dump, and that the school drop off and how to manage it all was just one of things I sent his way in my big-ass vent.

Me: *I'm intrigued.*

Sam: *I'll do it.*

Me: *What do you mean 'I'll do it'?*

Sam: *I mean that thanks to my 'situation', I have nothing else to do, while you have a lot to do. So, let me help.*

Me: *I can't put that on you.*

Sam: *It's nothing. It will be cool. We can bond over man stuff and shit.*

Me: *You almost had me until the 'and shit'.*

Sam: *K. No 'and shit', just man stuff.*

Me: *Let me ask Russ.*

Sam: *Sure. Keep me updated.*

I put my phone back in my bag and return to watching Russ on the swing set. A part of me wants to keep Friday all to myself for a bit longer, not wanting to taint it in any way, but I also need advice.

"Sam told me he wants me," I say, still staring straight ahead, not wanting to see Abby and Zoe's reaction in case they laugh and tell me it has to be a joke.

"Finally," says Zoe.

I turn to her, mouth wide open. "You knew?"

She looks at me like I've asked her if we should give up drinking coffee. "Er, yeah."

"Me too," says Abby, raising her hand in the air.

I look between them both, dumbfounded. "And you didn't think to tell me?"

Abby shrugs. "I kinda thought you'd have figured it out. I guess I'm not the only person who's hard work in this group."

I nudge her with my elbow. "Thanks for that."

"Just putting it out there. Plus, I owe you a ton of offhand comments for all the ones you've given me over the years." She leans forward and stares at Zoe. "You, too." She turns her attention back to me. "So?"

I give her a blank look. "So, what?"

"Do you want him back?"

My cheeks burn, giving away the answer as I try to stop myself from remembering one dream in particular that I had last night. One that involved Sam and chocolate sauce. I don't even like chocolate sauce, but I woke up tangled in my sheets, a hot, sexually frustrated mess.

"Well," says Zoe, rudely interrupting my daydream about my dream. "We have our answer."

Self-doubt kicks in and I play with a loose thread on the hem of my denim shorts. "I keep waiting for him to say he was messing with me."

"Soph," sighs Zoe, "does this have anything to do with Fitzgerald?"

"Actually," says Abby, sitting up straighter, with purpose. "We have more to talk about. What the hell were you thinking going with that idiot? For nine months?!"

"I dunno," I mutter. "It wasn't all bad."

"And that right there means it wasn't right," Abby replies, not holding anything back. "There shouldn't be any bad."

"Right," I scoff.

"Go on," she says, her eyes narrowing. "Say it."

"You and Jake have had plenty of bad times, so you can't really say that. At one point, you were like the king and queen of toxicity."

Abby shakes her head. "But our bad was from fighting the inevitable, Soph. More me fighting it than Jake, but we all know that. Our bad was because I didn't know what I wanted out of my life, and I was still hurting. It wasn't the relationship that was bad, per se. When we were together, we were always great. It was the bits where we weren't that was the issue, because we were fighting against what we both wanted."

I consider everything she's said and accept she's right. "Are you happy?"

Abby nods and her eyes glaze over like they do whenever Jake is around. "The happiest. Even when things are hard."

"Especially when 'things' are hard," says Zoe, wiggling her brows. I roll my eyes and she blows me a kiss. "So, Soph. When are you going to get happy with all the hard with Sam?"

"Please stop saying the word hard," I reply and Abby laughs. I don't answer Zoe's question straight away, trying to figure out how to tell them the one thing that's been bugging me since Friday. "He hasn't kissed me."

Zoe looks completely unphased. "He's probably just waiting for the right moment."

"Yeah …" I reply, not convinced.

She watches me. "If it's bugging you so much, just ask him why he hasn't."

"Just like that?"

Zoe nods. "Just like that. Don't overcomplicate things. Be open. Communicate. It's got you this far as friends. Just because he's told you that he wants to bone you, it doesn't mean there has to be issues."

"Thank you, oh wise one," I laugh. "If only you'd take your own advice with Shaun."

"Who?" Zoe stares at me, refusing to acknowledge what I'm saying.

"Be in denial all you like. You know what I'm saying."

"Oooo," says Abby, ending our back and forth. "Swinging is done. Time to go before Clara demands the zoo."

"Yeah," I agree. "I should get Russ back and ready for his first day at the new school."

"Is he feeling okay about it?" Zoe asks as we stand from the bench, while Abby busies herself re-organizing Clara's diaper bag on the buggy.

"Yeah." I watch him from a distance, helping Xavier with Clara, wishing it could be like this all the time. Hoping that with the months that pass, if he's with me that long, we'll get to a point where it is. "I think. I don't know. He's just … Russ. He doesn't really talk about any of it, but he's so little and I kind of think to myself, if I were in his shoes, would I really want to?"

"Give it time," says Abby, coming beside us. "If he needs to talk, he will."

Clara, Xavier and Russ walk our way, and just before they get to us, Zoe says quietly from my side, "Everything will be okay."

Things might feel rocky, and at times impossible, but I know that with the team I have supporting and rooting for me, that she's right, and eventually they will be.

The door frame to Russ's bedroom proves to be an excellent support as I use it to lean on and watch Russ, who's sitting at the small desk Sam bought him, drawing. He looks so peaceful that I consider leaving him longer; until he's ready to come out. Unfortunately, if the past few nights are anything to go by, it could be hours until then, and we both have an early start tomorrow.

I tap the door a couple of times to make him aware of my presence before speaking. "Dinner's ready." I don't get a response, so I raise my voice a couple of levels, making sure it's impossible for him not to hear me. "Hey. I said dinner's ready."

"I'm not hungry." He continues drawing, back to his sullen self, which only appears when it's the two of us.

Elayne's words echo in my head. *"Are you ready for what you might be faced with when the door closes and the two of you are left alone?"*

"Come on, please, Russ. You need to eat." I smile as I'm speaking, praying it reflects in my voice, hiding the alarm bells that are ringing in my head. I hate having to make him do things he doesn't want to. I want to be his friend and keep things happy and carefree, but equally my role right now is to be his parent, making sure he gets everything he needs, like food, and rest before his first big day at a new school.

When he doesn't answer me again, I walk over to his desk and stand at his side. My eyes trail to what he's drawing and what I find breaks my heart. Russ stills, making it clear he's sensed me by his side, but then he carries on working silently. It's when I see a droplet of water hit the paper that I decide to raise my hand and rest it on his shoulder.

"That's a really great drawing."

"It's my mom and dad." He pauses and the pencil he's holding stops moving. "My real ones."

I don't say anything straight away, just let him have his moment and take a few deep breaths. When he looks up at me, my heart doesn't just break like it has each time I've seen him this way since he moved in. It shatters. He shouldn't have to be going through any of this. It's all too much, and if I could, I'd take away every bad thing he's been through and carry the burden of each one myself if it meant he didn't have to keep waking up to this pain.

"It's okay to be sad," I say, when I think he's ready to hear it, needing him to know that even when he is, I will still be here. "We all get sad sometimes. You don't have to hide it around me."

I don't add all the extra stuff on. Like after how much shit he's been through, he's entitled to be sad for a lifetime. Those are the things he doesn't need to hear, and I hope together we can get him to a point where he never has to.

Russ swallows and nods, his eyes watering more than they already were. Then he does the thing I least expect, with a level of courage someone his age shouldn't need to have. He starts to build his own little bridge, ready to meet me somewhere along it. "I'm not trying to hide it. It's just … I don't want to be sad. I want to be happy with you. Like I was in The Parkapellas."

I reach and grab a tissue from the box sitting on his desk and wipe his tears away. "Would that make you happy? Going back to The Parkapellas?"

He nods. "I love it there. I love singing."

I smile and decide to help him finish building the bridge from the other side of the water where I'm standing, hoping

272

when it's done, we can meet in the middle and figure out our own dynamic. "How about you come and eat dinner, and we can discuss going back after this week?"

His eyes widen in excitement. "Seriously?"

"Seriously. But this week is about getting settled in school," I say sternly. It doesn't dampen his mood, and he looks ready to burst. I lean over and take hold of his drawing. "Come on. Let's go eat."

In the kitchen, I dish up the pasta I've spent the past hour making, full of hidden veggies in the sauce, because I've quickly learned Russ isn't a fan of them. I catch him wrinkling his nose as I'm loading up his plate.

"You haven't tried it," I say, before he can declare he doesn't like it. I consider telling him he's lucky he wasn't with me a few weeks earlier or he'd have been eating butternut squash noodles with a raw sauce and tofu.

He holds his chin up high, like he does when he wants me to give in to him. "I don't like pasta."

It's easy to forget when we're dealing with all the serious stuff, that really, he's still a child. One that's wise beyond his years but has the same reactions and behaviors in certain situations—particularly food-related ones.

"Have you ever tried pasta?" His mouth parts slightly, then closes again. A little bit of red creeps up his neck and I roll my lips together, trying hard not to laugh. I've got him. After sliding the plate in front of where he's sitting on one of the stools at the island, I lean forward, resting my weight on my arms so I'm at eye level with him. "I'm gonna up the stakes here."

"Okay …"

"If you try the pasta, I'll let you go to The Parkapellas on Friday."

273

He snatches up his fork and inhales a mouthful without saying a word until the plate is empty. It takes me by surprise when he doesn't drop the fork and push his plate away.

"Can I have some more, please?"

"Sure you can," I reply. With his plate piled high again, I leave him to eat and walk away with his drawing. After rooting through two drawers, I find some sticky tape and place it dead center on the refrigerator, then step back and take it in, pride filling my chest. When I turn back around, Russ looks confused. "It's a good drawing," I tell him, then ask, "Do you have any pictures of your mom and dad?"

He nods, but it's a hesitant one. I hate that it is, because it means he's uncertain why I'm asking, as if it could be for any other reason than the real one. The wariness in his eyes stops me from saying what I want to, initially. It's only later, as I'm tucking him into bed, that I decide I don't want to leave it as an unknown.

"If you want, we can get some frames and put them up … the pictures of your mom and dad."

My chest grows tight when he says, "Why?"

It feels completely natural to reach up and run my hand over his hair. I expect him to flinch, turn his head maybe, or worst-case scenario, grab my hand and tell me to stop. He doesn't do any of them and his brown eyes sparkle at me.

"I want this to feel like your home for as long as you're here. If you want pictures of your parents around, then we will put pictures up. If you don't, that's fine too." I take a breath, giving him a chance to digest what I'm saying before I continue. "You don't have to hide anything from me, ever. Including them."

"I'd like that."

"We can go pick out some frames this weekend. I know a great store."

He grins and pulls the thin bedsheet up to his chin. I don't turn off the night light sitting on his bedside table because he hates the dark. Instead, I ruffle his hair, then stand slowly.

He catches me off guard when he says, "Grams told me you're the best singer in The Parkapellas."

I hold off rolling my eyes at her prying. "Of course she did."

"My mom used to sing to me …" Before she died, he doesn't add on. "Do you think you could?"

His little voice bulldozes through my resolve, and even though I've never actually sung in front of anyone since the age of seven, I find myself saying, "Yeah. Sure." Needing something to make it feel less of a big deal than it is, I swallow over the lump growing in my throat. "Close your eyes."

Russ does as I say, the corners of his mouth lifted enough to encourage me to keep going.

I opt for one of my favorite songs from *Annie*, singing about all the promises that tomorrow will hold. I'm rusty at first and glad his eyes are closed so he can't see the frustration that must cross my face as I try to stop my voice from wobbling. Somewhere in the song, it starts to feel natural, and I forget all about my fears of singing to an audience.

One song runs into two, two into three and somewhere around the fourth, Russ's breathing grows heavy. My heart goes with it, remembering that I'm going to have to let him go, and that I really don't want to, because my life feels the most right it ever has with him in it.

Much later, when I finally have time to breathe, I cast a quick glance around the apartment, confirming that life is chaos.

There are clothes strewn everywhere, dishes piled high at the sink, waiting to be loaded in the dishwasher, and Russ's new car set we picked up on a detour home from the park today is scattered across the floor.

Deciding I don't want to deal with any of it, I sit on the couch, flinching at the crunching sound the cushions make when I settle. I block it out and rest my head back, closing my eyes. Exhaustion hits hard and, if given half the chance, I could easily pass out for the night.

My half a chance evaporates about ten seconds later, when someone has other ideas. My phone starts ringing, the tone sharp, too loud, and unwanted. When it stops and starts again, I accept I need to get up and source it from wherever it's hiding. I've covered half the kitchen without success, when I find it hidden beneath a towel right before it rings out for a second time.

My heart skips a beat when I see Sam's name on the screen. Is this the way it's always going to be now? Me swooning any time he's close by or just from thinking about him? Before he told me all the things he did, it was somewhat easier to block my own feelings out. Now, I don't stand a chance.

I'm about to pick my phone up from the counter when it lights up with a message.

Sam: *You ok?*

After he's made the effort to call twice, I figure the least I can do is call him back, so I do.

"You okay?" he answers, echoing his text.

"Hi. Yeah. Sorry. I couldn't find my phone."

"Things that good?"

"They're that good," I confirm.

We both go silent, and I don't know what to say. My pulse picks up and my hands go clammy. This is the first time we've actually spoken, besides texting, since Friday, when I packed his ass out of the apartment before the pizza arrived. What can I say? Hearing one of your best and oldest friends tell you they want you is overwhelming. I panicked. Sue me.

"You rang?" I say when the silence threatens to continue, and my nerves can't bear it any longer.

"Yeah." Sam clears his throat awkwardly. "Just wanted to check what's happening tomorrow."

"Tomorrow?" I blink at the mess in front of me and my mind comes up blank.

"Taking Russ ... to school?"

"Right! Yeah. I completely forgot." I cringe. That sounds bad, like I'm not fit to be doing this bad. "I mean I didn't forget, I ..."

Haven't got a clue how to explain my way out of this. If it weren't for Sam calling and saving the day again, tomorrow morning would likely have included a whole new level of panicking.

"Forgot," chuckles Sam. "What time does he need to be there?"

"Like nine. I think." I press the base of my hand against my forehead and squeeze my eyes shut, thankful he can't see the mess I look and feel.

"I'll pick him up just before eight thirty. Just in case."

"Yeah. Great."

The weird silence from the beginning of our conversation reappears, and I take the opportunity to contemplate how I can avoid seeing him in the morning if this is how things are going to be.

"Soph? You there?" Hearing the concern in his voice makes my stomach do a somersault.

"I'm here," I squeak.

A long sigh floats down the line. "Is this about what I told you Friday?"

"Kind of," I admit, because there's no point in not being honest. Zoe's right, this doesn't need to be an issue, but I'm making it into one and need to stop. "Why didn't you kiss me?" I blurt out.

Sam hesitates before replying and when he does, I wish he hadn't. "Why would I?"

There it is. The big humiliating truth. It's like I thought. Friday was a joke.

"Because you said …" I tail off, not ready to acknowledge out loud what I'm not even sure is going on anymore.

"That I wanted you. Which I do, and have, for a really long fucking time. What's the issue?"

I frown. So, he wasn't joking? I'm making this more confusing than it needs to be. "Normally, when people want someone or whatever, they kiss them."

"Did you want me to kiss you, or whatever?"

If Sam were here with me, I'd punch him in the arm for the laughter in his words. He's enjoying this way too much.

"I …"

My brain can barely keep up with what's happening.

"The fact you didn't say yes straight away is the reason I haven't, Soph."

"Are you mad I didn't say yes?" I'm ready to over-analyze all parts of this conversation as soon as we're done. Damn Zoe and her communicating crap.

This time, Sam laughs out loud. "I'm not mad. Stop overthinking it."

"It's a lot. There's a lot going on, generally. Do you blame me?"

"No," he replies seriously.

"Okay." I trace a pattern on the countertop with my finger, needing to do something with all the nervous energy. "I guess I should go. Busy day tomorrow."

Neither of us hang up and the sound of Sam's breathing suddenly coming out in small pants makes the hairs on my arms raise.

"Red?"

"Yeah?"

"Want to know the truth?"

"Yeah."

"I didn't kiss you because I've been waiting twenty years to. Believe me, I want to, more than I've ever wanted to do anything. But up until now, I've been able to put how I feel in a box, so if you didn't feel the same, we would still be fine, and we'd still be friends. If I kiss you … there will be no coming back from it. I need you to be certain you want it. That you want me back."

I want to tell him that if he were here right now, after everything he's just said, I'd kiss him in a second.

He isn't here though and there's something I can't put my finger on that tells me even though I want to, my head isn't quite there yet. It all feels so sudden and even though most of my body has gotten the memo that we're Team Sam all the way, my head needs more time to adjust. Basically, I'm terrified. Terrified of messing everything up and not living up to twenty years of Sam's expectations. I don't exactly have a track record that makes me feel like I'm worthy of someone sacrificing their time with a relationship. Brendan being a prime example of that.

"So, what now?" I ask.

"How about this …" Sam suggests. "We don't talk about this all again. *You* let me know if, or when, you're ready."

My throat grows thick, as I try to figure out if I'd ever have the courage to be as forward as he's been. "How?" I need him to guide me through what he wants to do, although I have a strong suspicion what it is.

"*You* kiss me," he replies, giving me the answer I fully expected. "The ball's in your court, Red. You just need to decide if you're ready to play."

Chapter Twenty-Two

Sam

Russ walks mainly in silence by my side, nerves for the day ahead wreaking havoc with his face. It makes me feel nervous for him, and if it weren't for the fact that I know Sophie will be checking in and would murder me if I didn't deliver him safely, I'd suggest we fill the day with fun and none-nervy things.

Everything changes when we arrive at the school. I take him inside, and although still quiet, he seems to take it all in his stride, saying hi to the principal, smiling at the receptionist and then his new teacher.

I have a suspicion the change is for two reasons.

The first: Sophie's given him a good pep talk.

When I got to their apartment, they seemed different together. What I witnessed firsthand Friday night, the tension and slight resentment on Russ's part, was nowhere to be found this morning. They moved around each other smiling, like they'd been doing it forever.

The second reason bothers me more than I want to admit.

I see it in his eyes, the way he takes everything in. Just like each time I step out on stage with the band, after years of working together and rehearsing, he's prepared. Nothing takes him by surprise because he's done it all before. I don't let myself think about how many times. It pisses me off.

With the morning drop off a success, I mentally high five myself while leaving the school premises, then respond to the ten missed calls and fifteen texts from Sophie, letting her know he's okay.

It's in the run up to after school, around two PM, when I start to freak out.

I'm due to watch Russ for three hours, maybe four, if Sophie gets tied up at the office.

That makes it two hundred and forty minutes at most, which sounds like nothing when you break it down. But for some reason, I'm sweating more than if I'd been sprinting for an hour.

Now I get how Sophie must have felt taking Russ into her care with no clear end or clue what she was doing. Terrified.

"Why do you look like you're going to puke?" asks Ryan, walking into my room.

"I'm picking up Russ from school."

I feel him watching me as I gather a couple of things that I think I might need.

"That's it?" He arches a brow and gives me a skeptical look. "You're more nervous than the last time you went on stage." Of course he'd reference that night with ease, because when he wants to, he can be the biggest ass of us all.

I stop what I'm doing and stare down at the things I've set out on my bed, letting out a frustrated huff when I realize it's all totally useless.

"I want to help Soph, but I don't know how to look after a kid." I throw my hands out in front of me. "I don't even know what he likes. The only thing I know is he's a character."

"A character?" Ryan's other brow raises, joining the other with intrigue. He sits at the end of my bed. "How so?"

I chuckle to myself, remembering standing outside of Sophie's apartment just a few nights ago, questioning what the hell she'd let herself in for when Russ bulldozed his way through every attempt she made for us to all have an enjoyable time together. "The first time I officially met him, he said 'Shit. It's Sam from S.C.A.R.A.B.'"

Ryan laughs. "Isn't he like eight?"

"Seven," I confirm.

We both go silent, then Ryan shifts his feet and claps his hands excitedly. "We're hardly One Direction. Only an eight-year-old who was into music would know who S.C.A.R.A.B. is."

"Seven," I remind him.

"Seven. Eight. What's the difference?"

"Erm," I scratch my head. "Like a year? It's like dogs. Kid years mean a lot. Anyway, that's not the point. What are you getting at?"

"If he's into music, why not do something music-related with him?"

"That's actually a really good idea." I grin as an idea starts to form.

Ryan picks up on my change in mood. "What are you thinking?"

"Band practice?"

I don't need to say anything else. Ryan's already walking out of my room, shouting, "Yo! Zach!"

"Yeah?" Zach shouts back from somewhere in the house.

"Change of plan. Band practice in …" Ryan turns and waits for me to give him a time. I mouth two hours. "Two hours!"

"Thanks, man," I call after him, as he walks out of my room to get ready.

He waves me off. "We're not just a band, we're a team, remember?"

Leaving behind all the crap I don't need on the bed, I grab my keys and phone, then head out to pick up Russ from school, praying Ryan's right and he likes our new plans for the afternoon.

"Why don't we go old school?" suggests Zach, dragging a hand through his dark, floppy hair, while his other arm rests against his bass.

I bang my head against the mic, making a *thud, thud, thud* sound through the speakers. "It's no good. I'm fucked."

Jake clears his throat and widens his eyes at me. At first, I'm confused about what he's trying to get across. When he tilts his head and I follow his movement to the side of the room, I curse, thankfully to myself this time. Russ sits watching us all with his mouth open and his expression excited.

"I mean, I'm screwed," I say, correcting myself.

At least Grams has got to him first and anything he repeats won't be worse than what he's heard from her.

Ryan hammers the drums with his sticks, letting out his own frustrations. "That mentality is gonna get us nowhere. Come on, we have to try."

I pull my head away from the mic and roll my shoulders, trying to relieve some of the tension building, accepting Ryan's right. "Fine, let's give it another shot."

Ryan counts us in, and the room fills with the opening chords from one of our oldest songs. It's more familiar than any of the new stuff. So familiar, we're usually able to perform it without having to practice. Gripping the mic tight, I tap one foot against the ground and try to block out my racing pulse. I let my mind go blank, pushing everything away. Sophie. Russ. My parents. They have no part in this moment; when the melody and beat flow through me and I forget everything around me.

One thing we've figured out in the past couple of weeks: scream-singing isn't my issue, something a few of our older songs contain, including the opening part of this one. When the sound comes out, my vocal cords ache in the best kind of way from the harshness of it.

The relief quickly dissipates when the next part of the song kicks in.

I take a deep breath, ready to sing, but then images of the crowds from the gig flash behind my eyes.

The disappointment covering their faces.

Sophie in the middle of them all with Brendan by her side.

My throat goes dry, and all that comes out is a croak.

"Dammit," I hiss, staring at the ground, forgetting the mic is in front of me, amplifying it for the whole room to hear.

Clapping starts and I look up, expecting it to be coming from Russ.

"I like the screamy stuff," says Sophie, leaning against the wall at the back of the room. Thankfully, she's kept up with the lack of designer black clothing, but the expression she's wearing makes her completely unreadable. I reach up and scratch the back of my head, giving her a sheepish smile. She purses her lips. "Can we talk?" My shoulders sink from those three words. Everyone knows they never mean anything good, and right now; they feel ominous. "In private," she finishes.

I glance at Russ and then at the guys. "I'll be right back." Sophie pushes herself off the wall and stands straight as I walk toward her. Even upright, the top of her head barely reaches my chest and I have to drop my chin so I can talk to her. "Outside? I could do with some air."

Sophie nods, giving Russ a small wave before following me out of the room. We make our way down a narrow set of stairs, avoiding the odd tear in the thread-bare carpet. It's a total trip hazard, and the place is a dive, but it's where we've rehearsed since we first started out back in high school, and we refuse to go anywhere else. We made a promise to each other, right before Orensanz, that no matter what happens, we won't forget where we came from.

The alley we step out to isn't much better than inside. Garbage cans overflowing with trash line the walls, and in the stifling heat, give off a questionable aroma. I take a deep breath, trying to drag as much air as possible into my lungs. With the summer humidity taking a firm grip of New York, it provides no relief whatsoever. I wait a beat before turning back to face Sophie.

"So …" I say, taking in her blank expression, trying to figure out, in the space of a few hours, which have been consumed with entertaining Russ and music, what I could have done wrong.

She folds her arms, looking super serious. "Nervous?"

"More nervous than when I lost my v-card," I admit, "and I don't have a clue why."

The tension between us breaks, and Sophie laughs. "Chill." She over-exaggerates the word, making it sound familiar. Like how I say it to her all the time when she's stressing over nothing. "There's nothing wrong. I just wanted to find out how today's been."

I frown. "You couldn't have done that upstairs?"

Eyes bluer than the ocean sparkle at me in amusement. "Not with everyone listening. No." She reaches over and pokes me in the chest. "Actually, I do have a bone to pick with you."

Before she can pull her hand away, I catch her wrist in my grip and tug her into me, so every part of her body is pressed against mine.

After our phone call last night, I promised myself that I'd do like I told her and leave the ball in her court to do with as she pleases. Unfortunately, the thing about Sophie is, when she has time alone to think—which she has a lot of currently thanks to the Russ situation—she over-analyzes everything.

I move my thumb back and forth along the inside of her wrist and her small pants tell me she's one hundred percent affected by it. I use the moment as a reminder of everything I've told her so far. A reminder of how it feels when we're together like this and we've barely even started. A reminder not to listen to the small part of her brain that likes to fuck with everything and is likely trying to convince her this isn't real. This is as real as it gets, and with almost everything out there, from my side at least, walking away from what I want—*her*—is impossible.

"Pick away," I reply, still circling my thumb against her skin.

She sucks in a breath, and the corners of my mouth tilt up, taunting her.

Kiss me. Do it, Red.

"H-how?" She snatches her wrist away. "Stop it."

"What?"

She scowls. "You're distracting me."

I can't stop myself, raising a hand and dragging the pad of my thumb over her bottom lip. "You're the one distracting me."

I'd love to distract her more, but she takes two steps back, shaking her head. "Why does it feel like Abby knew how you felt about me before I did?"

"Jake knows." I shrug. "I guess it was inevitable, because they tell each other everything now."

"So, Russ has been okay today?" she asks, changing the subject.

"Russ has been great," I reply, appeasing her. "He's had a great day at school. His teacher said he excelled in all the work she gave him and that he got along with his classmates. But you know that already."

The music filtering down the stairs from The Wreck, as Jake lets loose on the guitar and Ryan plays a catchy beat, all backed up by Zach, reassures me Russ will still be sitting there, more than fine. In the few hours we've spent together, I've learned we're more similar than I would have guessed. I keep trying to figure out what his story is and can't help wondering why music is his escape like it used to be mine.

"How do you know that I know?" asks Sophie.

"Because I know you."

"Oh really?" She cocks her head to the side, her uncomfortableness from a minute ago replaced with a playful edge. "What else do you know?"

She's referring to the other night when I didn't even touch the surface of everything that I've observed about her over the years.

"Hmmm, well …" I reach forward and pull her back into me. I'm hit with a wave of what can only be described as euphoria at the fact she doesn't resist. Anchoring her against me with one hand at the small curve of her back, I reach up with my other and toy with a lock of her hair, wishing it wasn't blonde. "I know," I say, rubbing the strands between my fingers, trying to figure out how they're so soft, "that you called two minutes after school started. Then around ten … and eleven. You usually have meetings over lunch, so I'm guessing you couldn't ring again until after one. And then, after school was chaos. I'm assuming my five missed calls were because there wasn't any answer from the admins."

"You know a lot," she muses, and I find myself leaning down into her. If she notices the gap closing between us, she doesn't comment, just smiles. "Some might say you've become a bit of a smart ass."

"I know one more thing."

I blame the heat pressing in for the fact I'm doing the complete opposite to what I said I would, pushing her over the invisible line that's always been between us. I don't just want her to be on the same side as me. I need her to be.

"What do you know?" she murmurs almost against my lips, her words making them skim mine.

"I know that I really, really, really want to kiss you right now," I whisper.

She turns her head to the side and presses a kiss against my cheek. It might not be where I want but I didn't expect anything less. Waiting for her to be ready is the slowest but best form of torture, and after waiting twenty years, I can wait as long as she needs.

"I should get back to Russ." She steps back with a heated look cast my way that pushes my resolve to its max, and almost has me saying 'fuck it'.

I want to show her all the reasons we shouldn't wait. With my tongue in her mouth, over her skin, against her breasts. I want to create circles more torturous than the ones I traced with my thumb on her wrist, over the place I know will guarantee an ending for her that fucking Fitzgerald was too selfish to achieve.

"Sam …"

"Yes?"

"Stop looking at me like that."

"Like what?"

She smiles sweetly, but what comes out of her mouth next is anything but sweet. "Like you want to fuck me senseless against the wall."

My mouth parts and I struggle to come up with a response. She smiles again, more of a smirk. "Like I thought."

I drag a hand down my face and groan. "You're killing me, Red."

"Wait," she says, her expression turning serious. "There's something else I wanted to talk about."

"Go on." I shove my hands in the pockets of my jeans, suddenly feeling uncomfortable, hoping there isn't anything bad coming my way.

"I really do want to help you." She's referring to what she witnessed before we came down here. Me being unable to sing in front of her for a second time.

"Do you not have enough going on?" She frowns at my response. "Soph, this isn't me thinking you can't help me, it's me saying you don't need to. When would you find time?" When she can't give me an answer, I give her a reassuring smile. "I know what this is to do with and that you want to help, but you don't need to. You don't owe me anything."

"I really should get back to Russ," she replies, disgruntled. I sigh and start to follow her back up to The Wreck. We're almost at the top when she turns around abruptly, and I almost slam into the back of her. She towers over me with determination in her eyes. "I *am* going to help you. I promise. And it's not because I feel like I owe you. It's because I want to. I'll find a way to make this right."

Chapter Twenty-Three

Sam

Ryan's idea for band practice to fill my time with Russ works great on the first day, but doesn't solve my issue for the rest of the week. Tuesday morning disappears, and then it's midday. I still don't have a clue what I'm going to do with Russ, so I pull out my phone and text Aunt Rachel.

> Me: *What do you do with kids?*
> Rachel: *Kind of vague. Need a bit more clarification.*

I smile at the text. Only she'd use such a long word in a message.

> Me: *I'm looking after a kid, and I don't know what to do with him.*
> Rachel: *Is this kid called Russ?*

Her message makes me pause, then I realize she'd obviously know about Russ. After all, she's been neighbors with The Parkers forever, and is one of Sophie's mom's close friends.

Me: *Yeah.*

Rachel: *You could take him to the park. For ice cream. Does he like games?*

An idea hits me.

Me: *Genius. Thanks, Rach.*
Rachel: *Love you. Good luck.*

A few hours later, I'm waiting for Russ outside the school gates. The bell rings and my pulse picks up as kids flood out, some to the school buses, some to their parents, others to the waiting cars parked along the roadside.

Russ is one of the last kids to come out and, unlike yesterday, he doesn't look excited to see me. His movements are slow, his face tilted down at the ground and shoulders slumped. He looks sad.

"Hey," I say when he finally makes it in front of me.

"Hi," he says quietly, without looking up.

Fuck. I don't know what I'm doing. I thought things were getting better. Then, I remember everything Sophie told me and feel like an idiot. I know better than anyone that unfortunately someone doesn't come along with a magic wand, wave it and then everything's better. Things aren't going to get easier for a long time. There are going to be ups and downs.

I drop down to my knees, reach over, and give his hand a squeeze. "Want to go do something fun?"

He looks up, his browns drawn into a small frown. "I have homework."

293

"First week doesn't count." He looks uncertain. "Plus, summer starts soon." His lips twitch, and knowing I've got him, I hold up my hand and whisper behind it, "Everyone knows the last couple of weeks don't count. Come on."

He giggles, and my chest feels warm. I jump back up and take his bag from him.

"Where are we going?" he asks, as we start walking hand-in-hand along the sidewalk.

"I thought we could go buy some games for your console. There's a new one out I think you might like."

His face drops and I wrack my brain, trying to figure out what I've said wrong.

"I don't like games."

"Huh. Okay. What do you like?"

He stops walking, and I watch him as he thinks about his answer. "Boats." He thinks again. "And singing. I really love going with Sophie to The Pa—" His eyes widen as if he's caught himself saying something he shouldn't.

As much as I want to probe, I want to make sure he's happy and we have a great time together more. Pulling out my phone, I hold a finger in the air, signaling for Russ to wait while I do a couple of quick Google searches, finding what I need. Luck's on my side and my couple of ideas could definitely work, but I don't want to do something without Sophie's permission, so I pull out my phone and call her.

"Hey," she answers. "Is everything okay?"

"Fine," I reply, then hold up a finger to my lips, motioning for Russ to keep quiet with what I say next. "So, Russ doesn't have any homework …" I wink, and he giggles. "I was wondering if you mind me keeping him out late? I know it's a school night, but there's something I think he might like." Russ's eyes widen and he looks more excited than when I told him he was coming to band practice, when I say, "It's a surprise."

"Actually," says Sophie, and for a second, I think she's going to say no. "A couple of new clients have signed on today, and Sooz is stressing."

"Sooz is not stressing," shouts Sooz in the background, sounding stressed.

"I could do with helping her, so that would work perfect if I can work late."

"Great."

"You're sure you don't mind?"

Russ tugs on my hand eagerly. Seeing him happy again does funny things to me. It makes me feel happy—lighter. "I don't mind at all."

"I don't know what I'd do without you," Sophie says, ending the call before I get a chance to reply that she'll never have to know, because I'm not going anywhere.

"Come on," I say, sliding my phone back into the pocket of my pants.

"Where are we going?" asks Russ, bouncing as we walk.

"Manhattan," I reply, and he almost pulls my arm out of its socket.

"A boat?" Russ screeches, catching sight of the Liberty Cruise boat as we hurry along South Street Drive toward the pier.

"Not if you don't hurry up," I laugh.

"My legs are tired," he whines, his pace slowing, even though I have a feeling this will be the equivalent of Christmas for him if we make it.

I can see a guy taking everyone's tickets and the line getting shorter. There's only five minutes until the boat is due to depart on the hour, and there's no way we're missing this. Russ's cackles can probably be heard for miles when I grab him, throw him over my shoulder, and race toward the boat. Lactic acid pools in my muscles and I think my legs are going to give way, but Russ's laughter is what keeps me driving forward, smiling so hard my face hurts.

We make it just in time and I set Russ down, bending over and panting as sweat drips down my temples, drying instantly under the blazing late afternoon sun. "Fuck, I'm so out of shape." Russ snickers, and I realize the mistake I've made, again. "Don't repeat that word."

"Grams says it all the time."

"Grams needs her mouth stitching shut," I say under my breath, then turn to the guy waiting at the gate. I hand over some cash. "Two, please."

When we have our tickets, we make our way onto the boat. I watch Russ in amusement as we stand in line to get the complimentary refreshments. He's so excited taking in every part of the boat that his head almost turns three hundred and sixty degrees.

"A cookie!" he screeches when we get to the front. "We get a cookie?! This is awesome!"

The woman serving behind the counter laughs at him when he starts to do a dance and slips an extra one in the bag with a wink. Russ looks like he's about to pass out from overstimulation. "I wish everyone got as excited as you about the cookies," she laughs and I mouth a 'thank you' as Russ darts off to the front of the boat.

Twenty minutes in, when he's eaten all three cookies, drunk his soda, and finally calmed down, I decide to probe about his day. We both stand, watching The Statue of Liberty getting larger as the boat slices through the almost-still water, with the Manhattan skyline shrinking behind us.

"How was your second day at school?"

"Fine," Russ replies quietly.

The shift I feel in his mood, despite what we're doing, tells me it wasn't.

"You can talk to me about anything, buddy. You know that, right?"

His brows furrow. "They were playing guns and shooting."

"Who was?" I ask carefully.

"Some boys. I've forgot their names." He stubs his toe against the ground, focusing on the movement as he does. "Guns killed my mom and dad."

Thank God I have Liberty's giant face to focus on as I process what he's just said, like it's nothing.

I lower my voice when a couple approaches the front of the boat.

"Guns?" I all but whisper for confirmation. I'm not sure why, because deep down, I already know the answer.

A couple of tears wet his cheeks. "Liam made me watch when he played them. He laughed and said it was them."

"Is that why you don't like games?" Russ nods. Without thinking, I drop to my knees and pull him into me as he starts to shake. "Was Liam at your old house?"

He nods against my shoulder and the damp material of my shirt rubs against my skin. "I don't like Liam. He was always mean and hurt me. Why? I didn't do nothing."

My heart cracks down the middle as I try to give him an answer I don't really know myself. "Some people aren't taught how to be kind."

Russ pulls back, and his brown eyes shine as they find mine. "Who taught you to be kind?"

I swallow hard and give him what he needs. The truth. "My Aunt Rachel and Uncle Matt."

He watches me intently, taking in my answer. "You don't have a mom or dad?"

"No."

"Are they dead?"

"Yeah," I reply, keeping my answer simple. "They are."

He doesn't need to know the ins and outs. Doesn't need to hear about the arguing. How Mom left and might as well be. How Dad did everything he could to make up for her walking out without even a goodbye. How he always made sure we had the best birthdays. How on one of Shaun's, he was killed in a car accident while he was picking up the cake.

All Russ needs to know is that, in his world, where it might feel like he's different, there's someone at his side who's the same. Who knows. Who gets it. Someone who understands what it feels like to be alone. Someone who understands what it's like to wonder if you'll ever have a home again. Someone who understands what it's like to be an orphan.

He buries himself into my chest again. "I don't want to go back. It's scary there. I want to stay with you and Sophie."

"I know you do, buddy," I whisper, rubbing his back as the boat turns and heads in the direction of the Brooklyn Bridge. "I know."

Russ grips my hand tight as he stares at the rainbow in front of us.

"Anything?" he asks.

"Yeah. Whatever you want."

His eyes widen, and we walk over to the giant candy wall. I grab a bag and hand it to him, then he moves to the blue tube. He glances over his shoulder uncertainly, and I nod, pushing out the implications of all the E numbers he's about to consume. Sophie can deal with that later. Our sole purpose right now, and after everything he told me, is to have fun.

He spends the next ten minutes filling the bag with candy of every color, and when we've paid, we leave M&Ms World behind, battling the throngs of people making Times Square virtually impossible to move through.

"Where are we going?" Russ shouts over a group of drummers we pass by.

"It's a surprise." A surprise I need to thank John West for in the morning, after he pulled strings I never would have access to on such short notice.

Ten minutes later, Russ tilts his head back and takes in his surprise. His face literally lights up from the flashing signs above us. "Singing! Yessss." He does a quick air punch and then races inside.

"Broadway," I call after him, laughing, ready to immerse myself in three hours of pink and all things *Hairspray*.

Chapter Twenty-Four
Sophie

Declaring to Sam that I was going to do whatever I could to help him wasn't the smartest idea I've ever had.

It's been over three days of him doing the school drop off and pick-up, basically whatever he can to make my life easier, and I don't have a clue how to help. There's not even a spark to ignite an idea.

It's Thursday evening, post-work and dinner, when I decide a trip home might help. Russ is more than on-board with the promise of another late bedtime and a chance of seeing his partner in cussing crime, Grams. Dressed in more suitable clothing for the humidity, we step outside and start the twenty-minute walk to my parent's place.

Five minutes into the journey, I pull off my red and gray checkered shirt, mentally high-fiving myself for remembering to wear a white vest underneath. I'm already sweating buckets, even with our pace set to an amble. Damn heatwave. There's nothing wavey about it. No peaks or breaks. New York in the summer is one giant sweat box. This one, in particular, has felt like a long slog and we're only at the beginning.

All the way, Russ chatters about the Broadway show Sam took him to and the S.C.A.R.A.B. practice he attended. The other main topic he keeps coming back to is, of course, whether he will get to The Parkapellas one tomorrow. I have to tell him twice that his attendance is dependent on how school goes the following day, to which I receive a disgruntled look.

By the time we reach my childhood home, my hair's plastered to the back of my neck. I stand at the bottom of the steps leading up to the house with Russ's hand in mine, staring at the yellow front door that's welcomed me since the day my parents brought me home from the hospital to my siblings. This moment isn't what I expected it to be—my first time going in with my child, which I guess Russ is. It's monumental and messy. I raise my other hand, shielding my eyes as the sun reflects off the paint, making the shade all the more blinding.

Noise filters out into the street. Shouting, singing, and then the sound of a guitar. I smile to myself, taking in the open windows. Dad definitely isn't home, because if he was, they'd all be closed. It's been a battle between him and my mom since they had air conditioning fitted throughout the house and it's the same with the car, making any long journey more painful than it needs to be. Dad is adamant there's no point in having the air conditioning running if they're open. Mom opens the windows any chance she gets, stating she prefers the fresh air. Ironic, considering there's nothing fresh about it in Brooklyn. One Sunday, they spent the whole day going between every room in the house, opening and closing them, just to piss each other off.

A loud clatter from inside the house that sounds like drums is our signal to go in. I make slow work of the steps, heat exhaustion threatening to take over. Russ's pace struggles to keep up with mine. When I swing the front door open and we step inside, I decide Dad's right. The sound of the air conditioning battling to keep the heat at bay greets us, but with all the windows open, the air is sticky, and I start to sweat more than when I was walking.

The front door clicks shut behind us, and on cue, my mom bustles into the entryway, fanning her face. The floor length boho dress she's wearing—a shade of yellow that matches the front door—swirls around her legs. "Damn heat."

"You could close the windows. That would solve the problem," I say, wiping the back of my neck. When I bring it away, I find my hand glistening. Sexy.

"Now, where would be the fun in that?" Mom muses, pulling me into her side and placing a swift kiss against my temple. "Glad to see the black has disappeared."

"You noticed that, huh?" I reply offhand.

"I'm your mother. I notice everything. Sweetie, you're far too colorful to be settling for something so bland." She isn't just referring to my recent choices of clothing. After letting go of me, she crouches, almost at eye level with the small, dark-haired person who's clutching my hand so hard it's painful. "Hi Russ. I'm happy you're here." She gives him a warm smile and when I glance down, I find him smiling back.

Mom stands back to full height and makes her way to the kitchen. "How's the album coming along?" I watch for a falter in her steps, but it never comes.

"Fine," she says absentmindedly over her shoulder as she continues walking.

Russ and I follow her into the kitchen. When she reaches the range cooker, she stirs something in a pan before turning back. I watch as she reaches into a ceramic pot filled with one of her herb concoctions, grabbing a handful and dumping it in the pan. The smell that fills the room makes me wrinkle my nose and I realize why the windows are open. Mom likes to pretend she's a connoisseur in the kitchen, but her cooking is as wild as her fashion and personality, and unfortunately, a little harder to stomach.

"You're lying," I say, smelling her deceit more so than her awful cooking.

"I want you to promise me two things before I respond," she says, grabbing a spoon.

I give her a hard stare as Russ shifts at my side, bored. "That depends on what those two things are."

Spinning around, she waves the spoon full of whatever it is she's making in the air. Something flies off and lands on the countertop, missing me by an inch, if that. "Number one. You draw the line under wearing all that ridiculous black clothing." She visibly shudders. "Two. In the future, when something's wrong, you talk to me about it rather than what you have been doing."

Tilting my head, I wonder how much she can possibly have picked up on when she and Dad spend sixty percent of each year touring. "Which is?"

"Hiding."

"I've not been hiding," I grumble, letting go of Russ's hand and grabbing a cloth to clean the countertop. "I don't need to."

"Is that so?"

Inhaling, I set the cloth down, along with my gaze. "Want to go find Xavier?" I ask Russ. He nods eagerly and scurries away. When he's gone, my eyes settle on my mom's brown ones. They're unusual, not dark like chocolate—they're lighter, richer. When she's excited, they almost look amber, clashing perfectly with her red hair and golden skin.

"Mom …" I bite my lip, unsure whether to give her the truth; truths I've told no one.

"You can't hurt me, Sophie," she says, reading my mind. "Whatever it is you're feeling, it can't hurt any more than watching my daughter not living her life to its fullest and not being true to herself."

I look around, taking in our kitchen, which hasn't changed one bit over the years. It's filled with an odd mix of Chinese lanterns hanging from the ceiling and mosaic covered ceramics, along with other random trinkets Mom has picked up from all over the world, scattered around.

"Mom, no one cares who I really am, or what I'm doing, unless I'm screwing up my life in one way or another."

"Is this about what happened in Berlin?"

"Maybe." Basically, a big fat yes. It's definitely what started this all. "I've not been hiding. I've just been … behaving."

She purses her lips. "Technically, you haven't been behaving, because you managed to get yourself and your *grandmother* arrested. She's got to eighty-six without a criminal record, and now she's got a mug shot."

I choose not to point out that Grams could totally be a criminal all on her own, but more of the mastermind kind. The reason she's never been caught out before is because she's too damn clever and spins everything in the exact way she needs to.

304

"It was her choice to turn up," I say. "She knew what she was getting into."

"Which was?" Mom watches me, waiting for my version of the story.

"A chance to fight for what's right. Russ was at risk. More than at risk." With my confidence building, I keep going. "Those marks on his face? They're not dirt or whatever people try to convince themselves they are when they see him. They're bruises, Mom.

"He's a seven-year-old child, and he's covered in bruises and scars." Her gaze drops. She can't even look me in the eye with the cold hard truth sitting in front of her. "Tell me, if you'd been there—seen what I did—that you wouldn't have done the same."

"You know you've always made us proud, right? But recently, the choices you've made, they've proved how strong you are."

"Thanks, M—"

On a roll, she cuts me off. "Apart from that guy. What's his name? Starts with a 'B'. From the Fitzgerald family."

"Brendan Fitzgerald," I tell her, because there's no point in lying.

"You might have made good choices recently, but he wasn't one of them. What do they call them in England? Banking wank—"

"Mom!" I cut her off before she finishes, partly out of fear of Russ adding another word to his long list if he's close by and hears her. "How do you know about him?"

"Eyes and ears everywhere." She winks and walks over, stopping directly in front of me. "Sweetie, fuck what everyone thinks. Be unforgivingly you and everything you were made to be. Leave a mark on this world and people's lives that's impossible to erase."

"Is that what you do?"

"Your father and I do it together with our music." Mom's eyes search my face. "You have a beautiful voice. It would be a shame for the world not to hear it."

"Mom ..."

Too many times we've had this conversation. Our family is made up of creatives, in every sense of the word. A mix of artists and musicians. It seems to be the Parker calling. The Parkapellas are as far as I've ever been willing to go.

The drumming from before I entered the house starts up again from above. Russ will be in his element watching him play. Him being my youngest brother—the one yet to graduate high school, A.K.A Xavier. Drumming is his new passion and Ryan, S.C.A.R.A.B.'s drummer, regularly comes over to give him lessons. Something only I know.

Mom says Xavier was the best fortieth surprise she could have asked for. Meanwhile, Dad almost had a hernia when he found out she was pregnant. Now, none of us could imagine life without him, but at the time, it was totally gross. Zoe and Abby snickered about it for weeks after I broke the news. My older sister, Aurelia, gagged any time Mom and Dad were in the room together and the eldest of our gang, my brother, Hale, refused to look them in the eye for the whole nine months.

Mom shakes her head at the ceiling. "We're looking into soundproofing. Your father tried to convince him to go for electronic ones, but he was adamant he wanted the real experience. That boy is a force to be reckoned with. Anyway, back to you. Why does singing need to have a purpose? Why can't you just do it for the enjoyment?"

"I want to do more with my life, Mom. I feel like I barely know who I am."

She reaches up and grabs my blonde locks, which I've been bleaching since I turned thirteen. "Probably because you've spent forever worrying about people's opinions of you and let it shape your choices. Just don't give a damn. Do you."

"Because it's that easy when the media plaster our mistakes everywhere for the world to see," I huff.

Mom's hand drops, and she looks at me sadly. "I won't apologize for the life your father and I have created for you all. We have our own dreams, too. But what I will apologize for are the actions and unkind words of others, which you've taken the brunt of. The world would be a much happier place if everyone spent less time judging. Who cares if you don't have your shit figured out by the time you're thirty or sixty? Who cares if you never do? Life isn't about having two-point-five kids and a white picket fence. Being unique and going to the beat of your own drum is what makes it exciting and worth getting up for each day."

Her words resonate somewhere deep inside me, just like she intends them to. This conversation has been a long time coming and the way her eyes sparkle at the end of her little speech tells me that she's happy she's got it all off her chest.

I'm about to ask her how she's managed to hide away for two weeks, when she says with a smile, "So, tell me about Sam."

"How do you …"

"Hey, sis," comes Hale's familiar voice from behind, interrupting me before I can figure out exactly what she knows.

Too lost in my conversation with Mom, I didn't hear him come through the front door. I turn and find eyes like our mom's staring down at me. His dark hair is longer than the last time we saw each other. My siblings and I are a mash up of our parents, although I'm the odd one out. Where the other three have our mom's eyes and dad's dark hair, I have our dad's dark blue eyes and, when I don't bleach it, mom's auburn hair. Hers never seems to gray. She says she's an earth mother and doesn't dye it, but I'm not convinced.

"Hey, you," I reply, unable to hide my smile. I might feel overshadowed by family who give meaning to the word 'bold', but I love them dearly—just like my best friends.

Hale wrinkles his nose in the same way I did a couple of minutes ago. "What the fuck is that smell?"

I snicker, and Mom rolls her eyes before walking back over to the pan containing the offensive liquid. "Language."

"You cuss more than Grams," Hale scoffs.

Aurelia appears at my side. I follow her lead and we air kiss in the way she has declared is her thing, then she throws her dark dreads over one shoulder.

The front door slams, and Mom straightens.

Dad's voice drifts through to us all. "Why is the air conditioning on when all the windows are open?"

Mom beams, rubbing her hands together, waiting for him to come into the kitchen.

Aurelia groans. "Seriously, no window foreplay, please. Remember how Xavier made his way into the world?"

"Unfortunately, my ovaries are past their sell by date," replies Mom.

Grams is the next one to enter, from a door off to the side. "I read an article just yesterday about a sixty-year-old woman giving birth to twins."

Aurelia makes a gagging noise at my side at the same time Dad appears through the other door to the kitchen with Xavier and Russ.

"What's that smell?" asks Xavier, eyeing the range top. "If that's dinner, I'm ordering pizza."

Russ's eyes widen in excitement. We haven't eaten pizza in almost a week after I laid down some veggie ground rules.

"Jesus, did I put out a war cry when I stepped through the front door?" I ask, looking around at all of my family members. It's a miracle we can fit in the same room. Abby thinks she has problems because her mom's a sex columnist, but at least there's only one. I have a whole clan of misfits to deal with.

"It's this," says Mom, gesturing to the pan. "My new family homing beacon. It's all in the herbs."

"Mom," says Hale, his voice more serious than I've ever heard it before. "If you want us to stick around, I strongly suggest that you don't cook."

"I built you off home-cooked meals," she replies, narrowing her eyes and daring him to say otherwise.

"Actually, that was Grams," states Aurelia.

Mom looks to Dad for help. He holds up his hands. "No comment. I just want either the windows closed or the air conditioning turned off."

Ignoring him, Mom turns to me. "So, what were we saying about Sam?"

"Sammy Sam?" asks Aurelia, brightening. She's had a soft spot for him ever since he moved in next door.

"I want to help him," I finally answer Mom, "but I don't have any idea where to start."

"Lovely boy," says Grams, maneuvering herself onto one of the kitchen stools with ease. I swear the woman is a carthorse and more agile than I am. "What's wrong with him?"

"He fucking bottled it on stage," snickers Xavier, stopping when Dad gives him *the look* while covering Russ's ears.

"What does bottled mean?" asks Russ, and I groan.

"It means he choked," explains Xavier, beaming down at him. I need to keep an eye on this situation. I love my brother, but he could be as bad an influence as Grams. "Here. See for yourselves." He brings up a video on his phone and my family, including Russ. All watch Sam, standing on stage, looking helpless. "Pussy." Xavier snickers again, and I clout him around the head. "Hey, that hurt." He pulls away, taking his phone with him and rubbing where my hand made contact.

"I don't know what to do. How to help," I say.

"You need to get to the nitty gritty of it," Grams replies.

"Nitty gritty?"

She rolls her eyes, as if the answer is obvious. "Where it all started."

"Duh," adds on Xavier. This time, Mom clouts him around the head. Yeah, he's definitely not spending any more time with Russ than is necessary.

I look at my mom and dad. "Have you ever had imposter syndrome?"

"No," replies my mom, at the same time Dad says, "Yes."

"I don't believe in it," says Mom, when I focus my attention on her first.

"Of course, you don't," I reply, then turn to Dad.

Mom opens her mouth to say something else, but Dad speaks first. "I suffer from it most days."

My brows shoot up. "Seriously?" He nods. "I never took you for being uncertain."

He winks. "I have a good game face."

"There has to be more to getting over it than that. Give me something I can work with."

He chuckles and pulls my mom into his side. "Every time it rears its ugly head, I ask myself if I could live without music, and the answer is always no. Sometimes, I have to delve deeper when it really tries to get a grip."

"What do you do?"

"I ask myself what I would do if I couldn't sing anymore."

"What's the answer?" I ask, voicing the question of everyone in the room, listening on tenterhooks.

He pauses, then says, "I'd do nothing. Singing is who I am. No matter how scary things get and no matter how much self-doubt creeps in … it's me and I am it. When you find what you're meant to do in life, there is no one or the other, you merge, and it makes you who you are. A bit like when you find your person. Even if they do waste money running the air conditioning with the windows open." He looks down dotingly on my mom, and she smiles back at him with the same amount of love in her eyes.

I clear my throat. "What would you do if you were me?"

Dad looks back over at me. "I'd remind Sam why he sings. Not for the accolades, but for the love of it."

Mom grins and says to him, "Remember when we took that first trip?"

"What trip?" I ask, looking from one to the other.

Ignoring my question, Dad chuckles. "That was a great trip."

"Are you going to tell us about it, or just keep saying how great it was?" asks Aurelia with a huff.

"We did a music tour," Dad replies.

I shake my head. "Yeah, I don't think that would help. Sam can't sing as it is."

"Not that kind of tour," says Dad. "We went and found music anywhere we could. We went right back to our rock and roll roots, so to speak."

Russ raises his hand in the air and the room goes silent.

"Yeah, buddy?" I say, encouraging him to speak.

"Why doesn't he go to The Parkapellas?"

"Sam doesn't want to go to The Parkapellas," I laugh. Everyone in the room gives me a blank stare, as if to say why wouldn't he. "He's a rockstar."

"He sings," says Russ, straight to the point, and I start to understand what he's getting at.

"Maybe it will do you *both* good to go back to your roots," comments Grams.

I narrow my eyes in her direction, willing her to, for once, keep her mouth shut and not announce to everyone something only she knows. Thankfully, she doesn't say anything else.

"You could be right," I say to Russ, as an idea sparks to life. I switch off from everyone, focusing my attention solely on him. "You really think he'd like it there?"

Russ nods eagerly. "I love it. So do you. Why wouldn't he?"

Self-doubt creeps in. It's a big wall to let down to let Sam see into this part of my life; the part I've kept from everyone who doesn't attend.

I know what my family is thinking. That I haven't told anyone because I'm embarrassed by The Parkapellas. Admittedly, to those who only know me at face value or through my social media rep, it would probably come as a

312

shock what I'm doing on the side. But it's not embarrassment, not even close. It's fear someone will turn around, laugh, and say I'm not the right person for the job.

I've never wanted to be the right person for a job more than I want to be for this one.

The Parkapellas, every single one of them, have a small piece of my heart. One of my fears when we started it all was that, with everything I gave, and what those who came to the rehearsals took from me, there would be nothing left at the end. But that's the thing about doing something you love with people you care about, it's just that—love. Whatever you give to it, it gives back in return, and over the years, my heart has kept on growing with our successes, so there's always more ready to be given.

The Parkapellas have been the part of my life the world hasn't been able to ruin. I've kept them close to my chest, cherished and protected them, terrified of what would happen if anyone found out and I lost them all.

It's not me feeling The Parkapellas aren't good enough to tell people about, it's me feeling completely inadequate and undeserving of them.

"I guess I could bring him along. See if he likes it."

Russ beams. "He could come to the competition!"

This is getting out of hand. Sam isn't even aware of anything yet and Russ is already planning out his travel itinerary.

"How about we take it one step at a—"

"I think it's a good idea," says Mom, interrupting me before I can stop Russ's overactive imagination going wild.

So much for locking shit down. Russ jumps up and down excitedly, more than I've seen him do, like ever, which is why I don't have it in me to say no.

"Sure," I say quietly, ignoring the feelings of dread taking over. "Let's just hope Sam is on board."

"Why wouldn't he be?" laughs Aurelia, an evil glint in her eye. "All his favorite people are going to be there."

"Even me," says Xavier, oblivious to the fact she's already speaking about him.

"And me," says Grams, spooning some of whatever Mom has made into a bowl, unphased that it smells like cow shit.

Great. This is going to be great.

Just in case the competition isn't going to be nerve-wracking enough, now Sam is going to be there, too. And what would this whole quest be without my family there, prying in ways only they know how?

Chapter Twenty-Five

Sam

It's almost five thirty PM, and Sophie still hasn't put in a food request for our usual Friday plans. I'm starting to panic.

Maybe I pushed things too far the other day outside of The Wreck? I thought it was what she needed, to have her eyes opened to what's been sitting in front of her all along, to really feel everything we could be. Now, I wish I hadn't tried.

I'm sitting in the living area with Ryan, sulking while he watches re-runs of Jackass, when my phone chimes. I snatch it up faster than if someone offered me a million dollars, while Ryan snorts into his bowl of Apple Jacks at something on the screen.

"That her?" he asks, not taking his eyes off the TV as he slurps murky-colored milk from the bowl.

"Yep," I respond, unlocking my phone.

Soph: *Can you meet me?*

My fingers become a blur as I text back.

Me: *Everything ok? No feast night?*
Soph: *Not tonight. So, can you?*

A lump forms in my throat. I definitely pushed her too far, and it feels like she's about to tell me exactly what she thinks about it. There's no point avoiding the inevitable, so I reply.

Me: *Sure. Where?*

I frown when she sends me an address. What the hell is she up to?

"Going out?" Ryan asks when I stand.

"Yeah."

"Cool. See ya later."

If I weren't so focused on what's going on with Sophie, I'd be more concerned by the fact he's barely said a word all night. Ryan loves the sound of his own voice and has been uncharacteristically quiet for the past two days. I don't have time to hash it out with him though, because Sophie's given me barely any notice to meet her.

Almost half an hour later, I find myself outside an unusually deserted Music Hall of Williamsburg. The building seems different without the crowds of people and paps swarming around it. After a second glance up and down the street, I still don't see any sign of Sophie, so I pull out my phone and message her.

Here. Where are you?

Three dots appear, and almost immediately, her reply comes through.

Come inside.

My brows furrow as I stare up at the Art Déco building. The night we performed here, it felt like the end of everything we've worked for. I swallow down the memories and push one of the doors. Finding it's unlocked, I slip inside and move through the entryway and toward the main hall.

Only the stage lights are on, which is why I don't see Sophie spread out across the middle of the floor until it's too late. Falling over her, I hit the ground hard. She giggles when I grunt.

I sit up and stretch my legs out in front of me. "Thanks for that."

"You should have been looking where you were going," she laughs.

"Soph, what are you doing?" I ask when it hits me that we're still on the floor.

"Lay back and see."

There's something in her voice, a playfulness that makes me smile, and my chest, which has felt tight for the past few hours, loosens. Doing as she says, I lay back and take in the plain white ceiling and lights.

"It's a ceiling."

She giggles again, and I turn my head to the side to look at her, watching as a peaceful expression covers her face when she closes her eyes and takes a deep breath. I want to ask why she's wearing a garish paisley headscarf, but decide to wait.

"Close your eyes." I drag my gaze away from her and close them like she says. "Walls don't just make a building.

317

They hold people's memories and experiences. Good and bad."

She lingers on the final word and a vision of me standing on stage with no one around creeps into my mind. Mom and Dad appear, waiting to hear me sing for the first time. Each time I open my mouth to try, nothing comes out. I bolt upright, sucking in as much air as I can, but nothing helps.

Sophie's arm falls around me, breaking through the anxiety threatening to swallow me whole.

"Tell me what you're thinking." Her voice is like a balm, and with the next breath I take, oxygen fills my lungs. I start to relax but refuse to look at her, humiliation taking over. When I don't say anything, Sophie pulls her arm away. "Sam, if I'm going to stand a chance of helping, you have to talk to me."

"I didn't ask for your help. You volunteered all on your own," I bite back, regretting it instantly. "Sorry. It's just … I'm embarrassed, Soph," I admit, glad for the dim lighting.

She reaches over, grabs my hand, and squeezes. Where she's touching warms and I feel my thoughts slipping into the gutter as I forget what we're talking about. All I know is I want her to keep touching me, everywhere.

Sneaking a look to the side, I really take her in, chuckling to myself again at the scarf she's wearing around her head.

"Are you auditioning for *Grease* or something?" I ask, moving the subject to lighter territory. She looks confused, so I gesture at her head. "The scarf. Is it a new look Zoe's trialing on you?"

She blushes furiously. "I finished work super early to make sure I could pick up Russ. I guess I had too much time on my hands, because I did a thing." She bites down on her bottom lip and my dick throbs.

I stare at the scarf, trying to stop my mind from wandering. "What kind of thing?"

"I thought it was going to be an empowering kind of thing," she says quickly on an exhale. "Now, I'm regretting it."

"Are you going to show me?" She looks down. "Hey," I say, dipping my head to try to catch her eye. "What's going on?"

She clambers to her feet and makes a show of dusting off her dress. "You'll laugh."

"I can't laugh if you don't show me," I say, standing myself.

"Exactly."

She shuffles back, and my pulse picks up with the challenge. There's no way I'm letting her get away without showing me what she's done.

"You're seriously doing this?" I smirk, matching her step for step.

"Yep."

"Okay, fine." I stop and hold up my hands, feigning defeat. "If you don't want me to see whatever it is you've done, then I won't ask again."

The second her body relaxes. I dart forward and my hand snaps out. I go to grasp the material and pull it away, stopped when Sophie grabs my hand.

I'm too stunned to move and remain frozen on the spot when her lips smash against mine.

Sophie pulls back, a weird mix of mortification and heat taking over her face.

"Y-you kissed me?" I stammer.

"I …"

She bites down on her lip again, and I lose what little control I have left. She's already played her card. I'm done holding back.

My hand snakes around her waist. My palm flattens against her back. I pull her in. This time when our lips collide, I make sure it steals her breath in the right way. My mouth moves against hers and I pour twenty years of wanting her into what should have been our first kiss.

She's hesitant and her lips move slowly, like her brain is struggling to catch up with what's happening.

The gentleman, best friend side of me says to take it slow, let her adjust.

There's no room for friendship here, because I've never wanted to just be her friend. I've *always* wanted more, and I'm determined to make it clear in every way I can.

Somewhere between my hand bunching the material at her back and my tongue sliding against hers, I remember how we got to this point. She's hiding something and I want to know what.

While she's distracted, I slowly move my hand—the one that isn't grappling with her dress—up her arm toward the paisley monstrosity she's hiding behind. I ghost the tips of my fingers against the goosebumps covering her skin. When my hand wraps around her neck, her pulse races beneath my thumb. I pull her hips into me, knowing she'll feel exactly how desperate for her I am. If I didn't have something else on my mind, I'd be trying my luck at taking her on the floor, so she can stare up at the ceiling she's weirdly fascinated by with a new kind of awe.

Before she can realize what I'm doing, I grab the material and pull it away. Her hair spills out and I move back so I can see what was so important to keep from me that she bulldozed through the barrier of our friendship.

I blink.

It clearly hasn't registered what I've done when Sophie gives me a lazy, heated look. "What?"

"Red …" I gawp.

She moves onto her tiptoes and against my lips, says, "Why do you call me that?"

It kills me pushing her away, but with both hands resting on her shoulders, I do.

"Your hair. It's … red."

She quickly figures out what I'm referring to when her eyes drop to the material in my hands that should still be covering her hair. It's out of my grip and she's storming to the side of the room to gather her things in a second.

I chase after her, knowing I've screwed up. I wouldn't change what I did, regardless. I'd do it again to see what I have.

"I hate you right now, Sam Riley," she snaps, picking up her bag.

"Is that so?"

With narrowed eyes, she looks up, and I swallow hard.

Fuck, I love her. I love her blonde. I love her red. I really fucking love it when she's angry with me, because her lips go all pouty and I start to imagine what they'd look like around my di—.

Suddenly, the space in front of me is empty.

"Soph!" I call, powering beneath the balconies that line each side of the room. Red silky locks flowing out behind her in the dark space add fuel to my movements. I catch up after four long, purposeful strides. "Stop!"

"Not until you stop laughing at me!" She spins around and stares at where my hand is wrapped around her arm.

"I'm not laughing at you, I swear. I missed the red."

"Sure." She laughs. "Like you even remember it."

An image of her sitting on my aunt and uncle's couch, her hair the exact shade it is now, flashes through my mind. The sound of her voice filling the Brooklyn sky each night for years reaches my ears.

"The first time you dyed it, we were thirteen."

"Another thing you know?" she quips, anger still swirling in her eyes.

"Yeah …"

"Right."

I decide to push a different way. "Want to know what I don't know?"

"What?" she sasses. "There are things you actually *don't* know?"

"I don't know why you kissed me."

Sophie rolls her eyes. "I think it's pretty obvious why one person kisses another."

I drop my hand away from her arm. "Maybe. But I want to hear it from *you*. The ball is still in your court, Red. Tell me why you kissed me."

She shifts her weight between her feet. Stares. "I want you, too."

"Oh, really?" I shove my hands into my pockets and the corners of my mouth twitch.

Everyone's always seen me as the joker. The truth is, I find enjoyment in every aspect of life. I have since things started to get better after losing my parents. People always assume hitting rock bottom is the worst. Sure, it's fucking horrific, but the thing is, when you get there, anything after that point feels incredible. You learn to cherish it all. Every single moment. No matter how small. They all become significant.

And I'm cherishing this moment right now, watching Sophie squirm.

"I—"

She watches me, bemused, when I slide into a chair, stretch my legs out in front of me and cross my ankles.

"I've got all night."

"I want you."

"You already said that. I think …" I uncross my ankles, lean forward, clasp my hands together and rest my elbows on my knees. "… I need more."

Her eyes widen. "More?"

I nod. "I want it all. Tell me what's going on under that pretty red hair."

She sucks in a sharp breath. Neither of us looks away when she walks toward me, only stopping when the tips of her low-rise Converse touch my Vans.

"I think …" she mimics, lifting the hand that isn't still clutching her bag and strokes the side of my face. She stops at my jaw, tracing a path back and forth through my stubble, thoughtfully. "I think that I've always wanted you. I just didn't know it."

"Tell me what you want, Red." I tilt my head back and hold her gaze. "*Please.*"

I need it spelled out. I need to know that if, when we do this, it's because she wants it, too.

In the darkness, I catch the movement in her throat when she swallows.

She leans in, and right before her lips press against mine, she stops, hovers, and says, "I want you to kiss me." She steps closer, drops down and straddles my lap. "I want you to fuck me," she murmurs against my ear with a slight roll of her hips. The tip of her nose skims my neck. "I want you to do whatever you want with me." Finally, she pulls back and all I see in her bright blue eyes is clarity. "I just want you to do it with me, Sam. Only me."

There's a loud thud as her bag hits the ground.

"Red …" I rasp.

A small yelp echoes off the walls when I thrust my hips up, letting her feel how hard I am. There's a reason this is one of the best places in New York for live music. The acoustics are superior, and the sounds Sophie makes when my dick presses against her for the first time, with just a few layers of material between us, are epic.

"It even smells red," I groan, burying my face in her hair.

Her dress jumps to the top of the list of things about her messing with my head. I love how thin it is, because I can feel the slightest curve beneath my hands. Equally, what I hate is how thin it is. I can feel all of her and if we carry on like we are doing, there isn't a chance in hell I'm going to be able to stop.

Before I can overthink it, Sophie's lips find mine. This kiss is different from the first. There's experience. Already we're learning what the other likes. She tugs on my bottom lip with her teeth, and I groan. I tangle my tongue against hers, then drag it out slowly, and she moans. Stars fill my vision and my world tilts on its axis as I become consumed by everything related to Sophie Parker; the woman I've wanted longer in my life than haven't.

Losing control of my hands, I bunch the material of her dress around her waist. I feel like I'm in a dream when Sophie shifts back in my lap, enough that she's able to fumble with the button on my pants.

"Soph." The button slides through the hole. It's the sound of the zipper, or maybe the vibrations when she pulls it down, shooting through my body, which makes me grab her hands. "Stop." No part of me wants her to.

"I want this." She kisses me again, and her hands pull from my grip, then toy with the band of my boxers.

Fuck the dream. I start to question my sanity when her index finger skims beneath the elastic. Her finger dips low. Too low.

"Soph," I warn, when her nail accidentally, or maybe not accidentally, makes contact with the head of my dick.

The rest of her hand disappears, and my eyes roll. It's when my head falls back as she strokes her hand all the way down, then back up to the tip, that I tell myself to get it together.

I grab her hand again, stopping her movements. "We have to stop."

"Why?" I don't have a fucking clue what the 'why' is right now, but something in the deeper parts of my brain tells me it's the right thing to keep saying. My mouth opens and closes. No explanation comes out. "Exactly."

She starts to move her hand again. Her strokes get harder, more confident each time. It feels too good to make sense of anything.

"Wait," I hiss through my teeth, almost coming when she lifts her hips and stokes me against the soaked piece of flimsy material, the only thing separating us. "St-stop," I choke, when she presses me inside her.

Fuck. I don't know what to do. I want this more than I could ever tell her. I just never expected it to happen this way.

"I want you, Sam." Then she says what only she would know could convince me. "Don't overthink this."

My last ounce of control evaporates, and I hook the lace of her pants with my finger, pull them to the side and thrust my hips up. She lets out a small gasp when I sink deep inside her, and my vision goes hazy.

Nothing, absolutely nothing, could ever have prepared me for what this would feel like. A faint ringing starts in my ears when I move my hips again.

Sophie might as well be my first, because I can't remember anything else before this. She feels incredible sliding over me, and in those first few seconds, my hands tremble against her hips. When she shifts them, electricity shoots through me.

I want to stand, take her with me, and fuck her senseless against the wall. I stop myself, every muscle in my body tightening as she rides me torturously slow, the ball still one hundred percent in her court. My hands skim down her arms, up the soft skin of her thighs, over whatever part of her they can get to. I touch everywhere, memorizing it all, imprinting how she feels against my palms.

"You good?" I ask when she stops moving and our foreheads rest together.

Our harsh breaths mingle.

The soft glow of lighting spilling over from the stage highlights the small smile she gives me.

"More than good."

"We can, you know, stop. If you don't want this."

My words sound unconvincing. God, I hope she doesn't want to stop.

Sophie lifts herself up, and for a second, I think she's going to agree and walk away. I forget about it all when she slides back down, taking me in deeper. We fit together like we were made for each other.

"I really don't want to stop," she whispers in my ear. "I really …" She kisses the skin just below. "Really." Bites. "Don't want to stop." Her tongue darts out, soothing a mark I know will be left for days. One I want there for a lifetime.

"Ride me, Red."

And she does.

Her soft, breathy moans are the only sound audible in the room. She moves up and down, finding confidence in her rhythm. When it starts to slow and she tenses, I know she's close to coming all over me.

"Sam …"

I tilt her back so I can see all of her as she circles her hips, pressing a finger over her lips to keep her quiet.

"Soph?" I thrust my hips up.

"Yeah?" She moans when I hit the perfect spot, and her legs start to shake.

My hands grab her ass and pull her against me as I stand. With her legs locked around my waist, I spin us away from the chair and press her against a pillar, making sure we're shielded in darkness.

"Can you be quiet?" I murmur at the shell of her ear.

My breath coating her skin makes her shiver.

"Yeah," she cries out when I slam into her.

"That's not quiet."

Silencing her with my lips, our tongues tangle and my hips move in a relentless rhythm.

Twenty years in the making, I want it to last forever, scared of what might happen when I stop. I block out the fear threatening to ruin the best moment of my life and move faster.

Each thrust, each kiss, has one purpose: to leave her needing me as much as I need her.

When she comes, I want her to shatter, knowing the only person who knows how to slot all the pieces back together is me.

Unfortunately, time isn't on our side and with the risk of someone finding us, I literally have minutes to make sure it's a moment she'll never forget.

Somewhere between my nails biting against the skin on her ass and my dick breaking through whatever walls there are left between us, her muscles lock and her breaths catch in her throat. When she falls apart, I swallow her cries, my legs buckling as I follow right behind her, coming long and hard.

Sweat trickles down my brow and lower back with my hips' last few jerky movements. Sophie sags over me, spent. I bury my face in her hair and inhale. Her smell overloading my already frazzled senses makes coming back down to earth a struggle, but eventually I find the strength to pull away.

"Hey," I say, warily, searching her eyes for any sign of regret. She smiles but doesn't say a word. I'm still buried deep inside her when my stomach churns. "What are you thinking?"

She tilts her head to the side, and her mouth turns into a slow grin. "That I would have dyed my hair a long time ago if I knew it was going to end with *that*."

I chuckle and peck her lips. "We're good?"

"More than good," she smiles, shyly this time. "Erm …
so when can we do that again?"

My chuckle turns into a laugh, and although it's the last
thing I want to do, I slide out of her, then set her on her feet
and make quick work of straightening her underwear and
dress before straightening myself out.

I pull up my zipper and fasten the button on my pants.
"Whenever you want." I kiss her and she leans back against
the pillar. "All day and all night." My lips move slower, and
she pants. Fuck. I'm ready to take her again and it's not even
been a few minutes. "Where's Russ?"

"Shit," she hisses, the cloud of lust disappearing and her
eyes dart around.

For a second, terror takes over and mine almost pop out
of my head. "He's not *here*, is he?"

Scooping her bag from the floor, she shakes her head.

"Shit," she says again when she looks at her phone. "He's
going to kill me. We're late."

"For?" She grabs my hand and drags me behind her.
"Where are we going?"

She points at the sign for the restrooms. "First, I'm
cleaning myself up, because your come is still inside me and
it's not appropriate with where I'm taking you."

My jaw drops, and I still hear her laughing when the door
to the restroom closes.

When she steps back out, she's a vision. Her cheeks are
flushed and her eyes glitter. Her hair spills in soft red waves
around her shoulders and I want to tell her it all. That I want
to spend a lifetime doing what we just did. I don't want
anything apart from her. I never have.

"Why are you looking at me like that?"

Because I love you, I almost say.

"Still taking in the red," I croak, swallowing the emotions threatening to spill out and focusing on what happens next. "So, really, where are we going?"

Sophie pulls me toward the doors, and we step out into the early evening. The noise of Williamsburg greeting us feels strange and out of place after everything that's just happened.

Leading me along the sidewalk, she glances over her shoulder at me. "To a place where I think I can help you."

"Okay," I reply, holding back from telling her that she already has.

Chapter Twenty-Six
Sophie

My legs shake, and not from the life-changing orgasm Sam gave me underneath the balcony at the music hall.

We're walking side by side into a new building, one where I definitely can't do all the things that I've been imagining on the way here. The dirty ones. It's like when I fell apart in Sam's arms, the person who came back was a massive horn-ball version of me.

It hits me. Sam's about to meet The Parkapellas.

Music and voices greet us halfway along the long corridor, and I stop. Sam stops right with me.

"What is this place?"

"This place," I reply, with a slight shake to my voice, "is really important to me." I pause. "I think it could be for you, too." I stop myself, not wanting to add an immense amount of pressure to however Sam feels about what is waiting for him behind the frosted glass door. "Even if it isn't, it's fine." I backtrack, nerves getting the better of me. "It's just …"

Sam squeezes my hand. "Why don't you show me rather than telling me?"

I nod, struggling with each step forward.

"Remember," I say, with my hand resting on the handle. "It's okay if you don't like it."

Sam smiles. "Open the door."

I press the handle down and push it open at the same time The Parkapellas start to hit the crescendo of the song they're rehearsing for The American Showcase. I hold my breath, praying they get it. I try not to wince when they miss the right note, the result a flat, pitchy ending. They haven't improved in my absence, they've gotten worse.

"Soph?" says Sam at the same time Russ shouts, "Sophie!"

Russ barrels over, taking the whole room by surprise when he throws his arms around me. His open show of affection after what happened with Sam is too much and the back of my eyes sting.

"Hey, you." I drop Sam's hand, so I can rest both of mine on Russ's back.

Russ pulls away and looks to my side, excited. "Hey, Sam!"

"Hey, buddy." Sam gives him a warm smile, then shoots a questioning look my way.

I'm about to explain everything, but Russ beats me to it. "What do you think of The Parkapellas? We're great, right?"

"Parkapellas?" Sam says quietly, the word coming out more of a question.

"Surprise?" I cringe.

Sensing the awkward vibes, Mom claps her hands from the side of the group. She's a vision in a vibrant orange maxi dress. It shouldn't work for her. It screams color clash as far as her hair is concerned, but in the way only she knows how, she pulls it off like she's ready to take on New York Fashion Week.

"Show's over," she declares. "That was pitchy as hell. Let's get back to it."

I make a mental note to remind her that subtlety is key when it comes to feedback. Too often, she articulates things in ways that are as bold as her fashion choices.

Russ gives an excited wave then rushes back to his position, puffing his chest out proudly when the opening chords of the song fill the room again.

"Erm, Soph," says Sam, dropping his head lower so I can hear him over the singing.

"Yeah?" I keep my attention focused on the group, not wanting to see his expression.

"Can we talk for a second?"

"Sure."

I mouth 'be right back' to Russ. His expression falls when he realizes we're leaving.

We're back through the door we literally just used to enter the room when Sam says, "The Parkapellas?"

"An a cappella group."

"I kind of figured that one out myself," he laughs. I can't decide if he's laughing because he's trying to take it in or laughing at how absurd it is. The thought of it being the latter makes me feel nauseous. He takes a step forward and pulls me into his arms. Brushing the hair away from my face, lines form between his brows and his expression becomes unreadable. "I thought I knew it all, but I guess there's a lot I still don't."

"You know most of it," I say quietly, not meeting his eye. "Just not this."

"Why?"

I chew the inside of my cheek, torn between the truth and a softer version of it. When I remember how it felt having him inside me, how he made me feel things I never have with anyone, I decide nothing but the truth will do. I don't want there to be secrets. Not that there ever really has been, but now, knowing how incredible we can be together, I don't want to risk even the smallest slip of a detail getting in our way.

"I was scared you'd laugh."

The lines between his brows disappear as they draw together. "Why would I laugh?"

I shrug. The movement is slow. My shoulders feel heavy with the pressure of saying out loud the negative thoughts I've been having about one of the best things in my life. "I dunno. I guess I feel like I shouldn't be doing this. Like I'm not cut out for it. Like someone else could do better."

"Sounds familiar." His eyes drop to my mouth a second before his lips do. Their warmth envelopes and reassures me. He chuckles when I try to part his lips with my tongue. "Later."

The way his voice drops sits low in my core. I keep asking myself how, like really, seriously, how, have we spent years without doing this? Suddenly, I can barely form a coherent thought from him just standing close by.

"I like to sing," I blurt out.

"Is that so?" he replies, stroking a hand through my hair.

He claims he doesn't know about all of this, but the amusement in his eyes suggests he knows more than he's letting on. I say as much.

"Why do I feel like you already know this?"

He takes a step back and, with some space between us, I feel like I can think straight again. "You're a Parker. It's a given." There's more to it, I can tell, but the muscle that twitches in his jaw tells me to leave it. "Tell me everything."

I take a deep breath and let some of the tension leave my body when I exhale. "We've been doing it for years. The group started out small and then turned into what it is."

"It's impressive." He smiles. "Whose idea was it?"

I look away. "My parents," I lie.

"Whose idea was it, really?"

"Mine."

"What started it all?"

The blood in my veins turns to ice. This is the question I've been expecting, waiting for someone to ask me for years. It doesn't matter that I've spent all the time leading up to this point preparing for it. The thought of answering it out loud is still terrifying.

My palms go clammy, and I finally admit, "You." I gesture to the door. "We should go back. Russ will want us in there."

"Russ will be fine waiting," Sam says, and his eyes turn to slits. "What do you mean, I started this all?" I need to sit. Or leave. Or something. Something away from the pressure of his gaze. "Red?" How can one word have such an effect on a person? A weight sits heavy in my stomach, full of dread. Meanwhile, my clit throbs at the way it sounds coming out of his mouth. He knows exactly what he's doing. "Tell me."

It's a gentle, yet firm request. One I can't avoid.

"I-I—" My head spins and I feel like I'm going to pass out.

Why is this so hard?

Because it's up there with telling him you've fallen in love with him in different ways, at different stages in your life, and that they've all built up to this, a little voice in my head decides to comment.

Shit. Love? The room spins and I sway. We've had sex once. I told Sam not to overthink what happened and here I am overthinking *everything*.

"Hey." Suddenly, I'm sitting in his lap on one of the chairs that line one side of the corridor, wondering if I've passed out because I don't remember getting here. "Soph, I'm sorry. I shouldn't have pushed you."

I definitely passed out.

"No, you didn't. Just almost."

"Do you think I'm crazy?" I mumble against his neck.

Thankfully, The Parkapellas are taking this rehearsal more seriously than the previous sessions. One song rolls into the next, their voices saving us from an awkward silence that would be the final nail in this coffin of mortification.

"I don't think you're crazy." I sigh with relief. "I *know* you are."

I sit up straight and flick his chest. "Ass."

He smiles. "Feeling better?"

"Singing helps them … feel better," I explain. "It helps them heal. I had this whole tagline planned for a business model if we ever needed one. 'Singing to heal.' I know it sounds cringe, but you were my inspiration. I wanted to create something. To use music in a way that helped people like it helped you. I guess I got a little excited when I saw *Pitch Perfect* and created a mashup with Otis."

Sam sticks his bottom lip out. "Otis got a look in before me?"

I can't be mad at his joke, because it's better than him telling me this is ridiculous. I should have known he'd never go against me. He would never tear me down, because he's always been there at my side, helping me build the foundations of who I want to be.

"Yeah," I laugh bitterly. "Don't be jealous. No one will be getting a look in if things don't improve."

Sam's hands trace a soothing pattern across my back. The past few hours have been a dream and the old Sam and Sophie feel like they were a lifetime ago. Everything between us feels natural; feels right.

When I lean into his chest, he's completely in tune to my change in mood. "What's wrong?"

"That song you heard them rehearsing, it's our required piece for The American Showcase. The one the judges pick. We've been rehearsing it for weeks and it's no good. They can't get it right. I think it's because they're scared."

"Of?"

"Losing."

Sam starts playing with the ends of my hair, and I could fall asleep from the soothing feel of it.

"But it's just a competition," he says, matter of fact.

I shake my head, forcing my eyes to stay open. "It's not. We need the prize money. You saw what it's like in there. We're bursting at the seams and more people keep requesting to join. We can't afford a bigger premises."

"Could your mom and dad not help? I don't mean to state the obvious, but they're global superstars."

"You're going to call me stubborn …" My lips form a flat line, ready to tell him the really selfish part I play in all this. "But I don't want them to. I want the group to run itself …"

"Like a business," Sam finishes, one hundred percent getting it, like I should have known he would.

"Right."

We both go silent, and the singing continues in the background.

"Soph, you can't work full time, care for a child, and run a business on the side. You can't be everything."

"I can try," I reply stubbornly, feeling his scowl when his body tenses. "We really should go back in."

Sam nods, then turns thoughtful. "Wait. Two things."

"Okay?"

"First." He raises one finger to hammer home the point. "You said this could help me?"

I contemplate my answer, thinking over everything my parents and Grams said yesterday.

"I think you need to strip it back."

"Strip you back?" He winks, and I punch him in the arm.

"I'm being serious." I laugh. "It's a win-win situation. I think everyone will listen and be inspired by your help. I also think if you go back to the reason that you started singing, the same reason I started The Parkapellas, and the reason they're all here, maybe you'll find your voice again."

He gives me a look. One I can't decipher. I think he's going to tell me something, but he simply says, "Okay."

I watch him, waiting until I have to probe him. "There were two?"

He frowns and his eyes darken. "I, um …" he reaches up and scratches the side of his head. "I forgot the second. Sorry."

"It's fine. Come on, let's go back in."

The nerves from when we first arrived are nowhere to be found now that he knows everything. My heart flutters with excitement. Anticipation knowing good things could come from this. At the door to the rehearsal room, I stop and take him in one last time before tossing him to the wolves.

"Wait! Your hair's a mess."

Sam stares at my lips, then looks up, eyes smoldering. "That's because you're a hair puller."

"Excuse me?" I scoff.

"When you came, you were pulling my hair."

"Oh." I chew my lip. "I didn't know I did that."

Sam's head swoops down. He stops right before my lips, and I feel his warm breath against them when he speaks. "Then clearly you've been with all the wrong guys, and they haven't done it enough."

"What?"

"Driven you wild." He brushes the tip of his nose against mine. "Fucked you like I did." I love soft, sweet-talking Sam, the one I've known forever. But this side to him, the dirty talking side, is quickly becoming my favorite. "Don't worry, Red." His hands tangle in my hair like he claims mine did to his earlier. "I'll rectify it for you. Just say the word."

I'm about to say 'word', but he steals it from me with a kiss that sets my body alight. Heat curls in my stomach just from the touch of his lips. His kisses are like earlier, but better. An ache builds between my legs when his tongue strokes mine. It's intense, unbearable, like he didn't just give me the best orgasm of my life under an hour ago.

He's a true musician, merging his body with mine, playing me like I'm his favorite instrument.

The door in front of us opens at the moment I attempt to dry hump his leg.

"My eyes!" cries Hale, spinning away. I want the ground to open and swallow me whole as every member of The Parkapellas, my family—Russ included—gawp at us. "Mom, I need bleach or something."

"Stop being dramatic," she responds, staring at Sam and I, then at my hair with a knowing smile. When my eyes dart around, signaling how uncomfortable I feel, she claps her hands together. "Break everyone. We will reconvene in …" she glances at her watch-less wrist. "Five minutes."

A young girl walks over to her. "What does reconvene mean?"

"It means we'll start singing again, sweetie," she replies, steering her and the other smaller members in the direction of the restroom.

The room disperses and Aurelia zeroes in on us. "Your cheeks are the same color as your hair. Impressive." The thing about Aurelia is that she likes to pretend her character is unique, like her style. Her mouth is smarter than her brain, which is impressive considering her IQ is off the charts. She spins the Parker creativity streak into her sideline of work, embedding her secrets in the tight weaves of her hair, but that's a story for another day. "So, this is a thing?"

Her eyes move between us, narrowed, assessing.

Sam goes to answer, but I beat him to it. "Yeah, it is."

There's surprise all around. Aurelia's from my answer. Sam's from the certainty behind my words. Mine when Aurelia's face cracks into a smile. She rarely smiles; she's too cool for it.

"Finally. It took you long enough to realize what was right in front of you," she says in my direction, then turns

340

her attention to Sam, who takes a couple of centimeters off his height when he shrinks, ready for whatever Aurelia-esque lashing is heading his way. "Sure you picked the right sister?"

He doesn't even blink. "I never had to pick. There was only ever one choice."

I totally swoon at his answer. It's what main male characters are made of. And he's mine. Mine. Sam Riley is mine. And I'm his. I mean, I need to double check that's where we're at. I don't feel like what happened earlier was anything close to a quick hookup, but you can never be sure. I tell myself I'm testing it all out in my head, ready for when I can confirm with him later.

It sounds great, better than great, but I realize he's right when I realize no one else ever stood a chance. The few other guys there have been in my life were simply there to help bounce me back onto the right path, serving as a reminder that Sam is like that rare pair of denim pants you find. The ones you cherish and take care of better than any other piece of clothing because they're a perfect fit, and if you destroy them, you won't find another like them.

And like the perfect pair of denim pants sculpting my post-thirties ass, which is struggling against gravity with each day that goes by, he sculpts me into the best version of myself.

He helps me to shine, inside and out. He's my perfect fit. My one.

I must be staring, because he gives me a weird look. I shake my thoughts away and smile.

Sam's words reduce Aurelia, often known as the person of many, to two simple ones. "Good answer." Because she always has to have the last word with anything in life, she

341

adds on to the end, "Fuck with my sister and I'll destroy you."

Sam salutes with a lazy smile that makes my heart flip flop. "Message received, oh brutal one."

"Xavier!" she balks, finally leaving us alone. "Stop flirting with Lacey and give me a hand with the refreshments."

"She's really something," Sam comments, as we both watch her physically pull my youngest sibling away from his target for the night. I remain silent. "Go on. Ask me."

"Ask you what?" I reply innocently, as if there isn't a single question running through my mind when there are hundreds. "If I'm sure I want in with your crazy family."

I follow his lead. "Are you sure you want in?"

I'm back to being engulfed in his arms and he kisses me quickly, a kiss that ends right when Hale calls out in the background, "Seriously? Again? Get a room."

Sam ignores him, refusing to let me go, then says so only I can hear, "I've been in since the first moment I saw you."

"Let's get back to it!" shouts my mom.

Sam and I pull apart reluctantly and he spends the final thirty minutes of rehearsals observing intently.

The room is almost empty when I ask, "So, do you think you can help?"

I pray he can help, because with each run through of the song, it gets worse.

"I have a few ideas. It could be fun."

"So, you want to help?" I grin. "We're really doing this?"

He nods, but because Russ is walking with the two of us as his target, he can't expand any further than, "We're doing it all."

My heart thrashes in my chest for hours after, trying to figure out what the hidden meanings might be.

Later, back at the apartment, with Russ in bed after a feast of pizzas loaded with veggies—much to his disgust—I try to entice Sam into my bed for the night.

He's stretched above me, his erection creating enough friction every time he moves that I could definitely get off with us both fully clothed. It's impressive, considering it's something pretty much all of my past boyfriends struggled to achieve without them.

I'm doing the hair pulling thing he told me about earlier when he draws away abruptly with a pained expression.

"Sorry," I pant. "Did I pull too hard?"

He snickers. "Red, you can never pull too hard."

I watch in total confusion as he climbs off me. "Um, what's going on right now?"

"I'm leaving," he states.

"What? Why? Are you sure I didn't pull too hard?" I jest, considering throwing in a jovial punch for good measure.

He laughs and his body shakes, causing some of his hair to fall across his forehead. He's the epitome of the boy next door, the one I was lucky enough to grow up and fall in love with.

"You've got too much going on for sex to be on the brain."

"After earlier, sex will be the only thing on my brain, ever," I declare.

"And there I was, thinking you wanted to be with me for our exceptional friendship and my great personality."

"The mind-blow orgasms sealed the deal." I wink and he shakes his head. "So, no sex, really?"

343

I'm more than disappointed when he says, "No sex. Not tonight."

I pout and his eyes fill with promises I hope will be as dirty as his mouth when he really gets going. He leans in and drops his voice to a low level that makes it vibrate through my body, amping how much I want him up by a thousand levels. "Red, it's true what they say. Good things come to those who wait. I promise, the next time we're together, the whole neighborhood will know my name." I can barely remember my name when he changes the subject entirely. "When's The American Showcase?"

"In the fall," I groan, plummeting back down to earth.

A final kiss finds my lips, and then Sam walks to the door. "Get some rest. We've got a lot of rehearsing to do."

Chapter Twenty-Seven

Sam

I'm four practices deep with The Parkapellas when the moment I predicted would happen, does.

Sophie wasn't kidding when she said we had our hands full. A week and a half disappear. The days blur into a cycle of working, school drop-offs and pick ups, Parkapella rehearsals and stolen moments when no one is watching.

The red head glued to my side is horny as fuck, and I love it. I love it even more at night when she begs for more. There's a bigger conversation we need to have, but time isn't on our side, and I struggle to find more than a minute alone with her to explain how I think things should go. She isn't going to be happy, but if the past nine days are anything to go by, we'll be limited in alone time for the foreseeable future, anyway.

My suggestion will simply be an extension. One I hope, if I get my way, won't be a long one.

"Okay," I say, walking into The Parkapellas rehearsal room at seven PM on our second Wednesday. "We're doing things differently tonight."

"Different?" frowns Russ, voicing the concerns of all the other members.

"No singing."

"But it's an a cappella group!" a female at the back shouts. I have a feeling it's Xavier's new love interest, Lacey. She's the type who makes it known she isn't happy, and also the only one loud and overbearing enough to compete with his family.

"I want us all to talk," I say, and there's a collective groan.

The younger kids already look bored, and I start to second guess myself at the same time Sophie steps into the room.

"Sam is leading the rehearsal." The room goes deathly silent. "He's here to help us win The American Showcase. Whatever we're doing *isn't* working. Be thankful he's here, giving you all a chance." There's more silence and Sophie smiles at me. I can't wait to tell her later how ridiculously hot that was, but for now, I have a job to do. "I personally love talking."

"I know you do." It tests my strength when I drag my eyes away from her and back to the group. "I want you to pair off." I wave a pile of paper sheets filled with questions in the air. "Work through these, and we'll regroup at the end."

"It's like school," I hear someone mutter. I ignore them, knowing in my gut this will help.

Everyone pairs off and it breaks me a little when I find Russ, the life and soul of the group, without a partner. He looks lost when he glances around uncertainly.

346

"Hey, partner," I say, handing him a sheet of questions.

"You want to be my partner?" he asks in disbelief.

I laugh at his constant awe toward me, despite the fact I drop and pick him up from school five times a week and spend the evenings in his home, struggling to keep my hands off his foster mom during the hours he's awake.

I crouch and gesture for him to come in closer. "Want to know a secret?" I whisper behind my hand. He nods eagerly. "I wouldn't want to be anyone else's."

He snatches the paper from my hand and races to save us two seats.

"You're great with him," says Sophie, resting her head against my arm when I'm standing again.

I place a kiss into her hair. "He's easy to be great with."

"He is, isn't he?" She smiles.

With every day that passes, they grow closer, the rocky start to their new relationship long forgotten. It makes my heart ache watching them together, knowing the ending this is going to have—the one I know Sophie is refusing to acknowledge. My stomach churns, twisting into a tight knot remembering all the things younger me believed, before all of this. That people always leave and that maybe happily ever afters aren't real. The thought of Russ going through it all, not once, twice, but over and over, experiencing what the perfect life could really be like and then losing it, almost destroys me.

"Stop distracting me. I have questions to work through," I say seriously, walking away.

"Yessir." She calls after me, not picking up on the change in my mood, made all the more obvious when I feel her wink against my back.

An hour later, we regroup.

"How are people feeling?" I ask no one in particular. A round of grumbles is my response. "Great," I say, even though no one has actually replied, deciding to poke the bear with a stick and really push them out of their comfort zone, "let's do some group Q and A."

There's another round of groaning that tells me The Parkapellas are a ship, bobbing in stormy waters, unaware they're about to sink if they don't start helping to patch up the holes in the framework struggling to hold them together.

"Okay." I scour the crowd, refusing to let my eyes find Sophie at the side of the room. I'm considering barring her from any rehearsals I'm in charge of, because having her close by, feeling her gaze on me, is distracting and unnerving. "Chase!" A guy in his mid-twenties with hair bigger and floppier than mine, pales. "Favorite song, hit me with it!"

"'Hosanna'," he replies.

His answer throws me, and I school my expression, refusing to give an ounce of my surprise away. "Dude. Serious?"

He shrugs. "I'm religious?"

"Okay." I hold my hands up. "We can work with this."

I grab my phone, already hooked up to the speaker system, and open my Spotify account. A quick search later, a South African choir version of Chase's favorite song reverberates off the walls. Every single person sits, listens, transfixed until the song ends. I couldn't have picked a better one, and I know fate is working on my side. I wouldn't have picked it, but it's right. It feels right. It's natural. Beautiful. Stripped bare. Music in its rawest form. The haunting harmonies remind me of a night sitting in my room, singing in unison with a completely unaware fiery Red, who's watching me from the side.

"Memorize the lyrics the best you can. Some of you can get them on your phones ready to share," I say, before hitting play again. Not one person protests and I take in every single face, focused solely on the music and the words.

This is why I started.

The butterflies in my stomach. The blood coursing through my veins. The lyrics resonating in my soul. The anticipation. The tingling in my fingertips that shoots down to my toes, right before the euphoria that hits when I open my mouth and the chords transform into a melody that, for some, can never be forgotten. Just like those we've lost, watching from above, waiting for us to make them proud.

This is why I sing.

I want it to be the reason why they do, and twenty effortless minutes later, The Parkapellas prove they want it, too. They create a perfect Parkapella rendition that sends a chill down my spine in a moment I'll never forget. Even if they don't win The American Showcase, they've proved their talent is superior to anything out there.

Well, until Russ hoots, "That's the shit I'm talkin' about."

Sophie shoots daggers at Grams, who's too busy blowing her nose into her hanky to care. I'm right there with her, wiping away a rogue tear, praying no one but Sophie, who's already clocked me, notices.

The group disperses for a break, and she wanders over.

"Sammy, was that a tear I saw?"

"Tell anyone and I'm depriving you of orgasms for a long, long time."

She makes a show of staring at her nails. "It's been over a week. What's a year or two more?"

"Try me, Red," I challenge when no one else is listening.

"I knew you could do it. *This*," she says seriously, excitement making her eyes the bluest of blue. "You're in your element. I can feel it."

"I love it here," I admit, at the same time the group congregates back together.

I raise a finger to my lips and with a quick 'shh', she's silent at the side again.

"Lacey, my main gal." I point in her direction, receiving a death glare in return. "Give me your fave."

"'Karma' by MOD SUN."

When the opening angry lyrics fill the room, I wonder where the song's going. I press pause at the words 'karma's a bitch'.

"Great song choice." I grin. "Not *quite* the vibe we're going for with kids around, but still great."

"You asked," she deadpans with slasher vibes in her eyes.

I start to sweat. She's bitchier than the karma in her favorite song. I can feel my grip on the group slipping, along with the animosity she's pushing my way. I need to rectify it, and fast.

"True," I agree. I decide to meet her in the middle. "It's your turn to ask." I lean back in my chair. "Ask me anything."

Her eyes pop and for the first time, her bitchterior vanishes, and she shows her real, vulnerable self. "But you're Sam from S.C.A.R.A.B."

"I'm just a guy who loves to sing."

"Bullshit," someone coughs in the group.

"Who was that?" says Sophie, sternly. A hand wobbles in the air from the least likely source. A guy our age who never says a word. She watches him, stares. Her lips form a flat line. "Ask him anything."

350

The guy swallows so hard the muscles in his throat pull tight and threaten to snap.

"Anything?" he croaks.

"Anything," says Sophie, the vein pulsing at her temple a clear sign she's struggling to keep her temper in check.

"Why—when did you start to sing?" he asks me, with two questions in one.

I block out the rest of the group and focus on him. "Ten. I was ten when I started singing."

The room falls so silent it feels like no one is breathing.

"Why?" he croaks. "Why did you start?"

"A tell for a tell," I quip. "You first."

I see it in his eyes. I feel it, the unhealed anger, the resentment that fueled so many of my younger years. He's lashing out, just like Shaun, because we all process in different ways.

"I lost my family," he answers, "every single one of them. Singing helps."

"Me too," chimes Russ.

"Me too," says a young girl.

"And me," says an older guy, closer to my age.

"I lost my one," says Grams, pain pouring from her eyes.

"I lost my first true love," says Sophie's mom, never taking her eyes off Grams. "My father."

"I'm sorry." Sophie stares at my original offender, but her gaze has softened with empathy. "I'm sorry for your pain. I don't want to … I can't even imagine …"

Her eyes flicker to Russ and it's then, as she shows nothing but humility, that my last wall tumbles and my heart knows it's hers. She reinforces, with her forgiveness, everything The Parkapellas represents.

"Red," I say quietly, wanting only her to hear, knowing everyone else can. "It was because of a girl with red hair." I stare at the guy. "I lost both of my parents for different reasons. And then, I moved to Brooklyn. It destroyed my brother and me. I thought we'd never get over it. And then I met *her*.

"She was so beautiful it hurt to look at her. Even at ten, I knew I loved her. I knew it the moment, when surrounded by the worst kind of grief, she really saw me and everything I could be when no one else could.

"I thought she couldn't get any more perfect ..." I pause. "Until I heard her singing into the streets of Brooklyn, like she did every night for eight years."

'*Sam,*' Sophie mouths when I steal a glance her way, and I decide to tell her it all. I'm halfway there after all.

"The first night I heard hers, I found my voice. It was her. It's always been her. The girl with red hair and eyes bluer than the sky is the reason I'm in front of you now. She was everything. She *is* everything. She taught me that even when you lose it all, there's still a chance you can have everything. You just have to open your heart to it."

"But why can't you sing now?" says the guy, cutting off my speech, gunning straight to the point and clarifying that everyone in the room knows about my issue.

My eyes move slowly, taking in everything in red. "Because I need her with me, to remind me why I started— why I still want to."

He nods and grins when my tense expression breaks into a smile of relief after letting it all out.

I turn my head back and focus my attention solely on her. "Sing with me, Soph."

Hale already has an acoustic guitar sitting in his hands. "Name the song."

"'Fields of Gold'," I reply without an ounce of hesitation.

I don't know if she's going to do it, but I really hope she does.

Hale's fingers pluck the strings, filling the room with the song I know best.

Dad's.

Mine.

Hers.

I hold my breath.

Sophie's mouth parts and the opening lyrics flow from her effortlessly.

Everything in the room disappears. All I see is Red.

Her voice floats through me, consumes me, coaxes mine to the surface. I feel it building, and then with her right by my side, I find it and grab hold of it.

My voice pours out with the emotions I feel for her and her alone, just like it did the first time. Our voices float through the air. The chords merge perfectly for everyone to hear, as we tell a story with the lyrics. One filled with questions, one with the hope of promises, some broken, remembering, anticipating, walking in golden fields.

I never want the song to end, but it does, too soon. My throat hurts in the best way and I can't wait to do it all again.

Sophie gives me a shy smile and I struggle to take my eyes off her. Reluctantly, we both look away when an applause that threatens to shatter the windows fills the room.

"That was epic," squeals Lacey.

Russ runs over to Sophie and wraps his arms around her. "Do it again."

Sophie throws her head back and laughs. "Another time."

"Tomorrow?" he asks, excited.

"Will you eat your veggies?"

"All of them," he replies eagerly, then rushes back over to the group, who are all standing, preparing to leave.

"Game faces Friday everyone. We're going to smash that song," I shout over all the noise.

Everyone cheers, and Sophie comes to my side. I want to talk about what just happened—I need to—but with everyone around, I don't know if I can.

Grams' sixth sense must be going crazy because she shuffles our way. "That was magical," she says with a dreamy expression, and I chuckle. "I was thinking of taking Russ for some ice cream ..."

"That would be great, Grams," says Sophie, her thumb tracing a pattern over the back of my hand. "Can you have him home in an hour? It's already late."

"Sure, sweetie." She leaves us and grabs Russ, who starts jumping up and down when she tells him about their new plans.

Almost all The Parkapellas have left, leaving just Sophie's siblings behind.

"I've gotta go," says Hale. "That was great. Russ is right. You should do it again."

I plan to, but I don't say it out loud.

"I've gotta go, too," says Xavier with a grin. "Got a date with Lacey."

"Great," mutters Sophie to herself.

Aurelia is the last to leave. "I had an idea," she says to Sophie. "I think you should sing with the group for the showcase. I think it's what's missing. Anyway, I need to go as well. Think on it."

She waves goodbye then disappears, leaving the two of us alone, finally.

"So …" I say, suddenly feeling nervous.

"So …" beams Sophie, washing the nerves away.

"That was fun."

She nods. "It was." A slight frown pulls at her brows, catching me off guard. "Why didn't you tell me you knew I could sing?"

"Because …" I reply, stepping forward and wrapping my arms around her. I lean down and kiss her like the world is about to end.

The kiss breaks when Sophie pushes me away. Her hands linger on my chest, and breathlessly, she says, "Because?"

"I didn't want you to stop if you knew I was listening."

She purses her lips. "Maybe I wouldn't have."

I chuckle and kiss her again. "You would have."

"Is that another one of those things you know?"

"Yeah," I reply against her lips, one hand skimming over the back of her neck, then tangling in her hair. "It is."

The kiss that follows is one that threatens to break my resolve of something I've been considering since the night at the music hall. Reluctantly, I end it, my body and Sophie both disappointed I do.

"What happened at the music hall … it shouldn't have," I pant.

Sophie's eyes widen and start to water. I quickly realize I probably should have led her into the statement slowly.

"You're breaking up with me?"

She stares at me like her world has just been broken and I stare back, confused. This isn't going how I imagined it.

"How can we break up? We're not technically together."

A small gasp leaves her lips, and I wrack my brain, trying to figure out what the hell is going on and what I'm saying that's so wrong. Sophie backs away, shaking her head, tears spilling down her cheeks.

"Hey," I grab her hand and drag her back into me. I reach up and brush her tears away, then kiss her in a way that makes it clear we are not breaking up, regardless of the technicality. "I'm sorry. What happened before, with the singing, it's thrown me. I'm sorry." I kiss her again.

"We're not breaking up?" she asks quietly.

"That's something we need to talk about. Not the breaking up part," I clarify when her eyes widen. "The us being together part. We never, you know …" My cheeks burn and I clear my throat. "We never said what we were."

Christ. I was smoother in high school and need to seriously assess my communication skills later when Sophie isn't around.

"So, we're not breaking up?" she repeats.

I laugh. "Why would I break up with you when I love you?"

Fuck. I guess that's one way of telling her. Who needs romance, right?

"Y-you love me?" she stammers.

I rub the back of my neck. "I mean, yeah. I kinda thought it was obvious. Especially after, you know … everything I said before."

"I love you, too."

This time I'm the one standing in shock.

"You do?"

"Yeah." Sophie gives me a warm smile. "I really, really do."

"So, we're together? We're doing this. You and me. Sophie and Sam?"

Sophie only manages to nod her yes, before I'm on her, kissing her like I've never kissed anyone. It's not just a kiss, it's a promise of everything to come.

Eventually, I pull away, but Sophie leans in and presses her lips to mine again.

"Don't stop," she moans.

She rolls her hips enough to make it clear what her intentions are, just in case the way she's toying with the hem of my shirt isn't obvious enough. I almost give in, until the image of what I want and where I want us to be flashes behind my eyes.

"We're stopping," I say firmly, gripping her hands so she can't lift my shirt like she's now trying to. "I want to run something by you."

"Okay?"

"I meant what I said before."

Sophie blinks. "Why would the best sex of my life be a mistake?"

"Really?" I wiggle my brows and puff my chest out like a goddamn peacock, but don't care after the statement she's just made. "The best sex?"

"Sam." Sophie rolls her eyes. "Concentrate. What are you getting at here?"

I swallow and do a quick mental run through of everything I want to say.

"I didn't mean what happened was a mistake. I just meant it shouldn't have happened like it did. It was our first time together, and I screwed you against a balcony."

Sophie laughs. "I don't get what the problem is."

"Soph, I'm in love with you. I think we should wait. When we do it again, I want it to be special. I want to make love to you." My man card is definitely going to be revoked after this.

"We can still fool around, right?"

I frown. "I'm trying to prove exactly how much I love you and you're asking if we can fool around?"

"I love you, too, but that orgasm was, like, really, *really* good."

"Head out of the gutter, Red."

"Okay." She rolls her shoulders back. "So, when do you want to, you know, wait until?"

"We're married."

"Married?" she chokes, then shakes her head. "I'm sorry, what? Say that again. I don't think I heard you right."

"I want to wait until we're married," I confirm.

"But ..." Sophie tails off. "Why?"

I laugh at the confusion covering her face. The whole moment is laughable, and I need to work it in my favor before Sophie refuses to take me seriously and throws the idea out.

"Because." I lean in and echo some of the words she whispered to me at the music hall. The words that changed everything. "I want you to always kiss me." I press my lips to hers briefly. "I want you to always fuck me." My eyes trail over her body, and she squirms under my gaze. "I want you to always want me as much as I want you, and I want you to do it all knowing you're mine, only mine, and always will be."

"Sam ..." she breathes. "I love you and everything you're saying, but marriage? It's only been a couple of weeks. Marriage could be years away."

I narrow my eyes. "Say yes. Say yes and I'll make you a promise."

"What kind of promise?" she asks, tilting her head to the side.

"This one." I swallow. "I promise I'm not gonna wait years to marry you, Red. I've been waiting. Twenty years is long enough."

"Okay," she replies, and my heart swells, knowing forever with her is there, waiting for us. "Yes."

Chapter Twenty-Eight
Sophie

Two weeks disappear in the blink of an eye, then Sam turns up at the apartment with bags and suitcases surrounding him.

A lot of them.

"You can't just rock up and declare you're moving in," I huff, folding my arms across my chest.

"I can do whatever I want. It's *our* apartment."

"You're not living here."

"Soph," he says lightly, treading carefully. "I stop every night, anyway. What difference does it make if my things are here?"

"Why though?"

He shrugs, clearly not getting what the issue is. "It's a pain in the ass having to pack a bag every day and do laundry at a home I'm never in. Plus, it will make the school drop-off easier."

"Russ finished for the summer two weeks ago," I remind him.

I've got him. I can see him trying to think up a response.

"Live-in nannies are a thing."

"Nanny?"

"I mean …" He stubs his toe against the ground. "I'm looking after him while you're working. I guess that's what I am?"

"Clutching at straws, Sam. You are not a nanny."

"What am I then?"

The look he gives me has me backing down. Dammit.

"Mine," I reply, walking over to him. I look around at all his things. "You really want to do this? The living together thing?"

"Yes," he answers instantly.

"Aren't there rules? Timelines we should be following?"

"We screwed up the timeline when I made you come a few minutes after our first kiss."

My cheeks flush, and I mutter under my breath, "It was more than a few minutes after."

"I know." He winks. "Right?"

"Ass," I huff, hating being reminded of the thing I really need and he's refusing to give me. "Well …"

"What?"

"Are you going to bring your things in or what?"

"Yeah." He kisses me hard; a kiss that makes heat surge everywhere and leaves me begging for more. "I am."

"He made you orgasm against a balcony?" Zoe stares at me in disbelief.

It's the day after Sam officially moved in. Next Level has lived up to its name and been next level busy, so much so, it's been weeks, and I haven't had time to tell the girls everything that's happened with Sam.

Sooz's going away drinks in Riffs have provided me with the opportunity I need.

"I always knew he'd be filthy," giggles Amanda, three Zombie Apocalypses deep.

"He moved in yesterday," I tell them all.

Abby chokes on her drink. "What do you mean, he moved in?"

"He turned up with his bags and refused to leave."

"Only Sam." She smiles. "It's kind of romantic."

"It's frustrating is what it is."

"Frustrating how?" asks Zoe.

"Frustrating because he lives with me, walks around shirtless with all his tattoos on show and his shaggy sex hair, and I can't do anything about it."

"Can't do anything about what?" asks Shaun, setting another tray of Zombies on our table.

"Sex," answers Amanda.

"I'm going to the restroom," says Zoe, jumping to her feet.

She moves away in a teal blur like she always does whenever Shaun is around. Shaun's eyes linger on her disappearing form until I clear my throat, drawing his attention back to us.

"So." He frowns. "Back to the no sex."

"Your brother wants to wait," I huff, swirling the straw in my drink, my sexual frustration at its absolute max.

"But I thought you already did the dirty?" says Amanda.

"We did," I reply. "But now he wants to wait to make the next time we do it special."

"That's sweet," swoons Amanda.

"Wait until what?" asks Abby, focusing on the detail I knew she would.

"We're married," I reply.

Three female faces gawp my way.

Shaun shifts uncomfortably. "That could be my fault."

I narrow my eyes at him. "You're responsible for my lack of orgasms?"

He grimaces. "Please don't use the word orgasm when we're talking about my brother again. It's weird."

"Explain."

"There may have been a conversation that involved me trying to push him into telling you how he felt. Some of the pushing involved telling him you'd end up marrying someone else. I guess that's where he might have got the idea from?"

"Free drinks," I say, and Shaun looks at me blankly.

"Sorry, what?"

"I want free drinks as payment for your involvement in this."

"Soph," he laughs. "You pretty much get free drinks, anyway."

"Yeah, 'pretty much'. I want them all free, forever."

He shrugs. "Sure. Whatever."

"That was easy," I grin. One of my life goals is complete.

"I mean, you're going to be my sister-in-law, anyway. Family always gets them free." He winks, leaving us with a "See you around, *Sis.*"

I watch him leave; mouth open wide. I guess he has a point.

Marriage.

Jesus. Life is literally a rollercoaster.

Sooz fans herself. "Well, this takes the edge off me leaving for the rest of the summer."

"You don't know when you'll be back?" Abby asks, mouth turned down.

Sooz's expression drops, and her mouth twists. "Less about me." She smiles, but it doesn't reach her eyes. "And less about the sex you're not having. I want to know more about The Parkapellas."

"Do we get to come watch?" asks Amanda. "I loved *Pitch Perfect*."

I take a sip of my drink. "I guess you could if you bought tickets?"

"On it," says Abby, pulling out her phone. "What's the competition called again?"

"The American Showcase," I reply.

"Ooooo it looks fancy," she says, tapping her phone screen. "Eeek, this is so exciting. Can I bring Clara?"

"Sure?" I can't keep up. It still feels weird talking openly about all the things I've been keeping to myself.

"Do you think you'll do it as a permanent thing?" asks Sooz. "You know, expand and things. It would be great if you won. It would really help."

I should have known she'd have her business head on with this. It's never switched off. Like, ever.

"I can't," I reply, playing with my straw again.

"Why not?" asks Abby.

"When would I have time to expand when Next Level is as busy as it is?"

"Simple." Abby laughs. "You quit."

I blink. "Quit what?"

Sooz rolls her eyes. "Next Level. You quit Next Level, Soph."

364

I look between the three of them. "I can't just leave you all."

"If it's to do something you love, sure you can," says Abby. "Life's too short not to go after what you want. Imagine how incredible it would be."

"You're all really on board with this? I mean, I'm not saying I will, but I could leave if I wanted to?" I watch them for any signs they're joking. I find none.

Abby reaches across the table and gives my hand a squeeze. "You can do anything you want to, Soph. It's your life. It's nice to see you finally living it the way you want to."

"Okay." My face hurts from smiling so much—something that seems to be happening more each day.

"Now," says Sooz, with a glint in her eye. "I want you to promise me something before I leave."

"What?" I ask warily. The last time she looked at me like she is doing, I ended up leading the opening for Babini's.

"That you won't have the wedding without me."

"Don't worry. That's not happening any time soon." My stomach sinks as I speak, knowing exactly what it means for my sex life. Nothing.

"Are you like … you know?"

"Pregnant?" Sam looks like he's about to pass out, and I laugh. It's nothing more than he deserves, because I know what he's referring to. "No, I'm not on my period." He doesn't relax in any way. I roll my eyes. "And I'm not pregnant either."

His shoulders drop, and he whistles through his teeth. "Okay. Yeah, that's good."

"What's wrong, Sam?" I smile. "It's all part of your end game. Babies come with marriage."

His arms come around me and he pushes his weight onto his hands on the counter behind me, caging me in. "I want babies." He stares at my lips hungrily. "Lots of them." He starts to move his face closer, and my lips tingle in anticipation. "After we've had lots of sex."

"Something we can't do until we're married," I remind him, and we're back to having the same conversation we have each day, where I still don't get my happy ending.

"You're being a bitch."

"I'm not perfect, Sam. I never claimed to be. You want marriage? You want it all? Then you need to take the good with the bad. The bad being when I'm horny as fuck and you won't help me out."

I push him away and past him, all but stomping my sexually frustrated ass to the couch where we're getting ready to watch a movie now Russ is in bed.

"You know if this carries on," I call out, but not too loud in case Russ is still awake, "I'll just have to get myself off."

The sound of the chips flowing into the bowl Sam is preparing stops. "You wouldn't."

I chew on the inside of my cheek, fighting back a smile. "I'll do whatever I have to."

Sam walks over with the bowl of chips, switching off the lights as he goes. It's late, but I'm too frazzled to sleep. I settle on a Marvel movie, partly to keep Sam happy, but also because I know it will have little to no sex references.

"What are you doing?" I ask when we're half an hour in.

Sam shuffles at my side, leans back against the cushions and stretches out. "Come here."

He curls his finger, motioning for me to lie between his now parted legs. I do as he says, and settle with my back to his front, my head close to his, and go back to watching the movie. Well, I try to go back to watching it. Sam's legs sit each side of me, stretched across the full length of the couch.

My heart thuds, the sound hidden by the explosions on the screen.

This isn't helping my situation. Him being close and pressed against me. Him smelling ridiculously good.

"Do you know what I think you need?" he whispers against my ear, and my clit throbs.

"No," I mutter. "But I think you're going to tell me, anyway."

He laughs, and the breaths that come out with it tickle the skin on my neck, making the ache between my legs—the one that's been there since the night at the music hall—literally unbearable. "I think you need to learn how to relax, Soph. You're wound up tighter than a ball of string."

"And whose fault is that?" I snap.

The tips of his fingers trail over my shoulders, then play with the straps of my vest first.

When he focuses on the straps of my bra, he asks, "Is this the green one? The lace one?"

I do my best to focus on the movie, which is proving impossible with all the throbbing between my legs because of all the toying he's doing.

"Yeah," I reply, "it is."

He sucks in a sharp breath, then lets out a long, ragged exhale. Touché, Sammy, I think to myself. I know he loves this bra. Whenever I wear it, he can't keep his hands off it, which is laughable, as it isn't even one of the fancy lingerie sets Amanda made me buy last year. I bought it in high school. It's one of those comfort ones you never let go of, and Target's finest is catnip for his dick.

Sam's thumbs start to circle over the tight muscles in my back. He's right; I'm tight everywhere, and with every circle, every little bit of pressure he applies to my tender muscles, I feel myself finally relax. When I become supple against him, I expect him to stop and focus on the movie. He does the opposite. His hands skirt up and down my arms, which become covered in their own little mountain range of goosebumps. He doesn't comment, but I feel his smile in the darkness as he continues the movement, up and down. Sometimes slow, sometimes a little quicker.

He sets the pace, and my breathing follows.

So much for loosening the ball of string. I'm a tightrope ready to snap.

I almost do when Sam's breath skims my ear again. "How much do you want to come?"

I freeze between his legs, scared to answer, not sure if I'm capable. My eyes drop to the black denim covering his legs, the ones that sit perfectly against his muscles. Who knew a pair of jeans could fit so well?

Sam doesn't fall for my silence. "Answer me, Red."

"A lot," I reply, swallowing hard.

His chest vibrates against my back when he chuckles. I feel it everywhere. Heat pools low in my belly and I shift, the small movement rubbing against him, where I feel his painfully hard erection pressing into my back. I don't move again. I don't move when his right hand trails down my arm to my hand, where he toys with my fingers. I don't move when the same hand steadily traces a path from my hand, along my hip, settling above my zipper.

My core aches when he tucks his thumb in the waistband of my pants. His fingers stretch out, the tips resting directly above my clit.

I stare at the screen. I've forgotten what we're watching. I can barely breathe, scared if I do, he'll stop whatever it is he's doing.

Tap. Tap. Tap.

Four fingers tap the outside of my jeans.

My ears start to ring. I try to switch off from the steady rhythm and how good it feels.

Tap. Tap. Tap.

Electricity courses over my skin. Fire roars through my veins. My muscles tense. Heat builds between my legs, and I think I'm going to explode.

Tap.

He slows the pace.

Tap.

I'm ready to grab his hand and tap for him when he takes me by surprise and circles two fingers over the denim covering my tight bundle of nerves. One small motion over two layers of material is all it takes. I start to tumble into bliss. My body tries to fight it, but the pleasure hits its peak, and the waves wash over me, making me tremble silently against him in the dark.

When the pleasure subsides, I sag into the wall of muscle behind me. Spent.

Sam removes his hand, and we go back to watching the movie.

I decide the green lace Target bra is the only one I'm wearing until I have a ring on my finger and the surname Riley.

Chapter Twenty-Nine
Sam

"How are you doing, Sam?" asks John West, leaning back in his swanky exec chair, framed by the billboards of Times Square just outside his window.

"I'm good." I grin as the past few weeks flash through my mind. "Really, really good."

He pauses, then asks, "Your voice?"

"Found."

He beams. "Great news. That will make this easy." I give him a confused look. "I called in a favor with someone I think you need to talk to." He glances at the door and gives whoever I'm about to speak with a warm smile.

I turn slowly in my seat, confused at who I find. "Mr. Parker?"

Sophie's dad grins and gives me a small wave. The movement makes the yellow floral shirt he's wearing appear even more psychedelic. "Hi, Sam."

Shifting in my seat, I suddenly feel uncomfortable. I can't decide if it's because I'm anticipating the reason why John wants the two of us to speak, or because I now have to face Sophie's dad when we're no longer *just* friends.

"Is everything okay?" I ask, glancing between two of the most influential people in the music industry.

"Everything is fine," chuckles John. "Don't look so worried. I just think it would be beneficial after what's been going on to make sure we're covered in the future."

"Okay …"

John stands behind his desk and steps out so Mr. Parker can take his place. When Sophie's dad sits down, his shirt blends with one of the ads on display in the background. I hear the door shutting behind me as John leaves the two of us alone, and then silence takes over.

"Sam …"

"Mr. Parker …"

Amusement flashes through his dark blue eyes, the only resemblance Sophie has to him. "It's Stu. You know that."

I rub a hand across my jaw. "This doesn't feel like a Stu situation."

"What kind of situation does it feel like?" He drags open one of the drawers and a bottle of Scotch appears with two glasses. Not the expensive kind John always has on display. The cheap crappy kind that I can only picture someone like Stu drinking, because he hates anything fancy. It hits me that whenever a serious conversation happens in life, there's usually some amber nectar involved. "Did I say something funny?"

I realize I've been smiling to myself. "I just thought it was funny how whenever I have a serious conversation, there's usually Scotch around."

Stu grins. "It's standard." His reply makes me relax as I remember who it is I'm talking to and that I have nothing to be nervous about. "You're singing again?"

I nod. "Thanks to Sophie." He gives me a knowing smile but doesn't comment. "Can I ask you something?"

"Sure." He finishes pouring us each a drink and slides a glass my way across the desk.

"Do you ever get nervous? Going on stage, I mean."

"A better question would be when don't I get nervous."

"Seriously?" I ask, unconvinced by his answer. He's been in the music industry for decades. Won hundreds of awards with Sophie's mom. They're royalty.

"Seriously," he replies.

Amicable silence passes between us, and I use it to think back on all the times I've seen him perform. "You never look nervous."

"Want to know the secret?" I nod. "You just learn to hide it well." He raises his drink for a toast, and I follow suit, wondering what it is we're actually toasting to. I don't have to wait long, because Stu says, "To being nervous wrecks."

I throw my head back and laugh, then clink my glass against his. "Understatement of the century." We both take a drink and Stu lets out a satisfied sigh. I try to hide my wince, because it really does taste like crap. "I'm scared it's going to happen again," I admit.

It's a thought that's been keeping me awake each night. It feels incredible to have my voice back—so incredible I'm terrified of losing it again. I know now that it isn't everything, but it's still a huge part of who I am. It helps me to feel connected to my past and although I know life would go on without it, I just don't want that to be an option.

"Don't let your fear of fear ruin this experience."

"Easier said than done."

Stu sets his glass down. "Loss comes in all shapes and forms. How we deal with the after affects everything."

"Are we talking about singing, or my dad?"

"Both," says Stu with a sad smile.

"I'm scared of letting him down."

"How about …" Stu taps his finger against the desk. "We flip it. Rather than being scared of letting him down, look at everything you've done and how far you've come, and how proud it would make him."

A lump forms in my throat. "He'd have liked you."

"I don't doubt for a second that I would have liked him, too." He pauses and his mouth remains parted. His brows pull together in a frown he rarely wears.

"I know what you're going to say next. That this is how things were meant to be."

"We can't change the past, Sam. But what we can do … is use it to guide us in the future. We can use it to learn from our mistakes and the mistakes of others."

My head tilts to the side. "I thought we were meant to be talking about singing?"

"Music. We're talking about music. Singing is just one part of what we do. We contribute to something much bigger. It's a collaboration. You have a team at your side. If you feel yourself slipping, don't switch off. Use them—let them help you."

"And what if that doesn't work? What if the next time I break there's no fix?"

"Then we try something new. Use a different play. It's all a game, Sam … life. You just have to decide how much you want to win and how hard you're willing to fight for the outcome you want." I take another drink, bracing myself for what I want to say next. "You want to marry my daughter," Stu says, beating me to it.

"I've loved her since the moment I saw her."

Stu raises his glass for another toast. "You had my permission since the moment you made her believe that just being who she was is enough."

I refrain from tapping my glass against his again. "She kind of lost her way for a while."

"But you were always meant to help her find her way back. Real love isn't always straightforward. That's what makes it worth it. Nothing in life worth having comes easy."

He moves his glass, and it clinks with mine. "Help each other be the best versions of yourselves. Love each other hard and unforgivingly. Nothing else matters other than the person standing at your side."

There's a knock at the office door, and when I turn, I find John waving eagerly. Stu gives him a thumbs up then pulls out another glass when he comes back into the office.

"Cracked out the good stuff I see," says John, laughing. He takes his glass from Stu. His drink turns into a splutter. "I don't know why I let you keep this shit in my office." He faces me, wiping his mouth with the back of his hand. "Everything good?"

"Yep," I reply, feeling some of the potent Scotch going to my head.

"Great. We can start thinking about booking the album and the tour for after the summer."

I can only focus on one word.

"After?" I ask with a frown. I expected him to jump all over my change in circumstances and get us recording the first chance he could.

374

John nods. "I think a summer break is something the whole band needs."

"Oh." My shoulders sink and I feel flat. "Do you mind if I ask why?"

The corners of his mouth turn up into an understanding smile. "You guys have been working for this since you finished high school. I've watched you all grind harder than most of the bands out there. You deserve the break. Burnout is a real thing, Sam, and you're all there sitting at the top, ready to take off. Once this starts, there won't be time for a break, so use this time to live your life. Live in the moment and catch your breath, because things are going to get crazy." His smile gets bigger. "Plus, a little bird told me you'll be busy planning a wedding," he says absentmindedly, smirking at Stu.

"Abby is turning into quite the gossip."

"She gets it from her mother," John says, then laughs.

"So, you're not dropping us from the label?" I ask, needing some final, clear confirmation from him.

He straightens and unbuttons a couple of the buttons on his shirt, giving me a peek at the S.C.A.R.A.B. t-shirt he's wearing beneath it. "Why would I? I'm the band's biggest fan."

"Can I ask you one more thing?"

"Sure."

"What are you doing in the fall?" My gaze darts to Stu, and he gives me a knowing smile. "There's something I think you need to see."

Feeling lighter than I have in a long, long time, a couple of hours after my meeting with John West, I arrive home.

Home.

It has a new meaning with the two people waiting inside the apartment for me.

After pulling out my keys, I make quick work of unlocking and opening the door, desperate to see Sophie. She had a late night working a club opening yesterday and then an early start this morning. Not seeing her for so long has almost killed me.

When the door opens, I'm greeted with noise and laughter. Noise from the speaker system, blaring out the *Hairspray* soundtrack, laughter from Russ, who is folded in half on the couch, almost at the point of wheezing.

And the source of his laughter … Sophie, dancing on the coffee table, belting out the lyrics into a hairbrush with bright pink rollers in her hair. She spins around, and when her eyes lock with mine, I love her more than I ever thought I could love anyone. She curls her finger at me as she shimmies her ass.

"Be my seaweed," she singsongs, as the music continues.

I drop my bag on the floor, forgetting to shut the door as I dance my way over to her and we fall in sync. We've had weeks of practicing this shit, as Russ has had the soundtrack on repeat since Broadway. He almost combusted when he found out there was a movie as well. Not wanting to miss out on the fun, Russ stops laughing and jumps to his feet, singing Zac Efron's parts with ease.

Because I know she loves it when I do, I jump straight into the next part of the song—the part with the Christmas ham.

"Travolta's got nothing on you, Sammy," Sophie laughs over the music. "You're wasted with S.C.A.R.A.B. Think big. Think Broadway, baby."

She raises her hands in the air and starts to spin.

It's one of the best moments we've had together. It feels like we're a family.

And then Sophie stops spinning abruptly.

"Elayne? Hi?" she laughs over the music.

Elayne, the woman from Child Protection, remains standing in the open doorway with a bemused expression as Russ waves at her happily.

Because the music is too loud to think, let alone have a conversation over, I say, "Alexa. Stop."

We're left standing, panting, happy and sweaty in the deathly silent living room.

"Did we have one of those assessments scheduled?" Sophie asks. "Sorry, I forgot."

My skin crawls when my gut tells me something bad is about to happen.

Elayne's expression turns grim. "No, we didn't."

Sophie looks at her, confused. "That's what you're here for though, right?"

Elayne can't meet her eye when she replies sadly, "No. Unfortunately, Ms. Parker, I'm not."

Sophie

This can't be happening. I say as much out loud to Elayne.

"You can't do this. You can't take him." It all comes out almost as a shriek. I want to crawl into bed and pretend this isn't real, wake up and it all be a horrible dream. Sam places his hand on my knee. I barely feel it. Numb.

"You knew he had a couple waiting to adopt him."

"But we just …"

We just got him. We just figured things out. We just learned how to be a family. I don't have the strength to say any of it out loud. It already hurts enough.

Elayne gives me a look that breaks my heart, and I think I see hers breaking too. "You never had him, Sophie," she says quietly. "This is the way things are. You're his foster mom. It isn't permanent."

"Then make it permanent," I snap.

"Sophie," says Sam from my side, his voice low. "You need to calm down."

I laugh bitterly. "You can't be serious?" A tear rolls down my cheek. "Calm down, Sam? Really? She's about to take him away from us."

"To a family. So that he can be part of a family."

"He's part of ours!" This time I do shriek, right before I feel like I'm about to puke. I turn my attention back to Elayne, too angry with Sam to talk to him. "When?"

"In the fall. Everything will have gone through by then," she replies, her tone solemn, like the world is ending.

I feel like mine is.

"The fall ..." I whisper, unable to speak any louder. "But The American Showcase? This means everything to him. He's worked hard for it. H-he," my voice wobbles, turning into a sob. I try to muffle the sounds that come from my mouth, not wanting Russ, who's in his room, to hear. When I manage to calm myself, I take a breath, then more calmly, say, "He has a solo."

"There's nothing I can do," says Elayne. "It's out of my hands."

My world tilts on its axis and I feel like things will never be the same again.

"I'll adopt him. I'll adopt Russ." It's a rushed decision, but one I'll think through later. All I know is that I can't let this happen.

"Ms. Parker …" says Elayne on a sigh. "The family adopting Russ, financially, they're—well, they're able to support him …"

"Better than I can," I finish for her, and she nods. "Married?" She nods again. "Is there a white picket fence?"

She shakes her head. "It isn't about that."

I glance up at the ceiling, willing the tears to stop. "Sure it's not. What else would it be about?"

"It's about what's best for Russ. Who can support him and give him what he needs."

"No," I snap. "It's about those hoops. I've jumped already. I've proved that I can give him the best thing. A home. Please, let me do this."

"I can't."

"Then we're done here. Goodbye, Elayne."

I stand slowly, and on shaky legs, walk to my room. Sam calls after me, but I block him out. I block everything out.

I want to be alone. I need to be. I need to prepare myself for it, for what it will feel like when Russ isn't here and I am. Alone.

Chapter Thirty
Sophie

I t's the first night in weeks Sam sleeps on the couch. I don't go back out to him. I don't want to see him, or anyone for that matter.

I wake up early and go for a walk, wandering the streets of Brooklyn, searching for answers that don't want to be found.

It's getting close to eight when I know I have to go back, and with a heavy heart, I do, ready to tell Russ that he won't be living with us in a couple of months.

He knows the second I walk into the kitchen.

He's sitting at the kitchen counter eating breakfast with Sam at his side. His spoon stops halfway on its path to his mouth.

"I'm leaving."

My throat goes dry. I can't speak. All I can do is nod.

His spoon clatters, and I'm left with an 'I hate you,' as he storms out of the room.

Russ doesn't speak to me for the whole day. He barely comes out of his room.

"Go in and talk to him," says Sam, pushing a glass of wine my way. "From the just-in-case stash."

I pick it up and take a long drink without a word. Like Russ isn't speaking to me, I'm still not speaking to Sam. I hate myself for it. Hate that I'm pouring my anger his way, but I can't stop myself. It's all too much. It hurts too much.

After another long drink, I set my glass down, deciding he's right. It's late, but with everything going on, I know Russ will still be awake. I jump down from the stool, and right before I go to find Russ, I walk round the island to Sam. I don't want to be this person and I know, deep down, him intervening like he did yesterday was his way of protecting me from myself, from saying something there wouldn't be any coming back from and making things worse.

Surprise crosses Sam's face when I wrap my arms around his waist. "I'm sorry. I'm so sorry."

"I know. I'm sorry, too," he says, stroking a hand through my hair, taking the edge off the pain.

I shake my head and look up at him. "You have nothing to be sorry for. This is all on me. I shouldn't have taken it out on you. It wasn't fair."

"We hurt the ones we love," he replies with a smile, "because we know they will still love us, regardless. And I am sorry. Sorry I can't do anything to make this better. I hate it."

"I know." My eyes drop to the ground. "Me too."

"Hey." He places a finger under my chin and lifts. I can't look anywhere but at him. "You're not alone in this. You won't be alone. You have me. Always. I'm not going anywhere. I love you."

I nod and my lip wobbles. "I love you too, so much it hurts."

"Speak to him before he goes to sleep."

He presses a kiss against my lips. A small, gentle one. One full of tenderness and more love than I've ever felt from anyone before.

"No couch tonight," I say before leaving the room.

"No couch," he agrees.

A couple of minutes later, I knock on Russ's door and get no answer.

I don't try again, because I'll only get the same response. Instead, I open it slowly and find him lying on his bed, staring up at the ceiling.

"Hey, you," I say quietly.

He doesn't reply, so I walk over to him and perch on the side of the bed. Hesitantly, I take hold of his hand. He doesn't take it back. It's another bridge we need to build together so we can meet in the middle. My stomach twists painfully when I realize we're on a countdown to our last.

"I don't want this. You have to know that."

He doesn't say a word.

"I love having you here. I love having you in my life. Maybe we can figure out a way we can stay in touch?"

He blinks. Frowns. "You didn't fight for me."

"I-I—"

"You're leaving me, just like they did."

"Russ," I sigh. "I'm not. But this … there's nothing to fight. It's bigger than us both."

"I thought all this … I thought you wanted me."

My chest goes tight, and my heart constricts. "I do. I do want you. I want you here more than I want anything."

He finally moves his bloodshot eyes away from the ceiling and looks at me. "Then why can't I stay here?"

"There's a couple that want to adopt you. You'll have a *real* family again. Just like you wanted."

He shakes his head and starts to cry. "I don't want them. I want you. I want you and Sam. You're my family."

I pull him into my arms, and we sit for a while, holding each other together before everything falls apart.

"You need to get some sleep," I say eventually.

He doesn't argue, just climbs back into bed and lets me tuck the covers around him.

Reluctantly, I make my way to the door, and when I turn back, ready to close it, his small voice finds me.

"I called you Mom in my head yesterday."

I stifle a sob and close the door before he can see me break in two.

Sam

"Fuck, man," says Ryan, taking a long drag from his joint while another circles the room. "That's fucked."

He blows smoke rings into the air, extending his arm out to the side so I can take the joint from him.

"So fucked," says Jake.

"Really, really fucked," finishes Zach.

I'm midway through taking a drag myself when all the F-bombs are thrown around, and I choke with laughter.

"Does anyone want to say fuck again?" I cough. Ryan raises his hand lazily in the air. "That was a joke."

Sophie called into work sick for the week. Needless to say, no one at Next Level has an issue with her feigning illness.

"Fuck," I say, joining the club, taking another long drag. "I still can't believe this is happening." But you knew it would from the get-go, my logical friend reminds me, the way I should have kept reminding Sophie.

Whatever they talked about last night, it cleared the air between them and Sophie has taken Russ to Coney Island for the day with Abby and Clara, wanting to do whatever she can to keep his mind off the news.

The empty, too-silent apartment taunted me for all of five minutes before I jumped into the S.C.A.R.A.B. group chat and requested an emergency meeting—weed compulsory. Because they're my team, like they keep telling me. They didn't ask why, simply agreed to meet at The Wreck within the hour, and Ryan confirmed he'd bring the good stuff. It's not even eleven and we're already gone, floating in the clouds, looking down on all the shit going on, seeing funny sides that don't exist.

"Wait, wait, wait, waiiiiit," says Ryan, holding up a hand and lingering way too long on the final wait. "Run it all by me again." So, I do, for the third time. When I'm finished, he frowns. "So, let me get this straight. Tell me if I'm wrong, but the reason Russ can't stay is because he's being adopted, yeah?" I nod. "And the reason Sophie can't adopt him is that … she isn't married?"

"That's part of it, I guess. If we were going to push to get him and stop the other couple, they'd look into everything. Financial security, all of it."

384

"Why don't you just marry her, then?"

"Just marry her." I inhale the last of the weed, then as I'm exhaling, say, "Just like that."

"I mean, it will help with the ridiculous sex ban you've put her on." I roll my eyes and choose not to comment, because he doesn't get it. "And you've already told her you want it all. So, why not? Do it and give her everything she wants."

"It's a good idea," says Jake seriously.

"And where exactly would we go on short notice?"

"Vegas," says Zach, waving his phone in the air. "There are flights still available for tomorrow morning. How many seats am I booking?"

"Booking? Like I'm actually doing this? We're assuming she's going to say yes."

"Technically, she already has," says Jake.

"Right …" Even with the amount of weed we've smoked, the pieces slot together, and it all makes sense.

Why can't we do this? We can. The why to the when is just a bunch of good old semantics.

"Eighteen," I say to Zach, pulling out my wallet and tossing my credit card at him. "Book eighteen seats."

"Who the hell is coming?" laughs Ryan.

"Everyone Sophie will want there," I reply.

Sophie

We have the best day at Coney Island.

I spend the entire time creating snapshots in my mind of moments I never want to get. Feelings I never want to go without.

It's around four PM when Abby and I decide to get Russ and Clara an early dinner while we're still out having fun, that it happens. It's right when Russ takes a huge bite of his hot dog and bright yellow mustard drips out of the end of the roll. He's put that much on. The kid won't eat vegetables, but he'll douse a hot dog in half a bottle of the cheapest, shittiest French M Coney Island has to offer.

He looks down at the stain, licks his finger and tries to get it out. All it does is smudge the yellow around, making it worse. His head snaps up, his eyes sparkle at me mischievously.

"Crapper."

It's then that I know I love him. I love him in ways I never knew I could love another.

The love I have for Russ is the selfless kind. It's the kind that makes you want to do anything for them. The kind that would make you sacrifice yourself, to tear down the world because of it, to make sure they're safe.

A motherly kind of love.

And it's when we're walking along the hallway to our apartment a couple of hours later that I sense something isn't right.

"You're sure you don't mind us coming back?" asks Abby. "I don't want to gatecrash, but Clara loves Russ, and I love seeing them together."

"Stop asking before I say that I do mind."

Abby sticks her tongue out, and I laugh, sliding my key into the lock. I'm about to open the door when I wrinkle my nose.

"Do you smell that?" I ask her.

"Yeah," she replies, looking around for the source.

"Smells weird," says Russ, yawning.

"Mommy, I go pee pee," Clara adds on the end.

"Sorry," says Abby. "Can we go in before she pee pees on the floor? We can figure out what the smell is after."

I open the door quickly before there can be any accidents, and step inside the apartment.

"Sam! What the hell? Are you trying to burn the place down?" I shriek, taking in the hundreds of candles.

My hair's gathered in one hand, protected from the flames, and I'm already blowing some of them out when Abby clears her throat. "Erm, Soph …"

"What Sammy doing, Mommy?" Clara asks, tugging Abby's hand.

I turn slowly, and when I'm facing into the living area, there he is, waiting on one knee. My heart flutters.

"Sam …"

"Soph …"

"What are you doing?"

"I want to ask you something." The candlelight flickers, highlighting his face and how nervous he is. "But I can't when you're standing on the other side of the room. Come here."

Six slow steps, and I'm in front of him.

"This is really messing with the timeline," I say. The words feel croaky and harsh against my throat, like they're the first I've said in years.

"Fuck the timeline."

I wrinkle my nose again; hit with the same smell I was at the front door. Sam keeps watching me with wide blue eyes and giant pupils.

"Wait." I sniff again, then slap him on the arm. "You're stoned?! You're actually proposing to me when you're high?"

"It was hours ago," he admits sheepishly. "Well, it was until I got nervous, and Ryan had some spare. I'm not that high."

"Unbelievable," I huff and my eyes move to the side of the room.

"I know you are." He grins, and my anger thaws instantly, because I could never, ever stay mad at him. "Marry me, Red."

My eyes move back and settle on his face. I could easily say yes to anything he says under normal circumstances. I could say yes to what he's asking right now, especially when he's looking at me like he is—like I'm his world.

"No," I answer.

His mouth parts, confusion lining his forehead. "What?"

I drop my voice, so that Russ can't hear. "I know why you're doing this."

He slides a small black box out of his pocket and stands. He doesn't open the box, and with him on his feet rather than down on one knee, the moment feels less intimidating. With him closer—close enough I could kiss him—my body warms, and I reconsider my no that was never really a no.

"That isn't why I'm asking. It's just semantics." I bite my bottom lip, and he reaches up, dragging it from between my teeth with his thumb. "I'm asking because I want to spend a lifetime watching you do that," he says, eyes lasered on my mouth until he looks up, and what I see then is the start of forever. "I'm asking because I meant everything I've told you. I want you. I want to love you. I want to grow old with you. I want it all, and I want it with you."

"I love these speeches." I smile. "Can we work them into the vows or some kind of marriage contract? I'm thinking they should at least be a weekly requirement."

Sam's expression turns serious, and he watches me intently. "Does that mean you're saying yes?"

I laugh lightly, knowing there was never going to be any other answer. Not with him.

"You're my best friend." His shoulders drop a little at my use of the one word that has got in the way of us being together for twenty years. I smile, knowing my words don't mean what he thinks they do and that I'm nowhere near close to being finished. "You're the one person who gets me." I take a breath. "You're the only one who will still watch *Annie* with me." I tilt my head. "You're the reason why, even on the shitty days, I want to get out of bed, and you're the reason why, when I climb back in at the end, it's with a smile on my face. I want all of it. The house, the kids-plural, including Russ. No matter how hard we have to fight. I want to celebrate all the holidays I know you hate, because I know things too, lots of them, and I want to do it all with you by my side."

"So?" he says, dipping his head and moving in closer.

I giggle. "So, after Shaun informed me that I'd get a lifetime of free drinks at Riffs if I became a Riley, how could my answer be anything else?"

"Say it."

"Yes. I'll marry you, Sam. Regardless of the semantics."

The black box falls to the ground at the same time Sam's lips crash against mine, moving desperately, pouring all the emotions he's feeling into every movement and every tease of his tongue. I'm tempted to try my luck with the bedroom for hot, steamy, celebratory engagement sex, but the opportunity is stolen from me when light floods the room.

We pull apart, startled, as the rest of S.C.A.R.A.B. spill into the living area from the coat closet, whistling and cheering, bringing with them the aroma of weed. I'm too happy to be pissed and figure the hundreds of scented candles still burning will eventually get rid of the smell.

"Congratulations," says Abby as she pulls me in for a hug.

Russ watches from the side, taking it all in. Sam and I join back together and focus only on him.

"Come here," I say, and he rushes over. We envelope him between us, and I consider staying like this forever, so we never have to let him go.

"Russ sandwich!" hoots Ryan in the background.

"So, when's the wedding?" asks Abby when we finally pull apart.

"Tomorrow," replies Sam, unphased, like he hasn't just dropped a major bombshell.

My eyes pop out of my skull. "Tomorrow? Where? How?"

"Vegas."

"Ooh!" squeals Abby. "I love Vegas."

"You know Russ can't come with us right …" I whisper in Sam's ear. He stills. "He can't leave New York."

"Dammit."

"Leave it with me," I say lightly, trying not to ruin the moment. "So, who else is coming?"

Sam grins. "Everyone."

It takes twenty minutes for him to realize he forgot to give me the ring—a white gold band with a small diamond.

Simple and uncomplicated, just like the two of us together.

Sam

The couple of hours after my official proposal to Sophie are a blur.

With a new and rapid timeline that works for us, but probably wouldn't work for anyone else, the celebrations start immediately. Zoe and Amanda arrive less than an hour after Sophie calls them with a garment bag that has Sophie squealing in our bedroom. Shaun arrives not long after that, bottles of champagne filling his arms.

"Thanks, bro," I say, taking some of them from him and setting them to chill in the refrigerator.

"Congratulations." He smiles.

We stand together, taking in the rest of the room, which is filled with laughter and promises of the future, with only one more Russ-shaped mountain left to climb.

"I don't just mean thanks for the Champagne."

"I know."

I don't say anything else; I don't need to. It's the way things have always been between us. Few words that only we know the meaning behind after what we've been through together.

"Do you think …" I think hard on what I want to say next, no clue how to say it without getting his back up. "Do you think you and Zo—"

"Champagne!" he calls out to the room, shutting me down.

There's no point in trying to get him to talk, especially when the teal-haired vision who's always owned his heart is close by. Where life has taught me that I want to fight for love, it's taught my brother that he wants to run from it.

He's already filled the glasses when Sophie comes back into the room, laughing with her phone held up in front of her. I watch, willing her to look at me, just for a second among all the chaos. She must feel how much I need her to, because her eyes move away from the screen and when they meet with mine, everything disappears. My galloping heart slows to a rhythm, not quite steady, but somewhere between a calm and storm that it only knows for her.

She walks over with her phone still stretched out in front of her, then nestles into my side.

"I said no wedding while I wasn't there," Sooz moans from Cape Town.

Sophie glances up at me, smiles, then looks back at Sooz and throws me under the bus. "Blame Sam."

Sooz glares at me through the screen, and I start to sweat. "We can video call you."

"Fine," Sooz huffs. "But when I'm back, we're having words."

"I'll be waiting," I wink.

"Sooz, baby, missing me?" grins Ryan, snatching Sophie's phone out of her hands.

"Like a hole in the head." Ryan laughs and laughs, then laughs some more. "You're stoned. How original. Put Sophie back on."

Ryan walks off with the phone still in his hands. "Not until you tell me you love me."

Sophie follows Ryan, laughing, ready to diffuse the ticking time bomb that is Rooz. Ryan and Sooz together. Ryan has a thing about merging names. Rooz ... Jabby ... he hasn't had a chance to come up with mine and Sophie's merger yet. I have a feeling the S initials are screwing things up for him.

When Sophie and Ryan are gone, I stand back and take it all in, grinning like an idiot until I realize Russ isn't anywhere to be found.

Knowing there's only one other place he can be, I head to his room and knock on the door.

"Yeah?" comes his voice, sounding small and defeated.

I slip inside, blocking out the noise and celebrations when I close the door behind me. I walk over to his desk where he's sitting and drawing.

"Everything okay?" I ask, knowing really, nothing is.

"Just tired," he says quietly, carrying on with what he's doing.

I take in what he's working on. "That's cool."

"It's for you and Sophie for when I leave."

The image he's working on is of the three of us, together—a family worthy of a perfect picture. I give his shoulder a squeeze, but I don't say anything, because there's nothing that I can say that will change things. I want to tell him that it might not be the end, that all of this, what's happening tonight, is really all for him. I want to tell him that it's Sophie and I fighting as hard as we can for him, and that I promise I will do everything I can to make sure he can stay.

It's the small boy inside me, the one who's been through some of the things he has, that stops me. The one who always wished that people wouldn't make promises they couldn't keep. Sometimes, silence is better than words that have no meaning.

I stay with him for a while, stand in a meaningful silence, watching as he finishes his drawing.

When I leave, it's without any promises being made, but I still feel hope.

Chapter Thirty-One
Sam

We're somewhere over Kansas the following morning when I sense there's something wrong with Sophie.

Over three hours of silence during a five-hour plus flight is her tell. I know there's more to it than the early start.

She's absorbed in one of the inflight movies, when I decide to broach the subject.

I clear my throat. When I get nothing in return, I tap her knee. She's fully aware I want to talk to her, because she looks at me out of the corner of her eye in a blink-and-you'd-miss-it moment. She still won't give me her full attention, so I opt for a non-subtle approach, lifting the old school flight headphones off her head.

"Hey," she pouts, attempting to grab them back.

I hold them in the aisle, out of her reach. "I want to talk to you."

"We can talk later. I was at the best part."

I raise a brow. "Later, when we're standing in front of Elvis saying our vows later?"

"Sam …" she huffs.

"There's a little thing called pause." With a roll of her eyes, she follows through with my suggestion and the movie on her screen freezes. "What's wrong?"

"There's nothing wrong," she replies, diverting her gaze.

"Yo! Soph!" whisper-hisses Zoe from the middle row. "Catch!"

A pack of blue Sour Patch Kids hit me in the chest.

"Thanks for that."

"Whoops, sorry," giggles Zoe, giving me a smile that says she isn't before going back to talking with Amanda.

I stare at the bright packet sitting on my fold-down table. "E numbers at this time in the morning? You only go for the hardcore stuff when you're …" It all starts to make sense, her snappy, huffy mood that only happens at key points in a month. I twist in my seat so I can face her fully. "Wait. Are you menstruating?"

The last part comes out louder than I intend, and Sophie cringes.

"Menstruating? Really, Sam? You could have said something a bit more discreet."

"Is that what's wrong? You're not having second thoughts or anything, right?"

Hearing the insecurity in my words, Sophie's hormone-fueled armor cracks and she kisses me. "I'd never have second thoughts. I'm just pissed off."

"Why? Do you have cramps? Are you worried about that bloating crap in your dress? 'Cause I swear, Red, you'll still look smoking."

"No, Sam, I'm not worried about bloating," she hisses. "I'm pissed because it's going to be my wedding night and I still won't get a screaming orgasm."

"Why did no one tell me we were talking about screaming orgasms?" Ryan whispers, as he peers through the gap between the seats.

"Screaming orgasms?" says Grams next to him, loud enough that half the plane can hear. "Shaun, are they off the new menu? Like those Zombie drinks you made me try?"

Shaun groans, shaking his head, while Ryan snickers as I mouth 'dick' at him.

"But no dick for Soph," he replies with a wink.

If he were next to me, I'd hurt him. It's probably a good thing he isn't, or we'd wind up getting thrown off the plane.

Sophie beats me to giving him a verbal whip lashing. "Asshole. I'm joining Sooz in the Ryan hate club."

His laughing stops abruptly. "It's hate fueled by love."

"Keep telling yourself that," replies Sophie, snatching the headphones from me and pressing play on her movie.

I can't hold in my laughter when we're flying over Colorado and the characters get a wedding night that Sophie, unfortunately, will only be able to dream about.

At the wedding chapel, Aunt Rachel appears behind me in my reflection in the mirror. I'm struggling to fix my bowtie, because my hands keep shaking.

"Want some help?" she asks with a hauntingly familiar smile.

A lump forms in my throat. "Sure."

I turn away from the mirror so she can fix the mess I've made. When she's standing in front of me, she extends her arms fully so she can reach, because she's gotten smaller over the years.

"Nervous?" she asks quietly, undoing ten minutes of pointless attempts.

"Nah." Her hands pause. "Terrified."

Rachel's laughter fills the room, a sound I didn't hear until a couple of years after we moved to Brooklyn. She loops one side of the material around the other. "He'd be proud of you."

I struggle to swallow when my mouth goes dry. "You think?"

"I know."

"I miss him," I admit. "Every day." My eyes move to where the sun is streaming in. The air conditioning whirring is the only sound there is until I continue. "But there are times when I forget. I don't want to forget, but sometimes I feel like I hardly knew him at all."

Rachel's hands continue working on the bow. "You know more than you think. You've just never realized it."

I frown. "What do you mean?"

"You're just like him. And your father, well ..." she laughs lightly, "he loved music, especially singing. He loved to laugh. He loved to live. But most of all, he loved to love. Just like you."

My gaze drops, watching as Rachel finishes pulling the bow tight. "But things didn't work out for him and Mom."

Rachel straightens the bow and gives it a final gloss over before dropping her hands to her sides and taking a step back. "Sometimes, love is messy. Sometimes, it's complicated. Sometimes, it's so easy it convinces you there's a fault somewhere. There are different kinds of love. Different ways of falling into it. Different ways of falling out of it. Your father didn't stop believing in love because your mother left … why would he? He still had you and your brother, and the best kind of love there is."

I look down, chewing on the inside of my cheek as I consider what I'm about to say next. "He promised things would never change, and then everything did."

Rachel reaches over and squeezes my arm. I look up and find her smiling. "Even though he broke his promise, I know if he were here, he'd make it again, even if he knew what the outcome would be."

"Why?"

"Sam, when you love someone, if it means it helps them and stops them from hurting, if it helps them to keep moving forward with their life, sometimes you have to make promises you know will eventually be broken. Nothing in life is a given. But most things in life are worth taking a risk for."

I let out a long breath and with it goes years' worth of grief I've never dealt with. I needed to hear her words more than I realized.

A quick glance at my phone and I see we have thirty minutes to fill.

"Can you tell me more about him?"

Rachel settles in a chair. "What do you want to know?"

I pull a chair up next to her and lean back, getting comfy. "Everything."

Sophie

I'll be the first to admit that I've always been way too judgmental when it comes to Vegas.

Weddings in Vegas, in particular.

I always pictured them being like what you see in the movies, *The Hangover* being the one at the forefront of my mind. The loving couple falling over wasted. Emotional strippers wearing too much glitter and not enough clothing. Cheap and nasty plastic floral arrangements with lights flashing in the background, while Elvis unites love with Ike and Tina blaring through the speakers.

Like I said: Judgy … and one hundred percent unjustified, because Vegas isn't like I expected at all.

Sam pushed the boat out, flashed his rockstar wallet and the next thing we knew we had the finest floral arrangements in Nevada. Unfortunately, Elvis is non-negotiable as far as Sam and Ryan are concerned. I refuse to let them know I'm secretly happy about it, or let on that he will be the only person standing at the front wearing white.

And a perk of being a Parker … we don't need Ike or Tina. I've got my pick of performers fighting over who is going to be the one to serenade me as I walk down the relatively short aisle.

"You look incredible," beams Zoe, as I skim my hands over my dress a final time.

"It definitely doesn't clash?"

"Not at all," says Abby, wiping beneath her eyes. "Gah! Why am I crying still?"

"Because it's what you do best," laughs Zoe. "Are you ready? I think we have to be out there in a few minutes."

I stare at my reflection in the mirror. I always thought that something as monumental as getting married, committing to a lifetime with someone, would be terrifying. But knowing it's Sam there waiting for me at the end of the aisle has never felt more right. All I feel is calm.

"Yeah. I'm ready."

Abby follows Zoe's lead, stands, and leaves the dressing room.

Zoe goes to follow her out but pauses by the dresser. "Hey, your phone is ringing." She picks it up. "Damn, it stopped."

"Thanks," I reply, taking it from her, frowning at the screen when I see it isn't a number saved to my contacts, but has a Brooklyn area code. I contemplate whether there's something wrong back home, then realize everyone is here with us.

"I'm gonna head out there. You good?"

I look up and give Zoe a quick smile. "I'm good."

My frown reappears and deepens the second Zoe steps out of the room, as my phone starts ringing again with the same number. I consider not answering, but I know it will bug me if I don't, so I hit accept.

"Hello?" I answer.

"Ms. Parker."

"Elayne?"

"Is now a good time to talk?"

I take in my reflection in the mirror. It couldn't be a worse time to talk.

"I have a few minutes," I reply, sitting down.

"Ms. Parker, I have something I need to run by you."

She's back to being her usual serious self, giving nothing away with her voice. I have a strong suspicion it's to do with our abrupt goodbye the other night—something that's weighed down on me since. I feel like, in the short time we've known each other, we've formed one of those weird connections that are sometimes found with the people you least expect.

Which is why I can't leave things between us as they are.

"Actually," I say, tracing a finger over the silky material covering my lap. "About ten minutes from now, it will be Mrs. Riley."

There's a long pause.

"Ms. Parker. There's someth—"

"Elayne, I owe you an apology for how I handled things the other night. I was hurting. You caught me off guard and I was wrong. I knew this was a possibility—Russ having to leave. I just didn't want to think about or face up to it.

"You forced my hand, and I hated it. But I should thank you, because you helped me realize something. Russ makes me want to be a better person. He makes me want to be someone worthy of being his mother. I know none of this is normal, and I know this isn't how things are supposed to go. But that little boy has changed my life in the best possible way, and I can't imagine living it without him. I refuse to live it without him.

"I love Sam. Marrying him under the circumstances is a bonus. We were going to end up here at some point, anyway, but whatever hoops there are … I'll jump. I'll keep on jumping if Russ is there at the finish line. But please help me, Elayne. I'll beg if I have to."

"Ms. Parker," says Elayne firmly. "There's a reason I've called."

"Oh?" Something in her voice lights the smallest flame of hope. "A Russ-related reason?"

"Yes." She pauses. It's a second at most, but it feels like an eternity. "Russ will be able to attend The American Showcase."

401

The flame burns a little brighter and I shuffle in my seat. There's a torturously long pause, then Elayne clears her throat.

"Ms. Parker, that night in the precinct ... I've already told you what I thought about what you said. But I never told you about how it made me feel. We're taught in this job not to let things become personal. It changes our actions, clouds our judgement over what is right and wrong.

"There's never been anything to cloud over when it comes to you and Russ. It's rare to see what I have between the two of you. A perfect match. Some might call it fate. But it's there, I can see it, and thanks to your words, I feel it. I feel inspired. Inspired to believe that things could change in my line of work and that the right people, regardless of what mold they fit, or don't fit into, can achieve the outcome they deserve.

"Children don't need perfection. They don't need a certain salary—although it helps. They need love. And thanks to you, there's been a ripple in the water beneath all the grays. The couple who was going to adopt Russ have pulled out. They want ... they want a baby instead. If you meant what you said the other night—that you would like to adopt Russ—then I would like to help you."

There's a part of me that wants to stomp my foot; declare how unfair the system is. How can people pick a child, promise them a future, then discard them? It's like they've gone to a store and picked up an apple, then decided they want the smaller one, or the one with red skin, not green. These are small people we're dealing with. Humans. It's not right, and I'm about to say as much, but then I focus on the last part of what she's said and what this will mean for us. All of us. Sam, Russ and I. Together.

I can't breathe. Can't move. Can't do anything apart from sit with my mouth hanging open.

"Ms. Parker?" says Elayne awkwardly after a minute of no response.

"I—" I seriously need to get my shit together and reply, which is reinforced when the door to the dressing room opens, and Zoe sticks her head through.

"It's time, Soph."

I give her an excited nod and a hold a finger in the air, asking her without words, for another minute. She nods and closes the door again.

"Are you being serious right now?" I screech when it finally sinks in what Elayne has said.

"Very serious, Ms. Parker," says Elayne, laughing. "Or should I say Mrs. Riley? We should probably say goodbye so you can go get married."

"Yeah, we should," I reply, beaming into the empty room, feeling like my heart's about to burst from my chest.

"We can organize the paperwork in the coming weeks. This isn't the end, it's only the beginning. We have a way to go, and it will take time. The process is long, sometimes frustratingly slow. But I'm happy to support and guide you both through it."

I don't hear any of the minor details, I just stand grinning. "Thank you, thank you, thank you," I squeal, not caring about the pitch I'm reaching. Elayne laughs. "Okay, okay, I'm hanging up."

"For the final time, goodbye, *Ms. Parker.*"

I feel her smile through the phone.

"Wait, Elayne, before we do actually hang up and I become a Riley, I just want to say I could have been Russ's parent on my own. I would have been fine on my own. More than fine."

Elayne doesn't pause before replying, "I know you would have been, Sophie."

Hovering in the main foyer outside Vegas' finest wedding chapel, my stomach does its first flip of excitement.

Footsteps come to a stop behind me, and I take a deep breath before spinning around.

"Sophie … you look beautiful."

My face breaks into a huge grin. "Thanks, Daddy."

"Ready to become a unit of two?" he says, holding his arm out for me to hook mine around.

I take it without any hesitation whatsoever. "Three." His brows shoot up, and my smile, which I didn't think could get any bigger, does. "A unit of three."

He nods in understanding, eyes glistening with tears—happy ones—and we turn to the door. Music filters through it, signaling that it's time, then Dad pushes it open and we step into the room. It's filled with an incredible display of multi-colored flowers that put Zoe's desk choices to shame, and a ton of fake Wisteria covering the wedding arch that's waiting for me at the end of the aisle.

The sweet melodies Hale creates as his fingers move expertly across the keys of a piano near the front fill me with warmth. The soft lyrics about love coming from Aurelia guide me onto a new path; one ready to lead me into a future without any limits, expectations, or pressure. A future that can be whatever I want it to. A future that's mine, and mine alone.

It's the familiar, deep blue eyes holding mine with every step I take, watching like they always have, that draw me forward. With Dad at my side, I move past the people who Sam and I love the most. The ones who have each, in their own way, helped us get to this point.

When I reach the front, and Dad lets go for a final time, Sam gives me a lopsided smile—one that makes my heart stop and race at the same time. It's then that I know it doesn't matter what we do or achieve tomorrow, next week, or in ten years, just being who we are is enough. Being together is enough.

Hale plays the final chords of the song as Sam takes my hand and we stand together in front of Elvis, dressed all in white. Right before the ceremony officially begins, I smile to myself as I flick my hair back off my shoulder. Sam gives me a sideways glance, tracking the movement, his gaze locking on the red, silk floor-length dress Zoe picked for me half an hour after I announced our plans yesterday, and what's peeping out from beneath it. The muscle in his jaw ticks. I smile straight ahead, refusing to look him in the eye.

The ceremony goes seamlessly, and Elvis proves he isn't just the king of rock and roll, but wedding officiants, too. And then come the vows; the only moment there are any signs of nerves … on my part, at least. Sam's busy giving a heated stare to the green bra strap I've left purposely on display. Because so far in our relationship, we've done things in our own unique way, we decided to with our vows as well.

At the last second, I take a deep breath and my hand trembles, just a little, in Sam's. He looks up, and all my worries slip away.

"I never thought I'd fall in love with my best friend." I pause. "I guess I didn't fall … not really." A small line appears between Sam's brows, stopped from growing deeper when I continue. "I loved you from the first moment I saw you. That love changed, was nurtured, grew and became what's us. Some people say love is hard. I wouldn't know. Sam Riley, loving you is the easiest thing I've ever done, because you help make it effortless just by being you.

"I want to love you through the good. I want to love you harder through the bad. You're the always I never knew I needed. The always I couldn't live without. And one of my biggest achievements in life will be being able to call myself your wife."

My eyes skirt to the side as I let out a ragged breath, finding even Ryan looking emotional.

"For the record," Sam says, turning to our family and friends. "I was supposed to be the one good at giving speeches." He scratches the side of his head as the room fills with laughter. "I don't know if I can beat that." He turns his attention back to me. "I don't need to."

His thumbs trace circles over the back of my hands, and my eyes start to burn. He frowns at where our hands join, and swallows. An awkward laugh crawls up his throat, and he glances away for a second, rubs beneath his nose, then clears his throat before focusing back on our hands.

"I had vows without promises planned, because the first promise someone ever made to me broke me when it was broken. I've spent my life never wanting to hurt people by breaking my own, so it was easier not to make any at all."

He looks up for just a second, then looks back at our hands.

"I don't want to live a life without promises any more. I want to make promises to you, Sophie Parker. I want to make a lot of them, and I want to spend my life doing what I can to keep them."

This time when he looks up, his eyes connect with mine, blue locks with blue, and he doesn't look away.

"I might not always do the right thing, but I promise I'll do whatever I need to do to make it up to you when I fail. I might not always do things you like, but I promise to learn from my mistakes. We might not always agree, but I promise to always meet you halfway. I promise to spend each day trying to be the best version of myself I can be, for us both. But the one promise I know will be easy to keep is that I promise to love you for as long as you want me by your side."

Somewhere among all his promises, tears start trailing down my cheeks.

Elvis does the official parts where we promise each other always, sealing it with a kiss I never want to end, but when it does, leaves me excited for the next, and a lifetime of ones after that.

Sam brushes his nose over mine, stares into my eyes, and then says under his breath so only I can hear, "The green bra? Seriously?"

Because I know exactly what the two combined do to him, I draw my bottom lip between my teeth, release it slowly, then reply, "Repayment for announcing to a plane full of strangers that I'm menstruating and want a screaming orgasm, *husband*."

Laughing, he pulls me into his side and presses a kiss against the side of my head as we turn to face everyone for the first time as The Rileys, and I can't keep the euphoric grin off my face.

We don't waste any time in Vegas. We hop straight back on a plane so we can get home to Russ who's being looked

407

after by Amanda. The second we step through the door to the apartment, wedding party in tow, I crouch down so we're at eye level, squeeze his hand and ask, "So, how would you like to become a Riley? Officially."

I get my answer when he jumps into my arms and flattens me at Grams' feet.

Chapter Thirty-Two
Sam

Unfortunately, there was no wedding night.

Technically, there was a night—just a long one that consisted of a late flight from Vegas back to New York. Even if Sophie had been able to, she wouldn't have had a screaming orgasm, because as soon as we arrived home, we all passed out and slept through most of the following morning.

"Hey, husband," Sophie says, sidling up to me in the kitchen around midday. "So, I was thinking we could do with a few days, just us. So, I figure let's just do it. No time like the present, right?"

"Just us?" I arch a brow and raise my glass of water, taking a small sip.

"I need you to pack a bag and leave."

I splutter. "Leave?"

"I've got shit to do, Sam."

I frown, trying to read from her face what she's up to, but she gives nothing away. "What about Russ?"

Sophie grins and grabs her own glass, turning on the tap and filling it with water. "Already covered. He's going to stay with my parents for a couple of days. He can't wait for unlimited time with Grams and Xavier. So, can you drop him off and then go stay with the guys or something?"

"Just like that …" I say, setting my glass down on the kitchen counter.

"Yep. Just like that." She stands on her tiptoes and her lips skim the shell of my ear. "I promise you'll like it."

"Fine." Before she can move away, I loop my arm around her waist and pull her in, sealing my mouth against hers. Her tongue sweeps against mine, and I groan, pulling her harder against me, needing her closer.

Hands find my chest, and Sophie pushes me back. "Go." The breathy sound of her voice keeps me rooted to the spot. I watch as she licks her already swollen lips. She giggles and kisses me quickly, then pushes harder, increasing the gap between us. "Tomorrow."

There's something about that one word that has me doing as I'm told. It feels like a promise. I hope it's a promise.

A few hours later, after dropping Russ at Sophie's parents, I make my way to Riffs to meet the guys. Inside, I find them sitting at what's become *our* table over the years.

"Here he is!" calls out Ryan when he catches sight of me. Jake, Zach, Shaun and a few of our other friends jump to their feet and cheer. I grin, walking over, feeling more at ease than I have in months. Impressive, considering the time of year it is.

The thing about Riffs is, it's like a second home. If we were anywhere else, the guys wouldn't be able to act like they are doing, because people are always watching, phones ready. But here, there isn't a phone in sight, just amused smiles being thrown our way.

"Sophie will kill me if I'm hungover tomorrow," I say when I reach the table, giving the four pitchers of beer and glasses a pointed look.

"What happens at your bachelor party, stays at your bachelor party," says Ryan, throwing an arm around my shoulders and giving me an excited shake. Jake fills a glass and hands it over.

"Are you going to tell her that in the morning? Her wrath is yours to face."

Ryan pauses and scratches at his jaw. "What time are you leaving?"

"Nine thirty, sharp."

He glances at his phone, and I watch the cogs turning in his mind. "Free for all until twelve. Anything goes as long as you stop at midnight."

I shake my head, laughing. "That's not how it works. Plus, I'm not a bachelor anymore."

"You didn't exactly give us much of a timeline to work with," says Jake.

"So," I say, sliding into the booth beside Zach and taking a long drink of my beer. Shaun stands and disappears without a word. I try not to focus on the hard-set line of his jaw; I don't need to think about why it's there. "What's the plan?"

The guys look at each other but don't get a chance to say a word, as the opening of one of my favorite songs filters in from the outside area.

I frown and turn toward the doors. "Is that …" as the opening continues on a loop and gets louder, I jump to my feet. "Live?" The guys all shrug, but their grins give it away. "You're kidding me?!"

Forgetting about my beer, I race from the table and out to the large terrace, which is set up, gig ready. The festoon lights Shaun saves for special performances are already glowing in the afternoon light, ready for the night ahead, and all the tables and chairs that fill the area during the summer months have been moved to the sides, leaving a huge open space. Crowds have already gathered around the outdoor stage.

My mouth drops open at the sight of Patrick Stump standing in front of the mic. "Fall Out Boy?" I almost pass out when Pete Wentz waves at me. "You got Fall Out Boy?!"

"As much as I'd like to take credit for this," chuckles Shaun, "*I* didn't do anything."

John West appears out of nowhere, wearing his signature S.C.A.R.A.B. shirt, holding a medium black box as the opening of "Save Rock and Roll" continues its loop. He gives nothing away, simply smiles and holds the box out in front of him. My hand shakes a little as I lift the lid off, and my shocked expression is replaced with a grin. I pick up the note.

Sorry I couldn't get Elton at such short notice. I guess you'll have to sing his part. Happy singing, Husband. X

I grab the mic from out of the box without a second thought and race over to the stage. When I've climbed onto it and turned back, everyone is there, even Russ, who is jumping up and down, unable to contain his excitement.

"Ready?" smiles Patrick, as the most important people in my life cheer for us to begin.

I nod, and as he sings the first part of the song, I mouth a *thank you* to Sophie.

She blows me a kiss right before I start to sing, with no doubts, no worries, no second guessing who I am or what I'm doing.

At the crescendo, I glance at Shaun then up at the sky, belting out the lyrics, so Dad, wherever he is, can hear what will forever be the best performance of my life perfectly.

Ryan's rule of not drinking past midnight went out the window.

I'm totally regretting it, when at precisely nine-thirty AM, there's a rumble from the street so loud it can be heard in the kitchen of the guy's place. The kitchen at the back of the house.

"Ooop, there she is," says Ryan, spooning a large pile of cereal into his mouth, looking totally fresh, like he wasn't the tequila instigator. There's another rumble, and he swallows. "What's she driving? A rocket?"

I shrug, push away from the kitchen unit, and grab my bags from the floor. "Let's go check it out."

Never one to miss out on excitement so early in the day, Ryan instantly jumps off the stool where he's sitting. We're walking through the entryway when Zach comes down the stairs, rubbing his eyes.

"Are they doing work outside?"

"No," answers Ryan, darting to the door, eager to be the first to find out the source of all the noise. "It's Soph's new ride."

He flings the door open and freezes. A second later, he folds in half, creased with laughter.

Zach walks up behind him, and the same reaction follows. I move them out of the way and stop in my tracks in the doorway. There was a small part of me that thought Ryan and Zach were overreacting. They weren't. Finding Sophie sitting in the driver's seat of an electric blue Ford F-150 Raptor is too much. I drop my bags and crumble to the floor, laughing so hard my stomach hurts and tears pour down my cheeks.

Each time I think I'm done, I glance up and find her peering through the glass at the three of us, and it sets me off again.

"Right," I say, holding up my hand to get the guy's attention. "No more."

"Okay, serious faces," agrees Zach.

Struggling to hold it together, Ryan wheezes. "She can barely see over the wheel."

His comment sets us off again, and when a now disgruntled-looking Sophie flings open the driver's door, and struggles to jump down, I laugh so hard I think I pull muscle.

She walks up the steps and towers over me, throwing one hip forward and folds her arms across her chest with a huff. "Are you done laughing at my expense?"

My mouth goes dry, and I can't answer her, as my eyes move slowly up her body. The sight of her in her hiking gear sucks all the humor out of me. It's one of my favorite attires to see her in, and it's been years since I have.

"Sam …" she says, making it clear with her tone what she wants me to do.

"Getting up," I reply, scrambling to my feet.

Ryan grins. "Nice ride, Soph."

414

"You're just jealous," she replies with a sniff.

He stands a little taller. "Actually, mind if I take a look?"

"Depends. Are you going to start laughing again?"

"No." He shakes his head and looks around her eagerly at the blue machine.

"Pinky swear?" Sophie waves said pinky in the air.

With a groan, Ryan links pinkies with her, then says, "Can I go check it out now?"

"No more laughing," she calls after him as he jogs down the front steps.

When he opens the driver's door, what made her make him promise not to laugh again is there, taunting him from the front seat.

He turns back, looks up at Sophie, and with a pitch he shouldn't be able to achieve, squeaks, "Cushions?"

Two pink cushions with glitter and tassels, to be exact, in a Raptor, which, sitting next to the rest of the cars on our street, looks like a monster truck's love child.

It's my turn to chew on the inside of my cheek. I look away from Zach when I catch his nostrils flaring, because if I meet his eye, I won't be able to hold it together.

"I just needed a bit of a lift," says Sophie, planting her hands on her hips.

"Bit of a lift? Soph, you might as well be sitting on a box." Ryan shakes his head and goes back to his perusal of the truck.

Sophie focuses her attention on me. "Hey, husband."

My chest swells. "Hey, wife."

"I'm gonna go check out the truck," mutters Zach, leaving the two of us alone and joining Ryan.

"I thought last night was what you were busy with?"

Sophie takes a couple of steps forward, and I wrap my arms around her. "And this," she replies, going up onto her tiptoes and placing a small kiss on my lips.

I glance over at the Raptor. "So, what is *this* exactly?"

"A mini-moon," she grins.

"Mini-moon?"

"I know you had plans to get away for the summer, which I kind of got in the way of …" she starts to explain.

"By marrying me."

"By marrying you," she nods. "And I know things are going to be busy with work and Russ. So, I thought we could do this. The mini-moon. We only get one night, but I figured it's better than no nights?"

She chews on her lip, and I can't look away. "Are you still … you know …"

"What?"

I drop my head and whisper, "Menstruating."

She pulls away as far as I'll let her and jabs me in the chest. "I swear, Sam, if you say that word one more time, I'll—"

I cut her off with a kiss that has her rolling her hips into mine. I stop it long enough to finish what she was saying for her, one hundred percent trying my luck and praying the newlywed gods are on my side. "You'll wear the green bra and spend all night punishing me?"

Sophie snorts and starts laughing. When she catches her breath, she steps back and dangles the keys to the Raptor in the air. "Can we go before Grams calls? Her and Mom were giving me stress hives with how many questions they were asking about how to look after Russ."

I whip the keys from her hand. "Come on, let's go."

"Hey! What are you doing?" Her voice carries after me down the steps. Instead of answering, I load my bags in the

416

trunk, then make my way to the driver's door. Sophie slides in front of me before I get a chance to open it, flattening herself back against the sheet of metal, the same color as her eyes. "I asked what you're doing?"

"I think it's obvious." The corners of my mouth pull up as I bait her. I love my wife feisty. "I'm driving."

"You can't. It'll ruin the surprise of where we're going."

"This is surprise enough. I love it. Now, move."

"I can drive, Sam." Stubborn as a mule, she still refuses to budge.

"I know you can," I reply, "but I don't want you to, because we just got married, and I'd like our marriage to last past today. If you have to sit on a cushion, it means you can't see over the wheel. It's not safe."

Sophie's gaze softens. "Fine."

She steps to the side, leaving the driver's door free for me to open. I get in and watch her walk around the front of the truck.

When the passenger door opens, Ryan says to her, "Need a hand climbing up?"

"No, thank you." The step up is huge for her small frame, but she makes it look effortless; the slight puff of air she lets out is the only sign of a struggle. Settled in her seat, she clicks her belt in place, then turns to me. "See, I'm a pro. I can totally handle the beast."

"That's what she said," comes Ryan's voice from down by her side. He winks at me across the cab, and dread curls in my stomach for whatever's going to come out of his mouth next. "My man might be a beast in the bedroom, but make sure you handle him with care. He's a softy at heart."

Thankfully, Sophie's switched off from what he's saying and is busy messing with the Sat Nav. Happy with whatever she's input, she leans back in her seat and throws waves of red hair over her shoulder, wafting her shampoo my way.

"Don't do anything I wouldn't," says Ryan, shutting the passenger door.

Sophie smiles down at him through the open window. "That gives us scope to do pretty much anything."

"You kids have fun." He winks again, then disappears back into the house.

"Are you going to tell me where we're going?" I ask before pulling out onto the road.

Sophie grins. "Nope."

"Not even a clue?"

"Nope."

"I'm probably going to guess."

"Guess all you like, husband. All that matters is that for tonight, you're mine."

I roll my eyes and pull out my phone. "One second, let me just text Shaun."

The lightness and humor are sucked out of the truck with the mention of his name, and Sophie gives me a tense nod.

Happy birthday, big bro.

After putting my phone away, I pull out onto the road. I don't bother waiting for his reply, because I know there won't be one.

Chapter Thirty-Three

Sophie

"Camping?" says Sam, staring at the sign for the campground where I've planned for us to stay the night.

"Yes, camping!" I say excitedly, hoping the enthusiasm in my voice will spill over to him. "I've planned it all. Well, as much as you can plan in a couple of hours. It took me longer to rent the Raptor than I predicted."

"Okay," he says, reluctance dripping from his voice.

I watch him pull out our bags and the tent from the trunk.

"Um, what are you doing?"

"Getting our things ready so we can walk to wherever you want to pitch up ..."

"Can't we just drive?"

Sam gives me a blank look, and points at the campground rules. The ones where it clearly states vehicles are to remain in the parking zone.

Crap. So much for planning. I plaster on a smile, take my bag, and head in the direction where I planned for us to spend the night.

Nothing will destroy our mini-moon.

"This is a disaster," I groan two hours later when I realize we've walked in one big circle.

Sam pulls me to his side and hides his smile in my hair. "Not a disaster. We've got a night together, right?"

His reminder and the little tidbit of knowledge I've kept to myself lifts my mood.

"You're right," I agree. "It's just I had all these pictures in my head of us hiking … fishing … making s'mores over an open campfire under the stars."

My vocal daydreaming is broken when Sam says, "Fishing?"

"I brought a rod."

"A rod … wow." He grins and mischief flashes through his eyes. "And tell me, Mrs. Riley …" He moves toward me, and I back up, right into a giant tree. Mischief is long gone; heat pools low in my pelvis when he rests his free hand next to my head against the trunk. "Do you know how to use this rod you speak of?"

I snicker. His flirting's wasted on me. "Did you just try to pull off a British accent?"

"Dan practiced with me after Abby's birthday. It's good, yeah?"

"Um …" I don't want to hurt his feelings, but I find myself admitting it, because we promised to always be truthful to each other, "It kinda sucked. But for the record …" I press my hands against his chest, then stretch so my lips skim the shell of his ear. "I know how to use the rod perfectly."

I push him away, hiding my smile as I put some space between us. I'd never tell him, but this whole waiting thing, besides being torture, has also been fun. The anticipation, the innuendos, the slight touches, and suggestions. He's got me all fired up and ready to go.

Speaking of fires, my plans for one fly out the window when Sam calls after me, "No fires, by the way."

I stop walking and turn back. "No fires?"

He rolls his lips, finding the whole mini-moon disaster way too amusing. "Them's the rules."

The ones he's referring to are the ones I didn't read because it was late, and the list looked long and boring.

"But that means no s'mores."

"And no hot meals."

The last one tips me over the edge, and I let out a small whimper. "I hate raw fish."

Sam slides the bags and tent he's been carrying off his shoulders onto the ground, then walks over to me. The next thing I know, my face is in his hands and he's stroking my cheeks with his thumbs. "Turn that frown upside down."

My bottom lip juts out. "You never say positive crap. That means this is a disaster."

He kisses the left corner of my mouth. "Red, I made you my wife forty-eight hours ago. I don't care about hiking …" He kisses the right corner. "S'mores …" He kisses the end of my nose. "Or fishing. I'm happy just being here with you."

"Okay." I nod away my bad mood. "You're right."

"I say we pitch up here."

I look around at the slight opening in the dense forest. All there is for fun is a patch of sky through the trees and a bed of pine needles. "And then what?"

Sam shrugs and takes a leaf out of Ryan's book. "You could show me what you can do with that rod?"

"It doesn't go there."

"Yes, it does."

"It doesn't, I swear."

I let out a puff of air, attempting to blow the red hair nest that has formed out of my face, which is impossible when I'm so sweaty it's stuck like glue to my skin.

"The instructions said it goes like this," I say through gritted teeth. Sam doesn't reply. When I look up through the hair covering my eyes, I find him rolling his lips. I dare him to smile in my head. "What? What's so funny?"

He smiles and walks toward me slowly with the instructions in his hand. He drops to his knees and slides the sheets of paper my way, pointing at one of the images. "This is what you're trying to do, but you did that with these bits." He points to another part of the tent I'd already put together over half an hour ago. "This is where you need to be."

He points at an image much further along in the instructions as his shoulders start to shake.

"Gah!" I drop the tent poles in defeat, and finally, with my hands free, manage to push my hair from my face. "I suck at this."

Sam brushes a strand I've missed out of my eyes, then presses a small kiss against my lips. I see it for what it is, a diffuser for what's going to come out of his mouth next. "I tried to remind you about Benicàssim."

422

He's referring to the tent-building race the group had years ago on S.C.A.R.A.B.'s first European tour. The one where there was no racing to be found, because we all sucked at building them.

"I came in second."

His eyes sparkle. "Second to last."

I glance around and take in the rapidly diminishing light. "It's getting dark. We haven't even eaten."

"You don't want raw fish?"

I scowl. "I've got s'mores ingredients and a couple of protein bars."

Sam laughs. "The perfect Friday Feast."

"It's a Friday?" The events of the past week have made time become a blur, and one emotional day has merged seamlessly into the next.

"It's a Friday, Red," Sam confirms, sliding around the back of me and shuffling forward so his legs stretch out along each side of me. When his arms sweep around my body, he draws me back into his warmth, then begins playing with the two bands of white gold sitting on my ring finger; the ones that mean I'm his and he's mine. "I think these could be my new favorite thing," he says, his chin resting on top of my head.

"Think we should give the honeymoon another go in a couple of months?"

"Nah." I still, questioning if I've messed it up that much that he doesn't want another. "I've enjoyed this one."

"You mean you've enjoyed laughing at me?"

His laughter rumbles through his chest, and I feel it everywhere. "With, Red. Always with."

I stare into the trees. "I just wanted things to be perfect."

He starts to trail his hands up and down my arms. "I don't want perfect, Sophie. I don't want a perfect life and I don't want a perfect wife. I want you. I want the woman that makes me laugh in the most serious situations, and also the inappropriate ones. I want the woman who fucks up, because it means I can fuck up, too. I just want you." His hands move from trailing along my arms to focusing on the waistband of the leggings I always wear for hiking; the ones that see the light of day roughly every twelve to eighteen months. His fingers slide just beneath the elastic, and I wriggle. "I know why you're doing this."

"I don't know what you mean," I reply absentmindedly.

"Bull. Did you think I wouldn't put it all together? The Raptor that looks like Uncle Matt's old ride. The camping …"

"Summer trips used to be the best."

"This one is up there with them."

"Yeah?"

Sam places a kiss against my lips, deepening it enough I start to forget what we were even talking about. "I spent every summer wanting to do that. Now, I can do it whenever I want, so I'd actually say it's *the* best."

A few butterflies in my stomach decide to take flight as his eyes sparkle down at me. "I just didn't want you to be sad."

He smiles, a sad one. "You know what day it is. I can't not be sad, Soph. It's a given. But … I'm also the happiest I've ever been."

"Promise?"

"Promise. I say we get the tent up before it gets dark and the bears come."

I focus on one detail.

"Bears?"

"How did you know your rod was going to get some action tonight?"

Sam blinks at me and continues chewing his deconstructed s'more slowly. "I never said I did."

"Please," I say with a roll of my eyes. "That is totally what you were getting at. All the talking about rods crap."

A smirk finds me as Sam sets down his food and removes the limited space there is between us in the tent when he crawls over me. He takes my small plastic plate from my hands and sets it to the side, along with his.

He stares with heat in his eyes and an intensity that steals the oxygen from my lungs, then says, "I knew, because if you were still menstruating, there would have been a homicide investigation this morning after me laughing at the Raptor."

"You're an ass sometimes, you know that, right?"

Sam's lips find my neck, just below my jaw line. His tongue trails a steady path over my skin to my shoulder, then over my collarbone. Small explosions are left everywhere his lips touch.

"Keep talking dirty to me, Red."

An idea forms, and I smile at the roof of the tent when his fingertips move in a whisper of a touch up my thighs.

"Want to know something you don't know?"

"Enlighten me," replies Sam, nipping my earlobe.

It causes the perfect amount of pain, making my nipples harden beneath my band shirt. I might not necessarily love rock music, but I know wearing a S.C.A.R.A.B. shirt is the equivalent to wearing a jocks number. I purposely chose it this morning, knowing it was the perfect play to guarantee the screaming orgasm I've been dying for.

"Right before the music hall, I had a dream about the two of us together. There was chocolate sauce."

The kisses Sam is trailing down over my shirt stop abruptly, and he looks up through hooded eyes. "I knew there was a reason you wanted to do s'mores. You hate chocolate sauce."

"Technically," I say breathily, when Sam lifts my shirt enough that he's able to begin placing hot, wet kisses against my stomach. "S'mores don't have chocolate sauce."

The sauce was a last-minute grab when I realized I'd forgotten to buy chocolate, but my imagination went a bit crazy when I instantly remembered the dream we're referring to.

"I know," says Sam, tugging at the waistband of my leggings. "It's what gave it away."

"Know it all." I lift my hips so he can pull my leggings down.

He tosses them to the side and his shirt goes next. My eyes linger on the tattoos covering his body that have been teasing me for weeks, settling on the small scarab beetle sitting by his right hip.

"Do you all have one?" I ask, nodding at it.

Sam smiles. "Yeah. It was Jake's idea."

"That's nice."

My shirt lifts, and Sam's eyes widen. "Not as nice as this," he groans, licking his lips as he takes in the green lace covering my breasts.

"All for you," I grin.

"Best." A kiss finds my belly button. "Present." A kiss finds between my breasts. "Ever."

The kiss that finds my lips isn't brief. It's languid, fiery, filled with love, and has too many emotions to name. My legs wrap around his waist and my heels press into his lower back, driving his erection between my legs, making the pressure in my core build.

Sam's movements slow and his body shifts low enough he's able to trace his tongue over the lace, around one nipple, then the other. "This can stay on." He moves lower, over my stomach, low enough I feel his groan vibrate against my clit when he finds more green lace. His tongue moves down through my slit, then traces back up. He looks up, torn between ripping them off or keeping them as a matching set.

I feel him everywhere. His hungry gaze on my skin. His breath, coming out in small hot pants against my center. Everything feels like it's being touched by him when nothing is at all.

"Want to know something?" he asks, hooking his thumbs under each side of my thong.

My hips lift on their own, a silent beg for more. The material drags slowly down my legs, leaving behind a path of fire as everything heightens and becomes more sensitive.

"I want to know everything," I moan, barely recognizing my own voice.

Sam grins, leans back on his haunches, and strokes a finger between my folds, watching intently. When his finger dips inside me, my hips buck. When it pulls out, I protest with a moan. A second joins in, and a third before he speaks again.

"I've spent every Friday dreaming one day it would be like this." His sweet words are swapped for ones I need more right now. "Open your legs, Red."

He settles between them, giving Friday Feast Night a whole new meaning. His tongue works in perfect rhythm with his fingers, until I'm crying out his name, telling him to stop because it's too much, while my hands hold him in place, begging him for more.

Somewhere in the time it takes me to come back down to earth, he removes his pants and boxers. Then he's there hovering over me with the promise of a forever with no more waiting.

When he pushes inside me, it isn't like our first time. He focuses intently on every kiss, every movement, every touch, and every thrust of his pelvis into mine as he makes love to me on the forest floor.

I smile into his neck, biting the taut muscles in his back with my nails. "I thought we were waiting for a bed?"

"Semantics, Red," he says, stealing the rest of my words for the night with the punishing thrusts from his hips.

And when I think it can't get any more intense, and he can't get any deeper, he pushes harder, taking everything from me and giving everything in return.

"Fuck," he says with a shudder. Dropping his face into the crook of my neck as his body collapses on top of me. "That was definitely worth the wait." I giggle, and he pulls away, giving me a lazy smile. "I love you."

"I love you, too," I reply, pushing the damp strands of hair away from his eyes. "So … about that chocolate sauce."

He shakes his head and places a quick kiss on my lips. "No sauce." I pout. "Unless you want to be eaten by wild animals instead."

Silenced, I decide then and there that the only camping trips we go on in the future will be the ones that have to remain PG.

Sam

We've only just fallen asleep when my alarm goes off.

"Wasat?" Sophie grumbles, burying her face into my chest. It feels like sand is scratching my eyes when I rub them and blink in the darkness. My alarm continues chiming, which Sophie makes clear she isn't impressed by. "Make it stoooop."

"Dramatic much?" I hunt through the tangled mess of sleeping bags and discarded clothing. Eventually, I find it underneath my sock and silence it.

Sophie's light snoring fills the tent and I shake my head. "Hey," I say, leaning over and kissing her bare shoulder. "We need to get up." She lets out a puff of air. "Soph." When I give her a little shake, she still doesn't acknowledge me.

Because needs must, I give her ass a slap. "Saaaam," she groans. "Stop."

"We need to get up."

"We don't need to do anything." She pulls my shirt over her face when I turn my phone's torch on. "We're on our mini-moon."

"I'm being serious." I source my boxers and slide them on. My pants follow, then I grab the material of my shirt and prize it out of Sophie's grip. She covers her eyes with her hands.

"Why are you doing this to me? We literally haven't slept."

"I want to show you something. Come on, get dressed. It will be worth it, I promise."

She lowers her hands and watches me put my shirt on. Her eyes make her intentions clear as day. "Come on, or we'll miss it."

"Fine." She sits up, and I try to keep my eyes away from the green lace still cupping her breasts. When I find her clothes, she reluctantly puts them on after seeing the time on my phone, making it more than known how unhappy she is.

I dismiss her questions when we get to the Raptor, and at some point during the drive, she falls back to sleep.

"We've got some walking to do," I explain, when she climbs out.

"Great," she grumbles, hair sticking up in all directions. My laugh doesn't do anything to improve her mood, and she scowls for the mile to our destination. "Oh, wow," she murmurs when we get to the top of the trail.

"Finished complaining?"

Sophie remains silent in the dim light. When the sun breaks above the horizon, it rises slowly, like the mist rolling through the mountains like cotton candy, and the sky becomes as fiery as her hair.

"Where are we?" she asks, keeping her eyes on the view in front of her. The awe that covers her face was worth every minute of her complaining.

"Blue Ridge Mountains ..." I wait for her to bite. She turns her head for a second and gives me a look. "Craggy Gardens."

With the sun higher in the sky, she looks around, smiling at the sea of white and green foliage clinging around the rocks. "Have you been here before?" I snicker, and she tilts her head. "Why do I feel like maybe I don't want the answer?"

"Uncle Matt brought me up here that first summer sleepovers were banned."

Sophie's eyes widen. "Ah."

Wrapping my arm around her shoulder, I pull her into my side while watching the sun crawl higher; the streaks of orange and red slowly turn light blue. "It was the summer I got *the talk* ... " I play with the strap of her bra. "I also think that was the summer this first made an appearance."

"Is this a thing?" she giggles, leaning her head against me. "Does it need a shrine or something?"

"I can think of a lot of 'or somethings' ..."

"You know you're being a goon, right?"

"And?" I place a kiss in her hair, then turn the conversation to something more serious. "Thank you for doing this."

"It was nothing."

"Fall Out Boy and a trip to the Blue Ridge Mountains aren't nothing." Pink covers her cheeks that I know isn't from the sunrise. "Replacing bad memories with better ones," I say against her lips. "The best ones."

"I could stay here forever," Sophie sighs.

"We have to leave," I say, deadpan, pulling back. "We have no food." Sophie jabs me in the stomach, which growls with comedy timing.

"This is a good memory. A really good one," she muses, right before we both know we have to leave. The mini-moon is just that—mini. With everything that's waiting for us at home and about to start in motion, she says, "Are you ready?"

I leave no uncertainty in my voice when I reply, "More than ready."

We walk back down the trail, hand in hand, and for the first time, I finally feel like I'm putting the past behind me, ready to start chasing our future together as a family, with Russ.

Chapter Thirty-Four
Sophie 3 Months Later

I t's the first day of The American Showcase and I'm a wreck.

"Can you have a drink or something to chill you out?" asks Zoe.

I roll my eyes and carry-on pacing the living area. "Zo, this is a big deal."

"Erm, duh." She grins, and I squeal, then do a little dance.

"I can't believe it's finally here."

Zoe looks around the apartment, which is empty apart from the two of us. "When are they coming back?"

I shrug. "Sam promised they wouldn't be late. They were going to get pancakes."

There's a knock at the door I know will be Abby. When I open it, Clara barrels through, almost knocking me off my feet.

"Where's Russ?" she huffs out.

"He'll be back soon," I try to explain. Her little face twists into a scowl, and I swallow. Her recent temperament explains why Abby looks like she's made her way through a storm to get here. "Want to watch some *Blippi?*"

Clara nods eagerly, and I let out a small sigh of relief, because her reaction could have gone one of two ways. Thankfully, it wasn't the bad way. Who knew toddlers could be so fiery? She races over to the couch and sits next to Zoe, who is more prepared than she's ever been for anything in her life. The remote is in her hand, ready to put on some mind-numbing television that will keep the small ball of fury happy until we need to leave.

"You've got mail," says Abby, walking into the apartment and handing over an envelope.

It's addressed to both Sam and me. Because I need something to do, I open it, rather than dumping it in the pile already sitting on the console table in dire need of attention.

"What the hell?" I hiss, staring at the sheets in my hands.

"Is something wrong?" asks Abby, peering over my shoulder. "Oh."

"Yeah. Big f'in oh," I mutter, praying Clara can't hear.

"Are you going to talk to him about it?"

"Talk to who about what?" asks Sam, walking in with Russ. The smile covering his face slips when he sees the papers sitting in my hands. "Surprise?"

"We need to go," I bite out, striding past him with determination into the hallway.

He grabs my arm before I'm out of reach and looks at me with his lips set in a flat line.

"We'll meet you there!" says Abby in a shrill voice, dragging a bemused-looking Clara and Russ past us. Zoe follows behind, none the wiser to something being wrong.

"Can we talk about this inside?" asks Sam warily.

"We're going to be late." I don't know what to do or how to take this. It isn't just something little. It's huge.

"Please, Red."

I pull my arm out of his grip and poke him in the chest. "Don't do that. Don't *Red* me."

"Come on …" He gives me a lopsided smile and tilts his head to the side.

Shaking mine, I walk back into the apartment and wait until he's closed the door. I glance around at everything, struggling to digest what I've just read. "You said it was an investment."

Some of the color drains from his cheeks and he shoves his hands into the pockets of his pants like he does whenever he's nervous. "It was the best investment I've ever made. I didn't lie to you."

"But you didn't tell me the truth …"

"Says the one who kept the a cappella group who we're about to go watch compete a secret for years." A smile tugs at his lips, then he grins.

"An apartment." I throw my arms out and take everything in one last time. "You bought me an apartment?"

Literally the day after I left the precinct, according to the finalized mortgage agreement I've just read. Sam walks toward me and I hold my breath, expecting him to pull me in and kiss me, until I forget what our minor tiff is even about.

"We would have gotten one, eventually."

I snort. "You don't know that." Realizing my mistake, I correct myself. "Sorry, I forgot you know everything." Sam drags a hand through his hair in frustration and his blond highlights catch the light.

"I knew you wouldn't have accepted the help, because I know you, and you're stubborn as fuck when you want to be. If I hadn't done what I did, we wouldn't be here now."

My eyes move down to the two rings sitting on my finger, and then over to his. The thought of not being here is enough to make me back down.

"Promise me something ..."

"Anything," he replies.

"Don't keep things from me."

"I promise." And I know he means it. He grabs my hand and tugs me toward the door. "Russ is going to kill us if we're late."

We leave the apartment, and Sam locks up. We're almost at the elevators when he stops.

"There's something else."

My eyes widen. "You haven't bought a house?"

He laughs, then his brows draw together, almost meeting in the middle. "Grace and I had an arrangement."

I swallow as my stomach sinks. "Arrangement ..."

His eyes widen. "Not like that."

"I walked in on you getting a blow job from her ..."

"Seriously. Nothing happened, ever. You definitely didn't walk in on me getting head. It was Ryan's idea."

I can't even pretend to look surprised. "Why?"

"To make you realize what you were missing. Did it work?"

I roll my eyes and continue walking toward the elevator. "Not in the way you planned." The doors slide open, and I step inside. Sam follows me in.

"I was expecting you to be mad. Why don't you look mad?"

As the doors slide shut, I press him back against the wall and kiss him like it's going to be our last, only pulling away briefly to press the emergency stop button and say, "Someone once told me it doesn't matter how you get to your destination, all that matters is that you get there in the end."

Sam and I walk hand in hand into the Weill Music Room, the designated rehearsal area for The American Showcase in Carnegie Hall. Butterflies swarm in my stomach as I take it all in. The rich floors are polished to perfection, not a scratch in sight, with a ton of overhead lighting that puts The Parkapellas rehearsal space to shame. It's swanky, and this isn't even where we're going to perform.

"Where've you been?" scowls Russ, standing in front of the floor-to-ceiling windows.

"Sophie lost something," Sam smiles, ruffling Russ's hair and winking at me when he backs away to meet with the rest of S.C.A.R.A.B.

Zoe and Amanda don't miss the meaning behind his words.

"Yeah, you're clothing, you dirty bitch," says Zoe when Russ is no longer in listening distance, adjusting my dress. A couple of other performers glance our way, and I raise a finger to my lips, shaking my head.

"How many orgasms did he make you scream through?" Amanda giggles, not picking up on my signal.

I decide to play both of them at their own game, knowing neither of them is getting the action they would like in the bedroom, and unless I give them something, any attempts at keeping them quiet will be a lost cause.

"Three."

Amanda's mouth parts as she huffs, pulling out her phone. "What's the best dating app for hook-ups?"

"Who's hooking up?" asks Zach.

Zoe and I turn, while Amanda keeps her attention focused on her phone. "No one apart from Soph. That's the problem."

"Just say the word, baby," grins Ryan, stopping beside Zach. He looks like all his dreams are coming true, missing the fact that hooking up with one of your best friend's exes is a red card.

Amanda finally looks up, and her eyes move between Zach and Ryan. "You're like sniffer dogs. I say the word orgasm, and there you are."

She walks off, shaking her head. Zoe follows, laughing.

"Christ, she really does need a quick hook-up, or ten," mutters Ryan.

"Guys!" I make a motion for them to be quiet when I realize Grams is heading our way.

"We're on third for the required piece," she says.

"How's everyone holding up?"

She grimaces. "They're nervous. Maybe a pep talk is in order?"

"Okay." I catch Sam's attention from where he's standing, still talking to Jake. He gives him a quick goodbye and walks over.

"Everything okay?"

"The Parkapellas are starting to sweat."

"Ah," he replies, smiling.

"I need your help. I'm not good at all this. I don't know what it's like. Do you think you could pep them up, to make them, you know … peppy?"

"I'll do what I can," he replies, giving me a quick kiss before walking over to the group.

Grams smiles at me. "You look happy."

"I am," I reply, taking in everything around me. There's an excited edge to the air as all the groups amp themselves up, and although I'm nervous for the group, I love it.

"Have you thought any more about what Aurelia suggested?"

I shake my head. "I'm not singing, Grams. I do the work in the background, not on stage."

"Just keep it in mind," she says, giving me a knowing look before leaving to join Sam.

Twenty minutes later, Sam finds me, and his expression isn't the one I want to see.

"Good warm up?" I ask, brows raised high in hope.

He rubs the back of his neck awkwardly. "Erm, maybe. Kinda, not really?"

"I thought you were supposed to be good at this?" I whisper hiss so the group can't hear me.

"No," he says with a frown. "*You* said I'd be good at this. I've been helping them practice, and it's been great, but I'm not their leader, Soph. You are."

439

He walks away, tension pouring off him. When I look around for help, for the first time in my life, I find no one but The Parkapellas. No family or friends who literally couldn't keep out of my business if their lives depended on it. There's no one.

With no other choice, I walk slowly over to the group. After Sam leading rehearsals for so long, standing in front of them like this feels alien. At first, no one notices me, apart from Russ, who's sitting cross-legged on the floor with the rest of the younger kids.

I clear my throat, and no one looks over. In fact, their chattering gets louder.

Knowing we don't have time for being nice or polite, I slide my thumb and finger into my mouth. A sharp whistle gets their attention.

"What's happening here?" No one answers, and I sigh. "I can't help if I don't know what the problem is."

"We're scared," says Russ quietly.

When I gesture for him to come to me, he does instantly, standing directly in front. I rest my hands on his shoulders before continuing to speak to the group.

"I know it feels a lot, putting yourself out there like this, but I need you to understand, the only reason we're here is because we love singing. That's it."

"We know the group needs the prize money," says Lacey from close to the back.

I'll have to kill Xavier and his big mouth later, because we have ten minutes until we have to go on stage, and half The Parkapellas look like they're ready for puking, while the other half look ready for walking out of the door without a backward glance.

"That's for me to worry about, not you," I say with a smile, then decide if I'm going to win them on my side, I need to be fully complacent. "Sure, the money would be great, but it isn't a game changer. If we don't win, I'll worry about the money side of things while The Parkapellas keep doing what they do best. Singing. All the money means is we can get a bigger place to rehearse in."

The faces of everyone in the group change, stress swapped with relief.

"How about we all warm up *together*?"

The warmup that follows is one that could win the competition alone, and I've never felt prouder of my not-so-little a cappella group than I do at that moment.

Well, until they sing their asses off in the required piece, blow the judges' socks off and get through to the final two for the following day.

"That was awesome!" screeches Russ, jumping up and down at my side. "Can we do it again?"

"Tomorrow," I laugh, pulling my arm out of his grip before he can pull it out of its socket.

"Impressive," says a deep voice from behind me.

When I turn around, I stare in shock at Abby's dad, John West, standing between her and Clara, who are both grinning.

"Thank you," I reply warmly.

"I hope you don't mind," says Sam, coming to my side, sliding an arm around my waist. "I invited him."

I want to ask him why and when, but I don't get a chance.

"Sophie," says John. "Would you mind going for a drink with me?"

441

I have no idea what he could want to talk to me about, and The Parkapellas need to start rehearsing for tomorrow, which is why I say, "Um …"

"Go," says Sam, close to my ear. "Don't overthink this. The group could do with a break. I'll start rehearsals in an hour, and you can take over when you get back." I give him a wary glance. "This is important."

"I know a good place," I say, as I turn to John with a smile.

"Great." He smiles back, but it doesn't stop my heart racing as we walk toward the door.

"It's nothing bad, right?" I ask, pushing against the glass.

"No, nothing bad," John chuckles.

Chapter Thirty-Five

Sophie

It doesn't take long for John and me to get to the bar I have in mind. It's the kind of place I think he'll like, with ping-pong tables, couches filled with multi-colored cushions, and a great selection of cocktails.

"Beer?" he asks, gesturing toward the bar. My mouth twists, and he laughs. "Something stronger?"

"Please," I reply, unzipping my bag to get some money out.

John holds up his hand. "These are on me."

He walks over to the bar, and it's only when I've found us a table away from the crowds of afternoon drinkers that I realize I never told him what I wanted.

When he slides into the booth across from me, I find myself smiling down at a Cosmopolitan. "I thought it was a little early for a Long Island Iced Tea."

I giggle, remembering one of the times he had to pick me up, along with Zoe and Abby, after we got fake IDs at seventeen and drank too many.

"You're sure this is nothing bad?" I ask, nerves kicking in again.

"Have I ever lied to you, Sophie?" he asks, his mouth tilting up.

"No," I reply, realizing he hasn't. John West is like a second dad to me and my siblings. He always has been, thanks to being so close with my parents—work wise and socially. I swirl the small black straw through the light pink liquid in my glass. "So, why am I here?"

After taking a drink of his beer and letting out a satisfied sigh, John says, "What do you know about Warped Records?"

"That they're warped for keeping my parents around as long as they have?" My joke falls flat and my laughter at my own failed humor stops when I take in John's serious expression. I raise my glass and spend longer than necessary taking a drink. "Not much," I admit. "Apart from they're one of the big guys in the music industry."

Weirdly, John laughs at the last part. "They weren't always," he starts to explain.

"How long have you worked with them?" I ask, trailing my finger through some of the condensation on my glass.

"Since the beginning."

"Wow. I didn't know that. I thought you'd worked at other places, too?"

"One hundred percent loyal to being a Warped employee." I can't decide if he's being serious or joking. "My friend Wayne started the label not long after we finished college."

"That's cool. And impressive."

"It is. What's even more impressive is where the label's at now after how it started. Originally, it was small. So small the artists Wayne signed were actually doing *him* a favor by signing on. A lot were from troubled backgrounds, or had major talent and no one believed in them, or major talent and a lack of funding to break into the business."

"A bit like S.C.A.R.A.B. …"

"Just like S.C.A.R.A.B.," grins John.

"Where does the name come from?"

"It's a reflection of the industry, but don't tell anyone I said that." John winks. "Wayne believed the industry was warped. That a lot of people were at the top who shouldn't have been, and that image was more important than the music being produced."

"Why are you speaking in the past tense?"

Pain fills John West's eyes, and for the first time, I take in how much older he seems. His face covered with the deep lines of life's experiences. "Wayne died three years ago after a long battle with cancer." He looks away for a moment and a thousand thoughts flicker in his eyes. I have a strong feeling that John and Wayne's friendship meant a lot more to him than he's letting on—that they had the kind of friendship I have with his daughter. One you hope lasts a lifetime, but sometimes doesn't work out that way. "When Warped Records really took off, he was one of the rare people in the industry who didn't forget where he came from. He used it to drive the label forward, picking artists for their talent alone. Apart from minor changes, he would never ask an artist or a group of artists to change their image. It's what makes the label special."

"Inspiring," I say with a warm smile.

445

John takes another drink of his beer. "Almost as inspiring as his last wishes for the label. Which is why we're here now you have all the back story." He grins. "Wayne believed in raw talent, but accepted a lot was missed because most didn't have the right people or means behind them to help them be noticed. He wanted Warped Records to go back to its roots, be present in more charities, and keep inspiring the industry to do better in helping those at the bottom. One of the things he always said was that a lot of people sing through their pain …"

"They sing to heal …" I finish, beginning to understand what he's getting at.

"Sam told me about The Parkapellas, about your ideas for expanding and helping more people with the group."

Even though I've heard every part of his story, the stubborn part of me that still likes to appear sometimes—usually when it's inconvenient—says, "I don't need a handout."

I expect John to frown and maybe be a little bit pissed or offended. Instead, he laughs.

"I've handled your parents' contracts for over twenty years, Sophie. Believe me, I know if you wanted a handout, it wouldn't need to come from me."

He has a point and I feel my cheeks burn from his subtle dig, even though I know what he's saying has no malice behind it. It's what I need to hear, but with what needs to happen for The Parkapellas, I could never hear it from my family. They're too close to this.

"Sorry," I mumble, taking another drink.

John reaches over and gives my hand a brief squeeze of reassurance, like my dad would. "You have nothing to be sorry for, but I will say this. Sometimes, to help others, you

446

have to accept help yourself. You can't be bold by being humble. You can't be brilliant by being stubborn. It's not a handout. It's an opportunity. Take it. Use it. Grow with it."

After a couple of deep breaths, considering everything he's said so far, I say, "What exactly are you suggesting?"

"That Warped Records become investors in the charity 'Sing to Heal'. We help fund bigger premises, better equipment, and bigger opportunities for those who come through the door. We provide you with a salary and benefits, because something like this will need all hands on deck to run it. And while you help people heal, you help us find talent. You help to find the people whose voices and stories deserve to be heard through music."

My shoulders drop as exhaustion kicks in. The past couple of months have been a lot, and this is one more thing added to the pile. But, even though it's been exhausting, and even though, at times, painful, that same pile has been full of positivity and life-changing opportunities.

I can't pass this up. This isn't about me. It's about The Parkapellas and what's right for them.

"I think," I say, picking up my glass, unknowingly to John, for a cheers. "That I would like to take the opportunity."

When I get to The Parkapellas rehearsal for the final, I walk in just as they're finishing the song we have planned perfectly.

I've never been prouder of them, but something about it doesn't feel right.

The group jumps up and down with excitement, while an audience that consists of S.C.A.R.A.B., my parents, and the girls, including Clara, applaud them.

Sam turns around beaming, but when his eyes settle on me, his smile falters.

He walks over and under my breath I say, "Can we talk real quick?"

"Sure." He follows me out of the room into the corridor. "What's wrong? Did everything with John go okay?"

"Better than okay," I say with a grin. Sam grins back, and I don't doubt for a second he knows all about John's plans.

"So, what's wrong, then?"

"The song isn't right."

Sam's face drops. "It's perfect."

I shake my head. "No, they might have performed it perfectly, but that doesn't mean it's right."

"For who? The judges?"

"Them. Sam, we don't *need* to win this anymore. When they go out on stage tomorrow, I want them to sing something that leaves them wanting more. That inspires them to keep going. That reminds them exactly why they started."

Sam rubs a hand along his jaw, dragging his fingers through some of his stubble. "I have a song. Something I've been working on."

My eyes widen and I gasp, "You've been writing? Why didn't you tell me?"

He nods, a little unsure. "I mean, I'm no Jake Ros—"

I stop him before he can finish, slamming my mouth against his, eventually pulling away. "You don't need to be Jake. You just need to be you, like you tell me I always need to be me."

448

"We'd need to start rehearsing now. The guys and your parents will need to help. It's gonna be a late night."

I jump up and down excitedly, then hurry back toward the room where The Parkapellas have been rehearsing. "Go hard or go home," I throw over my shoulder.

Sam chases after me, and right before we step through the door, he slaps my ass. "That's what she said."

The night that follows is a long one, and the younger kids, including Russ, work as hard as they can with the promise of an early morning rehearsal when Sophie forces them to go home to bed.

For the rest of us, it's a slog.

Without time on our side, we break into groups. The guys help me break down the song, originally intended for S.C.A.R.A.B.

I work on the lead melodies with Sophie and Russ, while Jake works on the chordal accompaniments that back up the leads. Zach spends time carefully making sure the vocal tones sound like a bass in all the right places and Ryan spends the night in his element, turning what would be his drum set into a pseudo-drum sound. I swear I'll be hearing the words 'boots and cats' in my dreams for the foreseeable future.

The final run-through still isn't perfect, and I see the disappointment on everyone's faces.

"You need to tell them," I say to Sophie under my breath, fifteen minutes before they're due on stage.

"You think it will work?"

I nod. "They need to know that they can just go out there and enjoy themselves."

Sophie chews her lip, and I know she's worried about all the minor details, such as the contracts with Warped Records. But if The Parkapellas win, she won't need to worry regardless—not for a while at least.

"Guys," she waves her hand in the air, getting everyone's attention. The group draws together. Sophie's parents stand hand-in-hand at the back, along with the guys, Zoe, Amanda, Sooz, Abby, Clara and, of course, Grams. "I have something I need to tell you before we go out on stage. I know I said yesterday that winning doesn't matter today, but I need you to know I meant it. It really doesn't …"

She pauses, looking to me for encouragement. I give her a reassuring smile, and she turns back to the group.

"Yesterday, The Parkapellas found an investor." Everyone remains silent. "The group will get bigger. There will be different types of music and other groups, because going forward it will be a charity, so more people can be a part of what we have here. But it means The Parkapellas are here for the long haul.

"Basically, what I'm trying to say is, go out there and sing without any pressure. When you step out on that stage, know you're doing it without any expectations from others. Go out there and remember why you started. Sing because you want to, not because you feel like you have to."

I pull Sophie to my side and kiss her head. Then, the last thing either of us expects happens. Every member of The Parkapellas joins us.

Russ, who's right in the middle, looks up at Sophie and whispers, "It's a Parkapella sandwich," then, testing the word out for the first time, finishes with, "Mom."

"Great," says Sophie, wiping beneath her eyes when the group disperses. "I'm going out there a mess." Then, she rushes over to Abby, and I hear her say, "So, how do I hand in my notice?" before disappearing backstage.

Sam

Something only those close to me know is that the first time I stepped out on stage with S.C.A.R.A.B. to perform, I had to run off and puke. The venue wasn't even big, not like what The Parkapellas are facing. Five stories filled with people watching. High. Low. No escape.

But, when Sophie steps out on stage to sing in public for the first time with The Parkapellas, she fucking owns it, casting a brief glance around the vast auditorium.

"What inspired your choice of song?" one of the judges asks her, the one right in the middle of the front row of seating.

Every year The American Showcase has a theme for the final, one the last two a cappella groups must base their song choice off. This year was a tough one.

The theme: inspiration.

"Singing," says Sophie into the mic. The judge must give her a questioning look because she goes on to expand. "Not just why it inspires us, but how, and what it means to us."

"And what does singing mean to you?" The judge looks down at the sheet of paper in front of him. "Mrs. Riley."

Sophie draws in a small breath at the extra question, the one she isn't prepared for, and I shift in my seat; the red velour material scratching against my arms. A second passes, and she exhales, her expression changing with a wave of clarity.

Her eyes source me in the crowd, and I give her a small wave. Then out loud, she admits, not just to the huge auditorium of people, but to herself, "It means everything."

At that moment, I've never loved her more.

The thing about love is that it knows no bounds.

It comes in different forms.

Means different things to each individual.

And when you find it, you have to face all the challenges that come with seizing it—it gives you no choice.

The judge gives Sophie a nod—not a terse one, but one of understanding. The nod he gives her is one telling her we're all here for the same reason, united by one of the things we all love the most, enough to put ourselves out there, on the line.

Music.

"When you're ready."

The auditorium goes dark and a silence thick with anticipation fills it.

Drumming my fingers against my thigh, I glance to my left, and Ryan winks.

Jake leans forward from further down the row and says, "She's got this."

When the lights pan down from the ellipse ceiling onto the stage, I question if they're needed, because the smiles on every single one of their faces could light up New York.

On my right, Elayne sniffles into her tissue when Russ steps forward and sings the opening.

Through the words, they sing a story about how melodies heal and bring hope. About how lyrics can mend broken hearts and open them up to love again. About how those who feel weak can find strength through their voice. About how singing can help overcome fear and open up a world of opportunities if people are willing to listen.

Sophie never takes her eyes off mine, pouring her heart and soul into the final, leading The Parkapellas through their winning performance, while telling the world my story.

Epilogue
Sophie 2 Years Later

Taking in my reflection in the mirror, I decide it's better to just not look, so I go and prepare breakfast instead. We're on a tight schedule for the day, which means I need to keep it simple, opting to mix up some eggs. A side of toast is a given.

I'm mid-whisk when a pair of hands come around my middle, then move down slowly.

"Tell me how wet you are, Red."

"Dripping," I reply. "It's almost a hundred degrees, and it's not even nine."

"Come on, you know I love seeing you like this."

I spin around with the whisk still in my hand and arch a brow. "I'm not having sex with you, Sam. Sex chafing is a thing you know."

He wiggles his eyebrows and glances down at my chest, which is threatening to spill out of my vest. "Just a quickie."

"No," I reply, making sure to add extra emphasis on the 'o'.

I let out a yelp when Sam's hands come around me, grab my ass, and lift me on the countertop.

"What are you doing?" I hiss, even though there's no one else in the house.

Russ left thirty minutes ago with Xavier, on what became known as 'Man Fridays' the week after the adoption was official. Sam refused to let me point out that neither of them were men, because it left our Friday's wide open. All puns intended.

Knowing he doesn't have much time, Sam goes all in, parting my legs and flattening me back against the cool marble with one hand, holding me in place.

"It's Friday," he says, skimming his lips along the inside of my thigh. I hear him lick them beneath the many taffeta layers of my skirt when he finds his target. "I'm feasting."

I roll my eyes and drop the whisk right before he works his magic with his tongue.

"We're going to be late," I huff, climbing into the Raptor thirty minutes later with Sam's help. He never had the heart to get rid of it after the mini-moon, claiming it held too many memories and that he loved that the color matched my eyes.

While Sam drives, I work my way through the many notifications that have built up during the night on my phone.

"Ergh, remind me … why do I let Grams run rehearsals for the showcase each year?"

Sam smiles at the road. "Because she's adamant that your first-year win was down to her."

"Right," I laugh. "As if it could because of the talent on stage."

My family is still intrusive in their own overbearing ways, especially when it comes to Sing to Heal. I don't mind, because I've learned over time that all they want to do is help, and their help means that sometimes, among all the crazy hours and the increasingly demanding schedule, I can take a break.

Usually, those breaks involve Russ and me following Sam around the world during school holidays while he tours with S.C.A.R.A.B., whose first major album was a bigger success than anyone could have imagined. Both songwriters' contributions were raved about in reviews, but they've decided to take a different direction with their new song, which is what today is about.

When we arrive, the venue is hot and busy—everything I currently hate. But when I step on set and sing like I never have before, beside the man who owns my heart, it makes all the discomfort worth it.

"You look beautiful," says John West, when we've finished filming the music video for S.C.A.R.A.B.'s new single; the one I've collaborated with them on.

"I look like a fat sugar plum fairy," I deadpan.

"Soph, you're not fat. You're thirty-six weeks pregnant," laughs Sam, placing his hand protectively over the balloon attached to my middle.

"Which makes me question why I'm here?" I huff.

"My fault," admits John. "The schedule couldn't be moved. There's one thing left. Just a quick interview, and you can leave."

Forty minutes later, we're almost finished, when the reporter says, "One final question. A more personal one." She glances between Sam and I. "Was it easy falling in love?"

456

I glance at Sam out of the corner of my eye and smile. I don't need to think about my answer, not for a second.

"There was never any falling. I loved him from the start. So, in a roundabout way, I guess my answer is yes?"

I've never meant anything more than I meant my vows.

Love came easily, because it came with Sam and every day, he makes it effortless.

It came easy because, although the love was always there, he was my best friend first.

When it was the right time, we already knew each other's best and worst parts. We knew we wanted to stand by and love each other, regardless.

Sure, there have been challenges, because life is never straightforward, and loving someone isn't a perfect or flawless task. But all the dramas, all the major hurdles, we'd already overcome together, as friends.

The easiest thing about loving my best friend was that when we were ready, all there was left for me to do was to fall in sync with him. Fall in sync knowing that I had a lifetime of sweet melodies ready to be murmured against my skin, and a forever of lyrics about our love ready to be whispered in my ear.

The End.

Acknowledgements

I have big plans for the rest of this series. Plans that wouldn't be possible without the army I have behind me, who each deserve a big thank you.

Mum and Peter, for your endless support.

Poppy, Marla and Rory. My inspirations to keep writing and chasing my dreams, so when you're older I can encourage you all to do the same.

Kris and Babs, to whom this book is dedicated. Your patience with me is astonishing, but I wouldn't be the writer I am today without either of you.

Cheryl, Aimee, Pauline, and Tess, thank you for all of your feedback.

My PA Carley, for helping me get my life in order and making it possible for me to keep doing the bit I love. Writing.

My editor Hayley, thank you for your hard work, expertise, and helping to make this book sparkle.

Finally, as always, thank you to you, my readers. None of this would be possible without you all. Your love for my characters inspires me to keep writing.

460

Want to know more about Abby and Jake?

Keep reading for more information about The Always Trilogy!

Always You

You never forget your first love, and mine and Jake's, was the kind songs are written about.

I thought we were forever …
He promised me the world …
Then tore mine in two.
With my heart shattered into a million unrecognizable pieces,
I ran.
Out of the city. Out of the state. Out of my life.
Now I'm back for one summer, with one life changing
decision to make, and one goal: steer clear of Jake Ross, the
person who ran me out of Brooklyn.
Unfortunately, fate has other ideas and when
our careers become entangled,
avoidance proves impossible.
Together we were magical …
Apart we're a disaster.
Everyone deserves a second chance.

**But what happens if that chance leaves you
questioning everything, even when he promises that it
was always you …**

Always Us

**What hurt more than losing Jake Ross the first time ...
was losing him the second.**

It's been two years since I turned my back on the one that
got away, doing what I thought was right
for both of us.
Instead, I'm more confused than I've ever been before,
fighting to forget what it felt like
being in his arms.
Now, it's another summer and another
life-changing opportunity.
This time I'm running around Europe,
surrounded by Rock Gods.
It's the life most would dream of, but things are never that
straightforward, and a chance meeting with a stranger is a
recipe for disaster.
The heart wants what it wants,
regardless of the consequences.
But just when I might finally be able to move forward ...
the tables turn.
The choice is no longer between my head or my heart.

It's a question of whether love, really is enough.

Always

My life's about to change and I can't decide if it's for better or worse.

There was a time when I thought meeting Jake Ross, was fate
. . .
When I thought our love, was written in the stars . . .
When I hoped we'd find our way back to each other . . .
Now I'm left wondering if the path I'm about to take, will be
one I'll walk alone.
The one I want. The one I need.
Doesn't want me back.
Then the person I least expect gives me exactly
what I need.
A break from reality.
But there's only so long I can hide, and when the truth
comes out, it's explosive.
They say what will be, will be.

But what if we were never meant to be together?

OTHER WORK BY LIZZIE MORTON

The Always Trilogy:

Always You
Always Us
Always

The Always Series:

Wanting You Always
Needing You Always

Fool Me Series:

Fool Me Once
Fool Me Twice
Fool Me Thrice

Summer Nights Series:

Just One Kiss
Just One Night
Just Once More – Coming Soon